Pride of Man

The Legend of Marcus Cesari, Book 2 of Legacy of Man

by David Lingard

A note from the author

I just wanted to say here, thank you, whoever you are for however you have arrived at this book and my story. It makes a big difference to authors like me, who like to feel as though their hard work and dedication is appreciated when our work is read.

Your investment of your own time and money is as always, well appreciated. It takes a long time and a lot of effort to write, edit and release a book, so please, I ask that you **rate** and **review** everything that you read – and not just this book, so that lesser-known authors can grow their audience and gain the credibility that they deserve.

Also, I have a website that is usually kept up to date with current works, reviews and a few extra little bits. You'll find it at: www.davidlingard.com

PLUS, Click HERE to get a FREE eBook!

Chapter 1 – Choose Your Battles

The Green Beret, Canada Road, Kent, UK. Marcus Cesari sat alone at the old-fashioned bar with both hands around a room-temperature ale. He hadn't been in the place for very long, but he often enjoyed the fact that being a military geared pub not far from an army barracks, not too many of the public came into the place. He liked to keep himself to himself, which by all accounts was not normal for most people his age.

At only twenty, Marcus was strong for his age, but his temper would sometimes get the better of him. He would often find himself in fights where somebody had annoyed him for simply existing, and keeping hold of a job was something that he couldn't quite figure out. He'd had a few of course, but gross misconduct hearings usually followed fist fights, especially when those fist fights were in close proximity to heavy machinery of dangerous chemicals.

Marcus hadn't ever settled down since his expulsion from school. It wasn't because he was unintelligent, quite the opposite in fact. Rather, the constant fighting and his short temper had finally proven too much for the school and its teachers to handle. His parents had thought about placing him into another school, but being fifteen and almost out of the education system as it was, they all decided that it was for the best if he found a job. Little did they know that it would in fact mean that Marcus was destined to take over the upstairs of his parents' small, terraced house just down the road from the fated pub, and opposite the active army barracks.

"You going to drink that, Marcus, or just stare at it all night?" The bartender and landlord of the Green Beret asked in a half-serious tone. He didn't particularly need to work hard for business, but it was quiet in the Beret this night, so he evidently had nothing better to do.

Marcus simply grunted. He wasn't in the mood, not since he'd just this day been sent packing from trying to go to work on a fishing boat. A fishing boat. What a joke. He should've known better than to try to find a job where he would be confined in close proximity to someone else. But thinking back, the other guy hadn't really been doing anything too wrong. He just couldn't stop making that sound after he took a drink. You know the one, a contented, loud exhalation.

Marcus had thrown him off the boat.

At least the guy had paid him for the three hours he'd managed, which incidentally gave him enough for this ale, and one more after it. And Marcus was in no hurry to exhaust his funds too quickly.

"Why do you always do that, Chris?" Marcus asked. "You know how this works: I lose my job and sit here and wallow, and you clean glasses and serve other people before me, pretending not to notice how long I take to finish a pint."

The bartender exhaled and looked down at the glass he was drying.

"You're not a bad guy, Marcus," he said with a half smile. "Just that temper of yours… it'll get you into trouble one of these days."

"It gets me into trouble all the time," Marcus grumbled back. "That's why I'm here and you're there."

"But it doesn't have to be that way," Chris replied. "Listen," he said, his shoulders dropping as though he knew what he was about to say was a very bad idea. "Helen's shift starts in an hour. I don't like leaving her on her own in here at the changing of the guard down the road. Nothing against those squaddies, but she's… well, you know… and they're… you know."

"Just say what you're saying," Marcus said, not really listening to the bartender and his attention falling back to his ale.

"Well, I need to run some errands, so why don't you come and sit on this side of the bar for the evening? Just keep an eye out for Helen and maybe pull a pint or two. I'll pay you for your time, and who knows, maybe you'll smile at a person or two?"

"You want me to babysit? No thanks," Marcus replied. "Got better things to do with my time than watch under-sexed army dudes try to hit on a teenager."

"Really?" The bartender asked. "You sure you're not going to sit right there and watch that happening anyway? But I'll tell you what. You can have a couple of pints on the house while you're round this side, and I'll let you give a piece of your mind to one person, but only if he deserves it."

Marcus looked up at the bartender, who was smiling warmly, and he gave a half-hearted smile back.

"OK, Chris, but I'm taking a bag of pork scratchings, and if one of those squaddies gives me any jip, then I'm going to split his lip."

"I don't doubt it," Chris replied. Then added as a purposeful afterthought: "Just… remember that they tend to travel in groups, so don't bite off more than you can chew, alright?"

Marcus frowned. "Just make sure you leave me enough rags. The amount of time you spend standing around with your hand in a glass… I'm not sure if I can match that."

The bartender threw the towel at him and smiled as Marcus jumped.

"There you go. But now you know you're going to have to use that, right?"

"Oh, I'll use it, alright," Marcus replied. "So soft and absorbent," he said as he passed the towel from hand to hand. "Much nicer than the cheap scratchy toilet paper you got back there…"

"Try it," Chris said.

Marcus smiled deviously.

There were only two other people in the pub, and they hadn't much cared for the conversation happening between the bartender and the annoyed-looking patron sat at the bar, but later that evening, the place would be so full that they'd barely have enough room to move.

Marcus resigned himself to the fact that his evening of wallowing would be rudely interrupted by something so trivial as work. Time passed quickly, and before any more patrons came into the Green Beret and the two other had already left, Helen arrived with a happy smile and a spring in her step.

"Hey, Chris," she announced as the door swung shut behind her.

"Hi Helen, you OK?" The bartender asked, and she nodded, giving a sideways glance to Marcus.

"Busy in here then," she said. "Good job I got here when I did; you look rushed off your feet!"

The bartender gave a half smile. "Yeah… about that…" he started.

Helen was a thin, blonde girl of only nineteen years. It was because of these facts that Chris had given her the job – if the punters had a good reason to keep coming back and to spend their money, then it was all good. So long as they kept their comments to themselves.

For the most part, they did. But as more and more drinks flowed, lips became looser and passions became boldened. Usually, it just took a word or two to the CO's at the barracks to ensure there weren't too many repeat offenders.

"Marcus has agreed to work behind the bar tonight with you," Chris said. "Now I don't expect he's going to be too much help, but a second body is a second body. I'm sure you'll be grateful when you're up to your eyes in empty glasses.

"Oh God no," Helen said sarcastically. "Does Marcus even know how to pull a pint?"

The bartender laughed. "I'm sure he'll figure it out once he gets thirsty."

"You got that right," Marcus replied under his breath.

"Well, whatever," Helen said as she made her way around to the back of the bar and poured herself a lemonade. "Just make sure you keep your hands to yourself, sailor."

Marcus looked up to see Helen smiling at him.

"Oh…" Chris said, still trying hard to maintain his smile, though he spoke in more of a hushed tone now. "Marcus didn't quite make it as a fisherman."

Helen frowned. "How do you not make it as a fisherman? Sit on a boat, catch fish... what's there to get? You fall in or something? Now that you mention it, you do seem a bit wet."

"Nah, it was the other guy," Marcus grumbled. "Couldn't stop being annoying, so he 'fell' in. Anyway, they don't want me back, so a sailor I am no longer."

"You ever try getting along with people?" Helen asked with a smile.

"Tried it, couldn't keep it up. People are just so annoying," Marcus replied. "Doesn't matter. I'll be your right-hand man tonight, and I'm raring to go," Marcus gave a raised fist in sarcastic solidarity. "Don't you worry, boss," he turned his attention back to the bartender. "I'll keep those nasty army guys away from your young employee here. I know how much her safety means to you."

"Uh… yeah," Chris replied slowly. "Just… don't do anything stupid. But I've really got to go. I think you two have everything under control."

"Sir, yes, sir!" Marcus announced, giving a rigid salute as he sat bolt-upright on his stool. "Ten-four, loud and clear, sir!"

Chris mouthed the word 'sorry' to Helen before he pulled open the door to leave.

"It's your fault if I end up killing him!" Helen called after Chris. He'd clearly heard her, but before he could reply, the door had closed and he was gone, leaving Helen and Marcus alone in the pub.

And as soon as the door had closed, Marcus stood up, picked up his stool, walked casually around the rear side of the bar, sat back down and began to refill his glass with a Gadd's No.4.

"What do you think you're doing?" Helen asked with a hand on her hip.

"Sorry boss, I just… I gotta take the edge off," Marcus replied in a very sarcastic and mock downtrodden tone. "Lost my job today you see."

Helen shot back a sarcastic smile but didn't mention the free drink again. Nor did she mention it the second time Marcus poured himself a pint of Gadd's, but before he had a chance to pour a third, the wooden door to the Beret swung open and in trooped no less than twenty uniformed soldiers all at once. Finally, it was time for the guard's rotation, which meant the pub went from dead to heaving in a moment.

"Six pints for me and my mates, darling," the first order came, followed by a cacophony of matching requests.

"She's not your darling," Marcus grumbled under his breath, but if the guy had heard him, he didn't let on.

The Corporal wore the usual olive green combats, black beret - which betrayed that he was with the Royal Tank regiment, and it was clear that the man was a Corporal because on his arms, his uniform bore two golden chevrons.

He looked like your classic army guy – smarmy and very, very assured of himself. Marcus hated him already, even before he'd called Helen 'darling'.

"Oh and, why not get something for yourself while you're there, darling," the Corporal said, flipping a single silver coin onto the bar. Now though, he was flanked by two similarly dressed soldiers, though this pair were both Lance Corporals, judging by the single chevron on their arms.

Marcus had always taken an interest in the army. Growing up opposite a barracks would have that effect on a young lad, though he'd never really ever thought about enlisting himself. Yes, he liked a fight, but no, he didn't like being shouted at or told what to do.

"I said, she's not your darling," Marcus growled, though this time louder so the guy could hear him over the background noise in the pub.

The soldier then finally turned his attention to Marcus, sizing him up with a smug grin. "And who are you, the lady's knight in shining armour?" he sneered. His comrades let out a laugh, and they, too, turned to face Marcus fully. They looked small for soldiers if anything, and being lower ranks as they were, Marcus had the feeling that uniform or no, he could take them. If memory served, they'd probably have been in the army for about two to six years, but hadn't progressed into the officer ranks via officer training. He wondered as he looked at them if they simply hadn't met either the physical or intellectual components of the training required to become Second Lieutenants.

Marcus clenched his fists under the bar but forced himself to stay composed for now.

"Just a concerned bystander," he replied evenly. "But I won't stand by while someone treats a woman like that."

The other soldiers in the group chuckled at the exchange, seemingly amused by the confrontation.

"And I suppose a civvie like yourself thinks you can do something about it?" the Corporal asked, now leaning forward and putting his elbows on the bar. "So if I were to tell this young lady that when she finishes her shift tonight, that a handsome, strong Corporal will be waiting for her so that she'll get to know what a real man can do then…"

"I'm warning you," Marcus said through gritted teeth.

Then the Corporal reached out and grabbed a hold of Helen's arm. She jumped a little at the contact, but it was nothing compared to what Marcus did.

He exploded.

Marcus pulled the Corporal's other elbow, the one that he was still using to prop himself up on the bar and the soldier's head smashed hard against the solid polished wood beneath. Within an instant, Marcus had placed a palm on the side of the Corporal's face and squashed his head flat against the bar.

"Tell me again how a civvie can't do anything about it," Marcus announced loudly.

The bar went silent.

"And that goes for the rest of you too. Anyone wanting to disrespect your gracious host can take it up with me, you got that?" Marcus peered around the room and watched the still pairs of eyes all staring at him, their owners listening to his words. It was either the way he said it or the look in his eyes, but nobody looked like they would argue with him.

A few moments later, attentions had turned away and the general chit-chat in the place resumed, and Marcus let the Corporal go. His two comrades had unsurprisingly done nothing to intervene.

"You're going to regret that," the Corporal growled, rubbing his reddened face. "You hear me? You just put your hands on an enlisted man, a soldier. And if you think that's something that's going to go unpunished, then you've got another thing coming."

Marcus didn't have the chance to respond. Helen placed a reassuring hand on his arm, trying to defuse the tension. "Come on, let's not make things worse," she said softly. "He's not worth it. Why don't we all have a drink and…"

The Corporal gave Helen one disgusted look up and down, then turned and walked towards the door. But not before muttering under his breath, loud enough for both Helen and Marcus to hear. "You two deserve each other. Damn civvies."

Helen glanced at Marcus, a grateful look in her eyes. "Thanks for standing up for me," she said quietly.

Marcus waved a hand at her nonchalantly. "Don't read too much into it. People like that just grind my gears."

Helen nodded, knowing not to push the conversation any further. But at least she had given Marcus her thanks.

Once the three soldiers were gone, the atmosphere in the pub returned to normal. Helen resumed their duties, serving drinks and chatting with the regulars, and Marcus returned to his ale and silence. Nobody else gave Helen any disrespect, and that made Marcus smile to himself. At least they all knew their place.

As the night wore on, patrons came and went, but eventually the last orders bell rang and the Green Beret began to filter out. Helen and Marcus' shift together had finally come to a close. She walked over to him, wiping down the counter with a tired smile.

"Thanks for sticking around and looking after me tonight," she said genuinely. "You didn't have to do what you did, and I appreciate it."

Marcus shrugged, trying to downplay his actions. "No big deal. Just doing what needed to be done."

"No, really," Helen insisted. "It means a lot to me that you had my back." She took a hold of his arm and squeezed it tightly. "So thank you." Then she added: "So get yourself away, I can clean up here."

Marcus gave a half smile and turned to leave. He hesitated for a second, but then shook his head, opened the door and left the Green Beret.

It was cold and dark outside, but nothing out of the ordinary for the great British weather.

"Well, well, well, if it isn't our little hero," a familiar voice taunted. "You think you can take on all of us, tough guy?"

It was the three soldiers from earlier, along with two more, standing near the exit, and they had clearly been waiting for Marcus to leave the pub.

Marcus didn't reply, but the anger inside him was simmering again. He knew he was outnumbered, but he wasn't about to back down from a fight.

Without warning, the Corporal swung a punch at Marcus, but he managed to dodge it on instinct alone. Marcus retaliated with a quick jab to the Corporal's gut, momentarily winding him. The other four soldiers rushed in, trying to overwhelm Marcus with their numbers but he dodged and weaved, landing a few punches of his own.

The fight quickly escalated, and the road outside the pub where once quiet had become a chaotic battleground.

The thing was though, that because there were just so many more soldiers than Marcus, they just kept getting in each other's way.

Marcus stepped back a few times when punches were coming at him, and some of the soldiers had practically hit each other. Then he saw the sneer on the face of the Corporal, and lunged.

Marcus didn't have any formal training, and he'd always relied on his strength and willingness to fight, so when he lunged at the Corporal, he did so with every inch of anger that he could muster.

He collided with his opponent's midsection before anyone could do anything about it, and he barrelled the soldier to the ground. He managed to land two punches into the Corporal's face before he was dragged off and thrown to the ground. The fight still wasn't over though, because Marcus leapt back up to his feet and before anyone could do anything about it, he'd launched his fist at his closest opponent knocking him clean out in one strong punch.

Then, buoyed by the small victory, he threw another haymaker and took down a second of the men. It was just all too easy.

But then he saw the Corporal still on the ground, and his vision turned to red. Even through a bloodied, possibly broken nose, Marcus could still see that sneer plastered across his face. And that would not do.

Marcus fell to the ground, his knees on either side of the Corporal and he clenched his fists as tight as he could ever manage. Then he let loose. He rained blow after blow down on the soldier until his opponent's pained cries died down to a whimper, and then nothing.

He'd done what he wanted to do. But now he was spent. Leaning back as the red faded from his vision, a knee impacted Marcus' chin from one of the two remaining soldiers, and then a fist from the other. Marcus flopped back onto the ground, unable to keep himself upright and between the pain exploding from his back on the concrete, and the assault coming as revenge from these two soldiers, Marcus couldn't help but let the pain carry him away into unconsciousness.

Chapter 2 – Night Watch

Colonel Jack Armstrong sat in the corner of the Green Beret after a long shift much like any other long shift. Ever since he'd figured out that he was able to blend in with the crowds in the place by taking off his uniform and hiding behind a large newspaper, he'd found his free time so much more enjoyable.

It was like the soldiers didn't even see people when they weren't in a uniform, but Armstrong, with his crown and three stars on his arms just had a way of putting people on edge when they saw him. Well, that or the implied twenty years of service that came along with the rank.

But he'd cracked the code. Get changed before heading out for his R&R, and when the local soldiers were out and about in their downtime, they kept themselves mostly to themselves, and were able to forego standing to attention. It was a win-win situation.

And the NCO's wouldn't recognise him anyway. Armstrong wasn't based at just one barracks, rather he roamed a few and oversaw their operation with more of an outside point of view. That meant that although the officers and base commanders knew who he was, his face wasn't immediately recognisable to the vast majority of soldiers. Especially in this particular barracks on Canada road, where he tried to spend as little time as possible because it was old fashioned and placed so far away from well, anything.

But Armstrong had been given a new task. The project was above his pay rank and the physical envelope had been handed to him by one General Carter himself. Needless to say that the information within was not to be shared with anyone else. Armstrong didn't even know who else was involved with the project.

The order was simple. 'Find exemplary individuals for a top-secret project that could change the future of warfare'. And then further down the page: 'Not to be discussed with any other individuals or parties. Once individuals have been identified, personnel files are to be presented to a top-level hearing on August 1st', Canada Road Barracks at 0900hrs.

And that fateful date was tomorrow. Armstrong had compiled dossiers of individuals that he thought were promising of course, but he didn't know if any were as extraordinary as the order had called for. If anything, the ten individuals he'd earmarked were more 'above average' rather than exemplary and with over one hundred years of military service combined, that really was to be expected. NCO's and Officers of varying ranks, the list covered as many bases as Armstrong could manage, not being entirely sure how long the list should be, what skills these individuals should have, or what ranks they should be. It was the best that Armstrong could do, but he felt deep down that it somehow wasn't going to be enough.

Armstrong sipped his lemonade and peered at the open newspaper before his eyes. He wasn't reading about what there was to say on the page, something about John Major leading the Conservative Party to a shock election victory or other such uninteresting drivel. Armstrong had learnt long ago that the articles were all the same, politicians and policies seeming to always work on some revolving carousel, coming and going, but nothing ever really changing.

He was thinking about what he was going to say in this meeting tomorrow, which in itself was a mystery. He had no idea who else would be there, who he would be presenting his information to, or even if he was the only one to do so. What if the mission had been to find thousands of soldiers who fit the bill? Or just one? He didn't know why he'd set ten as his goal, but it was what his gut had told him, and that was something he had relied on often. Usually to favourable results.

In fact, the whole thing seemed strange to the Colonel. Normally he would be given missions or orders through his usual channels, and they would be specific in their requirements. Not once, in fact had he been passed anything with the words 'Top Secret' at the top of the page. What was the need for so much secrecy anyway? The only thing that he could think of was perhaps this was a test. Maybe he was in line for promotion and the higher-ups just wanted to see how he would deal with this new and ambiguous mission. Whatever the reason, Armstrong was going to do what he could, even if he didn't fully understand the requirements.

His attention wandered from the paper when he'd heard a conversation at the bar that sounded as though it was escalating somewhat, and when he looked up, he saw three enlisted men bearing down menacingly on one of the two bar staff. He wasn't surprised. He'd seen this all too often: the local soldiers felt that they owned the town, so they'd cause trouble as they postured. Usually, the civvies would back down and keep out of their way, but what surprised Armstrong about this particular confrontation, was the fact that the young man on the far side of the bar didn't seem to care who these people were, not one bit.

The young man in fact, seemed like if things were going to escalate, then he was so assured of himself that he would defend himself without question. It happened, but every time Armstrong had witnessed such a thing, the soldiers would all club together and give the obnoxious civvie what for.

But something odd happened now. The young barman didn't back down, and in fact through either sheer ignorance or stupidity, he all but assaulted the young Corporal looking to make his mark and stamp his authority on the place.

Armstrong moved to put down his paper, sensing the need to intervene in the coming seconds. His pulse had increased, pumping adrenaline around his body. Not that he was worried about confronting the NCO's, just sometimes it took a few seconds while in a fight to realise who it was that was trying to pull you away from your adversary. Fists would fly and that was dangerous in itself.

But he was shocked again. The three soldiers didn't press the issue. In fact, they left without causing a scene, and that was something that was even rarer than a civvie standing up to a soldier.

Armstrong looked at the barman for a long second before letting himself relax and return to his thoughts. He might've been wrong, but there was something about that young man. Something he hadn't seen for a long time. The blonde girl behind the bar looked like she was used to this kind of thing happening, but the young man, who if anything, Armstrong thought was robbing the management blind what with his complete inattention to the job and obvious carefree attitude, was something different.

But all that had changed. The barman had taken umbrage with something and that had ignited something within him. He had a fire in his eyes that betrayed his total confidence in what he was saying. Not arrogance, but pure confidence.

The bar, as they tended to do, filled and emptied as the night drew on and there wasn't another altercation to speak of. The Colonel wondered if it was because of how the young barman had dealt with the last situation, but it could've just been one of those nights.

But before the Beret emptied completely, Armstrong made his escape. Not wanting to be last out through the doors, he slipped out a few minutes after the last orders bell rang.

He had planned to head back to the barracks and get in a good night's sleep before he'd come across an all too familiar sight. He sighed as he saw the three soldiers, one Corporal and two Lance Corporals loitering outside the pub in the road. These were the three men who the barman had taken issue with, and it was clear to Armstrong that these three were waiting for their new target to leave so that they could teach him a harsh lesson.

Moreso though, he watched as two more soldiers joined the threesome and as a five, they stood in wait for the young barman to appear from the door, alone and outnumbered.

Armstrong turned the corner around to the side of the pub and leaned his back against the brick wall. He wouldn't interfere, but if things got out of hand, he knew that he could at least shout out an order or two to stop things from going too far. A casual beating was fine, but anything more than that would just mean a bad wrap for the barracks.

Finally, the door had opened and closed, and Armstrong heard the soldiers greet the barman in their threatening manner. Peering round the corner, the Colonel watched as the beating ensued.

But things didn't go as Armstrong had assumed.

The barman dodged the opening flurry of punches and awaited his opening. He didn't seem scared or want to turn and run away, rather he waited and waited. He seemed to have a natural or primal desire to want to hurt his opponent, and even when he launched himself at the Corporal and took him to the ground, he didn't stop in his pursuit to cause damage. By the time two of the soldiers had managed to tear him off their comrades, the barman had floored three of his opponents, the third of which being the Corporal, who had been left unconscious and in a bloody mess.

But finally the wild man had been suppressed, and the two remaining soldiers taught him a solid lesson before they finished up, helped their friends to their feet and they all made their way wearily back to the barracks. The soldiers had won the fight, but to the Colonel's mind, the barman had been the true victor.

The young barmaid had been the one to find the barman unconscious and bloodied a few minutes later, and her scream could've woken the dead. Armstrong then appeared from around the corner as though he had no idea what was happening and immediately moved to 'check' if the young man was OK. He reassured the barmaid and told her that between them they would carry the young man to the barracks at the end of the road, where he would be seen to in the infirmary. The young girl had seemed cautious, though looking into the Colonel's eyes she saw nothing but honesty. The pair then carried Marcus Cesari the short distance down the road, through the manned security gates at the entrance to the barracks, and inside to the infirmary.

Chapter 3 – Unexpected Allies

When Marcus awoke, he didn't recognise the room he was in. The lighting seemed cheap to him and through his squinting eyes, it seemed to flicker in a frequency he knew meant quantity over quality for whoever had bought the light fittings. In short, the light hurt his eyes.

His bed had metal rails on three sides and it took him a moment to realise that he was on a hospital trolley of some sort. In the room, there were nine other beds, though none of them were occupied, and there didn't seem to be a nurse or doctor in the room either. He was alone. And judging by the sunlight filtering through the blinds, it was clearly morning, and probably early.

Marcus sat upright, not knowing exactly where he was or what he was supposed to do next, but the pain he experienced when he did so was far worse than he'd been expecting. It felt like his ribs and or nose had been broken, and it made his eyes water. It also took a fair amount of effort for him to remain silent.

He heard the footsteps before the door swung open and the sound it made echoed through the empty room.

Striding in with purposeful steps came a man in a crisp military uniform, his chest adorned with various ribbons and medals. The man had an immediately commanding presence, and it was clear to Marcus that he was a Colonel – denoted by the crown and three stars on his uniform.

The Colonel was in his mid-forties, with a strong and chiselled face that exuded authority. His hair was neatly trimmed and peppered with streaks of grey, indicating years of service and experience. His eyes, a piercing shade of blue, seemed to take in everything in the room like he could see more than what was on show.

The Colonel's uniform was immaculate, and every detail from the perfectly pressed creases to the polished brass buttons spoke of a man who valued discipline and order.

As he approached Marcus' bed, his expression remained stern but even. Marcus, where perhaps he should have felt intimidated by the high-ranking officer's presence, felt nothing more than curiosity.

"Assault is no light charge, son," the Colonel said, coming to a halt at the end of Marcus' bed.

"I think you're mistaken," Marcus replied curtly. "I'm not a soldier, I'm not in the army and I don't need to listen to you, or anybody else in this place for that matter. All you guys are the same… thinking you can…"

"Let me stop you right there, son," the Colonel interrupted Marcus. "Now I don't want to tell you how you should think, or even how you should address an officer – regardless of whether you're a soldier or not – but I'm not here to accuse you of anything."

"I know," Marcus said cockily. "You just wanted to see what your men did to me after I left the Beret, right? Maybe try to keep me quiet? I mean, two lemonades and the same page in the paper all night, you must've been concerned with something else… keeping an eye on your men to see what they do with their free time?"

Again, the Colonel was surprised. It was even less often that he would be on the back foot in any given conversation, but that's what was happening right now.

"I… it wasn't…" he started.

"And you come to me in newly pressed number ones, what, to try to scare me? Thinking this is some official business and that I'd better not say a thing?"

The Colonel looked down at the service dress that he was wearing and gave Marcus a half smile.

"I hate to say, son, that some things simply don't revolve around you, unfortunately. I'm wearing my ones for something else entirely. But what is amazing is that you remember me at all. Is that normal for you? To be so perceptive?"

"Sometimes," Marcus said with a cocky smile. "So can I go now or do you want to ask me any other meaningless questions?"

Armstrong didn't say anything for a long moment and Marcus wondered if the Colonel was going to simply turn and walk away from him, his interrogation complete, however difficult Marcus had made it. Then the officer looked down at his hands, where he held a brown file with no markings on the outside. Opening it, he began to read aloud.

"Marcus Cesari. Twenty years old, current occupation unknown. Threat level: Two. This individual had a short fuse and is arrogant to the point of self-destruction."

Marcus forced himself to sit up again, wincing through the pain of his ribs creaking.

"So what, you have a dossier on me? Sounds like your guys put a lot of time and effort into that one," Marcus said. But in truth, the file had opened his eyes somewhat. "Sounds like you know everything there is to know about Marcus Cesari, right?" He asked sarcastically.

"Mother: Adriana Cesari. Occupation: Primary school teacher. Threat Level: Zero. Father: Francis Cesari. Occupation: Unemployed on medical grounds. Threat Level: Zero. Current address of all three individuals: Seventy-One Canada Road." Armstrong looked up from the paperwork and stared at Marcus. "We know everything about the people who live near to our barracks, son. And you are no exception."

"And I'm supposed to what, be scared? Worried about you sending some guys to my house if I talk? Your men jumped me Colonel, five of them. And I think I have as good as I got if you ask me. So why don't you just leave me be and you don't have to worry, I won't say anything about what happened."

"Again, Marcus," Armstrong said in a far softer tone now. "Not everything is about you. Now I pulled your files last night after I saw what you did to those soldiers and after me and your friend Helen carried you all the way here after you'd been beaten to a bloody pulp."

"Helen's here?" Marcus interrupted the Colonel.

Armstrong shook his head. "Once I assured her you'd be safe here, she went home. I don't know why she likes you, but I'd try to be nice to that one if I were you, she might be the only friend you've got."

Marcus remained silent, sidetracked in wondering if Helen was actually his friend or not.

"But when I was looking through the information we have on you and your parents," Armstrong continued, "there's something I don't understand."

Marcus raised an eyebrow at the implied question.

"Just, why you don't seem to care to hold down a job when it would make life for your parents so much easier?"

"They get by just fine," Marcus said quietly.

"No, they don't." Armstrong interrupted curtly. "Your mother does what she can to put food on the table for you three and when you're working it's easier for them, but when you don't… you know they go without just to keep you fed, right? Your father can't work in his condition and it's only going to get worse…"

"Dad's in a wheelchair and he has been for years," Marcus replied quickly. "They said they don't know what it is but they know there's nothing they can do."

"Well son, that's not entirely true," Armstrong replied. "According to the medical records we have on file, your father has Neurofibromatosis type two. It's a rare genetic disorder…"

"I don't care what it's called," Marcus replied quickly. "They said they can't cure it and that's all that matters, isn't it?"

"Listen to me son, it's about time you take your head out of your ass and listen to someone when they're trying to tell you something. They do know what your father has, and it's a rare genetic disorder. It's hereditary, and even if you don't want to listen to me, maybe you'll hear that? Now there's not a lot that civilian doctors can do for your father, but the mutation in the NF2 gene responsible for this condition is likely present in your genetic makeup too. I can't help you outright of course I can't, but enlisted soldiers have access to better medical facilities, scans, technology that isn't available to the general public. Now I'm not saying that you should sign up specifically to gain the benefits of the medical care the military has to offer… but it's just something you should think about. Friendly advice from one man to another. Just… something to think about."

Marcus didn't know what to do with himself. His eyes had widened and his jaw had dropped. How could his parents not have told him this? And if it was true, then how could they have kept the fact that he could have this thing too from him? But then, was the army allowed to know all this information about him and his family? It all just seemed a bit much.

"…so is this some kind of new recruitment technique?" Marcus asked slowly. "You tell people they might have some genetic disease, then say only the army can help them? That's a bit desperate, isn't it?"

"Listen son… just think about it. Talk to your parents and maybe they'll tell you the truth. Join up, don't join up that's your choice, but it is a choice, so just think about it."

The Colonel then abruptly turned away from Marcus and walked out of the infirmary, leaving Marcus alone again. He let his body fall back against the bed and shut his eyes tightly. The Colonel had to be lying, didn't he? But he just knew so much about Marcus and his family.

Marcus slept through some of the pain, but when he awoke again it was still there. But he quickly concluded that he didn't want to be in this barracks for a moment longer than he had to be, so he forced his broken body up with a grunt, then onto his feet and he hobbled slowly towards the exit.

He found it a little strange that nobody seemed to be around to stop him from leaving, that was of course until he reached the front desk to the infirmary where a single nurse sat in her white pressed uniform. Marcus thought about trying to sneak past her, but she had evidently seen his reflection approaching somewhere and spoke without turning her head.

"Mr Cesari, are you sure you want to leave us now? You're welcome to stay for as long as you like of course."

Marcus stopped. They'd just let him leave? After he'd hurt the other soldiers in his blind rage? He wondered what the catch was.

"Yeah I uh… I want to go home now," he said.

"Of course, but if you change your mind and would like to rest more, please feel free to come back."

Marcus had no desire to do so, and walked straight out the door. A single soldier stood to attention at the door and smiled at Marcus as soon as he was outside.

"Right this way sir," the soldier said, gesturing towards the gatehouse and the pair walked in silence until the soldier opened the large metal gate for Marcus and he walked through, back to the outside world.

The air felt lighter and cleaner.

Marcus crossed the road and entered his house to find his father in the kitchen, sat in his wheelchair at the table with a paper, a cup of tea and a slice of toast. That meant it was most likely around nine or ten in the morning, and his mum had gone off to work already.

"Meet a girl then did you?" Marcus' father announced without looking up when he heard the door.

Marcus didn't reply, but walked straight into the kitchen.

"What's Neurofibromatosis?" He asked without greeting his father.

Francis Cesari slowly placed the paper down on the table and turned his attention to his son. His eyes filled with both anxiety and shame.

"Where did you hear that, son?" He asked. "And my God what happened to you!?"

"You know what it is?" Marcus replied without answering either question.

Francis peered up at his son, then his shoulders dropped.

"Who told you?" He asked.

"Does it matter?"

"I suppose not. Just… I didn't want you to worry."

"Didn't want me to worry? So you thought you'd lie to me? What if I have this thing too, dad? What if one day I came home and you… how could you think this was for the best?"

"They said there was nothing they could do so it didn't matter. Your mother and I made the decision not to say anything. If you did have this… this thing, then it's better you didn't know. God knows I wish I didn't know. It saps the hope from you, makes you less of a man. We just wanted you to have a normal life. Not one lived in fear."

Marcus sat down at the kitchen table and placed his head in his hands. This was just all too much to bear. It didn't help that his head was still throbbing. "There's always something they can do, dad," he said. "Different doctors, second opinions, new technologies!"

"I've looked. I've asked," Marcus's dad replied. "They aren't even close and the condition is so rare that the funding just isn't there. It'll be a hundred years before they think up something new to fight this but it won't be in my lifetime, Marcus."

"But the military…" Marcus said slowly. "They might have something new, right? Something they've developed for themselves but the rest of the country won't see for decades? That's how they work, isn't it?"

Francis' gaze was fixed on the table. "I stopped thinking like that a long time ago, Marcus," he said. "I know they say it's good to have hope, good to think like it's all going to get better in the end… but it's too late for me. But if you think the military has something hidden away that can help, then it'll be your choice to pursue that, just… I know if it was the other way around, I'd rather have not known about it. Ignorance truly is bliss. So you want to tell me who gave you all those cuts and bruises?"

Marcus sighed. "Just a couple of soldiers who couldn't keep their hands to themselves last night, down at the Beret. Don't worry I gave them as good as I got." He forced a smirk, and it eased the tension in the room. "A colonel took me to the infirmary afterwards… he's the one who told me about you actually."

"A Colonel?" Francis asked. "You must've done something pretty extraordinary to get his attention then."

"Not really, I think it was just the right place at the right time. He tried to get me to enlist this morning too. Thinks there's something there for me I guess. Or maybe they're short on bodies to throw overseas at their enemies or something."

Francis peered up at his son again. "Tried to get you to sign up? What was it this time, money? Or the promise of lifelong skills that'll be useful to future employers?"

"Neither actually. He said the military has access to better doctors and medical facilities. That if I signed up then maybe they could treat me if I..." he stopped, not wanting to finish his sentence.

"Well that's a pretty big draw," Francis said. "...I don't know if I would be able to turn that down if I were you."

Marcus was silent for a long moment. He hadn't been expecting his father to give that answer. In truth, he'd been expecting him to tell him that it was foolish, that the Colonel would've said anything just to get Marcus to sign up. But he hadn't. He'd said that he would've taken the deal and it made Marcus wonder why exactly that might be.

"What's it like?" Marcus finally asked after the silence became uncomfortable. "Does it hurt?"

"Sometimes," Francis replied. "But that's not the worst of it. It's the fact that you can't get onto the toilet yourself, in or out of the bath. This thing it... it makes you feel like less of a man Marcus, it saps you of who you are and that's the worst of it."

Marcus hadn't heard his father talk like this before and it sent a cold shiver down his spine. Francis had always been a stoic man, a strong man who didn't let anything get the better of him, but now Marcus could see in his father's eyes just how much he'd been hiding all these years. How much he wished he could change.

"Do you think they could cure it?" Marcus asked quietly.

"If there's anyone out there who can, it's going to be the military. But honestly son, I don't know," Francis exhaled. "I'm just saying if I had the chance to get this thing sorted, or if I could talk to myself twenty years ago, then I'd do anything I could, even if the chances were slim. I think you should take the offer seriously Marcus. It could be worth more than you know." Then his face morphed into more of a casual smile. "So tell me what the other guy looks like."

Marcus smiled weakly back. "He got what he deserved," he said. "Couldn't keep his hands off Helen in the Beret so I reminded him and a couple of his friends how they should behave outside of the barracks."

"You know you should be a bit more careful, those soldiers like to stick together and they aren't worried about giving a civvie a hiding."

"I know," Marcus grumbled. "But they've got something to think about, at least."

"So do you by the looks of it."

Marcus shrugged.

Francis then turned his attention back to his newspaper and grunted in a clear sign that the conversation was over.

Marcus took the hint and retreated from the kitchen, making his way upstairs. His mind was too full of questions to eat anything right now, and his battered and bruised body needed to rest..

Chapter 4 – Unlikely Candidate

"Please go through," the admin assistant said to Colonel Armstrong as he waited alone in the empty room just outside one of the mess halls. It was strange, the place must've been entirely cleared of personnel because every time he'd visited the Canada Road Barracks, this area in particular had been filled with soldiers coming and going, getting their daily meals. Now, though, it was silent, and Armstrong had heard the woman's footsteps approaching long before she'd arrived and made her announcement.

Colonel Armstrong nodded, stood up, straightened his number ones and pushed the double doors to the mess hall open.

It was not as he remembered it.

Ten tables had been pushed together to form a large 'U' shape, and behind them sat nine Colonels and three Generals. There was nothing else in the room, just a wide open empty space and twelve pairs of eyes staring at him as he entered the room.

"Colonel Armstrong, please take a seat," one of the Generals said. Armstrong didn't recognise any of them by their name tags, but the one who had spoken was called General Smith. The Colonel did what he was told and sat in the only free seat in the room.

"Now that we are all here, we can begin," General Smith said. "Now that you are in this room, I can say this to you all, once and only once. Operation Legacy, its mandate, directives and any details of the operation itself are not to leave this room. By remaining in this briefing right now, you are agreeing to this fact and it will be recorded that you agree to these terms. If you do not agree with this, then you are free to leave the room right now. But know that if you stay and you break these terms, then you will be court-marshalled and prosecuted to the full extent of the law. This will also mean you lose any pension accrued during your time in the British Army. Now is the time to leave if you would like to leave, gentlemen."

Armstrong looked around the room and saw not a single movement from any of the other Colonels. He couldn't help but feel a little pride in that fact.

"As was expected," the General continued with a slight smile. "Now, before we move onto the details of the operation, I would like each of you Colonels in turn to present the best of the best, the finest soldiers that you would each personally recommend to be a part of this operation. Colonel Johnson, please begin."

"Sir?" The Colonel, who had been instructed to go first, replied with a question. "In our orders, it wasn't specific on how many soldiers we should be recommending. Nor what they were being commended for. Would we be able to gain a little more insight into what this operation involves before we make our recommendations? It might allow us to give a better suited candidate for the operation."

The General gave a crooked smile. "It might do, but in this case, the orders were given in this manner purposefully, so present what you have and when you are all finished, we will review your thought processes and candidates."

Colonel Johnson didn't look happy, but he continued.

"I have shortlisted twenty soldiers from rank Sergeant to Major. With over two hundred years of combined military service, these men and women are what I believe display a decent cross-section of our military force today. These individuals are strong, fast, intelligent, brave and respected. I believe that whatever you might have in store for this operation, these twenty individuals could display what you're looking for."

"Very good," the General replied after the file of names had been passed along to him from the Colonel, and the man had taken his seat again. "I expected nothing less. A fair sample size and a cross-section of the brightest and bravest. Well done, Colonel, I will deliberate on these individuals."

Colonel Armstrong could read between the lines of that response. It was expected, ordinary even. But there was no exemplary to the individuals that Colonel Johnson had proposed. Nothing that could make him say 'this person is special'. And it was exactly how Armstrong had approached the task, too. He wished he'd taken a different approach. Taken a risk.

The next few Colonels gave similar responses, producing the dossiers of fifteen, twenty and twenty-five soldiers, all between the lower ranks and officers up to the rank of Major. It was only when Colonel Whittaker stood up that something different happened.

"I would like to put forward Hotel Company out of Catterick," Whittaker said. "They're two hundred and fifty men strong, and I can't fault a single one of them in the time I spent there. Well trained and disciplined, the entire company is an excellent example of what soldiers in today's army have to offer."

That was something that really caught Armstrong's attention. Could this Colonel simply recommend ten times the amount of soldiers that anyone else had?" It was an odd way to approach the assignment that each of them had been given, but at least it was something different. Perhaps novel, even. Armstrong awaited the General's response, wondering if he was about to reprimand the Colonel or otherwise commend him on his ingenuity.

To Armstrong's surprise, the General simply nodded and made a note on the paper before him.

It seemed that whatever anybody said, there were no differences in the responses the General gave, and that was strange; there were apparently no wrong answers.

The other two Generals gave identical responses to each of the Colonels as the declarations went on, nodding silently but never uttering a word one way or the other.

By the way the Colonels were presenting their cases around the table, Armstrong could tell that he was going to be last to speak, and he knew that unless he did something extraordinary, he would be just like the others, presenting his ten soldiers and considering the whole thing job done.

But that would be the smart thing to do, wouldn't it? Play it safe just like the others and be happy in the knowledge that everyone for the most part did the same thing, and he could get back to his duties.

"Colonel Armstrong," the General eventually spoke, giving the Colonel his chance to present his soldiers for the operation.

"Sir," Armstrong said as he stood up. "I took a similar approach to the rest of the Colonels here today, finding ten soldiers who I believed would be appropriate to cover a wide range of operations that you could put them forward for. I believe that we have enough of such individuals on the table here."

Every pair of eyes in the room fixed on Armstrong as he exhaled quietly and decided that what he was about to say next was the right call.

"With that being said, I met an individual this morning that I believe could play a vital part in this operation, and could offer something different to the soldiers we've all recommended here."

The General finally gave a response that wasn't the simple pleasantries he'd returned to the other Colonels in the room. He raised an eyebrow.

"Do continue," the General replied, clearly intrigued.

Armstrong took a breath. "Last night, I watched a young man display compassion, care and strength. A fighting spirit that I haven't witnessed in a long time. I won't go into details, but then this morning I had the chance to speak to the man, and he was both intelligent and perceptive." He paused to take a breath, but a part of him was telling him to stop, to stick to the plan and play it safe.

"Well, does this young man have a name?" The General asked. "If you are proposing just one soldier to join this operation, then I presume we might know him by name?"

Armstrong shook his head. "I doubt it, sir. Because this young man isn't a soldier; he's a civilian, living in the house directly opposite the gates to this barracks in fact. With his parents."

There was a shocked pause where nobody quite knew how to respond to that, and then one after another, the Colonels began laughing.

What mattered, though, was that as Armstrong stood there watching his equals laughing at his proposal, the General was peering up at him with clear curiosity in his eyes.

The General cleared his throat, and the mess hall returned to silence.

"Do you believe that you can enlist this man as a private so that he can join this operation?" The General asked.

"I believe I can," Armstrong replied right away. "I think that the army has just as much to offer him as he has to offer us, sir."

"Sir, do you really think a young man, who hasn't even passed through basic training…" one of the Colonels began to say, but the General quickly cut him off.

"Do not presume to know the first thing about this operation, Colonel," the General said. "And the reason you were all given this cryptic task was precisely so that we would have a pool of personnel that we believe as a group can be moulded to fit a situation that none of us have any experience in. In fact, this individual may well be exactly the kind of person we are looking for here."

The mess hall fell into silence again.

"Now, as you have all made your presentations, please listen to the following briefing with General Avery."

The General to Smith's left, a much thinner man, stood up and passed a brown folder to each of the Colonels.

"This is your non-disclosure agreement; please read, understand and sign it," Avery announced. "Then you will find your standing orders on the following page. These orders are not to be shared with anyone else, whether they are in this room or not."

Colonel Armstrong looked down at the documents. They weren't addressed to him by name, only entitled 'Dear Colonel'. The first page was a short NDA which he skimmed, ignored and signed. He'd read a few of them before, and this one said nothing more than what they'd all been told as they'd entered the room.

Then, as Armstrong turned the page over and stared down at a blank page, seven of the Colonels abruptly stood up, saluted and marched out of the room without another word. The three who remained watched them curiously but didn't say another word; presumably, their part in the operation had concluded.

The three remaining Colonels, Armstrong, Whittaker and Johnson, waited for the others to leave the mess hall before turning back to the Generals. They hadn't been given any orders in their files, and certainly none to suggest that they should leave.

"OK," General Avery announced once the mess hall was silent again. "This is how the operation is going to begin. We now have a pool of four hundred and twelve soldiers. Well, four hundred and eleven and one not as yet enlisted civilian, but you get the idea. Now the Colonels that have left have a duty to clear this entire barracks, which from this moment onwards..." a loud siren began to ring out and the lights in the mess hall dimmed. "...is to be for the sole use of Operation Legacy. Shortly, the soldiers that you've all suggested to us in this briefing will be transferred here and assigned new quarters until such a time as the Operation moves on from its preliminary stage. The details of this stage will be handed to you after the arrival of the soldiers." He had to raise his voice to above the level of the siren, but hearing him was just about manageable.

Armstrong had never before experienced anything like what was happening here, and his mind raced with the possibilities. The best that he could come up with was that perhaps it involved royalty. Or the Prime Minister? But he simply couldn't figure out why so much had been hidden from him and the other Colonels. Surely they could be trusted if they'd made it this far into the operation?

"I should not have to remind you," the General continued, still having to raise his voice, "of the non-disclosure agreements you have all signed," he peered meaningfully at the Colonels. "So with that being said, you can now consider this barracks and everyone inside of it mission critical. You may leave the barracks for the purposes of training exercises only, and leave of any individuals within the barracks has hereby been revoked – yourselves included. Lastly, any information that you are privvied to from this moment forwards, you are not to disclose to any of the candidates under any circumstances."

Colonel Whittaker raised a hand.

"Yes Colonel?" Avery asked.

"Are we going to get back to our barracks and stations to collect some of our things, personal items, clothes and the like? And should we tell our families that we won't be coming home this Christmas?"

General Avery smiled. "You three Colonels were picked because of your circumstances. You may not know each other, but the three of you are unmarried and have no dependents. Your personal belongings have already arrived, you'll find them in your new quarters. But believe me when I say that you and the candidates here are the only residents of the base. And that means cleaning, cooking, everything will be the responsibility of you and the candidates, and we expect you to pull your weight around here."

Colonel Armstrong's jaw dropped. They'd all but locked down the barracks for whatever this was, and relocated thousands of enlisted men, including the Colonels and even the barracks commander? Whatever this was, it was big big.

"You are now free to leave," General Smith said. "The barracks will have been cleared by now and it'll give you some time to discuss strategies for general rotas for you and the candidates. Though, Colonel Armstrong, please may we speak before you carry on?"

The other two Colonels quickly left the mess hall, shocked by the developments of the meeting and having their lives take a huge detour. Whittaker looked the most surprised - he'd asked about telling his family etc. But the General had made everyone aware that he'd had no such commitments. Armstrong concluded that the Colonel was a strange man, but he hadn't decided if he was going to like him or not yet.

"Jack," General Smith said in a conversational tone. "Is this civilian of yours really going to be up to the task? Do you think you'll be able to convince him to sign up?"

"I do," Armstrong replied confidently. Then, in an effort to lay all his cards on the table, he added: "His father has an illness that has him wheelchair-bound… it's genetic, and I've told Marcus that the army has access to better doctors and more up-to-date technology than civilian hospitals… I think he realises that it could be his only chance at a normal life."

The corners of the General's lips curled ever so slightly upwards at those words. "Well then, you best go and sign him up, Jack."

"Yes, sir!" Colonel Armstrong replied, and made his way out of the mess hall, back out of the front gate of the barracks leading out onto Canada Road and towards the address he'd read in Marcus Cesari's file.

Chapter 5 – New Recruit

"Marcus!" Francis Cesari shouted upstairs from the hallway leading to the front door. "There's someone here to see you!"

Marcus' head appeared over the banister, looking down to where his father sat waiting in his wheelchair.

"If it's Chris, then tell him I don't want to work in a pub again; it's too dangerous, too many soldiers, you see."

Francis sighed, "It's not Chris, Marcus. It's someone else. A soldier." He peered at the uniform and added: "Colonel".

Marcus furrowed his brow in confusion and spun around the banister to descend the short staircase into the hallway. His body protested as he moved, but he did his best to ignore it. His head still hurt too, but again the curiosity of what this man had to say got the better of him

Colonel Armstrong stood there, still tall and imposing, still in his finest, pressed number ones. His presence seemed even more authoritative in the humble surroundings of the Cesari home.

"Marcus," the Colonel announced, his voice steady.

"I haven't said anything," Marcus said quietly once he came face to face with the Colonel, and he couldn't help but notice a slight side-eye from his father.

"Oh, it's… it's not about that," the Colonel replied and scratched the back of his head. "Only… I wondered if you had the chance to think about the offer I made you?"

"I don't remember an offer," Marcus said. "But come through to the kitchen and we can talk specifics. All I remember is that you made some vague promises about better doctors and technological advances that the army may or may not have had, and that I may or may not have access to them – if indeed I have this genetic illness that I've only just been told about."

Marcus winced as he said the last sentence, seeing the anguish flash across his wheelchair-bound father's face. Then he raised a palm to his forehead in a dramatic fashion. "Unless in my beaten and bloodied state I'm suffering from terrible amnesia?"

Colonel Armstrong followed Marcus into the small kitchen without a word, his posture relaxed as he took a seat at the small tile-topped table. He cleared his throat, a hint of apology in his voice. "I apologise if I was a bit vague earlier, Marcus. Let me clarify things for you now."

Marcus leaned against the kitchen counter, his arms crossed over his chest. He met the Colonel's gaze with a challenge, but also with at least a small amount of hope that he was about to tell him something useful. He regretted crossing his arms though; their very presence caused his ribs to throb.

"Alright, shoot. Give me some specifics."

The Colonel's gaze didn't waver as he began to speak. "The offer is this: I will ensure that you are tested in every single way we possibly can for this illness in our own facilities – and as I said, these are significantly more advanced than the civvie sites," he winced at his own use of the derogatory term but continued. "In addition, I will personally extend the same offer to your father. We know that he has this condition already, and if there's even the slightest hope of treatment, then I promise you we'll try it. I can't promise you miracle cures, but I can assure you that we'll give this everything we have."

"Right," Marcus replied. "And what's the catch?" He noticed that his father had begun fidgeting like he wanted to speak, but he remained silent.

"Enlistment," the Colonel replied flatly.

"Enlistment," Marcus replied. "And I'm supposed to believe that I'm so important to the army that you'd go to all this effort and expense... just to sign me up as some Private?"

The Colonel smiled. "From what I saw last night at the pub, you demonstrated qualities that align with what we're looking for. Your courage, sense of justice, and willingness to stand up against adversity are traits we value."

"And you're telling me there aren't hundreds, possibly even thousands of other people with those exact traits, just waiting to sign up without all this bargaining?"

The Colonel's smile remained, but there was a seriousness in his eyes. "You're right; there are many individuals with those traits. But what sets you apart, Marcus, is that you're here right now, having this conversation with me. You have a choice to make, a decision that could change the course of your life. Let us do something here. Let us help you. Let us help your family."

Marcus glanced at his father, who was still listening intently. He could see the concern in the man's eyes, but also a glimmer of hope. The thought of better medical care and treatment options was undoubtedly tempting to the man who'd confessed to feeling less of a man simply because he was confined to a wheelchair.

Marcus turned back to the Colonel. "What if I enlist, and after all this, I'm not what you're looking for? What if I can't meet your expectations?"

The Colonel's tone was reassuring. "We'll provide you with training and guidance, Marcus. The process won't be easy, but we believe in your potential. And remember, this is a two-way street. You'll be evaluating us just as much as we're evaluating you."

Marcus bit his lip, his mind racing with conflicting thoughts. He glanced back at the Colonel. "Can I have some time to think about it?"

The Colonel shook his head and scratched the back of his neck again. "I… I'm sorry, Marcus. I need you to make your decision right now and come with me… there's something I haven't told you."

Marcus raised his eyebrows as though he'd been waiting for this moment. The one thing that would put all of this into perspective.

His heart raced.

"The barracks is effectively going into lockdown today. I can't say much about it – the truth is I couldn't even if I wanted to - but suffice it to say that even mentioning it could land me in a lot of trouble. Just, I want you to trust me Marcus. I want you to trust that I have your best interests at heart."

"Why?" Marcus repeated. "I still don't understand why this has to be me."

"Because I already put your name forward," the Colonel replied quickly. "It was a spur of the moment decision and I wouldn't change anything about it. I can see something in you, Marcus, something important. And needless to say, it's my career on the line here too, son, so please, think about this, and think about how we can help. You and your father."

Marcus's heart raced as he absorbed the weight of the Colonel's words. The idea of a lockdown, of something so significant happening that it could jeopardise the Colonel's career, was a revelation that pushed him further toward a decision. He looked at his father again, their eyes meeting in a silent exchange of hope.

"Alright," Marcus finally said, his voice steady. "I'll do it. I'll enlist and be a part of whatever this is. But I want it in writing that you'll do what you can to help my dad, right?"

The Colonel's face broke into a relieved smile, and Marcus felt a mix of emotions. If this really could help his father, then it would be worth it, whatever was in store for him. Plus, in the worst-case scenario, he knew he could always wait until his father had received whatever treatment they were going to try and then leave the army. It was one of those situations where whatever he chose to do, he would win. And he liked those, however fleeting they seemed to be.

"Thank you, Marcus," the Colonel said sincerely. "You're making a brave choice, and I believe you won't regret it."

Marcus turned to his father, who was beaming with pride, a kind of hope that had been absent for a long time. "Don't worry, Dad, I'll make sure they don't break their promise."

Tears glistened in Francis Cesari's eyes as he nodded, his voice shaky with emotion. "I'm proud of you, Marcus. This is a decision that you've come to on your own, something I couldn't possibly ask you to do for me. But if you're sure it's what you want, then I'm with you all the way."

"OK," Marcus said quietly. "What do I have to do? It's twenty weeks of basic training, right?"

"Twenty-six, actually," The Colonel replied. "But in truth, I think you're going to skip a lot of that, just you wait and see."

Marcus' palms turned cold. "Are we going to war?" he asked quietly. "Is that why you have to get as many people signed up as possible?"

"I can honestly say that I have absolutely no idea," the Colonel replied. "But what I do know, is that you alone are the single person that I have invited to enlist, Marcus, this isn't a mass conscription scenario."

The tension in the room was palpable as the weight of the unknown hung in the air. Marcus's decision to enlist had been made, but the uncertainty of the situation still gnawed at him. He glanced at his father again, silently reassuring him that he was willing to take this leap of faith, no matter the outcome.

The Colonel's expression softened as he saw the warring emotions on Marcus's face. "I understand that this is a lot to take in, Marcus. You're showing incredible courage by choosing this path. As for the situation, I wish I could provide more clarity, but some matters are beyond my station."

Marcus took a deep breath and nodded, steeling himself for the challenges ahead. "Alright then, Colonel. Tell me what I need to do next."

The Colonel's stiff professionalism returned as he stood up and straightened out his number ones. "You have to come with me now and say goodbye to your father for the foreseeable future. Oh, and Marcus," the Colonel said, his tone serious, "you'll need to keep the details of our conversation and your decision confidential. It's important for our security."

Marcus nodded, understanding the gravity of the situation. He could already tell that discussing anything related to the Colonel's actions would have consequences, both for him and for the Colonel.

Marcus extended his hand, shaking the Colonel's in a firm grip. "Thank you, Colonel. I'll do my best. I hope you keep your word."

With a final nod of affirmation and the simple order of "five minutes," the Colonel turned and left the Cesari home, leaving Marcus and his father alone in the kitchen. The room felt charged with a mixture of anticipation and anxiety. Marcus turned to his father, who was still seated in his wheelchair as always, his expression unreadable.

"You're really going to do this, Marcus?" Francis Cesari asked, his voice cracking and his throat dry.

Marcus crouched down beside his father, placing a hand on his shoulder. "Yes, Dad. I think it's the right choice. And if there's a chance that they can help you, then it's worth it, right?"

Tears welled up in Francis's eyes again, and he placed a hand over Marcus's. "I'm proud of you, son. You're stronger than I could have ever imagined."

Marcus smiled, his heart warming at his father's words. Then his expression darkened. "I won't get to say goodbye to mum!" he announced loudly. "What's she going to say when she gets home from work and I'm not here?"

Francis' face softened as he looked at his son, understanding the weight of his feelings. He reached out and gently squeezed Marcus's hand. "Your mother would want you to do what you believe is right, Marcus. She'd want you to make the decisions that are best for you."

Marcus's heart ached. He wished more than anything that he could share this moment with his mum, seek her advice, and feel her reassuring presence. But he knew he had to make this decision on his own, just as he was doing now.

"I'll write her a note," Marcus announced, "Explaining everything… she'll understand, right?"

Francis didn't respond. In truth, he didn't know how his wife would react to Marcus' sudden disappearance. But then, he knew that in time, and after he'd had a chance to explain everything to her, she'd come around.

"I'll come back, Dad. I promise. And I'll do my best to make you proud," Marcus eventually said through the silence.

Francis nodded, his eyes filled with more pride than Marcus had ever seen before. "Take care of yourself out there, Marcus. I'll be waiting for your return."

With a final embrace and a whispered farewell, Marcus turned and left the only home that he had ever truly known.

When Marcus looked across the road at the thick metal gates that stood between him and his surprise new future, he saw the Colonel waiting for him. He walked over to the man and gave him a nod.

"Do I need to bring anything? You didn't say..." Marcus started to ask but trailed off when he saw Armstrong shaking his head.

"Don't you worry, son, we've got everything you need right here. Anyway, follow me, and we'll get you kitted up just like everyone else. And between you and me," he lowered his voice and leant slightly closer to Marcus, "I'm glad you came. But don't tell anyone else that. Oh, and another thing: you may address me from this moment forward as 'sir' or 'Colonel', you got that?"

Marcus gave a cocky grin. "As long as I have something to blackmail you with later, Colonel sir."

Armstrong didn't reply, but he knew Cesari was joking. Well, at least he hoped he was anyway.

The pair walked on through the narrow corridors of the barracks and eventually came to a small room that had been filled top to bottom with oversized rucksacks. There must've been hundreds of the things in there, and it took a minute for Marcus to realise that he was being told to take one.

"They're all the same, son," Armstrong said to get him to hurry things along.

"Isn't there usually a guy handing these out?" Marcus asked, remembering what he'd seen on TV and learnt about the army recruiting processes. From what he could remember, it was much like a prison: you handed in all of your personal stuff, and they gave you the army-issue kit that you're supposed to have. Everyone was the same, every thing was the same.

"Usually, yes," the Colonel replied. "But not today, so pick one up and let's go."

Marcus dutifully obliged, trusting that all the packs were the same and left the room to follow the Colonel down the corridors once again. The pack was heavy, too heavy to be carried over a long distance, which Marcus hoped he wouldn't have to. Doors lined both sides of the hallways and occasionally stairs led off somewhere upwards. The doors were painted blue and had no glass windows to look through, so whatever was behind them would remain a mystery.

"The mess hall is through these double doors," the Colonel explained, stopping at the end of the hallway. "That's where you eat and sleep, got it?"

Marcus nodded.

"And to your right are the stairs that will lead you up to your quarters; that's where you sleep. You will be assigned a room number shortly."

Marcus nodded again. There was something wrong about all of this that he couldn't yet put his finger on, and he thought that if he spoke, then he might lose his trail of thought.

"Your dorm will house you and four other candidates, and ten dorms will share a head within your section of the barracks."

"And that's where we crap?" Marcus asked innocently. He couldn't help himself.

"That's where we crap, sir," the Colonel Corrected.

Marcus nodded.

"I don't really get along well with others," Marcus said quietly. He didn't mean it as a brag or some cocky response to the Colonel, but he felt like he needed to say it. "Have the dorms been assigned yet?"

The Colonel tapped Marcus on the back. "Don't worry son, I'm sure you're going to love your new friends."

There was a pause.

"And sir?" Marcus asked. "Where is everyone else? I mean, the soldiers that I assume fill this base from day to day? I assume I'm not the only person here, am I?" The thought had occurred to Marcus that perhaps he was the only one there and that this was somehow all one big joke, but he hadn't entertained it.

"You are not," the Colonel replied. "There are three Colonels in this base as of right now. Myself. Colonel Whittaker and Colonel Johnson. We three are to be the only senior officers within this barracks and we are not a part of Operation Legacy. Your fellow candidates will be arriving shortly, though again, very perceptive Cesari. Right now, there are indeed just four individuals present here in this entire barracks."

Chapter 6 – A Warm Welcome

The trucks carrying the new arrivals into the barracks streamed in like they were carrying colonies of ants. As each truck with its rounded tarp rear-end drove through the iron gates and came to a halt on the concrete, no less than twenty soldiers climbed off the back of them and fell into well-practised formations.

Marcus watched them from the side of the gate as the soldiers all stood there to attention, but he didn't follow suit; he hadn't been trained like they had, and he wasn't even wearing combat gear like they all seemed to be, proudly displaying their ranks on the tops of their arms.

From the flashes of colour that he could see, it was clear that these people weren't all privates like he was, or even ratings slightly above that rank. The scores and scores of soldiers he could see ranked from Lance Corporal to Major with a mixture of the ranks in between.

Eventually, the flow of trucks stopped, and the pavement was filled by the new arrivals. Then, from the door beside Marcus, the three Colonels emerged and walked straight to the front of the massed soldiers.

The Colonels stood to attention, facing the soldiers.

Then, from somewhere behind them, a fourth man approached. He looked older than the Colonels and his uniform was different, not one that Marcus recognised from what he knew about the British Army.

The man came to a halt and was silent for a long moment as though he was appraising the men and women before him. When he eventually spoke, his voice was loud, commanding and American.

"Candidates! My name is Vince Callahan, and I am your new base commander. Follow me into the barracks and we can begin the first day of the rest of your lives."

Marcus smiled. He'd nearly snorted but had managed to keep it in. All of this seemed just so overboard. Like it really was some huge elaborate practical joke.

Nevertheless, the soldiers trooped inside in a well-rehearsed fashion, their boots trip-trapping on the ground as they marched in unison, and then Marcus sauntered in behind them. He knew they'd be going to the mess hall of course – it was big enough to seat everyone as per its design, and they'd be close to the sacks of gear they would all have issued to them. Marcus carried his own with him like it was all he owned in the world. In actual fact, that wasn't very far off.

When everyone had found seating in the mess hall, which had seven convenient long bench-style tables running up to an eighth much shorter table for Callahan and the Colonels, the American spoke again.

"Welcome to Operation Legacy," he announced. "Now if you think that I'm going to stand up here and tell you everything there is to know about this Operation, then I'm sorry, but I'm going to have to disappoint you."

Marcus could now get a better look at the man, and could see that underneath his grey hair and his older outward appearance, the American looked like his gaze could pierce a balloon. His features were sharp and shaven, and his physique, though hidden by his uniform, looked large, strong and powerful. Marcus could tell that this was not a man to be messed with.

Callahan continued. "But I want to lay down a few rules before we begin, and don't worry, they aren't all bad. Firstly, I don't want to hear any complaints from any of you about the Operation. I don't want to hear your whinging or your whining about how difficult things are or about how the other candidates are treating you because frankly, I don't care. Life is hard, and the sooner you come to realise that, the better."

The room remained silent.

"Second, it will quickly become clear that this Operation is focused on finding the best of the best, so needless to say that you are all in direct competition with each other. If and when teams or squads are formed, you will still be in competition with each other, including your own teammates, so bear that in mind as we continue onwards."

The man surveyed the room for a short moment before he continued onto his third point.

"Thirdly, and this one might not be palatable for a few of you, judging by the ranks on your arms… your ranks, chevrons and insignia hereby mean absolutely nothing. You can, from this moment forward, consider yourselves the rank of Private in a new military branch that we have designated the 'Global Security Initiative' or the GSI."

There was a sharp intake of breath from the entire room. Marcus didn't particularly care that he was being made a Private – because technically that's what he was anyway – but he could feel the tension rising from the others. Years of service had just been effectively washed away with a single word and judging by the ranks he could see, some of these soldiers had been serving for more than ten years .They had just been busted back down to the bottom of the ladder through supposedly no fault of their own.

"Does anybody have a problem with that?" the man asked. It sounded like a question, but Marcus understood what it was: a threat.

There were a few shuffles of feet, but not a single soldier spoke up.

"Good," the man said. "You have all passed your first test: to not question the Operation. Now, as I have said, there is an upside to this. For the purposes of your pay and pension, the benefits are as follows: Whatever rank you were five minutes ago when you arrived in this barracks, you will receive pay to the equivalent of one rank above. In addition, you will receive pension contributions equivalent to one month of this new perceived rank for each week you spend within Operation Legacy."

That got Marcus' attention. He had been expecting to be on a salary at the lower end of the scale, somewhere around six thousand pounds if he remembered correctly, but if he'd understood it right, he now would be on a Lance Corporal wage, which should be at least ten thousand. But he wasn't in this for the money, and the announcement worried him. Why would the army give everyone here a pay rise? The only answer that he could think of, was danger. And the fact that they were effectively quadrupling their pension contributions with the caveat that it happened while they were in the Operation… it made Marcus wonder exactly how long the army expected them to remain in the Operation, or how they were expected to leave.

"And of course," the man continued. "You will have exclusive access to the world's foremost medical professionals. We wouldn't want our star pupils getting sick now, would we?"

Marcus found himself listening more intently now. The promise of higher pay was moot really, but better medical care was what he was here for. But this was also raising more questions in his mind. What exactly was this "Operation Legacy," and why were they treating it with such secrecy and seriousness? It was clear that whatever it was, it held a level of importance that went beyond regular military operations. And that was concerning.

Callahan's sharp gaze seemed to pierce through each soldier in the room as he continued to speak. "Now, I'm sure you're all curious about the nature of this Operation. While I won't disclose all the details at this moment, I will tell you this much: Operation Legacy is a test of your skills, your resilience, and your ability to adapt to unique challenges. You will be put through a series of trials, both mental and physical, that will push you to your limits and beyond. And rest assured, only the best among you will emerge as the true legacy of this initiative."

The tension in the room grew palpable. Marcus exchanged glances with a few of his fellow candidates, all of whom wore expressions ranging from curiosity to uncertainty, but everyone in the room was clearly acting professionally, just as soldiers were expected to act. This was a far cry from anything he had expected when he first stepped through the large metal gates into the barracks.

Marcus' head hurt and his body ached, but he kept his attention on Callahan.

"Your training begins today," Callahan declared, his voice unwavering. "You will be pushed, tested, and forged into an elite force that will redefine the standards of military excellence. You will learn skills that are beyond conventional military training, and you will be prepared to face challenges that no one else can or could possibly have imagined."

The hairs on Marcus' arms stood on end and his palms began to sweat. Something was wrong, he could tell. The words that Callahan used had been selected specifically to garner physical and mental responses from the soldiers, but he couldn't yet understand what or why.

But while the unknowns were intimidating, there was also an undeniable sense of purpose that emanated from Callahan's words. It was as if Marcus was being offered a chance to be a part of something greater, something that transcended everything he knew about the British army.

"You are all to report to your first mission," Callahan paused for a moment, then finished: "Medical examination. Each room through the doors behind you has been refitted and converted into a state-of-the-art medical facility, where doctors await each of you to carry out your medicals. Dismissed!" Callahan's command rang through the mess hall, and the soldiers began to stand up and disperse without another word.

Marcus followed suit, his mind racing with thoughts about the path he had just embarked upon. He had signed up for an opportunity that was far more unconventional and mysterious than he could have imagined.

As the candidates filed out of the mess hall, Marcus felt much more curiosity than he did apprehension; Everything that had happened so far just seemed so odd.

He followed the flow of soldiers towards the doors leading to the medical examination rooms. The hallway beyond was bustling with activity as soldiers made their way to the rooms and lined up on either side in fairly even groups.

Marcus' pulse began to quicken as he stood in line, waiting for his turn. The thoughts that had been nagging at him since the beginning of all of this resurfaced, gnawing at his mind. Would the medical examination uncover the genetic condition that had plagued his father? Would they discover something that he might've preferred to have ignored for most of his life?

Lost in his own thoughts, Marcus was startled when a voice next to him broke his pondering silence. He turned to see a young woman with vibrant red hair and hazel eyes standing beside him. She wore the rank of Corporal on her uniform, and her presence exuded nothing but confidence.

"Got a thing about needles? Or is it just doctors in general, huh?" She asked with a friendly smile.

Marcus managed a small nod, surprised that the girl had struck up a conversation with him. "Yeah, you could say that," he replied quietly, but didn't offer anything more.

She extended her hand towards him. "I'm Corporal Elise Ramirez. Nice to meet you."

Marcus shook her hand, offering a nervous smile. "Marcus Cesari. Likewise." He had no rank to introduce himself with, so he didn't, but he didn't make a point about it either.

Ramirez's eyes twinkled with something that Marcus couldn't place. It was like she was speaking with an equal, a peer perhaps, and he'd never really had that feeling before.

"It's all a bit weird, isn't it?" She said.

"Yeah, you could say that too," Marcus replied, trying to mask his nervousness with a hint of humour.

She chuckled. "Don't worry, you're not alone in feeling that way. These kinds of situations have a way of making everyone a little on edge. Trust me, I've moved around more than a few times and I'm still here. What doesn't kill you only makes you stronger that's what I say."

"Tell that to my dad," Marcus muttered under his breath.

"What?" the girl asked.

"Nothing… don't worry about it," Marcus said.

"Listen, you know you can always fall back on the old classic, right?" Ramirez said. "If you get too nervous in there, just imagine the doctor naked. Or is that public speaking? Doesn't matter really, the point is you'll be ok, there's nothing a doctor hasn't seen before."

Despite himself, Marcus couldn't help but smile at this soldier's words. Her easy-going demeanour and friendly approach definitely helped to ease some of the tension he had been carrying. But he hadn't sought it out, hadn't looked to strike up a conversation and yet here it was, some Corporal just trying to make him feel better for no reason. It was odd.

"Are you curious about what's going on?" she asked, her gaze shifting towards the examination rooms.

Marcus hesitated, then nodded. "Yeah, I am. And a bit anxious, too, if I'm honest about it."

Ramirez' expression turned sympathetic. "I get it. We're all in the dark, all in the same boat, you know? But the way I see it, we've been chosen for something big. Something that could change our lives and we wouldn't be here if we didn't deserve it."

Marcus grimaced. Did he deserve this? From what he'd seen of the soldiers, they had all given years of their lives to the army. All he'd done was have a fight with a couple of soldiers, and some Colonel had taken pity on him. Did that make him worthy, or did it make him more of a charity case? Whatever the reason, he certainly didn't feel like he belonged in whatever special force this was that was being assembled.

"Thanks," Marcus said, doing his best to offer up a genuine smile. "It's just… I have some concerns about the medical examination."

Ramirez raised an eyebrow, her curiosity piqued. "What's bothering you? You know if it's about…" her eyes dropped for a second to Marcus' crotch before returning a split second later.

"No!" Marcus interrupted quickly. Then he hesitated, unsure whether he should share his worries, especially to a stranger. But something about this woman's openness encouraged him to speak his mind. After all, if this was going to be his life now, he was going to own it.

"There's a genetic condition in my family. My father has it. I haven't been tested for it, and I'm worried they might find out that I do have it during the examination."

Ramirez' gaze softened, and she placed a reassuring hand on Marcus' shoulder. "Look, Marcus, you're not alone in having concerns. We all have worries and doubts. But this is a medical, not a complete scan for whatever it is you might have. No doubt it's just the same as all the other medicals we've been through, and if they've not found anything wrong with you yet, you're probably fit as a – terribly anxious - fiddle."

Marcus again skirted the truth. He'd never had a medical before, and this Corporal seemed to think he was something he wasn't: a soldier. He wouldn't correct her though; if the soldiers in the barracks knew he was really just some untrained civvie, his life could get far more difficult in all of this. As it was, if he could keep his head down, he might just be able to get through all this.

"You should try being a girl, though," Ramirez continued conversationally. "They're always wanting to get a good look at you, you know, downstairs?" She pointed downwards conspiratorially. "Sometimes I think it's a bit less medical and a little more… you know." She waved a hand around nonchalantly.

Marcus frowned. He hadn't really thought about the details of the medical, just the result. It made him wonder just how personal things would get in there and if it would be a male or female doctor who would examine him.

He hoped he could get some painkillers though. Perhaps the doctor would see how hurt he actually was and take pity on him.

Entering the room, Marcus was shocked at how pristine it all was. Shining stainless steel cabinets and counters, a very posh looking leather reclining chair in the centre of the room – much like a dentist's chair – bright white lights, a bed, and in the corner sat at a small podium-style desk, a middle-aged blonde woman smiling a warm welcome in his direction.

"Good morning," she said sweetly. "Name?"

Marcus blinked. He hadn't expected the doctor to be a woman if he was honest about the situation, and her friendly greeting took him completely off guard.

The doctor tapped the clipboard on the desk. "Just to make sure I put all the ticks in the right boxes, nothing invasive."

"Marcus," Marcus replied. "Marcus Cesari. But I don't know if you'll have me on there because I only just…"

"Ah, here you are," she said. "Well… that's going to be a problem," she continued, frowning.

Marcus' heart sank. They already knew. But how could they? This whole thing was going to be over before it even started.

"This is your first military medical, right?" the doctor said. "Not to worry, my name's Dr. Jones, and you have nothing to worry about. I keep my hands warm and my bedside manner caring. I presume that all of this," she gestured to his bruised face, "is nothing I should be concerned about?"

Marcus shook his head. "No, not at all."

"Good. Now I promise you, this isn't going to hurt a bit."

The doctor then pulled a pair of white latex gloves over her hands with a snap and Marcus' heart skipped a beat.

"Take a seat."

Marcus dutifully sat down on the leather chair, feeling a bit like he was in a futuristic sci-fi movie rather than a regular medical examination. He watched as Dr. Jones approached him, her demeanour calm and professional. She picked up a small device from a tray nearby and Marcus braced himself for whatever was coming next.

"First, I'll need to take your vitals," Dr. Jones explained, affixing a blood pressure cuff around his arm and attaching a small clip to his fingertip to measure his pulse and oxygen levels. The familiar tightening of the cuff and the rhythmic beep of the pulse oximeter eased some of Marcus' anxiety. It was a simple procedure, one he'd certainly heard about before and had seen in numerous movies.

As the doctor inflated the blood pressure cuff, she spoke again.

"Do you have anything I should worry about? Any conditions or illnesses that run in your family?"

The hairs on Marcus' arms stood on end as a wave of terror washed over him. This was it. If he told the doctor about his father and his own possible inherited condition, then he could be kicked out of the program altogether. But if he said nothing, then would he be passing up the opportunity he'd been given to get tested, or even cured?

"I…" Marcus pushed out. "What kinds of things do you mean?"

"The usual really," the doctor replied absently as she watched the blood pressure gauge. "Asthma, heart failure, dementia… the big ones mostly. The ones that come along later in life and suddenly the army realises that you haven't been worth the food they gave you." She gave a little chuckle.

Then and there, Marcus made his decision. He would have to keep what he knew a secret until he had his feet well and truly under the table.

"My dad's in a wheelchair, but it happened a long time ago. That's about it." Of course, Marcus knew that the best lie he could tell would be one that had its roots in truth.

"Fall off a bike?" The doctor asked.

"Something like that."

"Well, your blood pressure's good. Maybe a little high, but that's probably explained by your high pulse… if I didn't know better, I'd say you have a thing for me, Mr. Cesari." She smiled and winked, but Marcus could tell it was a joke.

With Marcus feeling far more at ease about his entire situation now, the doctor moved on to check his reflexes and range of motion. She used a small rubber mallet to gently tap his knee, causing his leg to kick out involuntarily. Marcus couldn't help but let his mind wander to how he was going to broach the topic of his possible condition in the future. He kind of just wished he wouldn't have to worry and that it would all just somehow sort itself out.

"Alright, Marcus, I'm going to listen to your heart and lungs now," the doctor informed him, picking up her stethoscope and placing it on his chest. It was cold and unwelcome, but Marcus did his best to remain upright and strong.

As the stethoscope moved over his chest, he let his mind drift for a moment. He remembered his father's stories of his time in the military, the pride he'd felt wearing the uniform, the camaraderie he'd shared with his fellow soldiers. His father had never talked about his health issues, but Marcus could now see the toll they had taken over the years. How could he have been so blind?

"Deep breaths for me, please," the doctor instructed, bringing Marcus back to the present. He followed her directions, inhaling and exhaling as she moved the stethoscope to different spots on his chest and back. The sound of his own heartbeat filled his ears, and his palms again turned wet.

"Giving you some grief, those bruises?" the doctor asked. "Not to worry, I'll get you some painkillers and you'll have forgotten about it in no time."

"Thanks," Marcus grumbled.

And finally, it was time for the last part of the examination. Dr. Jones prepared a metallic syringe and a small vial, her gloved hands steady and practised. Marcus watched as she carefully inserted the needle into his arm. It was sharp and it stung, but he resisted the urge to flinch. Then, the doctor drew a small sample of his blood. His heart raced a little, his anxiety resurfacing. Would this vial of his blood be the answer to his potential genetic condition? He could only wait and see.

"All done," Dr. Jones said with a warm smile, placing a bandage over the spot where she'd taken the blood sample. "You did great, Marcus."

"Thank you," Marcus replied, surprised by the genuine relief in his own voice. It was over, and whatever the results might be, he had faced this thing head-on. "But," he couldn't help but ask. "Aren't you going to ask how I got all the cuts and bruises?"

The doctor smiled. "Is that something I should be asking about? Is it a condition to be monitored, or did you just happen to walk into a door... one that opened and closed a few times on your face, admittedly..."

"No, nothing to worry about," Marcus replied shyly. He wasn't sure why he'd asked, but he felt a little silly for it now.

As he left the examination room, he then realised he hadn't given much thought to what came after the medical. Callahan's words echoed in his mind: "You will be pushed, tested, and forged into an elite force..."

Corporal Ramirez was waiting for him outside, a reassuring smile on her face. "All done?"

Marcus nodded. "Yeah, it wasn't as bad as I thought it would be."

She grinned. "Told you. Doctors aren't so scary once you get used to 'em. Except those mad ones who take your blood at the end. You don't want to even know what they do with that."

"What?" Marcus raised his voice in exasperation.

"Kidding," Ramirez replied.

Chapter 7 – Friendly Faces

"So I'm not usually one to pry, but how did you really get all those cuts and bruises anyway? And the black eye?" Ramirez asked as the pair made their way through the busy hallways. They'd been assigned rooms and it had been because Ramirez and Marcus were next to each other during the assignment that they had been placed in the same dorm. Number seventy-one – same as his house number, strangely enough. Marcus hadn't been expecting mixed-gender dorms, but he supposed that it was just the way it was.

"You should see the other guy," Marcus said as he shrugged.

Ramirez smiled but didn't reply.

"I uh… just got into a bit of a fight last night," Marcus continued to fill the silence. "Honestly, I woke up in the infirmary and they said nothing was broken, so I could get back to the real world."

Marcus was already clear in his conviction; he wouldn't be telling anybody that he was a civvie, and had spent a grand total of zero hours in the army. He figured that not only would it make him look stupid next to all the other ratings and officers, but it could also mean that he would be singled out and targeted. Something that he certainly didn't want to incite.

"And what do you think of this GSI business?" Ramirez asked. "I mean, I don't like the thought of being called a Private again, that's for sure, but I was a Corporal, you know? It took me a long time to get there, and it kind of feels like I've just thrown it all away."

"I wouldn't worry," Marcus replied. "They wouldn't do all of this if it wasn't something big."

"How so?" Ramirez asked. "I once watched a PT instructor make a new recruit do naked press-ups in the mud and rain because his trousers weren't creased enough. You tell me how there's any sense in that?"

Marcus snorted. "Well, look at what we have here: hundreds of the army's finest, right? A secret program that we aren't even being told about, communications blackouts, an entire barracks shut down for the purposes of whatever this operation is. This all has a point, and it's big."

"You're quite perceptive, you know that?" Ramirez asked. "Like, you think too much. What rank did you say you were again?"

"I'm a Private with the GSI thank you very much," Marcus replied with a smile that he hoped was just cocky enough to gloss over what he was leaving out.

"Well damn, me too!" Ramirez replied with an outstretched hand for Marcus to shake.

The pair reached their assigned dorm room and stepped inside. It was small, there were five single metal beds with thin looking mattresses on top of each. At the foot of each bed was a small locker and on top of that, a pillow and two sheets. Nothing about the place screamed either home or comfort, but at least the dorms weren't hundreds of beds long like Marcus had seen in the movies.

"I call top bunk!" Ramirez announced and leapt onto the bed closest to the door.

Marcus took the second bed and wondered exactly what he was going to put in the little locker, but when he opened it, he found three identical outfits complete with shining black boots. The outfits were a black and olive green overall, and on the right shoulder they each bore crest displaying a globe and a single vertical red line underneath – presumably this was the GSI emblem along with the Private rank indicator.

"Sexy right?" Ramirez said as she held up her own outfits. "One size fits all, boots n'all!"

"What?" Marcus asked. He hadn't even thought about how they'd sized everything, not knowing where the soldiers would locate themselves within the dorms.

Picking up the shiny black boots, he looked them over to figure out what size they were, though on thorough inspection nothing came to light, so he put them on the ground, sat on his bed and pushed his feet into them, one at a time.

The boots felt amazing. Like nothing he'd ever worn before. They fit perfectly before he'd even touched the laces, and he had to stop himself from asking if all army boots were like this before he looked up at Ramirez, who he was happy to see was staring down at her own boots with similar wonder in her eyes.

"They… they fit so well," she said quietly. "Like nothing I've ever worn on my feet before. Like they weigh nothing at all, but still they're solid as steel… what… what is this?"

"They must be something new," Marcus replied slowly. He knew now it was OK to be weirded out by the boots. "Like the next generation in combat gear or something…" then something clicked in his mind. "This is what Operation Legacy must be all about!"

"Boots?" Ramirez asked incredulously.

"Not boots, testing!" Marcus said. "They must test out updated technologies with soldiers, mustn't they? But if something's dangerous then they couldn't do it at a live barracks… so we're… guinea pigs?" his mood quickly changed from happy to concerned as he finished his statement with a question mark.

"Oooh, I hope it's more stuff like the boots," Ramirez replied, clearly choosing not to rise to the guinea pig thing. "You think all the gear…"

Marcus looked down at the overalls and shrugged. These would've been easier to size than boots, but now he was curious. So he stepped into the overalls – not removing his boots first as would have been proper – and pulled them on surprisingly easily.

It was like the overalls had been tailored specifically for Marcus. Even after he slid his booted feet through the leg holes, nothing was difficult or too tight, but somehow, once he'd zipped the front up, it was like the whole thing had shrunk down to fit him as well as could be.

"Yeah, it's the overalls too," Marcus announced as Ramirez watched him with her mouth gaping open. Marcus had put the overalls on top of his regular clothes, and it didn't even seem to have caused even the slightest issue.

Ramirez then quickly pulled her combats off and over her head, removed her boots and trousers and picked up the strange overalls, now standing before Marcus in just her bra and pants.

And then the door swung open.

"You uh… want us to come back later?" a deep male voice said. It was owned by what Marcus could see was a Lieutenant, judging by his pair of pips. The man was tall, well-built and had short brown hair with hazel eyes that seemed friendly, yet disciplined.

"You know you're supposed to put your cap on the door if you're doing that sort of thing," a second male voice came, this one from a stocky Corporal, who barged his way into the room.

Once the pair of soldiers had made it into the room and Ramirez had quickly dressed herself in her new gear, a blonde female Lieutenant walked in and stood to attention by her bunk.

"At ease Private," the male Lieutenant said. You heard the Colonel, no ranks here, so that meant no ceremony. We can consider this boot camp."

The Lieutenant took a moment to appraise the room, then visibly relaxed.

"Sorry," she said, "Kind of a force of habit at this point. Do you have any idea what this is all about?"

"Not a clue," the Lieutenant said with a smile. "Just got this order to ship out, no questions asked, and here I am. Damn long ride to get here but it's not my money so you know, it is what it is." He paused for a moment after realising that four people were now watching him. "The name's Ethan McCulloch, and I suppose I was a Lieutenant. I like woodworking and vintage cars. Seems like we should all get to know each other if this is our digs?"

There was a moment of silence before the remaining four roommates realised that they were supposed to then offer up their names and interests.

"Corporal Liam Foley," the stocky Corporal said. I like rugby."

"Emily King, Lieutenant," the blonde woman announced. "I like sports and uh... nature."

"Ramirez, Elise, Corporal," Ramirez offered the group. "Bit of a martial arts buff. And I like reading too. We can't all be killing machines."

Then all eyes fell to Marcus, who hesitated for a moment before speaking.

"Marcus Cesari. I grew up around here, and I don't know if I have too many interests past movies and sports." Then he gestured to his face and added: "Don't worry about all this, the other five guys got it worse."

"Well that's the five of us I guess," McCullock stated, clearly breezing over the cuts and bruises on Marcus' face, and Marcus let out a quiet breath, happy that he hadn't been asked for his rank. "We're all privates in the GSI now, so we should just take whatever beds we can and get changed?" he peered at Ramirez and Marcus, who had both already changed into the strange overalls denoting their new rank.

"Looks like we caught these two red-handed," Foley smiled, indicating Marcus and Ramirez."

"Oh, don't be jealous, Corporal," Ramirez shot back. "I'm sure you'll get to see a lot more of me if we're living here together. The problem is, I just don't think you'd be able to handle it."

King covered her mouth, and Marcus could see from her cheeks that she was hiding a smile whilst Foley turned bright red.

"Have you ever seen anything like this?" Marcus asked, indicating the gear he was wearing. "I mean, I don't know how to describe it… just put it on and see what you think."

"I've worn my fair share of overalls working on the cars," McCulloch said absent-mindedly as he pulled his legs into the overalls. "Once you get used to them…" then he abruptly stopped speaking and his eyes grew wide. "Did they just…"

Foley furrowed his brow. "What's the matter? Too tight around the gonads?"

"N… no," McCulloch stuttered. "They… it was like they just resized themselves. They were way too big, but as soon as I got them on… they just, well, fit."

"Shut up," Foley said. "I may look like someone you can pull a fast one on, but I'm not falling for it this soon. What do you four all know each other, and this is the hazing of the new guy or something?"

"Just try it, new boy," Ramirez said. "You're going to make yourself look like an idiot if you keep talking."

Foley abruptly shut up and pulled his own gear on. His movements became more cautious as he experienced what McCulloch had just described. As he zipped up the front of the olive green and black outfit, his eyes widened in surprise, and he glanced around the room as if expecting someone to jump out and reveal the prank. But there was no one else there except for the group of newly recruited privates.

"It's true," Foley muttered, his voice tinged with amazement. "These things are like magic. They just fit perfectly."

Ramirez grinned triumphantly. "Told you so. These overalls are something else. But don't you find it a bit tight around the crotch?" she asked earnestly.

"No, not even a little bit," Foley replied slowly.

"Oh… then I just must have more down there than you then I guess."

King snorted this time as she attempted to hide her laugh, and Marcus raised an eyebrow. Foley again turned bright red, but didn't reply.

Last of the group, King stepped forward, her own bundle of gear in her arms. "Well, no use just standing here talking about it. Might as well see for myself." With that, she changed into the overalls, her expression shifting from doubt to surprise as she experienced the unusual fit for herself.

Each member of the newly formed dorm then put on their boots and experienced the exact same sensation that Marcus and Ramirez had already. The group exchanged glances and words of wonder, and even Foley couldn't hide his amazement, but nobody said another word until they all wore the new outfits.

"This is unreal," McCulloch said, shaking his head in disbelief. "I've never seen anything like it."

"Definitely not your typical military uniform," Marcus remarked, his earlier tension easing as he shared this strange experience with his new companions.

"Marcus thinks that this is why we're here: to test new gear for the army. It makes sense, right? Especially after putting these things on."

"It seems like a lot, though, doesn't it? Just for some new tactical gear?" McCulloch replied. "I mean, they could just hand out a few of these to soldiers in the field and see how they do, couldn't they? Why go through all of this?"

"Guns," Ramirez said with wonder in her eyes. "Untested, big, dangerous guns… it just has to be! And these overalls are just another thing they want testing!"

Foley's eyes had lit up at that, but King looked like she wanted to be anywhere else but there.

"That… sounds dangerous," she said quietly. "I don't know if I want to be testing something that could blow us all up. I mean, look at the atomic bomb. Is that something you would've wanted to be a part of?"

The group fell silent again, thinking about just how dangerous this all could be for them.

"Well, we're here now," McCulloch announced. "So we just have to see what we can do, and if it all gets too much, then we just request transfers. But that pension contribution… that's something I haven't heard of before. I mean, I don't know about you guys, but I plan to keep in the program as long as I can so that when I retire, I do it the right way."

"Retire?" Foley said. "What are you like fifty? We got another twenty years of service in each of us at least. And I plan to make the most of it."

"What about you, Cesari?" Foley nodded at Marcus. "Thinking about retiring already, or are you a real man?"

"Hey!" Ramirez interrupted. "Don't make me and King here show you what a real man looks like."

King smiled at Ramirez' words, and Foley nodded in apology.

"You know what I meant."

"Actually," Marcus said, moving the conversation along. "I just want to get through whatever all this is, and then we'll see later. Who knows, they may want to retire us after anyway, you know… if we know too much or something."

"You don't think they'll want to kill us, do you, you know, keep us quiet?" Foley asked.

"That actually sounds… pretty likely," King said quietly. "I heard about a secret program up Colchester, and when it was all over, it was like a national security risk or something. Nobody ever heard from any of those guys again after the cleanup."

"Really?" Foley asked, turning a shade paler.

"No you tit!" King laughed. "Out of all the candidates here and we get Sergent gullible!"

"Corporal, actually," Foley said.

"Private actually," McCulloch corrected. "And listen, it doesn't matter what we think. We're all enlisted to do a job, and no matter what it is, this is what we do. If it makes us into some supersoldiers, then all the better, but if it's just testing to see how many parades these shiny new boots can stay shiny for, then that's what we do and we smile while we do it."

"Ooh, I hope it's a new bayonet, one that heats up when it's attached or something," Ramirez said with a sparkle in her eyes. "No wait, one where the bullets never miss!"

Marcus couldn't help but smile. Ramirez was clearly a soldier, but she spoke with wonder in her voice, like everything was exciting and new. It was a feeling he hadn't experienced for himself for a long time.

"Ivan Drago," Foley said. "That's what I want. Turn me into a machine with some medical program, and I'll give them what for."

Marcus was the only one who apparently knew what Foley was talking about.

"Didn't Drago lose?" he said.

"Well… yeah, but that was just Hollywood. In real life, Drago would've knocked Rocky's block off. What do you think is going to happen anyway, smarty pants?"

Marcus thought for a moment before responding. He had been taking in what everyone had said, but he still couldn't make his mind up.

"Well, it has to be something big. And something dangerous, otherwise they wouldn't have gone to all the trouble. At first, I thought it had something to do with the queen or the PM, but after seeing this gear, I'd say it was something more advanced, technology based maybe. Something we don't want anyone else to know about. Most likely, I'd say it's a new rifle, maybe something that's never been done before?"

"I knew it!" Ramirez cried. "I knew you'd agree with me!"

"And what, the outfits are just a side project?" McCulloch asked.

"Maybe," Marcus said. "Like I said, I don't really know, but if it was just the outfits, you were right when you said they'd just throw a few of them out into active duty and see what happens. This has to be something much bigger than that. Something important."

The dorm fell silent again as each of the Privates thought about what the Operation could have in store for them. They knew there was no way of finding out, other than just waiting to see what came next.

"What do you think's going to be for dinner?" Foley asked to eventually break the silence.

That was something Marcus hadn't thought about yet – he would never have to worry about food ever again, because he would be provided with not only clothing and lodgings as a soldier, but also meals, along with being told what to do, when and where to be, at all times.

It didn't actually sound all that bad.

Chapter 8 – Baseline Testing

It wasn't long before something happened that nobody could ignore. The light in the dorms, the hallways and, by all accounts, the entire barracks turned to red, and a siren wailed at an uncomfortable level. It was exactly the opposite of what Marcus needed for his headache.

"That's the call," McCulloch announced a moment after the sound started, and the four trained soldiers leapt for the door. Marcus was last to make his move, not entirely sure what it was they were supposed to do in a situation like this, but happy he at least had a group to follow. But blending in wasn't going to always be so easy, and he knew he was going to have to learn fast if he wanted his true past to remain a mystery.

"Where are we going?" Marcus asked Ramirez as they entered the hallway and quickly joined the other scores of newly-uniformed privates rushing to get where they were going. He was sure that nobody else could hear him over the sound of the periodically wailing siren.

"Parade square," Ramirez shot back. "Must be something good otherwise they'd just send a runner to the dorms."

Marcus wasn't so sure about that. He'd been listening at that first briefing, and he remembered that the barracks wasn't properly staffed, so he doubted that there were any 'runners' to be found.

The group were assaulted by the bright sunlight contrasting against the dim red light inside the barracks, and it took Marcus more than a moment to get his vision back to where it needed to be.

"Listen up!" the sound of the American-accented base commander Callahan hit Marcus' ears, and even though he had no formal training, the sound certainly made him stand a little straighter.

Marcus did his best to copy the rest of the soldiers in the way they stood, their feet firmly pressed together and their arms flat against their sides. Nobody wore berets, though, which Marcus assumed meant that the uniform simply didn't include them.

"I told you that this operation would test you all to the best of your abilities. I see that you have all found the uniforms that we have assigned for you, and I presume that you're all comfortable in them?"

The question was clearly rhetorical, and nobody responded.

"Good. Now, your testing is to begin immediately. Does anybody have a problem with that?"

"No sir!" came a loud, chorused reply from every single soldier on the parade ground except Marcus. Thankfully, the response had been so loud and well-coordinated that nobody could've noticed.

"Good. Now how is your running pace?" Callahan asked with a smile and this time nobody responded.

"Then something easy to get us all acquainted then," he said. Then his voice raised into a shout. "You will run out of these gates in a four-man column. Turn left and run straight until you see the pebbles on the beach. Then make a right turn and keep going until you reach the sign for the Zetland Arms, at which point you will make an about turn and run all the way back here. This is a six point seven five kilometre, or as you Brits like to say, four-point two-mile run, so I would expect you to be there and back in thirty-three minutes or less. What are you waiting for people an invitation? Move move move!"

The soldiers seemed to move as one as they all turned on their heels and formed into a four-man column that spilled from the barrack gates and made their way to the seafront. They made no sound other than their boots hammering the pavement as they moved in unison.

It took Marcus a little while to get the step right to fit in with the rest of the soldiers, but he'd placed himself near the back of the column so that he could watch what everyone was doing, and if the pace proved too quick for him then at least not too many people would notice.

Running was painful though, and right from the beginning, his body protested.

Canada Road, up to where it met the beach was easy. Marcus kept in step and up to pace without too much hassle, but when he turned the corner and had a moment to appreciate just how far they were expected to run, his heart sank.

He tried. He really, really tried but after the first mile was done, Marcus' lungs burnt with the effort of keeping his aching body moving in the right direction. He hadn't tried running in a long, long time, and if anything, he was pretty unfit although he didn't look it, and the beating he'd taken just made everything so much harder. He was pleasantly surprised, though, that his boots gave him no trouble at all and were as light and as comfortable as the moment he'd put them on.

"Come on, Marcus," Ramirez encouraged. He hadn't noticed her next to him, but he would've preferred she wasn't there at all. "What's wrong? Stone in your boots?"

Marcus turned to look at her. Not a bead of sweat or the slightest sign of exhaustion on her, where he felt like he wanted to lay down and die.

"Its… been… a… while…" Marcus managed to wheeze back, to which Ramirez looked at him with an expression of both surprise and disgust.

"Not even a mile, Marcus," she said. "You better remember who you are and lift those boots."

Marcus fell back another place in the squad. Then another and another as soldiers overtook him with ease.

"God dam it you worthless, half assed, waste of a uniform and med kit excuses for a soldier! Do you really think that what you are doing right now is worth the money that it costs to simply keep you alive?" Cesari! Lift those boots off the ground and keep pace with the rest of the squad before I come up there and give you a reason to run!"

Callahan's voice was what Marcus heard approaching from behind before the thundering footsteps bearing down on him. He tried to push whatever he had left in the tank into his legs and for a moment, he did manage to cut a little of the distance between him and the back of the pack, but it was too little too late and after a moment, he came to a halt, doubling over and struggling to breathe.

Marcus heard the base commander's boots approach and come to a halt next to him. He could see how shiny they were and how they exactly matched his own boots.

"Are you playing with me son?" Callahan asked at a slightly higher than civil volume. "Are you seriously telling me that you aren't capable of running two miles without having to stop for a rest? Is this the best of what the British Army has to offer? Because I tell you what: If you were a member of my unit, you wouldn't have had to worry about the enemy pointing their guns at you, I'd be more worried about getting in the way of my allies. Now you can get yourself back on your feet and make it to that God damn building and back again no matter what it takes, or you can get the hell out of my operation right God damn now!"

Marcus wasn't sure what made him do it. It was either Callahan's degrading of him and the British Army, or the fact that he simply wanted to prove the man wrong. But he unfolded himself, and started jogging. At his own pace now, without trying to keep up with the rest or even to close the gap.

Callahan continued to pace Marcus from a few strides behind until a few minutes later when the rest of the group passed by Marcus in the opposite direction. He didn't know how far he still had to go, but he was determined to make it no matter how long it took. Thankfully, Callahan left him alone when Marcus neither replied, slowed or sped up at his shouts or insults.

More than a few of the soldiers gave Marcus confused looks, some even raised their eyebrows as they passed him, and some even shook their heads. He managed to spot Ramirez as she approached too, but kept his gaze on the ground so that he couldn't see the disappointment in her eyes. He knew there would be no explaining this one away.

Marcus finally made it to the Zetland Arms alone, and as soon as he reached the sign, he curved his slow jog and began the journey back. His pace was now so methodical that it was almost robotic. He kept his eyes fixed on the ground and just concentrated on putting one foot in front of the other over and over. His throat was tight, his chest hurt and his muscles burned, but he kept going with nothing but sheer stubbornness fuelling his desire to get this all over and done with. But he wouldn't give up. He needed to stay in this at least until he was sure that his parents were going to be looked after properly. That was the thought that came to him over and over each time he just wanted to stop.

'Do this for dad,' he thought. 'Just a little bit further.'

Do this for dad.

And then finally, it was over.

Marcus practically fell through the gates, where the rest of the soldiers were standing to attention in the parade square once again and in silence.

"Private Cesari," Callahan boomed from the front of the amassed soldiers. "It's so nice of you to join us. Now, have you heard the expression that a chain is only as strong as its weakest link?" he paused as though awaiting a response, which he didn't get.

Callahan turned his attention back to the soldiers. "Well, for the purposes of these baseline tests, not only are you all being assessed individually, but also as a fighting force. And do you know what that means, ladies and gentlemen? Well, that means that your entire unit has just recorded a time to run four miles and change, of fifty-one minutes and twelve seconds. Congratulations people, you just made a laughing stock out of the British Army."

Marcus could see eyes shifting to look at him, but no heads turned. He felt embarrassed, ashamed and above everything else, like he didn't belong there.

"And if you're all feeling refreshed and ready for your next test, I would like you all to prepare for something that I like to call The Gauntlet."

Marcus' head began to pound again immediately. It was like he'd been beaten to a pulp, hadn't had any sleep and then thrown into a top-level army fitness test. Which, of course, was exactly what had happened. None of the real soldiers seemed to care though, as they didn't seem to respond in any way to the announcement.

"Over there," Callahan gestured to a green hill behind him, nestled neatly in the centre of the barracks, "we, your instructors have painstakingly arranged The Gauntlet. Now this is an obstacle course in which you will be judged on your speed, decision making, tactical awareness, and ability to work as a unit. Set between two hills which will be treated as impassable, you will be fired upon by myself and the three Colonels here in the barracks. We will be armed with SMG-60 select fire paint guns. Six hundred rounds per minute with an effective range of one hundred feet. Now, if you are hit, you are dead. If you leave a man behind, you have failed. If you take too long to complete the course, you have failed. Do you understand me?"

"Sir, yes sir!" the call returned, and this time, Marcus had enough wits about himself to respond on time and in the correct manner.

"Now this course will be taken in groups of five, and surprise surprise candidates, those groups will be denoted by your dorms, of which the number will be your designator.

Marcus thought back to his own dorm, number seventy-one, just like the house he'd grown up in. It was a bit of a coincidence, sure, but it wasn't something he was going to put too much stock into.

"First squad, go!" Callahan shouted, and five of the soldiers clacked their boots together and ran towards the grassy hills. Marcus couldn't tell if it was by design, but he couldn't actually see anything of The Gauntlet because of where all the soldiers were left standing.

"The rest of you at ease," Callahan ordered, to which all of the soldiers visibly relaxed where they stood. "You will be called when it is your turn to face The Gauntlet and until then I expect you to display just how patient you Brits can be."

Second squad was called just three minutes later, but first didn't come back to tell the rest of the soldiers what to expect. They must've been moved along to whatever Callahan had in store for them all next.

The squads were called in numerical order, and each took up to about five minutes to take their turn, with some taking as little as a minute before the next was called. In the meantime, Marcus had the chance to group up with his dorm mates and devise their plan of action.

McCulloch was the one to round up the squad, and he was the first to speak.

"Alright, it can't be anything too different to what we're used to, so I say we tackle it as we normally would – two groups, a two and a three. Me and Foley will stay left, King, Ramirez and Cesari you take to the right. One group covers and the other moves, alternating the pattern until we make it through."

"What?" Marcus asked while the rest of the group nodded. "How do you know there's going to be a left and a right path? And what if it's nothing like the others?"

Seventy-First squad looked at Marcus like he'd grown three heads.

"They're always the same," Ramirez said. "Unless you know something we don't?"

"No..." Marcus replied. "I mean, they can't all be the same, can they? Otherwise, what's the point? If this operation is completely geared to us being tested with some new weapon... and these new outfits... then why would they want to just do the same thing over and over?" He was backpedalling and he knew it. Of course, it made sense that it would be the same as the others; that was the point of baseline testing, wasn't it? But after his slip, he didn't want to be asked questions like 'haven't you done one of these before?' Or 'how long have you served for anyway?' There was only so much he could blame on his cuts and bruises.

Nobody seemed to challenge Marcus though, a fact that he was very thankful for.

"But that all sounds good to me. Do you think they'll give us weapons?" Marcus asked, changing the subject.

"Some do, some don't," McCulloch said. "But if we need to adjust on the fly then that's what we'll do, agreed?"

The squad nodded again.

"Seventy-first for the win!" Ramirez announced, and Marcus couldn't help but see Foley break into a grin. McCulloch remained the picture of stoicism, and King looked quietly confident about the whole situation.

It was only a few hours before the seventy-first were called by Callahan from the grassy hill, and Marcus, along with the rest of his squad, made their way to the start of The Gauntlet.

It was so much more than Marcus had been expecting.

The Gauntlet was a valley carved out between two grassy mounds with sheer dirt walls on either side. Along the dirt walls were a number of fixed firing positions aimed at the valley's centre that were clearly for Callahan and the Colonels to use to pepper the squads with their paintballs. But the main event was what ran through the centre of the valley.

Four clear sections separated the squad from the start of The Gauntlet and safety at the other end. The first was a section of small staggered walls that were clearly placed to be used as cover – and Marcus noted that there were indeed left and right paths in this section.

Next came a cargo net suspended no more than two feet from the ground, and underneath it was a pool of murky and very cold-looking water.

Third stood a high wall. It looked to Marcus like it was around ten feet tall, and the top had a small sheltered section about a foot thick.

And then there was the last section. Another series of staggered walls to the left and right, but this time there was a single fixed gun pointing straight forwards at an opposing firing position. It looked like at this point, the squad was finally supposed to fight back – presuming they weren't to be given weapons for the rest of the course.

But what was worse was the fact that not only was the entire Gauntlet a cesspool of wet, squelchy mud, but it was also covered in splotches of red paint where the course had already seen fire.

"Seventy-first!" Callahan announced as the group stood ready to take on The Gauntlet. The three Colonels, Armstrong, Whittaker and Johnson, stood behind him at ease as he spoke. "This is to be treated as a live fire scenario. If you are hit, you will remove yourself from the course. Your goal is to breach the far end of The Gauntlet as quickly as possible with as few casualties as possible. Is that understood?"

"Sir, yes, sir!" The seventy-first replied in unison.

"Your Gauntlet will begin as soon as I touch the first firing position. Stand ready!"

Callahan then ran the short distance to the first fixed position and picked up the paintball gun resting there.

"Split up!" McCulloch ordered, and as they'd planned, he and Foley knelt down behind the leftmost blockade whilst Marcus, King and Ramirez threw themselves to the right.

It only took a second for the first paintballs to thud against the wooden barriers, and with each, a splash of red paint splattered up into the air. Callahan was focussing all his fire on Marcus's cover.

McCulloch held a flat palm up so that the entire squad could see, and the order was clear: wait.

As the paintballs impacted the cover in bursts, McCulloch counted them off on his fingers until a pattern emerged: Callahan was firing in bursts, three shots, three times and then a pause.

Marcus caught on immediately – the paintball gun must've had a limitation that caused an offbeat in its firing pattern. He wondered if he would've caught it without McCulloch there to point it out, but it didn't really matter.

Marcus looked down at his feet and could see that his boots had already sunk into the ground by a few inches. They squelched as they resisted his pull to bring them back up to the surface, and in that moment, Marcus hit some kind of serenity and understanding. The world around him had changed from regimented order to simulated chaos – and that was exactly the point of the course: to remove the soldiers from comfort and make their hearts pound. Marcus felt both as he looked across the course to the other pair of soldiers in the seventy-first.

McCulloch then, having waited for the third firing round from the Commander, pointed to Marcus' group and mimed for them to move forward. Marcus wasn't exactly an expert in unspoken commands, but it was fairly intuitive, so he quickly got the idea.

He, Ramirez and King spared no time at all in pushing themselves around the barricade and to the opposite cover one row in front of McCulloch and Foley. They dove behind the cover just in time for another round of three paintballs that impacted heavily on the wooden barricade.

Pop, pop, pop.

Marcus felt relief wash over him that he was back into safety, but he could also feel the sick in the pit of his stomach starting to rise. This wasn't like the long run to the Zetland Arms and back; this wasn't to test their endurance. This was to see how the squads would work as a team and work together to achieve a shared goal – all the while under fire.

Yes, they were only paintballs, but Marcus had never been shot before, even by one of those, and by the sounds of them hitting the woodwork, they'd hurt if they hit.

The pattern repeated again in the Commander's firing sequence, three bursts and then a short pause – and again the fire was directed at Marcus, King and Ramirez's wall.

Marcus thought that behind cover he might have felt safe, but with each impact against his barricade, he couldn't help but wince. He looked to the two women and they didn't even seem to care that they were under fire, both of them watching to see when McCulloch and Foley were going to make their move.

They didn't have to wait very long.

The pair of soldiers leapt into action on the next brief pause in the peppering of paintballs and crossed the path to fall into cover opposite Marcus and his team. Their dive into cover was far less dramatic than Marcus' own, though, with the pair of soldiers simply moving quickly into position and then kneeling down behind the barricade.

It felt like it took forever to Marcus, but two more manoeuvres saw them safely out of the first section of The Gauntlet and at the beginning of the second section. It was a welcome respite that the fixed firing position the Commander was using didn't turn all the way along the course, so he was forced to leave his weapon and move away. The second part of the course was then covered by Colonel Armstrong, which Marcus was pleased about. He wasn't expecting leniency, but perhaps the Colonel would be a little more forgiving than Callahan.

He was unpleasantly surprised.

The group stood together, looking down at the waterlogged mud pit before them. The cargo netting – which they could now see was also tangled together with razor wire – was only around a foot from the surface of the water – so that meant they'd have to completely submerse themselves in order to pass through the section. With Armstrong manning another paintball gun, too, this next section wasn't going to be pleasant.

"Opening fire!" Colonel Armstrong yelled and McCulloch immediately pushed Marcus face-first into the mud. Marcus would've objected, but as he fell, three paintballs blazed over his head so closely that he felt the wind as they passed him by.

"Seventy-One, down!" McCulloch ordered, and the squad all fell to the ground behind Marcus as one.

"Move!" McCulloch ordered, and Marcus knew what he was supposed to do. He pushed his arms out before himself and dragged his body along the mud until he slid into the cold, wet puddle underneath the netting.

It wasn't a motion he was used to, and he did the best he could to both keep his head above water but also keep his ass down low enough so it didn't present itself a target to Colonel Armstrong, who was covering the top of the cargo netting with rapid fire to hit anything that protruded up out of the mud.

Each time a paintball impacted one of the stakes holding the netting up, again Marcus couldn't help but wince and drop his head.

By the time the second section had been completed, Marcus had fallen right to the back of the squad, despite starting first.

"Cesari move your ass!" McCulloch shouted from the end of the section. Again the fixed firing position that Armstrong was using wouldn't turn away from the bulk of the section, so that left Marcus as the one and only remaining target.

Paintball after paintball flew just inches overhead again and again and it made Marcus drop his head and cover his ears with his hands. It was just all so much. He wanted to move, to summon up the willpower to ignore the incoming fire, the shouting and the screaming, but his body had just entirely taken over. He would stay there until the gunfire stopped.

"Come on, Marcus!" He heard Ramirez's voice now. "You can do this, just move your arms and legs, one at a time!"

"Yeah, you can do it, Cesari!" King shouted. "We know you can do it!"

Marcus let go of his head and looked up. He had been expecting to see Ramirez and King egging him on, but what he saw was all four of his squad mates, McCulloch, Foley, King and Ramirez all standing there just outside of the Colonel's firing range, their arms outstretched, willing to pull him out of there as soon as they could.

Marcus felt the surge of determination swell inside him.

He pushed his hands down into the water and dragged his body forward with all his might. There was no technique to this any more though, just sheer willpower. Inch by inch and foot by foot, he closed the distance until, eventually, a hand grabbed his own and pulled him free of the mud and water with a loud, wet slop. He had done it. He had passed the second stage of The Gauntlet.

But next up was the biggest challenge so far: a flat wooden wall with a top clearly out of Marcus' reach. It towered over the squad, and it made Marcus feel so small just standing next to it.

Marcus was just wondering if he could run and jump at it when McCulloch ran forward and braced his back against the wall. In a moment, Foley had spring-boarded up with the help of his very stable squadmate and lay flat atop the wall with a single arm dangling down.

King and Ramirez both sprang into action, using McCulloch as a boost while Foley pulled them up and over the wall one by one. Marcus could again hear the impact of paintballs on the covered section of the wall – it was clear that they all needed to stay low to the top, and then quickly drop down to the ground on the other side.

Marcus launched himself at McCulloch and was surprised at just how much force he felt from the soldier's boost up. And then the pull from Foley too, it was like Marcus hardly had to do anything. He let the momentum carry him over the top of the wall and fell down to the ground on the other side, letting his legs fall away beneath him when he hit the soft wet mud and splashed his entire body into the ground.

Before Marcus righted himself, he was being dragged up and into cover by McCulloch and Foley.

It was at this point that Marcus had a moment to stop to breathe, and his entire body reminded him of just how much pain it was in.

He'd not yet recovered from his beating and although his weird outfit was going some way to keep every part of his body tight and where it should be, there was only so much mitigation that it could manage.

Marcus looked up at what lay before him next. It was another corridor of barricades, and at the far end, Callahan was manning a fixed paintball gun pointing down the range. This time, though, the squad had an opposing paintball gun to use to return fire with. The only problem was that there was just one, and it, too, couldn't be moved or carried.

"I'll provide covering fire, then it's the same as last time," McCulloch announced as he took hold of the paintball gun. "Foley head to the left and keep your head down, you three on to the right and don't move until you hear the break in fire."

The soldiers all nodded. Marcus wanted to ask why they wouldn't split the teams equally to the left and right, but thought better of the question in case he'd missed something obvious.

A moment later, the firing started. McCulloch began peppering the base commander with bursts of paintballs, and immediately Foley darted away to the leftmost cover. The fire that Callahan returned thankfully seemed to be aimed solely at McCulloch, who presumably posed the only threat at the moment, so drew all of the attention of the enemy.

McCulloch's fire was not regimented like Callahan's had been though, as he seemed to purposely obfuscate his bursts and pauses. Marcus couldn't help but think that was a stroke of genius, as their opponent wouldn't be able to work out when there would be a break in the firing pattern and therefore it would be difficult for him to know when it would be safe to return with his own shots.

Under McCulloch's covering fire, the squad took their turns to continue along The Gauntlet until they each reached the end, past the point where Callahan could hit them and out into freedom. When they came to a halt, each of them clearly exhausted and Marcus folding himself over to try to catch his breath, Callahan left his firing position and approached the group.

"Good job Seventy-First," he announced with a smile. "You just failed your first attempt at facing The Gauntlet. How do you feel?"

Marcus could've sworn he'd misheard. Failed The Gauntlet? But they'd made it through to the end, hadn't they? He opened his mouth to ask that very question when Callahan spoke again.

"If any of you would have taken the time to listen to our briefing, then perhaps you might've stopped to wonder why exactly your squadmate was left behind to face oncoming fire alone, or indeed how exactly he was supposed to make it through The Gauntlet under fire once the rest of you had found your own selfish way to safety?"

As one, the Seventy-First squad turned to look back at the fixed firing position where McCulloch had provided covering fire from, and they were all surprised to see their de-facto leader covered head to toe in red paint, where Callahan was entirely free of anything but a little mud around the boots.

Chapter 9 – A Fine Steak Dinner

"You want to start talking?" McCulloch said to Marcus as soon as they were out of Callahan's earshot. "You think we can't tell when a soldier doesn't know the first thing about what we do? What rank were you before all this anyway, Cesari? Private?"

It was the one question that Cesari didn't want to have to answer, but he knew that if he lied about it now and was found out later, then it could make things much, much worse for him.

The squad had been told to walk to the far side of the barracks where the rest of the soldiers who had already completed The Gauntlet were waiting.

"Just leave it, will you?" Ramirez answered on Marcus' behalf, though even he could hear from the tone of her voice that she wasn't so sure about him any more either.

"No, I want to hear this," Foley said. "If we've got a rookie holding us back, then I want to know about it. We're soldiers and we need to know that when we get dropped into combat, the man standing next to us…"

"Or woman," King interrupted.

"What?"

"Or woman," King repeated. "We need to know that the man or woman…"

"Right then. Or woman," Foley corrected himself. "Is just as well trained and as ready for battle as the rest of us. You know it's not a joke when they say a chain's only as strong as its weakest link. It's real."

"That's a fair point," Ramirez conceded. "Marcus? Can you tell us what rank you were before we all joined the GSI as privates?"

Marcus' mind raced, but he knew that there was no way out of this. He simply let his shoulders drop and spoke quietly.

"I wasn't a soldier," he said.

"OK, then navy? Or air force? Just give us a number," Ramirez pressed, but McCulloch placed a hand on her shoulder to stop her.

"You weren't in the military at all, were you Cesari?" he asked, though it was more of a statement than a question.

Marcus shook his head but said nothing.

"Oh, brilliant!" Foley announced. "Couldn't make it up, could you? Get a squad together to be the best of the best, get onto some secret Operation and… and we get some civvie who doesn't know his arse from his ones!"

"No, that can't be right…" Ramirez said. "You'd have told me if that was the case, right? You'd have said?"

Marcus didn't look up from the ground as he spoke. "It… It sounds bad, I know… and believe me when I say that I didn't want this to happen..."

"Well, that makes all of us," Foley interrupted. "I swear to God, if you get me shot out there or pushed down to the bottom of the rankings, then I'm coming for you, Cesari. Then those bruises of yours will be the least of your concerns."

"Then maybe you can tell us how it was Cesari's fault that we failed The Gauntlet? That it was his fault we all left McCulloch behind?" King asked, pushing Foley on the shoulder.

"Well maybe if he knew how to be a proper soldier, or even run further than I can spit…" Foley started, his face twisting into one of disgust.

"Well, maybe you should've opened your damn eyes and kept an eye on McCulloch! Then we wouldn't be here right now, would we?" Ramirez said. "We all failed. And it wasn't just Marcus' fault or anyone else's; we all left McCulloch there with that gun to cover us as we moved, and we're all to blame."

The group went silent for a moment as they digested what Ramirez and King were saying. It was true of course, if Marcus had been faster, stronger, more tactically astute even, it wouldn't have made a difference. Yes, perhaps they'd have finished The Gauntlet a little quicker, but they would still have left McCulloch behind.

"No… it wasn't that," McCulloch said finally and in a small and thoughtful tone. "We failed The Gauntlet alright, but it wasn't because of Cesari and it wasn't because you left me back there. I didn't get hit by Callahan out there. It was the paintball gun I was using. It worked well for the most part, but eventually the thing just exploded and covered me in red paint. I don't know if it was rigged to do it or if it was some weird lesson in not using weapons you aren't familiar with, but we'd have lost either way. Whatever happened, as soon as I used that paintball gun, it meant we'd failed The Gauntlet."

"What?" Foley asked in shock. "You mean to say we went through all that and the course was rigged against us? What kind of crap is that supposed to be?"

"I don't know," McCulloch replied honestly. "But we might get a better picture when we see how the others did on the course. But I doubt many would've passed if it was rigged like that. Maybe we were just unlucky."

The time to find out was now though, as the group approached the open double doors to the inside of a sports hall where they could see the squads who'd already taken the course dossing about. Most were sat on the ground in their groups, deep in discussion about what had happened, but others were keeping themselves separate and standing nearer the edges. Marcus tried his hardest to find a squad without one of their members covered in red paint, but found the task challenging.

"No, we didn't pass the course and yes, the gun was rigged," a young man announced as the Seventy-First walked through the doors. It was clear that as each group had arrived, they'd quizzed the rest on what had happened and if anything, the announcement made Marcus feel a little better about himself.

"Well, that settles it then," Ramirez was the first to reply. "We were supposed to fail. And that means we can't blame anyone, right?" She peered at Foley, who didn't reply and, if anything, looked a little ashamed.

"Oh yeah, most of the guys here were fooled by that backfiring paintball gun. Seems like it was moved around the course each time through, so some would fail right at the start and others at the end. How was it for you?"

Ramirez filled the man in with what had happened and he let out a short whistle.

"Such a shame to happen right at the end. If you're wondering, only five squads passed the whole course, and most of that was luck. Two of them had so much mud in their faces that they just missed the gun altogether. If you ask me that should count as a fail anyway – imagine being in combat, unarmed, and you miss a perfectly good gun just sitting there."

"But it wasn't perfectly good, was it?" Marcus said. "And that was the point, right? Don't use a weapon you aren't familiar with because you just don't know what could happen."

The soldier clicked his tongue and extended a hand for Marcus to shake.

"Liam Johnstone," he said with a smile.

The squad introduced themselves and then split away from the main bulk to find a corner of the hall to themselves.

Before they even found a quiet space, another squad had arrived, and one of them, too, had been accosted by the malfunctioning paintball gun. The sight made Marcus again feel like the weight of their failure wasn't squarely on him. A feeling that was quickly dissipated by Foley, who, as soon as they were in a quiet area by themselves, went straight back onto the offensive.

"You were telling us about how exactly you got here," he growled. "Tell us all how a civvie managed to get onto Operation Legacy?"

"Oh shut up Foley," Ramirez said. "You don't know what this Operation is any more than the rest of us. Maybe Marcus is here as part of a control group to make sure this new equipment does what it's supposed to do regardless of the individual – and that's why there's such a wide range of ranks here too. You ever think about something like that you great lummox?"

"Or maybe he just faked his way in here and now he's been caught out," Foley growled.

"Why don't you just let him speak?" McCulloch asked, and by all accounts, with the gravitas with which he spoke, it sounded very much like more of an order than a question.

Marcus sighed. He would have to tell his story now and leave nothing out if he wanted these people to trust him, or perhaps even simply tolerate him.

He told them about the soldiers in the bar, the fight, the Colonel, his father and the possibility that he may also have been harbouring the genetic illness that could potentially one day rob him of his ability to walk.

He blurted everything out in one long sentence and didn't look at any of his squad mates as he did so. He'd never been one to share anything with others – even the few friends he'd managed to make in his short life – and if anything, he was surprised that when he finally finished speaking, he felt like the weight of the world had been lifted from his shoulders.

When he finally looked up at his squad mates, who didn't seem to want to respond to his truth, he saw them all staring at him in stunned silence. It was like they had no idea how to even begin to respond, and in that moment, Marcus wondered if he'd just made a huge mistake in telling them.

Foley was the first to speak. "So you're saying that Colonel Armstrong gave you this opportunity as a way to help you and your dad?"

Marcus couldn't place the tone in Foley's voice but nodded.

"Hell, I'd have done the same thing," he continued, placing a firm hand on Marcus' shoulder.

"And I'll tell you what," McCulloch said with a smile. "You don't have to worry about trying to fit in, or that you're doing things wrong. We're a team, and we'll turn you into the finest soldier this barracks has ever seen, you mark my words."

Marcus smiled, though it didn't reach his eyes.

"Thanks," he said. "But I don't know how long I'll be able to keep this up. I argued away the running pace because of my cuts and bruises, and I can just about figure out how to stand to attention and those kinds of things… but I'm not a solider. I have no training, and once everyone figures that out. I'm done for. I mean, it took you what, all of four hours or so to find me out?"

"I can get your running pace up," King said without missing a beat. "It's not going to be easy getting to the level of the rest of mind, but I think it's doable if you really want it. Loads of it is just in your head, so once you get past that, it's easy street."

"And we'll bring you up to speed on the rest," McCulloch said. "You don't have to worry, we'll keep all this between us and you'll be a proper soldier before you know it. Besides, we're all Privates here now anyway, correct?"

"Besides, if the worst comes to the worst, we'll just make you pick up the self-destructing paintball gun when we're on The Gauntlet next," Foley said with a smile. "You know, sacrifice yourself so that the rest of us can live."

Marcus looked at Ramirez, who was peering at him with a strange look on her face.

"Why didn't you tell me?" She asked. "You think I would've judged you?"

Marcus could tell she was hurt, but he had no other explanation for it than the truth.

"I… I didn't know you," he said honestly. "All I know about soldiers is that they stick together when they fight, and if I was just a civvie, I'd have been an outsider."

"Well, you're right about that," Ramirez said. "We do stick together, that's how we survive out there in the real world. And you know what?" She stepped a half pace closer to Marcus, who swallowed. "You're a soldier now too, so that makes you one of us, regardless of whatever you were yesterday, you got that?"

Marcus nodded and gave a cautious smile.

"And that means no secrets from your squad. Because that's how you'll get us all killed when it hits the fan."

Marcus lowered his gaze slightly, but Ramirez cupped his chin and directed his face back upwards and towards her own. "Soldiers don't feel sorry for themselves, that's lesson one," she said. "And you better pay attention because there are loads more lessons like that on the way. I can tell McCulloch is dying to turn you into a super soldier."

"What?" McCulloch asked, not entirely sure how he'd suddenly been dragged into all this.

"Oh, come on," Ramirez said. "You're dying to tell him how to act to be a proper soldier, aren't you? I can practically see you vibrating at the idea."

"I have no idea what you're talking about," McCulloch said, looking genuinely confused.

"Well whatever happens…" Marcus said. "I guess I have to say thank you to all of you. You've already done a lot for me, and I know this thing isn't going to be easy."

"Don't worry Marcus, you can always make it up to us later by saving our lives. You know, take a bullet or throw yourself onto a grenade, that kind of thing," Foley said with a smile.

"Alright! Listen up!" Callahan's unmistakable voice brought the entire sports hall to silence and the soldiers as one stood bolt upright and to attention.

"If you are the best of the best of what this army has to offer, then we have a lot of work to do, don't we?" he continued. "A total of five squads have passed The Gauntlet, Twelfth, Twenty-Second, Twenty-Ninth, Forty-First and Sixty-Second, but don't worry because in a short while, there will be a leaderboard set up for you all to follow how well you're doing in your squads, or in the case of some of you, how far you have to go to match your peers."

Marcus looked at his squad to see what their reactions were going to be, but not a single movement was made, not even a flicker of the eyes.

"This course, The Gauntlet, was not only a test of your tactical competencies, but it was also to serve as a warning about the dangers of unfamiliar or convenient enemy weapon placements. I trust that it is a lesson that many of you will remember, but if you ever need reminding, just think about the next time you try to remove those new boots of yours."

This time, a few of the soldiers shuffled ever so slightly.

"That was a joke," Callahan said after a short pause. "But my point stands. The unknown is dangerous, and it will serve you well to remain vigilant at all times, even if you think you're in a comfortable situation. Now, with that being said, when you leave this hall in a moment," he gestured to the double doors they'd all entered through, "you will pick up a paper bag. This bag contains your squad's supplies and food for the afternoon, and it falls to you all to find a way to cook said food. If you happen to be within one of those five squads that passed my Gauntlet, you will find a lighter within your bag. I say this now and only once: do not share this lighter, or any fire you happen to light with any other squad. Do you all understand your orders?"

"Sir, yes, sir!" The call returned from the room.

"Then you are all dismissed," Callahan said and took a step to the side to allow the soldiers to pass back outside.

When Marcus' squad found themselves back outside, McCulloch had picked up their pack and moved them away to the side as a group. He had opened the brown paper sack and was passing items out to Foley, who was practically dancing, so eager to see what was inside.

In the end, they'd counted out five large steaks, raw, five new bayonets, no rifles or pistols, five canteens of water, lukewarm, and a handful of mixed salad leaves, washed.

"I take it none of you are vegetarian?" McCulloch asked once they'd emptied the bag. "Because if you are, then this task is about to get a whole lot easier for you."

Everyone shook their heads.

"Then this one's just going to be a basic survival test. Callahan hasn't said anything about shelter, but it wouldn't surprise me after this. So first we make a fire, then decide on the best way to cook the meat. The rest is already done for us."

"You think this could be another trick?" King asked. "Like the meat is poisoned and it'll teach us we shouldn't just eat whatever we're given, trusting it's safe?"

McCulloch scratched his chin. "I don't think so, this one doesn't have so many layers as The Gauntlet so I think it'll be OK. Besides, they have to feed us proper food, and what better way than to make it into a task? I guess we just go out there and get a fire going."

Marcus, of course, knew generally how to start fires without the help of a lighter. The premises of magnifying glasses, flints, rubbing sticks together, but as a resident of an up-and-coming first-world country, it had never been something he'd attempted in practice. Thankfully for Marcus, he'd been teamed up with the best of the best.

"Right, we need kindling, firewood, and a few stones or rocks would go down well," Foley said. "And does anyone have a lighter, or any matches?"

"Oh yeah, I always keep a lighter in my bra," King replied, "along with my handgun, knife and hardback books. You heard what Callahan said: no lighters for the rest of us."

"Calm down, it was just a joke," Foley said. "But the rest of that stuff would be good. And I mean, take a look around us, there are plenty of trees around, dry leaves and stuff, so I say we just get to work and cook us up a nice dinner. I like my steak medium rare by the way."

"And I like my men not to be pompous assholes," king replied. "You can cook my steak once we get the fire going, and if you're lucky, I'll let you eat your own in peace."

It didn't take long for the squad to find everything they needed and for McCulloch to get the fire going by spinning one stick into another with kindling pressed against the friction point, along with Foley occasionally blowing into the thing. They used the paper bag that everything had arrived in as a form of kindling, which turned out to be extremely effective and Marcus had to admit was pretty ingenious. Once it had caught, they made a small stone surround like it was a campfire and started adding progressively bigger sticks until they had a roaring fire.

Marcus couldn't help but be impressed, and he wondered if this was something that he would've been able to do alone. In truth, with all the finer details that he hadn't known, he doubted it.

The group opted to balance three of their new bayonets across the fire to act as a pan to place the steaks onto, and once it had browned, the other two blades were used to cut the meat before sharing it all out equally.

King waited for Foley to go for his share of the steak, but took it right off his knife, biting into it herself. It wasn't a selfish act, and Foley saw the funny side, laughing as he waited for his turn.

The meat was good, and the salad was fresh and crisp. It seemed like they hadn't been tricked again by Callahan, and the supplies were exactly as they seemed: fit for consumption.

Marcus ate his steak quietly, but as he did so, staring down at his own feet he noticed something. Something he wouldn't have noticed if they hadn't been sitting quietly on the ground.

"What do you think they made these boots out of anyway?" he asked aloud. "I mean look at them, the mud falls right off and they look as new and shiny as the minute I put them on."

McCulloch smiled. "I noticed that too. And the overalls. I know they look mudlike , and mine are a bit painty… but they just wipe clean, and they fit so well. It's like I'm not wearing anything at all."

"Nobody wants to see that," Ramirez said. "And I don't thank you for the mental image either."

King snorted, and it made Marcus smile.

"Whatever it is, I bet these aren't the only things that we'll be seeing that'll blow our minds," Foley said with a glint in his eye. Then he picked up one of the bayonets and peered at it. "I mean, what if this isn't just a knife? What if it... uh... shoots lasers or something?"

"Then we probably did the wrong thing by putting them in the fire," McCulloch said.

"Nah," Ramirez said. "They're just bayonets, nothing special about them I don't think. But I do think there's more to come... and if it's something that's just one per squad, then I'd like to think that I'll be the one to give it a go."

The squad quickly descended into a heated discussion of who should be the first to test whatever it was that they'd decided they would be given next, but in the end, they agreed to disagree. The only thing that they could all agree on, in fact, was that Marcus certainly wouldn't be the one to get his hands on this fictitious new tech first.

Chapter 10 – Final Rankings

After eating their well-cooked steak and salad, the squads were then given new orders: to make their way to the firing range. It was clear that this was just another of the baseline tests of the abilities of the soldiers and in this one, Marcus was at least a little happier because pointing and firing a gun, he thought, would at least require a little less skill and physical effort than running or general soldiering.

Marcus quickly found out that firing a gun, and firing a gun properly, were two very different things.

The Seventy-First squad took to the range in a group, and as the others had before them, they were expected to take their three single shots together. The target down the range was arranged in coloured rings with a number from one to ten going into the bullseye.

The guns they'd been given were not some futuristic laser guns or anything of the like that Marcus had seen in the movies. In fact, they'd been handed the standard L85A1, or more commonly the SA80, as Colonel Whittaker – the firing range instructor handily pointed out to the Privates.

"The rifle in your hands is compatible with standard NATO ammunition, which is used by many allied forces across the globe. You should all be familiar with this weapon, however help is on hand should you require it."

Marcus looked down at the rifle in his hands. The weapon was short and had a magazine already loaded into the base behind the trigger. Most of the gun was a dark metallic material, though the stock and hand guard were lighter green and more plasticky. A long sight on top of the SA80 looked to Marcus as though it was going to make this whole task even easier.

"With a thirty round magazine and a fully automatic firing rate of three hundred rounds per minute," the Colonel continued, "you can see how it will be beneficial in most cases to keep to burst or single shot modes."

Marcus and his squad moved forwards to arrange themselves behind the firing stockade, and as one they raised their weapons to face the targets down range.

"You may fire your first shot when ready," the Colonel announced, and after a short pause, four shots rang out from around Marcus. He heard the sound of paper tearing as the bullets hit their marks.

Then Marcus took a deep breath, aligned the crosshair inside the scope with the target down range and pulled the trigger.

There was no sound of paper tearing.

"Thirty-eight points in round one," Whittaker announced loudly. "Cesari, your shot was about a foot too high to hit the target. Is there a problem with your rifle?"

"No sir," Marcus was forced to reply, though he didn't offer an excuse for his performance.

"Very well. Seventy-First, prepare for your second firing," Whittaker announced.

The guns fired again, and again Marcus' squad fired before he had the chance to properly line up his own shot.

This time, Marcus had adjusted where he thought he was supposed to be firing, and to his delight he heard the satisfying pop of his bullet impacting the paper.

"Forty-three," Whittaker announced loudly. That's a perfect ten four times over, and a three for you, Cesari. You fired two inches to the right this time, but your height was on. Getting used to that crooked sight then?"

Marcus could hear the sarcasm in the Colonel's question, but didn't respond. All he could do was think about how he was the only thing letting his squad down.

He hit a seven on the third try, and with only King missing the ten for a nine, it meant that the third round had netted the squad forty-six points. Their grand total after the firing range was one hundred and twenty-seven out of a possible one hundred and fifty, and that sounded pretty good to Marcus.

"Damn, Cesari, have you never fired a gun before?" Foley was the first to ask as the squad moved away from the firing range.

"Actually, no," Marcus replied sheepishly. "But the score wasn't too bad in the end, was it?"

McCulloch quickly interrupted before Foley had the chance to say something else that looked like it would be degrading.

"One hundred and twenty-seven over fifteen shots," he paused for a moment as if thinking what to say next. "Averages out to sevens and eights, maybe a few nines in there. But these guys should be well trained enough not to miss by too much. I think the miss and the three will hurt us, but not the seven."

"Yeah, I was way off on the first one," Marcus agreed.

"Yeah, and at least you got better," Ramirez said, tapping him on the shoulder. "And you don't have any bad habits like Foley over there."

"What do you mean bad habits?" Foley asked, looking shocked. "I got three bullseyes and didn't even have to try."

"Yeah, but you open your mouth before you shoot every. Damn. Time. You know how annoying it is seeing your big gob in the corner of my vision every time I'm about to shoot? It's a wonder I hit the target at all with that kind of distraction."

Marcus saw King smiling to herself and Foley looking a little put-out.

"You just have to trust the process," Foley countered. "If I'm getting the tens, then does it matter what I do with my face?"

"Do I seriously have to answer that?" Ramirez asked. "It's like you want me to insult you."

"Maybe I do," Foley replied with a wink.

"You're disgusting," Ramirez said.

"Disgustingly good at firing a rifle."

"Nope, just plain disgusting," Ramirez said.

"Right, you two, that's enough," McCulloch announced with heavy authority in his voice. "You're going to have Cesari here thinking we act like animals! What kind of impression are you trying to give him?"

"Nah, it's OK," Marcus replied. "I know you're animals. You're just a little more well-trained than I'd been expecting."

King laughed, and Foley looked like Marcus had slapped him in the face.

"Did Whittaker say where we're supposed to go next?" King asked.

"Nope," McCulloch replied, "so you know what that means: stay put and wait for orders."

The group did not have to wait long. In fact, it was only a few minutes before the next of their 'baseline tests' was to occur, and it was far from the next generation in modern technology that Marcus had been hoping for. Nope, this test was a simple one, and to test the strength of the Soldiers, they were going to have to do pull-ups.

Marcus had done a pull-up once or twice in his life, generally when he was much younger, and the kids in school all wanted to show off what they could do for the girls. But his confidence evaporated as he looked up at the round metal bar just out of reach above him.

The bar was long enough for a squad of five to all hang on at once – which was a good thing otherwise, this exercise might have taken all day, but the premise was simple: do as many pull-ups as possible and your squad's total will be recorded and added to the mysterious leaderboard that Callahan had already spoken about. And as if to make things more interesting, while the soldiers did their pull-ups, Callahan shouted insults at them all the whole time about how they were going too fast, not going low or high enough, or that his grandmother could do better than them. All in all, before Marcus's squad took to the bar, most soldiers could do twenty or thirty pull-ups, meaning the average squad score was somewhere near one hundred.

That was all about to change when the Seventy-First took their position, though, and each of the squad jumped a few inches up to hang onto the bar. The soldiers all seemed happy with performing pull-ups, with King doing the most at just over thirty. Ramirez completed twenty-two, and Foley and McCulloch both maxed out after twenty, each of the squad dropping back down to the ground once they were spent.

Marcus though, he was still up there after the others had finished. His arms burnt, his heart raced, and he knew that he needed to give this everything he could to prove to everyone that he was worthwhile.

Thirty seconds after the rest of the squad had finished, Marcus was still there. The only problem was though, that he had only managed a grand total of three pull-ups, and judging by Callahan's screaming, they couldn't really be counted as 'full' pull-ups anyway.

So Marcus dropped to the ground.

As Marcus landed, his arms felt like lead, his chest heaved and he struggled to catch his breath. Had it really been that long since he'd done a handful of pull-ups?

Callahan's harsh comments continued to rain down on him, mixing with the pounding of his heart. He felt embarrassed and frustrated, not only for this poor performance but also for the fact that he had drawn attention to himself once again, and blaming his injured body simply wasn't going to keep working. He felt worse for the squad though, because Callahan had annoyingly announced that the total for their squad had been ninety-four. It was the lowest score that Marcus had heard announced, and it must've meant that Callahan had only counted one of his pull-ups as a complete one. What an ass.

"That was an embarrassment, Cesari? You call that an effort?" Callahan's voice boomed across the training area. Marcus gritted his teeth, his face turning red as he fought to control his breathing and ignore the mocking remarks. If this had been anyone else, anywhere else, he'd have given that guy what for.

"You are a disgrace, Cesari, and it is nothing short of an insult that you stand here dressed in the same uniforms as the rest of the soldiers around you! How in God's name did you make it onto this program boy? If I was your dad, I might've just put you up for adoption and be done with it, you useless sack of…"

And that was it. The point at which Marcus could take no more.

"It's not like I'm not trying!" he barked back. "Have you seen my body? The cuts and the bruises? I'm trying to complete your stupid tasks as best I can, and maybe if you'd shut up for just a moment, then you might be able to see what's happening right in front of your face!"

"Do you want to hit me son?" Callahan replied, looking very much like nobody had ever spoken to him like that before.

Marcus hadn't noticed it, but his fists were now clenched tightly, and his face had turned a deep shade of red.

"Because it looks like you're about to attack me, so you better be able to back that up."

Marcus realised what was happening and remembered why he was in this situation as it was just in time. He closed his eyes, concentrated on his breathing and slowly let his fists unclench themselves. It wasn't without a monumental amount of effort though.

"Oh no you don't Cesari. Just because you can calm yourself down doesn't mean you don't owe me a fight. So I think I'll ask you straight up: you think you can take me?"

Marcus stared at the base commander, not entirely sure if the question was rhetorical or not.

"Because it sure looks like you think you do," Callahan continued. "So I'll ask you this one more time: do you think you can take me?"

Marcus then realised that Callahan was indeed waiting for an answer, and for the first time, he really looked at the man standing before him. Callahan was wearing loose-fitting dark green overalls, so Marcus couldn't quite see the man's physical stature. The pair were about the same height though, and Callahan's hair was grey, which went well with his wizened face. His skin was scarred as though he'd been in battle at some point in his life, but if pressed to say it, Marcus now thought that the commander was probably well past his prime.

"You want me to go get your mom to answer for you boy?" Callahan asked with wide eyes. "Answer my God damn question! And I swear to God, if I have to ask you one more time, you'll be out of this program faster than you can do three pull-ups!"

"Sir, yes, sir!" Marcus shouted once Callahan had closed his mouth.

"And what exactly are you saying yes to, son?" Callahan replied, squinting one eye.

"Sir, I think I can take you, sir!" Marcus clarified.

"Oh, is that so?" Callahan said. "Well, that sounds like a fine thing to put to the test then, doesn't it?" he raised his voice so that all of the soldiers could hear. Marcus hadn't realised, but they'd all moved closer to see what was happening between Cesari and the base commander.

"Next up is hand-to-hand combat!" Callahan called. "Pair up with another Private and make a circle on the ground. The first one out of the circle – by any means necessary – is the loser. Give your results to Colonel Whittaker once done. You will all be pleased to know that Cesari here is the first to volunteer, and he will be fighting against me. Any who wish to watch this round, feel free. You might just learn something."

Callahan then used his boots to scrape a circle into the mud with a diameter of a few metres and came to a halt facing Marcus, who hadn't yet moved.

"What do you need, a written invitation?" Callahan asked after Marcus did nothing but stare at the base commander for a long few seconds. "I'll make it easy for you; you can take the first hit, a freebie on me."

"Do it, Marcus!" Ramirez's voice was the only one that came besides Callahan's, and it really, really helped.

Marcus raised his fists as a boxer would and widened his stance. Then he moved in to close the distance between him and Callahan, who still hadn't changed his posture to anything remotely resembling a fighting stance.

Marcus wasn't sure if he was allowed to fight Callahan, with him being a superior officer or whatever, but he guessed from Ramirez' words that it was somewhat OK.

He threw a jab at the commander's chest. Nothing too hard, just so he could be sure he was allowed to do it, but when it made contact with the commander, the man's chest may as well have been made of steel. There was no give underneath the overalls, and Marcus saw Callahan smile.

"That was a waste of your free hit, son," Callahan said.

"Move Marcus!" Ramirez's voice rang out again, but it was all too late. Like it had come from nowhere, Callahan's fist crunched into Marcus' nose with a loud crack and blood immediately strayed out in a cloud between them. Pain followed the surprise.

Marcus scrunched his face up as he fell backwards to the ground. How could he have been so stupid? This man was clearly a trained killer, and he had failed to look past his grey hair.

Blood was already wetting his lips, and Marcus could taste it seeping into his mouth. He could feel his heart beating faster and faster, but above everything else, he felt the anger rising within him. How dare this man make a fool of him?

Rolling over and planting his hands firmly on the mud, Marcus turned to his front and forced his body to do as he commanded. The pain that he had almost forgotten from the beating the night before was back with a vengeance, but Marcus did his best to ignore it; he had a task to complete now. Revenge to seek.

As Callahan watched, Marcus' nose dripped fresh blood onto the ground. It was clear that that first punch had probably broken it, but Callahan was surprised to see that Marcus was not giving up. In fact, it was the opposite and he could only raise an eyebrow as Marcus retook his boxer's stance and stared directly into the commander's eyes.

"Now you know that nose is broken boy?" Callahan asked.

"I'm still in the circle," Marcus growled. "So this isn't over."

"Well fine, if that's the way you want to do this," Callahan said.

Marcus knew that he needed to be smart now. He knew that he wasn't going to win in a straight-up brawl against the commander, but he didn't need to win; he just needed to get Callahan out of the circle.

And with that in mind, Marcus lowered his head and charged at his opponent. The thought was that if he impacted Callahan hard enough, he'd be thrown backwards and out of the makeshift circle.

But Callahan had other ideas. When Marcus' shoulder impacted the man's midriff, he didn't stumble backwards as expected; Callahan had planted himself well enough to feel like Marcus had just run into a brick wall.

Marcus barely had the time to feel the pain radiating from his broken nose as the impact shocked him to his very core, but a second later, Callahan had snaked an arm around Marcus' neck to put him in a headlock that Marcus couldn't even blink in it was so tight.

Then up came the knee. Callahan showed Marcus no mercy and planted his knee into Marcus' chest once, twice, three times and on the third, a loud crunch made many of the watching soldiers let out an involuntary 'ooh'.

Marcus wanted to straight up die on the spot because the pain was simply unbearable, and stumbling backwards, he looked at Callahan with confusion because the commander was smiling. He was smiling! Like all of this was some game to him, and he was enjoying it.

His vision blurry and every part of his body screaming with agony, Marcus mustered all of his energy into keeping his eyes open and remaining on his feet. He wouldn't give this man the satisfaction of surrendering now, and if Callahan wanted to win, he was going to have to work for it.

Callahan took one step forward, span on his left foot and planted a spinning back heel into Marcus's jaw. The world turned black as Marcus fell to the ground, and he felt the cold, wet slap of the mud against his cheek. The kick had been so fast that he hadn't even seen it coming.

"Maybe that will teach you something about manners, Cesari," Callahan said as he stared down at the defeated Private, but to his shock, the boy who he was sure he had just dealt a beating most would not want to be on the end of, was again clenching his fists.

"Seriously Cesari," Callahan exhaled. "You enjoying this?"

Marcus didn't reply. He forced his eyes open and willed his upper body to obey his command to come to all fours again. It wasn't pleasant or pretty, but after a moment he managed it and again the base commander loudly exhaled.

"You will submit Cesari, and it's either going to be easy for you or hard for you, so what's it going to be?"

Marcus didn't answer, instead choosing to continue working his way back to his feet – which, by all accounts, was taking all of his concentration anyway.

Callahan then slowly walked over to Marcus, spanning the short distance in a second and took hold of the Private's arm. For a moment, Marcus thought the Callahan was going to help him up.

But that was not what happened.

Callahan threw his left leg over Marcus' shoulder, falling into a forward roll and all the while keeping a hold of Marcus' arm. The position that they fell into, was that of Marcus on his back with his arm outstretched, and Callahan pulling away to bend the arm in a direction that arms just weren't meant to bend in.

"You tap now, son, or I'll break your arm," Callahan growled.

Marcus did nothing. He could feel the pain, of course he could, but he was way past the point of caring now. He'd lost the fight before it had even begun, but all of the merit – if any – that he was going to gain from this encounter was in his resilience and longevity. With that in mind, he closed his eyes and gritted his teeth. He knew what would happen next.

Without hearing a single sound from Marcus, Callahan then had no choice. It wasn't something that he was going to enjoy, but he had no qualms about it either: he put his strength into his armbar and pulled until the loud crack that followed turned every soldier in the barracks silent.

Marcus didn't even let out a cry of pain; he simply lay his head back on the ground behind him, and let unconsciousness carry him away to a world without pain.

Chapter 11 – A Strange Doctor

"Well, this will simply not do, will it?" A very strange voice reached Marcus' ears before he had the chance to open his eyes. "I mean, how am I supposed to assess baseline statistics if that big dope changes what the baseline actually is?"

"I don't think you should be calling him that," a female voice replied.

Marcus opened his eyes.

He was in one of the medical rooms, he was sure, but although he could see a dark-haired woman in a white lab coat standing over him, the strange male voice didn't seem to have an owner. When it spoke again, Marcus realised it was coming from a speaker in the corner of the room.

"I want to come and have a look at the damage he's done. I swear to Ka… never mind. I'm coming in."

"I don't think that's a very good idea," the woman said. "I can report from here, you know you aren't supposed to…"

"I don't care what I'm supposed to do. This wasn't part of the plan, so if that oaf can do things off script, then so can I."

"Uh, what's going on?" Marcus managed to wheeze out. His nose felt like it had been smashed between two bricks, and it was so painful that it was hurting his eyes to simply keep them open. His ribs too, sent a searing hot, stabbing pain all the way from his stomach to his throat every time he took a breath.

"Don't worry, it's nothing," the woman replied. "You've just taken quite the beating, and the doctor in charge of this Operation wants to come and see you for himself, but that really isn't supposed to happen."

"Why?" Marcus asked. He was hurting badly, but that didn't mean he couldn't tell something was off here. He could tell there was more to the simple fact that it 'wasn't supposed to happen'.

"I can answer that for you," the speaker in the corner of the room said happily. "But you're going to have to become rather understanding about a few home truths really quite quickly. I trust that's OK?"

Marcus started moving his head to nod but then experienced how much pain that caused him. Then he also remembered that he was talking to a speaker somehow and didn't even know if the voice's owner could see him or not.

"I have a pretty open mind," Marcus said.

"Is that so?" The speaker replied. "That'll make it easier for me to just reach in and scoop out some of that delicious brain of yours then, won't it?"

Marcus was still trying to place the accent, but it was proving impossible. He remained silent at whatever the doctor meant by that last statement.

"Oh, trust me, Marcus, if you were standing right next to me right now, you'd see how funny that was. Well, perhaps you wouldn't, but you get my meaning. I mean, you will get my meaning once I've explained more about what's going on."

"I don't think that," the woman started to say, but she was interrupted again by the absent doctor.

"Now, Marcus, tell me, do you believe in aliens? And no, I don't mean little green men running around with those oh so convenient probes as your media would have us imagining. I mean, seriously, why would aliens enjoy probing things so much, and even if they did, why would they choose that particular entrance?"

"Doctor I…"

"Please do be quiet, Ms. Lang. I am trying to have a conversation with one of my subjects."

Marcus looked up.

"Subjects?"

"Well, yes, of course you are!" The doctor replied. "What else would you be here for?"

"The boots? Or the overalls?" Marcus replied slowly, trying to remember if there was anything else he'd missed. "It's some kind of testing ground for new equipment, right? Maybe new weapons?"

"That is quite perceptive of you, Marcus," the doctor replied. "But I am afraid you are living a half-truth. Yes, the boots and overalls you have all been given are far, far more advanced than anything you people have now, technologically speaking, but for most of the known universe, such items could be considered almost prehistoric."

"Doctor, please, I really don't think…"

"Right, that's it!" the doctor announced. "If I keep getting interrupted like this, then I'm coming in, and we're all just going to have to talk face-to-face. It was always going to happen anyway because I will have to look at those broken bones. It's not like any of you backwater unenlightened humans know what you're doing anyway, is it?"

"No, I…"

"Then I'll be right there. But Marcus, please remember that you were the one who said you have an open mind, and when we meet face to face, I want you to try your best – I mean really try – not to freak out. Do you understand?"

Marcus again went to nod but caught himself.

"Yes, doctor," he said.

"I really mean this Marcus. You're going to want to freak out, you may even be tempted to attack me, but remember that I am here to help." Then he added as though it was an afterthought: "And in your state, I would absolutely be able to hold you down, cut your chest open and lay eggs in the cavity left beneath, only for them to hatch later on and burst out like little spiders when you least expect it."

"What?" Marcus asked in a very small voice.

"I'm coming," the doctor replied in a sing-song voice.

A moment later, the door opened rather slowly, and Marcus took in the absolute absurdity that sauntered into the room.

The lizard-like creature walked on two legs like humans did, had two arms and legs but had some kind of yellow scaled skin – like a reptile – and his eyes were also bright yellow with a small central pupil. It was also clear that it had pointed teeth much like a dinosaur or a crocodile, and instead of a nose, it had two small slits in the middle of its face.

That wasn't the most absurd part of the whole situation though. No, the strangest thing that Marcus witnessed, and what made him think that this was all some kind of dream – and that perhaps he hadn't even awoken from that fight last night – was the fact that this lizard-man-thing, was wearing a regular white lab coat, and had a stethoscope wrapped around its neck. Just like people.

"Hello Marcus," the thing said in its weird yet still somehow well-to-do accent, "I told you that you would have to get really open-minded about all of this. My name is Dr. Kono, and if I'm not too much mistaken, I am the first alien being that you have encountered? I mean, of course, to me, you are the alien. Though as we are currently on your home planet and inside one of your military institutions… I guess that I can, as you say, 'take one for the team'."

Marcus looked at the woman in the room, then back at the lizard thing. Then back at the woman and tried to ask her with his eyes if all of this was real or if this was all some kind of terrible joke. She didn't say a word.

"I guess you have some questions for me," Dr. Kono said. "But let me start with a few of the simplicities. Yes, the boots and the overalls that you are all wearing have been provided by extra-terrestrial means. But as I have already said, you must understand that although they seem advanced to you, in the grand scheme of things, well… not so much. Let me try to put it in a way you might understand." The lizard tapped his chin a few times in a very human-esque gesture and then said: "Ah, here's one. It's like giving a caveman a knife. On a cursory glance and to one who doesn't understand who or what cavemen were, it would seem like nothing out of the ordinary. But to the caveman, it would seem like it was something so far out of their ability to produce, it may as well have been magic."

Marcus stared at the creature, still trying to decide if this was real or a pain-induced nightmare.

"I'm sorry," the doctor said. "Is there something wrong with your ears too? Can you hear me?"

Marcus slowly looked back to the woman, who sighed.

"Yes, this is a real alien being," she said slowly. "He is the scientist behind this entire program, though we are all under orders from the highest possible command not to divulge his identity, and he has been told not to show himself to any of the candidates in Operation Legacy. I know it must be hard, and it's a lot to take in – believe me, I know – but it is what it is. You kind of just get used to it."

"Ah, come on, I'm not that bad," Dr. Kono said. "I don't take a lot of getting used to really. I studied your race, your popular cultures and your histories, and I think I have a pretty firm grasp on what's important. Wouldn't you say so?" He peered at the woman, who sighed again.

"We aren't all just movies and war," she said.

"You could've fooled me."

"Doctor?" Marcus asked, and the lizard man turned his attention back to the patient lying on the bed.

"Yes?" Kono replied.

"No, I meant to say: You're a doctor? Like you went to medical school? Here?"

Dr. Kono peered down at Marcus and raised a single eyebrow. "Damnit, Jim, I'm a doctor, not an alien lizard creature!"

Marcus remained silent.

"Wasted on you," Dr. Kono muttered. "But yes, I am a Doctor… of many things actually. The translation module I am using gave me that title as the most appropriate for me in your language, and so that is what I am called. Again though, some of the things that I am able to do as a 'doctor' in your eyes… well you may as well call me a wizard. But please don't. It'd run the risk of people going around calling me the 'lizard wizard', and I just don't need that kind of thing in my life right now."

"OK," Marcus replied simply.

"OK? Don't you have anything else to ask me? This is the first time you have definitive proof that advanced lifeforms are out there, that the human race is neither alone nor at the apex of universal sentience, and all you have to ask me is if I am a real doctor or not?"

Marcus blinked. Then said: "No."

The doctor's lizardy mouth hung open to reveal his pointy teeth and dark red tongue. The woman in the room covered her mouth with her hand in a failed attempt to hide her wide grin.

"Can you get me another one? I think this one's broken?" Kono said to the woman.

"Maybe he's just shocked?" She replied. "It's not every day you get to meet a big, bad alien being. It's almost like you're disappointed he didn't go running and screaming out the door."

"Well, I am a little disappointed, to be honest," Kono replied. "Is it too much to ask for a little scream? You know what, it doesn't matter; the moment's passed."

"Sorry for asking," Marcus said, "But now that I've seen you… they aren't going to throw me in prison, are they… or kill me?"

"What?" Dr. Kono asked clearly confused. "Why would they do that?"

"Because it's clear that you don't want anyone to know what you're doing here, and I'm guessing that's not limited to humans? I mean, you've given us these boots and overalls to try out – things that we couldn't possibly make on our own - but by your own admission, they'd go unnoticed out there in the bigger universe. You would only go to that trouble if you weren't actually allowed to give us advanced technologies. So that means the fact that I know all of this… means I'm a liability."

The room fell silent for a long moment again.

"Are all humans this perceptive?" Dr. Kono eventually asked the woman.

"Not that I'm aware of," she replied. "Is what he said true?"

Dr. Kono nodded. "Actually, he's right on the mark. My race – the Kanaan – has known about planet Earth and the human race for a very long time. But technically, we're supposed to go through the 'proper channels'," he air quoted with four very long and green fingers. "But I, along with some of my colleagues believed that in this instance, there is something more to be gained from working with the humans in the early stages of their development, you know, before the Council cover you all in red tape. Don't worry, I don't expect you to understand all of this, of course, but the bigger picture is, well, how Mr Cesari put it: It's a secret that I'm here."

"Are there more of you?" Marcus asked.

"In the universe? Hundreds of billions. On Earth? I believe that I am the only Kanaan, though I could be mistaken; my people do tend to be wily."

"Are there other kinds of aliens out there?"

"Oh, dear boy, there are an infinite number of races out there in an infinite number of galaxies, star systems and planets. Surely after learning that humans weren't alone, you didn't think there would just be two races out there?"

"What are you doing here?" Marcus asked. It was the one question that he really wanted to know the answer to, and he had saved it until last just in case he really was just dreaming.

"Why don't you try to figure it out, Mr. Perceptive?" Kono shot back. "Tell you what, if you get close, I'll throw in some extra details."

Marcus stared at the alien for a long time before he spoke. There were so many theories just swirling about his head that he had a hard time trying to focus on how all of these things fit together.

"You're not here because of the boots or the overalls," Marcus said, speaking quickly as though he was on autopilot. "They are nothing to you, and they're probably little more than uniforms to keep us identified as candidates in Operation Legacy. I say this because you've referred to them as technologically inferior a few times, so you wouldn't be here in person if it was just about giving us some fancy new gear. The fact that you've identified yourself as a doctor – and I assume your 'translation' has taken that to be more of the medical kind than the mad scientist kind - means one of two things: You're either here because you know there's something here that's dangerous – something that could hurt a lot of people… or because you want to do something to us."

Dr. Kono blinked five times in quick succession.

"Seriously," he said again to the woman, "Does he know more than he's letting on or is he just super perceptive?"

The woman shrugged.

"You were very close, actually," Kono said. I'm not here for the clothes, although they do handily send real-time biometric data about all of the candidates to my terminal so I can keep my beady little eyes on all of the progress you'll be making in the program. But you were slightly off about the medical doctor versus mad scientist assumption. In reality, I'm both." The doctor then grinned. It was kind of horrific, showing off his rows of sharp, pointed teeth. "So now, what do you think?"

"Well..." Marcus said. "In that case... taking those baseline tests into account, the fact that you just said the outfits will tell you how much 'progress' we'll be making and the fact that you're a mad-scientist doctor..." Marcus curled his legs up and moved away until his back met the head of the bed. "Y... you're..."

"See," Kono said to the woman. "This is what I wanted to see from the start: a little fear."

Marcus had entirely paled, he was sweating and his heart was racing. The two conclusions that he had come up with were either this thing was going to turn them all into lizard-monster things, or it was going to try to 'upgrade' them by cutting bits off or adding other bits on. Neither of which were things that Marcus wanted.

The pain Marcus was in was stopping him from covering his face with his hands, so all he could do was watch and cower.

"Now you listen here," the woman started.

"Fine," Kono interrupted. "I am more of a medically biased doctor," he said. "And I'm not here to do strange experiments on you all. Well, I mean, there is one experiment, but that's kind of the whole point behind Operation Legacy. But it's not going to hurt you, and it's not designed to change your physical appearance except perhaps your physique. But again its to be nothing outside of the human 'scope of existence'," he airquoted again.

Marcus relaxed slightly, but he wasn't entirely convinced.

"Then... what is Operation Legacy?" He asked.

The lizard smiled widely once again and opened his arms wide.

"Operation Legacy is my finest ever work," he said.

Marcus immediately felt terrible again.

"It is simply put, a program of gene editing with the sole purpose to allow human beings to punch through their genetic ceiling in order to take one huge step along their evolutionary paths. It is an evolution in a bottle, plain and simple. Operation Legacy is here to give all of you candidates a way to become, well... the strongest, fastest, smartest human beings ever to walk the Earth."

Marcus couldn't help but let his mouth hang open.

"I mean on a universal scale, you're still right down there with some of the other child races, but from the human perspective, I believe that the candidates of Operation Legacy will be delighted with the results."

"And you do this by…" Marcus said slowly.

"A series of injections and nothing more," Dr. Kono said. "No surgery, no radiation, no getting bitten by a spider and no toxic waste. It really is just that simple."

"When," Marcus asked. "When is this going to happen?"

"When you least expect it…" Dr. Kono said. "Or, you know, tomorrow probably. The baseline tests have all been completed now, so I think we're ready to rock and roll."

"I… I'm not a soldier," Marcus admitted quietly. "I don't know what that means if you want me to be a supersoldier."

"You're here and that's all that matters," Kono said. "Besides, if you don't match up, I'm sure the others will all just eventually eat you as the weakest of the species. Or is that just my people? Either way, I'm sure it doesn't matter. By the way, does your nose hurt? I'm sure it's broken."

Marcus blinked, trying to separate all the information thrown at him.

"What?" He said.

"Does your nose hurt?" Dr. Kono asked again, stepping forward and taking hold of his stethoscope.

"Yes," Marcus said, "but not as much as my arm." He knew his arm was broken, but he only suspected the same for his nose – not being able to see it and all.

"Arms down," the lizard ordered as he arrived within touching distance of Marcus. Marcus dutifully obeyed.

"How does it look?" Marcus asked.

"Well I'd say it looks like you're going to be the first to me," Dr. Kono said.

"First?'

Marcus didn't have the chance to get a reply to his question because as quick as a flash, the doctor's balled fist impacted his face so hard that his vision immediately turned black and he fell back onto his bed without so much as a kiss goodnight.

"Really perceptive that one," Kono said. "Kind of disconcerting actually. Really puts you on edge, doesn't it."

Chapter 12 – The First

"I still don't think you should've hit him," the same woman's voice roused Marcus from his sleep.

His first instinct was to cringe in readiness for the pain that was surely about to wash over him. From either the beating from the group of soldiers, the broken nose or arm courtesy of the base commander, the punch from the strange alien lizard-doctor thing, or the culmination of everything that his body had been put through over the last couple of days. In short, he was expecting pain.

But it didn't come.

There was no pain, and that in itself presented Marcus with a fair amount of worry.

"Well, it's done with now anyway, isn't it? And besides, look at the boy, sleeping like a baby. Does it seem like he cares about how he got there?"

"That isn't the point!" The woman replied. "I took an oath to do no harm!"

"Then what would you do if you had to cause harm to one person to save ten from getting hurt?"

It sounded to Marcus like the doctor was asking the question sincerely rather than sarcastically, and he kept his eyes shut so the pair didn't recognise that he was conscious.

"Because that is exactly what is happening here, you know? The candidates are going to have a bit of a rough time, but in the long run, this Operation could save the lives of literally billions, and not just human lives either."

The woman exhaled loudly. "I know," she said. "But… did you really have to hit him?"

"Well, no, but it was just so much fun," Kono replied. Then after a short pause added. "If I had introduced a chemical anaesthetic into his system, it could have had an effect on the genetic modifications and trust me, this isn't the kind of thing you want to introduce unknown variables into."

Again a short pause followed, and Marcus took the opportunity to open his eyes for the first time.

"Uh… what happened?" he croaked out, choosing to walk the path of ignorance rather than have to talk about what he had just heard.

"Oh hello Marcus, back with us then I see?" Kono replied. "How are you feeling?"

"I feel like you punched me," Marcus said.

Dr Kono grinned deviously. "I know. But how do you feel?" he asked again.

"I feel… OK?" Marcus replied, and it was much more of a question than he'd been planning to come out with. The truth was that he did actually feel OK. Not perfect, not happy and healthy, just OK.

"OK…" Kono replied slowly. "And what does that mean? Given the fact that you are still in the same room you were in when you, ahem, passed out?"

"It means you did something," Marcus said. "You… fixed my broken arm and nose? Or just gave me so many painkillers that they just don't hurt any more?"

"Well fractures do tend to heal in a couple of months in humans…" Kono said, trailing off at the end of his sentence.

"A couple of months?!" Marcus almost choked on his own words.

"That will never get old," Dr. Kono said with a grin. "Usually, human bones will take that long to heal. But you've only been out for less than a day… and you aren't actually healed. But I haven't given you any painkillers either; I don't want anything in your system that could interfere with my own little project."

Marcus then looked down at his broken arm. It didn't feel like it was broken any more, and the other pain that he had been in was all but gone. His arm was purple, brown and yellow already though, as the bruises had made their way to the surface. Though that in itself was sooner than usual, wasn't it? Then he brought his other hand up to feel his nose. That too didn't feel exactly right, but the searing pain had been reduced to almost nothing, though when he touched it, it did hurt a little.

"I… it doesn't hurt as much any more… but if it's only been a day. How can that be?" Marcus asked.

"Well, it's because I'm Jesus," Kono said.

Marcus blinked.

"You know, came down from up high, healed the unhealthy, performed miracles?"

"Seriously?" Marcus managed to say. "Is everything a joke to you?"

"Well, not everything," Kono replied. "Just I find it better to cope with the monotony of life if I inject a little humour into things. You probably don't get it with your human lifespan of what, less than one hundred years? Try living for five thousand years, and you'll find that amusing yourself tends to help pass the time."

"Five…" Marcus started.

"Doesn't matter," Kono said. "What does matter is the fact that you are now patient zero. And by that, I mean you are the first candidate to have become a full participant of Operation Legacy. I will note down here for the official and timeless records that you are feeling 'OK' about it."

"The… what?" Marcus asked. It was like the doctor always seemed to talk three steps ahead of him, like he was never fully up to date with what was going on in the conversation.

"Well, you are the first to receive the treatment that Operation Legacy is all about. And that is namely a gene modification serum that will allow you to break your racial and genetic ceilings. Or at least that is the hope."

"Gene modification?" Marcus asked, feeling his hands turn sweaty and his skin very cold. A shiver enveloped his entire body as he processed what the lizard man was saying.

"Gene modification," Kono replied. "You said you wanted to turn into a lizard, didn't you?"

Marcus opened his mouth to object, but the doctor spoke again before he had the chance.

"Just kidding," Kono said. "Not about the gene editing, but about the lizard thing you understand. Well, let me explain a few things to you so you can understand what we're trying to do here with Operation Legacy. Human beings, and well, pretty much any creature or race in existence, have what is known as a 'genetic ceiling'. Now, these ceilings can vary from individual to individual, but in general, their scope is somewhat confined to the race that the individual belongs to. Is your monkey brain following?"

Marcus nodded.

"Good. So these ceilings come in many shapes and forms. Strength, speed, intelligence, creativity, those sorts of things. The easiest way for me to explain this is to take strength. Let's say we have a weight sat on the floor with us here now. If it is ten kilograms, then most humans would be able to lift it up without any issues. If it was one hundred kilograms, then a lot would still lift it, but not as many. At two hundred, there would be far less, and at five hundred, there would be none."

"Like the world records then," Marcus said flatly.

Dr Kono looked at him like he was annoyed that there was an easier explanation than the one he had given.

"Yes," Kono finally said. "Let's just say that world records are the current genetic ceilings for humans. And, of course, like records, these ceilings can be broken. But it's not so easy to measure things like conceptualisation, intelligence, situational awareness, or perception. Now what we are trying to do with Operation Legacy, is raise, or possibly even entirely break through those ceilings. Understood?"

Marcus nodded.

"I think so… So that means you want to make us stronger, faster, or smarter?"

"In some cases, perhaps all three," Kono said. "But again, it will vary on the individual. Plus, I don't want to make you anything. I want to give you all the ability to make yourselves those things. I can open the doors for you, it is up to you to take those steps to walk through."

"Not to be rude or anything," Marcus said. "But that sounds a lot like pretentious crap."

Dr. Kono's mouth dropped open, and Marcus couldn't help but notice that the woman in the room was covering her mouth, trying her best not to laugh.

"Seriously though," Marcus continued. "So your whole idea is to say to us 'the sky is the limit', and then just make us try harder? Honestly, I could've come up with that one myself."

"Not really," Kono replied. Besides, the sky isn't the limit. My plan is to remove all limits, but as I said, you do still have to put the work in. I know you may think I'm capable of performing miracles – and from some perspectives I am, just like Jesus – but some things are universally impossible. For example, I can't just give you a pill to make your muscles bigger overnight; those cells have to come from somewhere, you know. What I can do, is make it so during the normal procedure of your muscles becoming damaged and repairing themselves slightly thicker or stronger, they won't stop when they hit your predefined genetic limit."

Marcus wasn't exactly sure how to respond to that. He was already half convinced that whatever experiments this alien doctor was planning to run, they seemed like they weren't exactly cutting edge on the universal scale of things. And it very much sounded like there weren't going to be laser guns, huge destructive WMD's or anything else that the British Army was going to unveil as the thing to change the world. No, this was more like Rocky IV, where the government seemed to be sponsoring some kind of steroid program whereby the soldiers were going to be turned into machines but inevitably would lose to good old-fashioned grade-A human meat. Somehow through all of this nonsense, Foley had been correct.

"So how are you feeling?" Dr. Kono said after a while of Marcus thinking through this whole situation. "Knowing that you're the first human being to ever exist without limits. To know that you can do anything, be anything."

"Honestly? Not really different at all," Marcus said. "I mean, it's like this: If I put the effort in, I could play the piano. But I haven't, and you know why? Because I don't want to put the effort in. I don't not try because I don't think it's possible… so why would I put the effort in to get stronger, or faster, or smarter?"

Kono stared at Marcus again, though this time there was something different in his eyes, something that Marcus hadn't seen before: a challenge.

"I know you aren't a soldier, Mr. Cesari," Kono said quietly. "And the others may just want to be the best that they can be because that's the way they've been trained. But you have something different to fight for. I had the chance to test your blood samples and I want you to know that you don't have any secrets from me."

Marcus' heart skipped. The doctor knew.

"You… know?" He asked.

"I know," Kono replied. "I know what you have, and I know why you are here. I even know about your father."

"My…"

"Don't worry," Kono said. "I do like a challenge, so I have already begun work on synthesising a cure for the condition, though I don't deny that it will be difficult and take some time. What I can say, are the following two things: One, if your body grows in the way that I think it should within this program, I doubt that you will have very much to worry about from your condition in the future and two: If you keep me happy, I'll keep wanting to cure this condition not only for yourself, but for everyone."

It was clear who he meant when he said everyone.

"Where is he? The little piss-ant? Where is the Private who has no idea when to back down when faced with a superior opponent?" Callahan's voice came booming through the corridor outside the room before the door behind Dr. Kono swung open and the base commander strode in. Marcus watched as Callahan's entire body went rigid once he realised the man in the white medical coat had scaly yellow skin and a rather long tail.

"Doctor," Callahan practically stuttered. "I didn't realise that…"

"This is now my nest, Callahan," Kono replied in what could only be described as a sinister tone. "Do I come to your mess hall and interrupt you during your meal times?"

Callahan looked at Marcus as his skin paled.

"Are… are you OK, Cesari?" He asked as quietly as Marcus had ever heard him speak.

Marcus nodded.

"Very good… I… I just wanted… I'll be going then," Callahan said as he retreated back out the door and closed it gently behind him. Kono looked back to Marcus and smiled.

"You owe me for that one," he said.

Marcus couldn't help but grin.

"Just hates lizards," Kono explained. "Any type of reptile, I mean. I found it out entirely by accident, but it's a rather fun coincidence, isn't it? I mean, imagine the chaos I can cause around here."

"I'm sorry," Marcus said, interrupting the doctor's monologue. "But what's going to happen to me?"

"Ah, of course," Kono said, clicking his fingers. "First, your skin will turn to yellow scales, and then…"

"Doctor, please," Marcus begged.

"Fine. My studies have shown that the first course of action my gene therapy will take is to repair damaged or stressed cells. Then, well, in the most basic terms, many of your receptors will be switched off. You know, things like when your muscles have grown enough so they shouldn't grow any more, that kind of thing. I mean, none of my studies have been carried out on live subjects until now, of course, but I doubt it will be too dissimilar. And by the way, I believe that this is the reason the pain you should be experiencing from your broken bones has been reduced to a dull ache, so I guess… you're welcome."

"Right," Marcus said, making sure not to give the automatic response of 'thank you' to the doctor who had basically violated him in his sleep. "But… what do I do next?"

"You can stay here for a night if you like. I can keep that Callahan away with stories of nightmare lizards to give you some breathing room and you can heal up. But know that the sooner you can return to training, the better. The others will receive the same treatment over the next week or two, so this is a good chance for you to put some distance between you and them."

"Or catch up to them," Marcus said.

"Yeah, I wouldn't worry too much about that. I think that you're going to be pleasantly surprised at what the human body is capable of, given the right circumstances."

"You don't know how far behind I am," Marcus said. "I feel like a little kid out there with that lot."

"Oh, I've seen the initial test results," Kono said. "Though I haven't yet put names to the squads. Am I to assume, then, that you are a member of the seventy-First?"

"I am," Marcus said, sitting bolt upright. "Are they doing OK without me?"

"For someone who can be so perceptive, you sure can be a dimwit," Kono replied. "If there is one squad that I was asking if you were a part of, what might you think be the reason for that? Don't answer that it was rhetorical," he added quickly. "It would mean they are doing exceptionally, wouldn't it, either exceptionally well or exceptionally poorly. Which do you think is the more likely?"

Marcus let his body fall back down to the bed. He knew he didn't need to answer the question, and the fact was that he was just letting his squad down. He felt guilty, useless, and weak.

"But like I said, when you get back out there, I think you're going to be pleasantly surprised at the speed you can improve yourself. Seriously, just wait and see."

And with that, the lizard doctor turned and walked out of the room. Marcus looked up at the woman who had been standing there silently the entire time and raised his eyebrows at her as though to ask some unvoiced question.

"I know he's an ass," the woman said. "But we've been assured that he's quite brilliant. He... wouldn't be here if he wasn't, would he?"

Marcus shook his head slowly.

"Do you trust him?" He asked.

"Not even a little bit."

Marcus closed his eyes. All he could do was wonder how exactly he'd managed to get himself into this mess.

And what was going to happen to him next.

Chapter 13 – The Secret's Out

Marcus took the opportunity to rest his body for a day. To his surprise, the woman he had spoken to was very pleasant once she wasn't all stressed about dealing with the overbearing Dr. Kono.

In his day in the doctor's office, Marcus was fed and watered, and even had the chance to just lay back and listen to the world outside passing him by. It was a nice change not to have to run, cook his own food or be constantly shouted at by the commander, and after the few moments he took to get used to it, he actually found it all rather relaxing.

"How are you feeling?" the doctor asked. She'd asked the question routinely, and Marcus had always thought he had to be more descriptive than just replying with 'alright'.

"Alright," he said, sitting upright. "But… Ms Katherine, should I be alright? I mean, I don't know about my nose, but my arm was definitely broken. Shouldn't it be hurting a lot more after just one day?"

The doctor smiled. "Absolutely. You should be in a fair amount of agony, and I doubt you should be moving around as confidently and as quickly as you are. That being said, that Dr. Kono is as good at being an ass as he is at being a doctor, from what I've been told. I know everything seems a bit weird, but it's one of those things you just seem to get used to the more and more ridiculous things get."

Marcus nodded. "Do you think we're going to be alright?" he asked.

Ms Katherine gave a shy half smile. "I think we're all going to get through this one way or another, Marcus. I just hope the higher-ups know what they're doing with all of this."

"Do they ever?"

"Mr Cesari, how dare you," the doctor said with a grin. "But seriously, just keep your head down, do what you're told and you're going to be fine. That's what I'm here to make sure of."

Marcus wanted to ask why the doctor hadn't thrown herself in the path of Dr. Kono's punch like some kind of rabid bodyguard, but decided it was better to just leave it. She'd been nice to him after all.

"And well, I think you're ready to go back and join your squad. It sounds like you have some catching up to do because, trust me, this isn't one of those places where you want to be at the bottom of the list."

Marcus knew that all too well, though he'd always had an aversion to the top of the list too. 'Never stand out because the tallest grass gets cut down', he'd thought to himself on more than one occasion.

Spinning on the small bed, Marcus planted his bare feet onto the ground and pushed himself up. It wasn't the same as he'd remembered. In fact, he pushed himself so hard that he nearly went up and over before he quickly replanted his foot in front of himself. He seemed lighter somehow, like he was filled with helium or something. It must've been the extended period of relaxing, sure, that was it he thought.

Ms. Katherine chuckled at Marcus's slightly wobbly attempt to stand. "Careful there, Mr. Cesari. It seems like you've got a bit of extra bounce in your step. Just remember, you're still solid enough to fall flat on your face."

Marcus grinned sheepishly, feeling a bit embarrassed by his unsteady start. He steadied himself and stood up properly, still feeling the subtle difference in his movements, as if his body was more responsive and agile than before. He wondered how much he had actually needed that day's rest – after all, it had all been a whirlwind ever since the beating outside the Berry.

"Thanks for everything, doctor," he said sincerely. "It's been... interesting."

"You're welcome, Marcus. I hope to see you again soon! Just try to avoid getting into too many fights if you can."

Marcus nodded, frowning. "What an awful thing for a doctor to say," he mumbled.

With a final nod to the doctor, he turned, replaced his boots and overalls and walked out of the medical bay, re-entering the barracks where he was immediately unsure as to what he was supposed to be doing.

All around him, squads seemed to be doing something different. Some were running, some were sat, he could see some running The Gauntlet and in the distance, he could hear the telltale pops of gunfire from the firing range.

Marcus walked up to the closest of the squads and tapped a soldier who was sitting on the ground to get his attention.

"Excuse me," Marcus said. "Can you tell me where the Seventy-First is?"

"You're Cesari, aren't you!" The soldier said, turning to stand up. "Eh, Hunter, come have a look who it is!"

A second soldier stood up, and as soon as she saw Marcus, he broke into a wide grin.

"I've got to shake your hand," Hunter said, beaming. "I've never seen someone take a beating like that before. I mean, honestly, it was hard to watch, what with you not really knowing how to fight and all, but to just never give up? You've either gotta be stupid or just plain stubborn!"

"Mostly stupid," Marcus replied quickly. "But can you tell me where Seventy-First is? I really need to get back."

"Yeah, you do," the first soldier said. "Your mates are bottom of the list, and according to Callahan, that makes them just about fit to peel potatoes – so you'll find them in the kitchens, through there," the man pointed behind Marcus.

"Right… thanks," he managed to reply. His throat had tightened at the mention of the punishment, and the familiar pang of guilt was back, biting the nape of his neck as he very much knew that his squad was paying the price for him being out of place.

As he made his way back to his squad in the kitchens, he couldn't help but reflect on the strange twists and turns that his life had taken recently. From his initial shock at being enlisted into the army, to the intense training sessions and encounters with an honest-to-God alien being. It felt like he was in some strange dream he couldn't awaken from.

Entering the kitchen, he was greeted by the sight of his squadmates engaged in peeling a veritable mountain of dirty potatoes. Ramirez looked like she'd done it a thousand times before, but Foley looked like he was having trouble keeping the pressure off, as his pile of finished potatoes seemed to be a lot smaller than anyone else's.

McCulloch was taking his time, producing perfectly round spuds, though at a much slower rate than Ramirez, and King was just throwing one up in the air over and over, not even bothering to peel it.

"Hey, look who's back from the land of the injured," Ramirez called out with a grin as she noticed Marcus.

Marcus chuckled and approached the squad, immediately looking around for a spare potato peeler. "Yeah, it turns out my superpower is not knowing when to give up."

"I'll say," Ramirez said. "I mean, look at the state of your face! And shouldn't your arm be in a sling or something?"

"Probably," Marcus said, "But I don't think it's as bad as they thought before. Something about being hard as nails or something."

"Pfft," Foley said. "More like stubborn as a mule. You want to try round two with me?"

Marcus winced.

"Can't you leave him for even a second?" King said. "Besides, we all watched you get floored by Chloe."

"Listen, O'Connell's not human, I'm telling you."

"Not human?" Marcus asked, his ears pricking up.

"Oh, don't listen to him," King said. "He ran at the girl and she suplexed him right out of the circle… and onto his face! You should've seen it!"

"I tripped and…" Foley descended into annoyed mumbling, and the rest ignored him.

McCulloch chuckled. "Well, at least we're back to a full team, so now we can work on moving up the leaderboard. This time it was potatoes, but you don't want to be there if next time it's cleaning the heads, or even on laundry. Soldiers are animals."

Marcus found a peeler and picked it up along with a decent-sized potato.

"Did I miss anything exciting while I was away?" he asked.

Ramirez shrugged. "Same old, same old. More training, more mystery."

"More mystery, huh?" Marcus said, beginning to peel his potato with a fair amount of focus. "I feel like we're collecting more questions than answers in this whole operation."

King nodded, catching the potato she had been tossing in the air and beginning to peel it as well, though with a lot less care than anyone else. "You're not wrong."

"Well, I'm hoping they'll let us in on the big secret soon. Maybe we're getting close to being let in on the real action," Foley offered.

McCulloch chuckled. "I think we'll be lucky if they even let us in on what's for dinner."

"I… I might know something," Marcus said slowly. "But I don't know if I'm supposed to say or not. I guess… well they didn't say I couldn't so…"

"Jesus Marcus spill the beans," Ramirez said. "It's like listening to a politician being asked why there's so much pollution in a lake!"

"It's… well, it's not going to be easy to believe," Marcus said. "The doctor who treated me… he's an alien."

The room fell silent for a long moment.

"You know, if you want to make an impression," Ramirez said, "I think you should go back to getting punched in the face over and over."

"I'm being serious," Marcus said. "The thing's like a weird human-lizard creature. And he speaks English. And makes jokes and… and he punched me!"

The room remained quiet as Marcus' words hung in the air. The squad exchanged bewildered glances, seemingly unsure of how to respond to such a strange statement.

"Funny," Foley finally said, breaking the silence, "I was wondering which one of us was going to go mental first. Should've known really."

Ramirez burst out laughing, and the rest of the squad couldn't help but join in. The tension in the room dissipated in a wave of laughter.

"Come on, Cesari, an alien doctor?" King said between giggles. "You've been watching too many sci-fi movies."

Foley wiped a tear from his eye. "Yeah, next you'll be telling us he has a UFO parked behind the barracks."

Marcus couldn't help but chuckle along with them, realising how absurd his story must have sounded. "I know, I know, it sounds crazy. But I swear, it's true. I couldn't make this up if I tried."

Ramirez playfully punched Marcus' good shoulder. "Alright, alright, we believe you… not. But it's a good one, I'll give you that."

McCulloch chimed in with a grin. "So, when's your next appointment with Dr. Zorgon, the alien healer?"

"I'm telling you, guys, there's something weird going on," Marcus said, still chuckling. "I might not have all the answers, but I do believe there's more to this than meets the eye. And his name is Dr. Kono."

The group broke into hysterics for the second time. And it took much longer for them to return to normal this time.

Foley was the first to speak. "Okay, let's say for a moment that your alien doctor is real. What's his angle? Why would some shape-shifting lizard be interested in fixing up a bunch of soldiers?"

Marcus leaned back, crossing his arms thoughtfully. "That's what I've been trying to figure out. And he's not really a shape-shifter, it's hard to explain but you'll get it once you see it."

King's amusement clearly began to fade as she watched Marcus refuse to back down from his story. "And you trust this… alien's words?"

"I don't know if I'd say 'trust,' but there's something about him," Marcus replied. "It's hard to explain. He seems genuine, like he genuinely wants to help us succeed. But I think it's because this is all his experiment or something. He said so much that I don't know what he was being serious about and what he wasn't."

Ramirez leaned in, her tone serious. "Marcus, you have to be careful. We're in a highly classified program that we barely understand. Trusting an alien doctor who conveniently speaks English... it's a lot to swallow." Then she reduced her volume to a whisper. "Did he... did he probe you?"

"NO!" Marcus shouted and Ramirez' shrill laughter filled the room.

"Come on, Marcus!" she coughed. "You don't expect us to believe this, do you?"

"I know it's a lot to take in," Marcus admitted. "But it's the truth. Listen, let me tell you everything he said, and you can make your own minds up."

Marcus then reeled off everything he could remember that Dr Kono had said about genetic ceilings, physical and mental advancements, and the Operation in general. He was pretty sure he hadn't missed anything out by the time he'd finished telling his story.

"No genetic ceilings, huh?" Foley said. "If this is all true, we could become the most famous soldiers in history. Seventy-First: The Best of the Best.'"

Everyone chuckled again, the scepticism not completely gone, but the mood significantly changed.

"Hey, even if Dr. Zorgon turns out to be a fraud," King said with a grin, "at least we'll have a good story to tell once we're out of this place."

Marcus chuckled, feeling grateful for his squadmates' ability to find humour even in the most bizarre situations.

"But then know your nickname will forever be 'Lizard Boy'," Foley said. "And that's for life."

"So how's your arm holding up?" King asked Marcus to change the subject, a genuine note of concern in her voice.

Marcus flexed his arm experimentally. "Surprisingly well. I can move it without much pain, and it feels... different, somehow. Lighter, maybe."

Ramirez chuckled. "Well, if you start floating around, let us know. We've already got a lizard infestation, the last thing we need is birds."

"You sure?" King asked, taking a step towards Marcus. "I've seen arms break like that before."

"Yeah, I think..." Marcus started, but was interrupted by King poking him at the elbow. He flinched, but didn't yelp as clearly King had been expecting.

"Show it to me," she said.

Foley opened his mouth to make a comment, but a stern look from King made him shut it again.

Marcus took his arm out of the overall to reveal its heavily bruised form. King then took a hold of it and started squeezing it and moving it around.

"It's… it's not broken," she said with wonder in her eyes. "But how?"

"It's that doctor," Marcus said. "I told you he can do things that we just can't comprehend… and healing a broken bone looks like it's one of those things – that's if you were sure it was broken."

"I saw the bone, Marcus," King said. "I know what I saw."

The room fell into a contemplative silence as King continued to examine Marcus' arm. Everyone was processing the implications of what he had just shared, the boundaries of what they considered possible expanding in unexpected ways.

McCulloch broke the silence, his voice sceptical. "So, an alien doctor who can miraculously heal broken bones... this is what, like a sci-fi movie come to life?"

Ramirez leaned in. "Did he say anything about how this... healing ability works? I mean, did he just wave his alien hands and voila?"

Marcus thought back to his interaction with Dr. Kono, trying to remember what exactly had happened, and then he remembered one detail he'd left out.

"He punched me," he said. "Right in the nose. I mean, it was so hard that it knocked me out, and when I woke up, it was all done."

"So he could've probed you!" Foley announced with a wide smile.

"Shut up, Foley," King said. "The question is then, is this a part of whatever the gene-editing program is, or did he do something different? Because believe me, I wouldn't mind the ability to heal broken bones overnight."

"I don't know," Marcus answered honestly. "And he didn't say when anyone else is going to get the treatment. But when you do see him, I'd say cover your face."

"I'd like to see some alien try to put his greasy green paws on me," Foley said.

"Well, they were more yellow and scaly rather than greasy," Marcus said.

"Whatever, you get my point!" Foley complained.

"Oh, whatever, Foley," Ramirez said. "One look at the vial of super potion and you'll be cuddling up to that alien like he's your bed-time bear."

Foley turned red, but didn't say a word.

"Anyway, I think all we can do is just carry on as we're ordered," McCulloch announced. "And right now, that means peeling potatoes. Then maybe tomorrow we'll get a chance to lift ourselves from the bottom of the leaderboard just in case, you know?"

"Right," Ramirez said. "But if there's a vote to be taken on who has to put their hands down the blocked toilets first, I vote Foley."

"Ay," King agreed.

"What? Why?" Foley asked.

"Because it was probably you who blocked it anyway you great lummox!" Ramirez replied.

Foley shrugged and grinned in somewhat agreement.

"Do you have any idea what we're going to have to do to get off the bottom?" Marcus asked.

"Actually, it isn't that bad," Ramirez said. "We can challenge any other squad in any of the baseline tests. You get points allocated again just like we did the first time, but bonus points for beating your opponent based on where they are in the table… so…"

"So nobody wants to challenge us?" Marcus asked.

"Exactly. If they win, they don't gain much, and if they lose, then it's a big deal." Ramirez agreed. "Except for one thing. You lose points for turning down a challenge. So, all we need to do is pick some of the lower-ranked squads and beat them – we'll be off the bottom in no time!"

"Just beat them?" Marcus repeated. "Can we do that?"

"If we're smart and pick the right tests," Ramirez said.

"The right tests…"

"You know Cesari ain't half the soldier as any of the others out there," Foley quipped and Ramirez glared at him.

"And that's exactly why we're going to work as a team to turn him into the best soldier that we possibly can," Ramirez replied through gritted teeth. "One without any bad habits like your God damn fish mouth!"

Foley shut his mouth with a click.

"So the standing orders are seriously just to go forth and do whatever we want? Doesn't that sound a bit… uh, easy?" Marcus asked, trying very hard to change the subject.

"It would be strange," McCulloch said. "But you have to remember who we are. Some of the new Privates have been serving for decades – we know what we're doing - so all of this is more like a test than a training thing, right? They want to see how we do, how we think and what we do without constant orders. Well, that's my take on it anyway."

"I think you're right," King agreed. "On the battlefield, we won't always have someone telling us which way to walk. Or better yet, we'll be the ones telling the others. We aren't just grunts here. Uh, no offense Cesari."

"None taken," Marcus said. "Just I always knew soldiers were a lazy bunch..."

King punched him in his good soldier. "Just you wait. You think pretending to be a soldier is hard? Just wait until we turn you into the real thing."

Chapter 14 – The First Day of the Rest of His Life

The next morning, all eighty-three squads stood in their groups on the parade square, facing the base commander and the three Colonels: Whittaker, Armstrong and Johnson. They had been called to attention as soon as they had all finished their breakfast – porridge, which Marcus felt wasn't enough for his rapidly repairing body – and the Colonels had followed them shortly after.

"Good morning, Privates," Callahan announced loudly to no response. "Now I expect that today, your squads will face off in a number of tasks in order to better position yourselves on the leader board. It may not come as a surprise to you that at periods I deem necessary, the squads closer to the top of the board will be provided with bonuses, whilst the squads near the bottom will be handed punishments. But this does not mean that you are safe in the centre of the leaderboard. Because those who fail to improve their ranks can and will be punished, do you understand?"

"Sir, yes, sir!" The call returned.

"Now that we all have good reasons to strive for greatness – God forbid you all be able to carry out your orders without a carrot and a stick – let's move along to organising this mess I see before me. I want each squad right now to elect a squad leader. The squad leader shall then take one step forward to indicate his or her separation from the rest of you grunts."

It was the first time that the candidates for Operation Legacy were unsure of themselves. It seemed that they knew they had previously worn ranks as soldiers and officers, but if they were to take their new ranks in the

GSI literally, then technically there was no superiority to be had, other than what the squads would give their new leader. Thankfully for the Seventy-First, it was an easy call.

"Get out there," Ramirez nudged McCulloch in the back. "And don't give me that. We all know you're the squad leader."

McCulloch dutifully took a step forward and turned back to look at Marcus, King, Ramirez and Foley. Marcus was sure that he stood a little taller, knowing that he'd been chosen for such a prestigious position.

After a few moments, the shuffling stopped and every squad had nominated their leaders. Colonel Whittaker then walked the line and noted down each of the nominated squad leaders.

"Now," Callahan announced loudly. "If you would kindly afford me a little of your attention, there is one more announcement that I wish to make before the day's festivities begin." He paused purposefully before continuing. "Each squad commander is hereby promoted to the rank of Lance Corporal. Congratulations people, your new uniform will be delivered to your dorms."

Marcus couldn't help but notice the wide grin spread on McCulloch's face. The man clearly took great pleasure in his career advancement, and truthfully, Marcus was happy for him.

"Your squad leaders are the individuals who will make and accept challenges from other squads, so ultimately, your final place in the ranking system will be determined by their actions. I hope that you have chosen well."

The squads were then dismissed, and after a few minutes, McCullough had been to the dorms and back, returning wearing almost identical overalls to what he had been wearing before, only now on the shoulder the single angular chevron that sat there was red with a dark black background.

"Do you want to start issuing challenges?" McCullough asked before he even stopped walking towards the group.

"Thirty-Eighth would like to challenge Seventy-First in hand-to-hand combat," a nearby soldier announced loudly before anyone had the chance to reply to McCulloch.

The Lance Corporal turned to stand face to face with a man about a foot shorter than him, though his expression was clearly full of confidence.

"Why?" McCulloch asked in a far less official tone.

"Do you accept or do you reject our challenge?" The man said.

"Maybe if you answer my question," McCulloch said. "You're a good ten places higher than us on the leaderboard, so why would you risk it?"

Marcus stepped forward. "Because he thinks that we'll reject it on a count of my injuries. Then they get to look like the big dicks, and we lose points for turning down a fight. On the other hand, if we accept, then they have the advantage that I can't really fight in this state," he gestured to his arm. He was pretty sure that he could fight, but a little overconfidence wouldn't be such a bad thing for their opposing team to fill up on.

"I say take the challenge," King said, balling her fists. "Just let me take two of them."

"You know the rules," McCulloch said. "We all fight, one on one. No double-ups and no teams."

The Lance Corporal from the Thirty-Eighth was now clearly grinning, like he'd found the most wonderful loophole to this entire situation.

McCulloch turned and looked back at the rest of his squad with a questioning expression on his face.

"We turn it down and we lose anyway," he said like he had no other choice. "You all ready to fight?"

It was clear that the question was aimed at Marcus, though King answered for the group.

"Hell yeah!" she announced and moved into a boxer's stance, throwing two punches in quick succession.

"Not here, on the grass," McCulloch said. "We don't want any more broken bones, do we?"

The other Lance Corporal, at this point, looked like the cat who'd got the cream. Presumably, knowing that Marcus had suffered breaks only served to bolster his conviction.

"Well, what are you waiting for?" the other Lance Corporal said. "Let's go!"

The squad followed the man over to a makeshift circle on the ground, and as they walked, they quietly discussed what was going to happen.

"You going to be OK, Marcus?" Ramirez asked. "I mean, you could forfeit your match, and as long as the rest of us all win, then it won't even matter."

"I can fight..." Marcus replied. "Just put me in there first so we can get this all out of the way, OK?"

McCulloch paused for a second, looking into Marcus' eyes, and whatever he saw there must've convinced him that it was the right thing to do.

"OK, you first, then me, Foley, Ramirez, and King last. I know you're going to want to go mad, King, but try not to bloody them up too much, right?"

King smiled. "No promises, sir."

When they all came to a halt facing the other squad, Marcus stepped forward and into the small ring and a moment later his opponent followed.

It was obvious which one of the Thirty-Eighth it was going to be – the smallest soldier in the group stepped into the ring, clearly they thought that Marcus would either be a pushover, or that he was going to forfeit, even if he was to face off against a woman.

Marcus, though, had no intention of forfeiting, and even though he was a good head taller than his opponent, he knew that she was most likely a well-trained soldier who should not be underestimated.

So he put one arm up and left the other down by his side to punctuate his injury. By now though, it wasn't painful, but again, it was best to control the narrative of the fight.

"I think you should just forfeit," the woman said. "I really don't want to hurt you but… well, you know."

"It's alright," Marcus replied. "Just make it quick, would you?"

The soldier shrugged, and then lunged.

Marcus took a step back just before his opponent reached him and presented his good arm for the impact. What would've been a full-on tackle quickly became a glancing blow, and the soldier's face changed from confidence to surprise in a single second.

The surrounding soldiers were cheering loudly for their own squad members, but Marcus didn't hear any of it. From the moment his opponent had taken a single step towards him, it was like the whole world had melted away. The world around him was dulled, and his vision focussed on the fight he was now a central feature of.

"What the…" he heard his opponent whisper to herself, and moved out of the way of the second attack coming his way: an elbow aimed directly at his face.

But Marcus saw it coming. Again, the strike and his opponent's movements seemed easy to read and in a kind of slow motion, like she was moving through water and this time Marcus dropped to his knees to dodge the incoming appendage.

The follow-up took a lot of work to avoid, though. Even though Marcus could seem to watch the fight happening at this new reduced speed, it did nothing to change the fact that he was still both slower and weaker than pretty much anyone else in the barracks, not to mention entirely untrained. The woman took the opportunity whilst Marcus was on his knees to drive a strong kick into his chest, causing him to bring his arms up to defend against the strike.

Unfortunately for Marcus, it seemed that he was yet to heal from his last fight fully, and the one kick hurt more than he had expected. It wasn't because it was so much more powerful than he would've thought; rather his bad arm just couldn't seem to take the impact. As soon as he dropped it back down to his side, another kick arrived.

"Get up, Marcus!" he finally heard King's voice permeate his combat bubble. "You can't fight on your knees!"

Marcus looked up to see where the voice was coming from, but that proved to be an even bigger mistake than dropping to his knees.

A shiny black boot impacted his cheek and sent him spinning to the ground. At least this time he didn't pass out; he remained just conscious enough to feel his body dragged from the small circle and deposited gently onto the ground.

"That's one for us then, agreed?" Marcus heard the opposing Lance Corporal announce with a fair amount of cockiness in his tome. "Fancy a go, you and me?" the soldier continued.

"Alright," McCulloch replied. "Just let me make sure Cesari here is OK."

Marcus grunted.

"He's fine," Ramirez said. "He likes it down there, just make sure you beat his ass, right?"

Marcus opened his eyes in time to see McCulloch nod at Ramirez and enter the circle.

It was clear from the start that both of the squad leaders were well-trained in hand-to-hand combat. It was one of those situations where they both had so much respect for each other that neither wanted to make the first move and put himself in a vulnerable position.

Inevitably, something had to give, so McCulloch made the first move. He feigned a jab at his opponent's face, and, as expected, the opposing squad leader moved to block it. However, the attempt had clearly been a distraction because McCulloch quickly followed with a swift kick to the other man's midsection, catching him off guard.

The strike was executed perfectly, and the opposing squad leader staggered back, momentarily winded. McCulloch didn't let up, pressing his advantage and moving in. He closed the distance between them and unleashed a series of rapid punches and kicks. His opponent, still recovering from the initial blow, struggled to defend himself, blocking and dodging where he could.

The other squad's leader tried to counter, but McCulloch was on the front foot. McCulloch then landed a powerful punch to the man's jaw, sending him sprawling to the ground. The Lance Corporal rolled out of the circle, clearly accepting his defeat.

"That's one each," Ramirez announced. "Great work McCulloch, I knew you could take him down."

McCulloch smiled back at Ramirez as Foley stepped into the ring.

When Foley stood against his opponent, Marcus had never thought such a mismatch would've been allowed. The woman wasn't much bigger than the soldier Marcus himself had fought, but when she stood opposite the hulking silhouette of Foley, the size difference was almost comical.

Foley though, didn't even get the chance to raise his fists in readiness, with the female soldier charging him down at waist height. She clearly knew what she was doing, judging by the two steps back Foley had to take to mitigate her momentum. Inevitably, though, Foley was stronger and heavier, and once he'd stabilised himself, he placed the woman in a tight headlock and simply walked her out of the circle with nothing exciting happening.

Marcus looked at the opposing squad and saw that they had now realised their mistake. They may have had Marcus easily beaten, but they would have to beat at least two of the rest of the squad to win the fight overall. And they'd already lost to McCulloch and Foley.

The score stood at two-one in favour of the Seventy-First, with Ramirez and King left to fight.

The problem was though, that in order to try to sway the advantage of the fight in their favour, the opposing squad looked like they'd kept their most skilled fighters (or at least their largest) back for last, to fight the women of the Seventy-First.

Ramirez' opponent was a full head taller than her, and if she needed a place to hide like a cartoon rabbit hiding from an annoyed pig with a shotgun, she'd have been able to stand behind this guy happily.

"Well, you know what they say, the bigger they are, the harder they fall," Ramirez said loudly. "What the hell do they feed you anyway? The bones of your victims?"

The soldier cracked his knuckles and gave a smirk, though to Marcus, it didn't look entirely jovial.

"I mean, if that's what you look like, I wouldn't want to see your parents. I mean, one must have been a troll and the other a giant. Seriously, man, if you wore a black hood, you'd make the perfect executioner. Plus we wouldn't have to look at your ugly face either."

"Don't let her get to you," the opposing squad's Lance Corporal called out. "She's just trying to get you mad."

"Mad?" Ramirez said. "Hell, if he gets mad, I'm worried he might turn green!"

And then the soldier ran. More like he charged. Like a rhino. An angry rhino.

Ramirez, smiling all the way, pirouetted on the spot just as her opponent came into touching distance and happily sent him on his way out of the circle. She'd won the fight, but without throwing a single punch or even touching her opponent. And Marcus was seriously impressed.

"Watch yourself, he's coming back," McCulloch warned. The giant soldier was about to attack again when his own squad leader barked an order.

"Reed, STOP!"

The soldier halted and stood to attention like he had been electrocuted.

"Sorry about that," the Lance Corporal said. "Bit of a livewire that one. Hell of a fighter, though."

"Not as good as me though!" Ramirez cheered back as she sauntered out of the circle. "And just one more to go, so it'll either be a draw or you lose. Bet you regret picking on the weaklings now, huh?"

"We'll take a draw," the Lance Corporal said. "Saved the best for last of course."

"Oh, well so did we," Ramirez gestured with a thumb to King. "This one's uncle is Lennox Lewis."

The Lance Corporal peered at King with a fair amount of confusion, wondering how the very blonde and very pale, sleight woman could have been related to the boxing legend, but eventually he shrugged it off, catching on that Ramirez was joking.

King stepped into the ring, and the man who was to be her opponent, although not as troll-like as Ramirez', was still bigger than her and looked far more athletic than the last. Marcus could tell that King needed to fight well if she wanted to bring home the win for the Seventy-First.

King didn't try goading her opponent like Ramirez had done so effectively; rather she took a stance more likely to be seen in a judo match than in a boxing ring. Her hands were open, and she stood far more face-on than Marcus would've assumed for a fistfight.

King was the first to close the distance between the pair, and she immediately grabbed her opponent's collar and cuff. She clearly knew what she was doing, but Marcus worried that getting in so close and personal with a much stronger opponent was probably a bad idea.

There was a moment where it looked like the guy was just going to overpower King as they fought each other for positional superiority, but after a moment of what turned out to be a feigned difficulty, King spun her back into her opponent, lowered her posture and threw him over her shoulder and to the ground in front of her with a loud thud.

It all just looked so effortless, and Marcus couldn't help but let his jaw drop at the sight of the smaller woman felling such a large opponent.

The fight wasn't over, though. The man stood up again, brushed himself down and now looked determined not to fall for the same trick twice.

King stepped in and threw two quick jabs that connected with the man's face, though it proved a little too much as he managed to throw his own hands out, pushing King to the ground. She didn't have time to get up again.

Her opponent leapt on top of her, and King managed to wrap her legs around his waist just in time to lock the pair together. Again, it looked like her technique would control the narrative as she held the larger man in position, but he pushed her away, arching his back to break her hold on him.

Then he cocked his fist and threw a punch directly at King's face.

It would've been the end of the fight for sure, but at the last moment, King redirected the strike and pushed the arm away. Then she raised her leg over the man's shoulder and locked it into place with the back of her other knee, causing her opponent to turn instantly purple in her well-executed triangle choke.

But the man still wasn't done. He raised himself to his knees with the choke still applied and forced his legs beneath him to stand fully up with King still attached. He was going to slam her into the ground. Marcus held his breath.

King knew what was coming, so she did the only two things she could: She pulled the choke on tighter, and elbowed the man in the face with her free arm.

It proved effective.

King hit the ground hard as the man couldn't keep them both upright any longer, but it wasn't a slam; it was a passing out. She let her choke go and turned to help her now-defeated opponent come around. Clearly she'd done this before.

"I believe that's our win," McCulloch announced loudly.

"Yeah, better luck next time!" Ramirez called out. "But not really. I hope you're bottom of the board after that display!"

"Come now, Ramirez," McCulloch interrupted. "There's no need to be bad winners."

Ramirez smiled back at him. Not because they were bad winners, but because they were winners.

Nobody else dared challenge the Seventy-First that day. Not because they thought they would lose, but because they knew that Marcus was injured and there would be no honour in that victory. They also knew that if for any reason they lost, it would mean harsher penalties for their own squad because the Seventy-First were at the bottom of the table and therefore, had nothing to lose themselves.

But that wasn't strictly true. Because when the squad decided to take a break from teaching Marcus how to stand when he fought, and the others took part in light sparring matches, the Seventy-First visited the leaderboard. The Thirty-Eighth were now at the bottom of the table, with Marcus' squad just one single point above them.

Of course, it was a mystery how points were truly being allocated now because of how the opponents in the challenges were being scored based on their difficulty, but the lion's share of the squads' scores were still being dictated by the baseline test results, in which Marcus had performed abysmally, and was a clear hole in his squad's points bucket. If they really did want to start moving up the table, he was going to have to get better at everything, not just fighting. And fast.

Chapter 15 – Overnight & Planning

McCulloch, King and Foley spent the majority of the day trying to teach Marcus how to be a proper soldier, but also how specifically to score higher in each of the baseline tests. This was done by watching the techniques of the other soldiers as they competed against one another, with a background narration of what was happening under the hood.

For example on the firing range, as they watched the two squads taking aim, McCulloch pointed out how the shots were taken on a short pause in the breath after an exhale, and not with a held breath as the movies would have people believe. This apparently led to a steadier shot and would lead to more points.

The hand-to-hand combat section was something they were going to have to work on later, but King assured Marcus that he'd be able to fight anyone of any size soon enough, and mainly because he had no bad habits to hold him back. She seemed excited about it, but Marcus didn't care for it too much.

Pull-ups and running were two things that relied on strength and fitness for the most part, but breathing and pacing did also play a role in their execution. Marcus promised he'd do his best to practise, but he knew that he wouldn't have very long to do so, so he feared it might not have been within his reach.

Inevitably, the group decided that during the following day, they would try to focus their efforts on the firing range. They hadn't done too poorly to tell the truth, and if they could get Marcus up to a solid eight with each shot, they knew they'd probably rank within the top ten or fifteen squads overall. And they knew that points meant prizes.

"I really think it's a good idea to throw out the challenges ourselves," McCulloch said as the squad lay in each of their beds. "That way at least we get to choose the test and our opponent rather than the other way around. And if Cesari listens to what we have to say, he'll be up there with us in no time."

"I don't see why we can't just keep fighting hand to hand," King said. "If three of us win, then it doesn't matter if Cesari loses. Or even forfeits."

"Yeah," Foley agreed. "Make Cesari sit on the side and let the real men do the work."

Ramirez had to stretch, but she just about managed to hit Foley in the chest with her boot, which she picked up off the floor.

"And wouldn't you just say that the real men, I.e., King and me, did a great job today?"

Foley didn't answer, and a distinctive snicker came from King's bed.

"The range is our best shot," McCulloch said. "Plus, there's no real physical component, so we can train the rest independently and compete on the targets. I'm not saying Marcus will be able to keep up on a run any time soon, but we can start with him not chucking his guts up next time he tries."

"Chance'll be a fine thing," Foley said.

"Do I need to give you the boot again?" Ramirez asked.

"Anyway," McCulloch interrupted. "We should all get some sleep and tomorrow we'll have a good go at it. I don't think we'll be anywhere near the bottom once we really get going."

"Not a word, Foley," Ramirez warned. Foley kept his mouth shut.

Marcus hadn't realised how much his body needed rest. It was one of those times when he was so immeasurably hungry that all he wanted to do was find anything to eat. But at the same time, he was so tired, beyond exhausted even, that just the thought of getting up out of bed was a mammoth task not worth starting.

Besides, the mess halls were closed, and Marcus didn't even know if there was any food to be had out there. In the end, he chose sleep, and drifted off just a few moments later.

"Cesari," the soft, female voice said. "Cesari, you need to get up," she whispered again. This time, Marcus recognised it as belonging to Ramirez.

"Slap him in the face," Foley said. "If he can't get his lazy arse out of bed at a respectable hour, I'm not getting dragged down with him."

"Slap my face, and when we're on the range, I'm going to shoot you," Marcus groaned. He couldn't yet open his eyes properly, but he forced his words out well enough. "Too early," he moaned.

"You've had your eight hours," McCulloch announced. "So if you aren't dressed and ready to go in three minutes, we're leaving you here. And that means no breakfast. Are you OK with that? I heard it was pancakes."

The word pancakes made Marcus' mouth water. He was still ravenous from the night before, and perhaps if it was possible, even more so, He felt like he hadn't eaten in a week.

"Please let me slap him," Foley said when Marcus didn't move.

"You can slap him," Ramirez said. "But then I'm going to slap you."

"I'm up, I'm up," Marcus groaned, spinning his body around on the bed and forcing his eyes to part.

"Woah," Ramirez said, staring at Marcus. "Did you not go to sleep at all last night? Your eyes are redder than Foley's face the first time he saw King getting changed."

"Hey," Foley said.

"Don't make me slap you," King said.

"What?" Marcus asked. "My eyes?"

Marcus knew there wasn't a mirror in the room. In fact, he hadn't seen one since he'd arrived at the barracks, so he would have to take Ramirez' word for his bloodshot eyes. What he did notice as he appraised himself was the fact that he no longer felt any pain. And that really was something new.

He had no pain in his chest, ribs, arm, nose. No headache, no nausea, in fact, this was the best Marcus had felt in a long time. That was of course other than the tiredness and hunger – but those he felt were fleeting, and after a big breakfast, he felt that everything was going to be OK.

"Pancakes, you say?" he asked with a smile.

"No, not really," McCulloch said. "But by the sound of your stomach - all Goddamn night I might add - I guessed you'd be hungry. Come on, let's go see what they're making for us today. I heard it was Twenty-Four on breakfast duty."

The squad gave Marcus his three minutes and then made their way into the mess hall. The place was packed with the soldiers all sitting together in their groups, and the Seventy-First picked up their food trays before finding an appropriate place to sit and eat. Each of the soldiers got their food and then sat together at the end of one of the long tables.

"Toast," Ramirez announced, holding a half-toasted piece of bread in her hands. "I know it's something we all have to do… but cooking for everyone, knowing we all have to fight and train and stuff… and they make us toast."

"I bet they're eating like kings back there, laughing at us," Foley said.

"They might be," McCulloch agreed. "It would be a good way to get an advantage over us, wouldn't it? And damn, Cesari, did your parents never teach you any manners?"

"What? Marcus forced out past the three slices of toast that he had stacked up and forced into his mouth. He'd stopped counting how many he had eaten after the seventh, and he was still going.

"Seriously, it's like sitting next to a horse," Ramirez said. "Just try to keep some of the crumbs actually inside your mouth."

"Mmmhh… sorry," Marcus said, taking another huge bite. "I don't know… what it is… but I feel like… I haven't eaten… in a week…"

"Well, maybe you should go and ask Doctor Zorgon," Foley said. "I bet you're overdue a probing by now."

Marcus clicked his fingers. "That's it!" He swallowed everything he had in his mouth. "It must be the gene editing thing; it's making me hungry!"

"Not this again," Ramirez sighed. "Didn't we all decide that you were having some kind of trauma-induced hallucination?"

"No?" Marcus replied.

"Oh yeah," Ramirez replied. "We all decided that. You were too busy recovering from a broken arm and nose."

Marcus couldn't help but feel hurt by that. He had been spoken about behind his back, and apparently, he looked just as hurt as he felt.

"Oh, don't give us the hurt puppy look," Ramirez said. "What were we supposed to do, believe that you really did have some encounter with an extra-terrestrial doctor from Mars?"

"He never said he was from Mars," Marcus grumbled. "And anyway, if it wasn't some alien doctor and advanced gene editing program, then how do you explain my broken bones being fixed already? Do you know of any medicines that can sort those out?"

"Maybe," McCulloch said slowly. "What if it's another thing like the boots, or the overalls? What if there's a healing drug they wanted to test, and that's why we're all here? Explains the need to fight each other, doesn't it?"

"No!" Marcus protested through another absently bitten piece of toast. "It was an alien doctor. His name is Dr. Kono, he has yellow scaly skin, a long tail and he looks like a lizard. Oh, and he has a weirdly dry sense of humour. Even dryer than yours Ramirez."

"Well crap," Ramirez said. "I'm going to have to up my game. What's brown and sticky? No, wait, that won't do. Come back to me in a minute. I'll think of something."

"Whatever happened," King said. "We have a plan for today. Let's just chalk this up to something weird happening and figure it out later. I'm thinking we take today by the balls and start working our way up that leaderboard. You all in?"

"Hell yeah!" Foley replied overly loudly, and a small section of soldiers around the squad turned immediately silent. After a moment, the usual sounds of knives hitting plates, and low chatter resumed.

"I say we go for Twenty-Four first," Ramirez said. "Take them to the firing range and show them how real marksmen… uh people, work."

"Why? Did they get a low score?" McCulloch asked.

"I have no idea," Ramirez replied. "But it's their fault that I'm now covered in toast crumbs and I'm betting they wanted to fight today, not stare down the iron sights. I think a little payback's in order. And if we're quick with the challenge, they won't have time to ask anyone else."

"OK, sounds good to me," McCulloch replied, standing up. "I'll go make the challenge, you lot…" he looked back down at the soldiers who all stared back up at him. Everyone except Marcus, who was eyeing up his next piece of toast while still chewing. "Make sure he doesn't choke."

"You mean like he did last time on the range?" Foley said.

"No, he means like how you're going to choke on my boot when I ram it down your throat the next time you fall asleep," Ramirez said.

"Why do you always do that?" Foley asked as McCulloch walked away. "Do what?"

"Defend Cesari. You two aren't… you know… are you?"

For the first time, Marcus stopped chewing and looked firstly at Foley, and then at Ramirez. Foley seemed to be asking a genuine question for once, and Ramirez had turned bright red.

"He's like a baby deer," Ramirez said finally. "He was sent here, never even been through basic training, told to fight against trained soldiers, some of whom with decades of experience. Shouted at, beaten to a pulp, made to run until he was sick… and you don't think he deserves a little pity?"

Pity. Marcus knew what it was, of course he did. But to hear the word out loud. It made him feel so small.

"Let the boy become a man," Foley said. "It's not like I ever really mean anything I say, you know that, right, Cesari?"

Marcus swallowed his toast and looked at Foley. The soldier certainly didn't look like he intended Marcus any harm, physical or not. In fact, the way that he was looking back at Marcus and the sincerity in his words… Marcus felt a little gratitude to Foley.

"I know," Marcus said. "And Ramirez… I know it might sound strange or ungrateful… but I can fight my own battles. I know you're trying to help, but I do need to stand on my own two feet here. Otherwise, I'll never learn."

Ramirez looked shocked, and Foley gave a wide smile.

"I knew you were one of us!" Foley announced loudly and slapped Marcus on the shoulder. "Now let's get out onto that range, and you can see how a real soldier fires a gun!"

"I'm telling you," Ramirez said. "Watch his mouth when he shoots, it's like a cartoon."

Chapter 16 – A New Perspective

"How are you even walking?" Ramirez asked Marcus as the group made their way to the shooting range. McCulloch had arranged for the squad to face off against Twenty-Four, and they would meet them there shortly.

"I mean, I watched you eat at least twenty slices of toast one after the other. Are you not in pain? Bursting at the seams or something?"

Marcus shook his head and took a bite of another slice of toast he'd brought along with him. "Could do with some coffee… or tea… something sweet maybe…"

"You're insane," Ramirez said with wide eyes.

When the group made it to the firing range, they all huddled closely so that they could all give Marcus a little last-minute inspiration.

"There's no pressure Cesari," McCulloch said. "Do the best you can, keep calm and don't get frustrated. When that happens, people rush and their aim suffers. Just remember what we said about your breathing, and take your time."

"And try to hit the target," Foley added. "Really helps the points if you hit the target. You know, that piece of paper down there with the numbered rings on it?"

"Oh…" Marcus replied. "I was supposed to hit that?"

"What?" Foley almost shouted. "Of course you're…"

"As you can see, sarcasm is lost on this one," Ramirez said. "Sometimes it's funny, but most of the time it's just annoying. He's joking, big mouth," Ramirez explained. Then she turned back to Marcus. "But it is true, you're supposed to hit the target with all your shots."

Marcus smirked. "I'll do my best."

"Going to have to do better than that," King said. "Because if you don't up your game then I'm going to disown you."

"Noted," Marcus said.

"Right, are you lot ready?" McCulloch asked.

The group gave their readiness and turned to the range, where their opponents had turned up and were preparing for the first round.

"Let's get this over with," the opposing squad leader announced with an exhale.

"Don't worry, this won't take long," Ramirez called. "You can get back to your master plan of malnourishing all your opponents so you can take them on in hand to hand soon enough!"

The man went bright red, and turned away from Marcus' squad. Clearly, he hadn't expected to have had his plan seen through so quickly.

"You get up there first, Foley," McCulloch ordered. Then King, Ramirez, me and then Cesari. Try to learn something from us Cesari, we're going to need whatever points you can bring to the table."

Marcus felt a little pressure at those words, but that all quickly dissipated as he watched Foley take his shots. The task was a little different to the baseline testing, with Foley and a single opponent facing off head-to-head, so that did make things a little quieter, but the overall points score was still going to be the main factor in determining the winning team.

He couldn't help but laugh as he watched Foley as he shot though. He did indeed open his mouth rather comically before every shot he took, but the results were undeniable. A nine and two tens in three shots, it was kind of amazing, particularly because Foley's opponent only managed three straight eights.

King's performance was a little less amazing, racking up a total of twenty-five points versus her opponent's twenty-eight, and Ramirez pushed herself to a respectable twenty-seven, though her own opponent hit an almost perfect twenty-nine.

McCulloch produced three nines with three holes in the paper that actually overlapped each other – something that Foley commended him for by way of announcing that McColloch had 'excellent grouping' – but the feat was matched by his own opponent who also fired in three nines.

Marcus had been keeping a count of how the teams were doing and regardless of the individual battles so far, both squads were on level pegging with an overall score of one hundred and eight each. That meant that Marcus had to do better than his own counterpart if they wanted to win this thing.

Stepping up to the small wall that served as the firing position, Marcus picked up his rifle. It was warm in his hands, given that it had been picked up and held a number of times already, and McCulloch had been sure to check that there were enough bullets in the magazine for Marcus to take his turn.

He had barely lifted the rifle to his eyeline when he heard the telltale pop of his opponent taking his first shot. Glancing over at his opponent's paper, Marcus could see that he'd hit the eight. It was a good shot, and Marcus knew he had a difficult hill to climb.

Marcus brought the weapon up to his eyeline and centred the iron sights on the target. He remembered how it had felt the first time he'd taken a shot and missed.

But this time, something was different.

The small rectangle of paper that seemed so far away was now somehow different. Where once he had the feeling that lining up a shot was less about hitting the bullseye and more about hitting the paper altogether, he felt something.

As Marcus peered down the sights, he ignored the second shot that rang out from his opponent's rifle and concentrated on his own target. Because now, somehow, the paper seemed to be growing.

Well, that wasn't entirely true. It was more like the paper was becoming the focus of Marcus' attention and as he watched and squinted, trying to figure out what was happening, he realised that the target was so in focus, that he could now see the tiny little numbers printed within the circles as clear as day. It was like he was looking at the target through a telescope.

Steadying his aim on this new, clear and focused target, Marcus exhaled, held his breath out, and squeezed the trigger. The target popped, and Marcus peered through the sights to see that he, too, had hit the eight ring.

"Great work Cesari!" Ramirez practically squealed.

Another shot popped from Marcus' opponent, but he ignored whatever the score had been; he didn't need that kind of pressure.

"Take your time, there's no rush," McCulloch ordered and Marcus brought his rifle back up to his eyeline.

Again, as he focussed, Marcus watched as his target became the centre of his world. It was again like he was looking through a telescope, and there was nothing else in the world that mattered. This time he adjusted his aim based on where his last shot had landed, and fired again.

Pop.

The target was torn dead centre, right through the bullseye in a shot that couldn't have been any more perfect. Marcus heard the cheers from his squad, but kept his firing line and quickly fired again.

This time, the paper did not tear, and Marcus peered at it, somewhat confused.

He turned to look back at his squad, who looked like they were all in shock.

"What happened?" Marcus asked. "I shot in the same place, but I didn't hit the target?"

"Oh, you hit the target alright," Foley was the first to reply, and he had a huge grin on his face. "You hit the target in exactly the same place as your second shot. You went through the perfect ten, twice!"

Marcus looked back at the target, though he couldn't see any evidence of the perfect shot. Though perhaps that was exactly the point.

"You did it, Marcus!" Ramirez shouted. "Beat him by one and with three great shots! What happened, you suddenly figured out which way round to hold a rifle?"

"Must just be your teaching…" Marcus said, deciding not to share what he had truly experienced just yet. Placing the rifle down on the firing position and stepped away from it.

The opposing squad quickly made their exit, presumably to go and enact their master plan.

"I'm going to have to eat more toast," Foley said as the squad all moved away and back towards the main part of the barracks. "There's just no other explanation for it: eat twenty pieces of toast and become the perfect marksman… not that I'm not pretty perfect as it is."

"Well, you did hit a nine," King said. "Doesn't sound too perfect to me.

"Hey I hit twenty-nine out of thirty. Remind me what you got again?"

"I got twenty-five, but I kept my mouth shut the whole time. And I reckon if we sent you and Cesari up there together, there wouldn't be much between you."

"I'll take that bet," Foley said.

"No, that's not what we're doing here," McCulloch interrupted. "We work as a team and if we're good at something, then we should just be happy about it. We don't need to compete with each other."

"Right," Ramirez said. "Let's just all agree that Cesari's better and be done with it."

Foley turned red with anger.

"Only kidding," Ramirez finished.

"But seriously guys..." Marcus said once he was sure that no other squads were nearby and could overhear him. "I think… I think it's the gene editing thing… you know, with the… doctor?"

"Ohh, you mean the ALIEN?" Ramirez practically shouted. "Seriously, we aren't still talking about that are we? You were tired, exhausted even, broken. You saw things in a state of semi-consciousness, and it's just your mind trying to explain it all."

"No, it's not that," Marcus said. "I feel different. I couldn't even hit the target properly last time and now, now it's easy. I could see the target so clearly. And it's not just that. I feel good. Much better than I should. And stronger, faster. Somehow more perceptive. It's hard to explain, but this isn't normal, you have to believe me."

"Faster and stronger huh?" Foley said and immediately whipped an arm up to slap Marcus in the face.

Marcus caught Foley's wrist and held it tightly before letting him go after a momentary struggle.

"You… what?" Foley said, not entirely sure what just happened. "You know, maybe we should all go to that medical bay and talk to this doctor?"

His face was filled with concern. He'd happily been about to smack Marcus around the head, but Marcus had just caught the slap like it was nothing. The rest had seen it, too, and they all turned pale and quiet.

Ramirez was the first to try to lift the mood.

"At least your eyes aren't bloodshot any more," she said. "And your arm seems a lot better too."

"I'm telling you, it's all related," Marcus urged. "Seriously, this isn't something I've made up for some sick joke. I think it's a good idea for us all to go and see, well… you know."

"Fine," Ramirez said, though her heart wasn't in it. "We'll go see the doctor and if he doesn't have a tail, then you're up first in every round of hand-to-hand from now on, you got that?"

Marcus nodded, though didn't reply.

The squad then worked their way across the fields and to the medical bays, where Marcus led them all into the room where he'd met Dr. Kono. In truth, he was tired of just telling his story only to be told that he was at best crazy, and at worst straight up lying.

There was a man in the room dressed like a doctor, white coat, stethoscope and all, but he was definitely human and perhaps a little younger than most of the soldiers in the barracks.

"Show us your tail!" Ramirez said loudly to the doctor as soon as the squad entered the room.

"What?" The doctor said.

"Never mind that," Marcus said. "I want to see Dr. Kono. Can you get him in here so I can prove to these guys I'm not insane?"

"Doctor… Kono?" The doctor replied. "I don't recall there being a…"

"Cut the crap," Marcus interrupted. "I've met him, spoken to him, had him fix my broken bones and inject me with some alien concoction. So go out there, tell Kono that Cesari is here to see him and we can all get on with our day.

"Listen," the doctor replied. "I don't know what you think…"

Marcus tuned out the doctor and looked around the room for any signs that Kono had been around. Not that he knew what he was looking for, of course, a photo, an alien gun or something, but then he remembered the speaker set in the corner of the room.

Focussing on the object, Marcus could definitely hear a very slight crackle coming from the speaker, like it was a two-way radio that someone had left on.

"I know you can hear me, Kono," Marcus announced, startling everyone. The room turned silent.

After a short pause, McCulloch spoke.

"Listen Cesari… I don't think that this is all going the way you thought it was going to go, so why don't we all just take a breath…"

"I swear, Kono, if you don't get your tail out here in ten seconds, I'm going to start spreading rumours that all lizard-like aliens are partial to a probing, and if anyone ever encounters one, they should scream and run."

This time, Marcus' announcement got a reaction, and the entire squad turned to look at the speaker in the corner of the room when it crackled and broke into speech.

"Alright, Marcus, you don't have to go there," Kono's voice came from the speaker. "Just tell your friends to move back, I wouldn't want the little mouth inside my head to get excited, pop out and eat their faces."

Foley visibly paled. "T… that's a thing?"

"No," Marcus said. "Kono likes making sarcastic jokes – usually about what humans think about aliens. I think he's watched too many movies."

"Or have I?" Kono replied, then let out a stereotypical evil laugh. The speaker then clicked off, and no more than ten seconds later, the door opened, and in walked Dr Kono in all his lizard's glory.

"Told you," Marcus said,

Nobody said a word.

"Boo!" Kono announced, holding his hands up in a mocking gesture.

"What in the actual…" Ramirez mumbled.

"So should I eat their brains now or later?" Kono asked Marcus. "And how's our plan going to take over the world? Is your mind fully controllable yet? I'll accept 'yes, master' as an appropriate answer, but if you don't want the others to know, just give me a wink; we can talk later."

"Will you just be serious for one second?" Marcus asked through gritted teeth.

"Oh, fine. But you're no fun," Kono replied and turned his attention to the Seventy-First squad as a whole. "Yes, I am an alien – a Kanaan, if you must know. "Yes, I look like a lizard. Yes I'm a real doctor, no I'm not here to hurt you, neither will I eat nor probe you," he looked pointedly at Marcus. "I'm sure Mr. Cesari here has told you what the deal is and well, it's true. Unless he told you I'm here for some secret nefarious means, in which case it isn't true… but I think Marcus and I are good enough friends to know what the other is thinking by now."

"Friends?" King asked Marcus.

"Don't listen to everything he says," Marcus said. "Like I said, he's got a bit of a weird sense of humour."

"Probably all the human brains I keep eating."

"See."

"Anyway," McCulloch said slowly to bring the attention back to what they were there for. "You're an alien, right?"

"Well, technically, to me, you're the aliens, but I guess, seeing as I'm here on your planet, I'll take it your way."

"And you're really here to give us some gene editing thing?"

"That's exactly right," Kono replied. "A gene editing thing. I couldn't have said it better myself."

There was a silence in the room again while everyone internalised how ridiculous the whole situation was.

"Are you going to give us all the treatment?" Foley asked shakily, still not having regained his colour.

"I would," Kono replied. "But I fear we wouldn't have enough food here in the barracks if Marcus is anything to go by."

"You've been watching me?" Marcus asked.

"What, you think I'm the kind of alien doctor-cum-scientist that starts an experiment and doesn't keep his beady lizard eye on it? I thought we knew each other better than that buddy."

It made Marcus feel a little violated, but also a little angry. He hadn't even stopped to think that he might have been under surveillance, but after he thought it through for a moment, it made a lot of sense.

"But yes, the experiment is to enter its second phase over the next couple of days, so while you're all here, I suppose I can induce the gene therapy drug into your systems. If you are all OK with that, of course. But even if you're not, because you all signed the waivers I can do anything I want to you all anyway. Even probing, which is still on the table. But not really, because that's just gross."

"Now?" Ramirez asked. "And what exactly does that entail?"

"Well it's just a simple injection into the neck," Kono said, producing a long needle from his pocket attached to a vial of luminous pink fluid. "But I can't say exactly what will happen as each human will adapt to the serum in different ways depending on your physiology, current state, positioning along your genetic path, proximity to your genetic ceiling and so many more factors that it's just mind-boggling. Suffice to say, you get injected and just wait and see."

"So you want us to let you stick a needle in our necks and hope it makes us into super soldiers? Forgive me if we have some reservations," Ramirez said.

"Well, the proof is in the pudding, isn't it?" Kono said. "Look at Mr. Cesari here. Stronger, faster, a better shot on the range, eats like a horse. If you think he's not already a better soldier because of the therapy, then you're free to walk away right now. But you'll be back tomorrow with the rest of them, and it won't be a choice then… so this is kind of your one chance to get a leg up on the competition. So tell me, do you feel lucky? ...Well, do ya, punks?"

"So let us get this straight," McCulloch said. "You want to give us an injection – just one – and afterwards, we'll be better soldiers? What's the catch?"

"No catch," Kono replied. "Well, there is the slight chance that the therapy will have no effect on you, especially if you're already touching that genetic ceiling – hypothetically, of course. And as always with experimental treatments, there's always the chance of sudden and horrific death. But I'm like a good ninety per cent sure that's not going to happen. Weeell eighty-five."

McCulloch peered at Kono again, trying to divine what was a true statement and what was his own unique style of humour.

"But again I say look at Mr. Cesari here. Body and bones broken, unable to hold a rifle straight and now look at him. He's a sharpshooter with all his bones in the right place, and I would say they're a little stronger than they were before. If you need a shining beacon of hope, then look no further because I present to you, my star pupil."

"I'm in," King said quickly, and the squad turned to look at her as one.

"If this gives me the advantage that I've been searching for all these years, then I'm going to take it. Plus, you know what those other countries are doing, if someone like Russia, who's been experimenting with steroids for God only knows how long, comes up with something close to this…"

"Well, yes, we've all seen Rocky Four," Kono said. "But thinking on an 'Earth scale' is a little short-sighted. Think of all those alien races out there that have the ability to crush your fragile little skulls in one claw like it was a grape." He held out his lizardy hand and mimicked the crushing motion in front of King's face, which only served to bolster her reserve.

"Are you alright Foley?" Marcus asked, having watched his squad and the doctor as they'd spoken.

"Y… yes, why?"

"Only you haven't taken your eyes off that needle since the doctor brought it out. And you look a little pale."

"I… I don't like needles," the big soldier said. "Never have."

"Oh, we've found something that gets the big boy's skin crawling!" Kono announced loudly. "You'll just have to go first." And with those words, Kono pulled the needle to neck height and took a step towards Foley, who started backing away.

"I'll go first," McCulloch said quickly, stepping forward. "I'm the highest rank here and the squad leader. I mean first after Cesari, of course, but that is what it is. Plus, from what we can see, you're right; Cesari has benefitted from the treatment, so if we all do so in a similar way, then I think we'll all be happy with the results."

"I like this one," Kono announced with a wide lizard grin. "Always so keen to play the role of the perfect soldier. I think that with a little leg up, he could go all the way. And if not, at least all the way into a hole in the ground."

"Could you just be serious for one second," Marcus said to the doctor. "I know it might not be such a big deal for you, but this is our lives, and we're not exactly used to dealing with alien doctors and weird injectables."

"Well, I do recognise that sometimes I do try to diffuse tense situations with humour. But saying you aren't used to putting weird injectables into your bodies is just plain untrue. You listen to your doctors and health services with an almost blind eye. They tell you to put leeches onto your throat when you're nauseous and away you go, happy to oblige. They tell you this one serum prevents mumps, measles, and rubella and there you go, presenting your arm like you've been ordered to do so by Jesus. Just… seems a bit unfair to me that if I was a regular human doctor telling you the exact same information, that you'd be lining up with smiles on your faces."

Truthfully, Marcus couldn't argue with that. But this was different, wasn't it? This was almost a cosmetic or elective procedure, not something that would prevent infectious diseases or work towards wiping them out altogether.

"And I know what you're thinking," Kono continued. "But you'd be dead wrong. The human race is going to have to come a very long way in a short space of time if they want to hold themselves well out there in the greater universe because, let me tell you, right now, you're nothing but ants inhabiting a rich and fertile land of opportunity. And one of these days, a big kid with a magnifying glass is going to show up and take what they want from you. There's nothing you'll be able to do to stop them, so you better step up to the mark and get started right now."

"Christ just inject us already!" Ramirez said, annoyed. "We're on board, just do what you've got to do and let us get on with our day."

"Well I'm not one to stand in the way of an individual bettering him or herself," Kono said, took a quick, large step forward and plunged the syringe into McCulloch's neck. The squad leader winced and let out a slight yelp, though otherwise kept his cool. A moment later, the vial was empty and McCulloch stumbled away from the doctor.

"Alright, who's next for a stabbing?" he asked. "Or if you'd prefer, there is the option of a suppository".

Official Records – Thoughts from Marcus Cesari during initial testing.

None of us thought things were going to happen the way they did. It was like we were in some kind of sci-fi movie where they wouldn't really tell us what was happening, but we were just told to get on with it. And in this case, the carrot was just too much for most of us to turn down. We'd go on this special operation and after a few months passed by we'd have enough money in our pensions to retire and never have to think about being a soldier, or taking orders ever again.

Of course, my situation was a little different. There would be money there for me in the aftermath, but nothing compared to the pension pots of some of the guys and girls that had spent decades fighting for queen and country. My only hope was that my dad would get the help he needed, and perhaps that one day I wouldn't end up in a wheelchair like him.

It's probably common knowledge, if this account is ever to be read by anyone, well at all really, but it seems that I inherited a genetic condition from my father that causes tumours to grow and sometimes press on nerves or something. I'm not really sure about the specifics, but if it continues then it's likely I'll eventually lose the ability to walk too.

But there's a doctor here, and he has a plan. Well that's what he said anyway. I don't know how much I can actually say here, but screw it, if I say something wrong they can redact it later.

The doctor is an alien. I didn't believe it either and if I hadn't seen it for myself then I wouldn't be saying it here. But that's just how it is. He promised to turn us all into super soldiers and the Seventy-First, although sceptical, were on board. I think it was because they'd seen what the therapy has already done for me.

I was constantly hungry. And I don't mean just for food. The therapy made me *want* to do better. To be better. So that's what I did. I threw away all ideas of life on the outside and I did everything I could to become the best human being I could be. If the doctor was telling the truth about the universe and the alien beings that inhabit it, then this whole thing was bigger than me. Bigger than I could even comprehend and I was going to do whatever I could to help turn our fighting men and women into a force that the universe was afraid of.

I never did like bullies.

As for the rest of the squad, they took their medicine after a little coaxing. It didn't bother me either way, I had my job to do and they were either going to help me or not. But they did it.

Sometimes when I look back, I wonder if they made the right choice.

Chapter 17 – Consumer Rights

The squad all received their injections and were sent along on their way. None of them had been punched like Marcus had been, something that Marcus felt a little hard done by if he was honest about the situation, but at least they were all in it together, as a team.

They were told not to partake in any exercise until the following day, something that King alone took issue with. Where most were content to rest, she wanted to test out her new genetic ceiling.

"I just don't get why we have to wait," King said. "It's not like we're going to get hurt, and we already saw that Cesari healed really, really quickly."

"Just relax and do what you're told," McCulloch said. "Besides, once whatever happens happens, I doubt that we'll be getting much time to sit and take the weight off. Best to make the most of it while we can."

"Don't worry," Marcus said. "Once it sets in, you'll know. Apart from an appetite that you can't seem to satisfy, you'll be feeling a bit lighter on your feet."

"I don't need to feel lighter on my feet," King said. "What I need is to see if I can run faster, hit harder or shoot straighter. I want to see the look on Foley's face when I beat him on the range, now that's going to be something."

"Just wait," McCulloch said again. "In the morning we'll all get out there and make our way to the top of the leaderboards, I can feel it. Right Cesari?"

Marcus hadn't been listening to the conversation around him; something else had caught his attention. Foley hadn't responded about King beating him on the range and in fact ever since he'd been injected, he hadn't said a single word.

"You OK Foley?" Marcus asked. "Pretty sure you should have something to say about King beating you on the range."

Foley's gaze had been fixed on the floor, but he brought his head up with a fair amount of effort and looked at Marcus. His eyes were bloodshot, and his skin was still pale.

"I really don't like injections," Foley managed to wheeze out. Then he abruptly stood up and ran out of the room, holding his stomach.

"What a big baby," King said. "The size of him and he gets all gooey over a needle in the neck. Remind me to bring this up next time he needs putting in his place."

"Come on, let the man be sick in peace," McCulloch said.

"I think we should all get some rest," Ramirez said. "If we really want to kick some ass tomorrow, better to get in a good night's sleep, right? Especially if we're to carry Foley if he's still being sick."

"Hey Cesari?" McCulloch asked. "You know how you said you feel lighter…"

Marcus nodded.

"Well, do you think that's real or more like a conceptual thing?"

"I think it's real, why?"

McCulloch looked up at the ceiling where a wide metal pipe spanned from one side of the room to the other, hanging about a foot down.

"How do you feel about pull-ups now?"

"What do… Oh!" Marcus caught on. "Hang on."

Marcus then stood up from his bed and jumped to hang from the pipe.

"It does seem easier even just hanging here."

"Pull yourself up," McCulloch ordered.

Marcus followed the order and pulled himself up until his head nearly hit the ceiling.

"Again," McCulloch ordered.

Again, Marcus complied.

"And keep going. I want to see what this stuff can do."

Marcus kept pulling himself up and dropping down to his full arm's length. He closed his eyes and eventually lost count before he felt like if he carried on, he was going to pass out.

When he opened his eyes, he saw Foley in the doorway, staring at him and the rest of the squad with their eyes wide and mouths open.

"Sixty-four," Ramirez said. "You go from basically nothing to sixty-four pull-ups in a day? I feel like I've wasted my entire life."

Marcus allowed himself a sheepish grin. "I didn't count, but if you say so."

"Seriously, let me get out there!" King shouted. "This is such a waste on Cesari, let me see what I can do!"

"No King," McCulloch said. "You have your orders and they're to rest. So rest, and I don't want to hear any more on the subject."

King didn't reply, but lay back on her bed and exhaled loudly.

"Just remember what Kono said," Marcus said. "He doesn't know what's going to happen to each of us, how long it'll last or anything. So maybe we'll all wake up tomorrow, and I'll be just as weak as you are now."

King sat up with a look of absolute disgust on her face. Marcus couldn't help but laugh, and she let herself flop back down onto the bed.

"Feel better Foley?" Ramirez asked as Foley sat back down on his own bed.

"A bit. But I didn't even eat carrots. Why's there always carrots in it?"

"One of the mysteries of the universe," Ramirez said. "Hey, maybe that's something we can ask Kono the next time we see him."

The squad then descended into conversations about the lizard doctor, what he was doing on Earth, what the rest of his race was like, and indeed what other races of beings the universe had to offer.

Eventually, sleep took the entire squad, and the following day, they all awoke with a new desire to deprive the barracks of its entire food supply.

Breakfast was a far more mixed offering than the toast had proven. The squad who'd been placed on kitchen duty had thankfully not followed in the footsteps of the previous day's team, and where they'd provided nothing more than toast, this squad chose to cook a buffet of everything one might find in a traditional English breakfast.

In reality, for the Seventy-First, it was a Godsend.

Even Foley, who still looked rather pale and by all accounts had experienced quite the night of sweating and the occasional vomiting, couldn't help but fill and empty his plate no less than four times. It was clear to the entire squad that whatever this gene therapy program was doing, it required calories to do so.

"You know what we should do first?" King announced with her mouth full of bacon and sausage. "Go for a run. I feel like I've got so much energy to burn off and you're right Cesari, I do feel lighter on my feet."

"I'm game," Ramirez agreed. "Then we hit the pull-up bars afterwards. I want to wipe the smirk off some faces around here, and the best way to do that is to make Marcus here wipe the floor with them."

"Well, we don't want to let everyone know all our secrets right away, do we?" McCulloch said. "I'm thinking Cesari just takes his time and beats his opponent by a few, rather than go all out. That way at least we might get some repeat business, rather than everyone avoiding the ringer."

"What, so we're like, sharks now or something?" Ramirez asked. "Got to maintain the illusion that we can be beaten, while all the time narrowly taking the wins?"

McCulloch nodded. "That's exactly it. If we have an advantage for a day or two, we'll use it to get to the top of the board. By then, everyone else will know what's happened and will probably start catching up again. Just, if we don't have a limit any more, they'll never be able to catch us up, will they?"

"So you're saying," Marcus said through his own mouthful of breakfast, "That none of you will be able to catch me up either then?"

"You were so far behind that all it's done is bridge the gap a little, "King said. "You'll never be as fast, nor as athletic as me, no matter what you get injected into your neck."

"Oh yeah? You want to put that to the test?" Marcus asked.

"As a matter of fact, I wouldn't mind it," King replied.

The pair then both stood up, apparently oblivious to the world around them and darted towards the door. McCulloch and Ramirez quickly followed soon after, and Foley looked down at his plate longingly before standing up and following the rest of the squad out the door.

"Come on, Cesari, pick up the pace!" King shouted behind her as the squad filtered through the main gates out of the barracks. She didn't have to tell Marcus twice, though, who raced past her at a speed that made her raise an eyebrow.

"No way you'll be keeping that pace up the whole time Cesari!" She called out. "You got another four miles to go and if I know you, you'll be chucking your guts up before you even make it to two!"

Marcus didn't look back. Nor did he respond to King; he was too amazed by the feel of his own body as he ran. His legs pumped hard into the ground but gave no signs of fatigue. The wind rushed by his face as he ran, keeping his skin cool, and his breathing was both calm and natural. This was nothing like he had been expecting, and something with running that he'd never experienced. Enjoyment.

When he hit the Zetland, he turned back and oriented himself on the path once more. A minute or two later, he passed King, followed by the rest of the Seventy-First as they tried to catch him up. He could already tell, though, that he was way too far ahead of them for any of that. Overnight, he'd become the fastest member of the squad. Possibly even the entire barracks.

"How… quick was that?" King asked when she passed back through the gates to find Marcus standing there waiting for her. "Got to be around twenty minutes, right? That's… insane." It took her a moment to catch her breath, but she managed it a moment later.

"You were twenty minutes. I was seventeen minutes and three seconds," Marcus said. "Want to try again?"

"Seventeen minutes… for just over four miles…" King replied slowly. "But that's…"

"It's like a world record or something, isn't it?" Marcus said, beaming. "Some might say I'm like a super soldier."

A moment later, the rest of the squad entered through the gates and joined Marcus and King. Although they hadn't managed to catch up to Marcus or even keep up with King, they had all shaved a significant amount of time off their initial run times.

"Are you two happy now?" Ramirez asked. "No, we know who's got the bigger tackle, so can we just get on with the day?"

"We'll put a pin in the rematch," King said, nodding once. "Well done, Cesari. I didn't expect that." She held a hand out for Marcus to shake, which he did with a smile.

"Always ready when you are," he said. "And weren't we supposed to be doing pull-ups or something today?"

"Yes we were," McCulloch replied. "So let's get over there and see who we can get to face off against us. Cesari, try to look like you're still a little bit in pain – like Foley there. He looks terrible."

Foley did indeed look terrible, but the group just ignored it. He'd get over it eventually.

"Now that is what we call an improvement, guys and girls," Callahan's unmistakable voice met the squad as they regrouped. "Good job."

Marcus thought he'd misheard the base commander at first, given that this was the first time that he'd heard any praise coming from the man, but there he was, and as it turned out, he'd timed Marcus and the squad as they'd ran.

"Now the thing that you are all now a part of, and the things that I know you know, those are things that are best kept to yourselves for the time being, you got that?"

Marcus was the first to nod, though the others replied with a quietened 'Yes, Sir!'

"Now because of your improvements, I expect to see you at the top of the leaderboards and no less within a day or two, you got that?"

This time, Marcus remembered that he was supposed to give his answer verbally, and the base commander seemed satisfied, turning and walking away a moment later.

"You think he's on the juice?" Ramirez asked when the commander was out of earshot.

"What a guy like that?" Marcus said. "I don't think so. They'd have to remove the stick from his ass first, wouldn't they?"

It was like Marcus had just insulted Jesus or something as the whole squad turned to face him in stunned silence.

"What?" he asked. "Don't you think the guy's a bit much? I mean, what's he even doing here anyway? An American commanding a British army base? Seems a bit suspect to me. And you haven't tried to hit the guy; it's like punching a brick wall that hits back."

"I think we can let that one slide," McCulloch said slowly, not taking his eyes off Marcus. "The commander did break his arm and nose after all."

"And he hurt my feelings," Marcus said.

"Seriously?" Ramirez asked.

"Nope."

"Anyway," King said, clearly changing the subject. "You think we can go rack up some points on the pull-up bar now because if I don't either do something active or eat my weight in red meat, I think I'm going to scream."

"You know what?" Ramirez said, "that sounds like a great idea.

The plan went without a hitch, with the Seventy-First narrowly beating no less than five other squads on the bars. For the first few goes, they didn't even have to issue any challenges; they just had to hang around in the general area until another squad tried their luck with the runt of the litter. But eventually, the word started to spread that they weren't such easy pickings, and they had to not only issue challenges of their own, but to higher and higher ranked opponents.

Not that it made much of a difference, of course. Marcus was pretty sure he could pass seventy if he really wanted to, and the others could hit forty quite comfortably. That meant that there wasn't a squad in the base that could match their total, and by the time they found other squads giving them a wide birth on the apparatus, they decided to move along to the next task.

The firing range didn't provide as many challenges as the pull-up bars had. Mostly because all of the soldiers had been pretty close to each other in terms of scoring to begin with anyway, but also partly because in the two rounds that the Seventy-First squad had been a part of, they had all scored perfect thirties. It was clear that they weren't going to be beaten, and so they weren't even given the challenges.

The Gauntlet at least provided something different. The Colonels who had been manning the guns along with Callahan were nowhere to be seen, so the object of the course was for one squad to fire upon their opponents whilst they completed The Gauntlet, and once they were done, they'd swap places. This time before they started, McCulloch reminded the entire squad not to pick up the backfiring paintball gun near the end, and just to make their way through as best they could. Marcus found that with his enhanced perception, speed and strength, the course was easier than it had ever been, and within just a few minutes, the Seventy-First had all made it through to the end without so much as a drop of paint on them.

Something they hadn't been expecting, though, was the fact that when they manned the paintball turrets to take aim at their opponents, their new enhanced perception really made a difference. It was like they could anticipate the movements of the opposing squad, even before they knew which way they were going to turn. After a few paintballs had flown, they could also accurately predict the flight of the ammunition, as well as the speed and the parabolas of the shots. In short, they could take out their opponents before they even got to the final showdown with the rigged gun.

What none of the group had been expecting was the fact that by the end of the day and countless victories, the amount of opponents that were available for them to face off against, had reached zero. And that could only mean one thing: that they had all been taken away by Dr. Kono or any of the other doctors, to receive their gene therapy treatment.

And that meant that the advantage that the Seventy-First had was about to be severely diminished.

"I think that's the day," McCulloch announced with a grin.

"And if we aren't top now, I'm going to have a few words with Callahan," Ramirez said. "We beat everyone at everything, and even Marcus has changed from useless to, well, a little more use, I guess."

"Shut up Ramirez, I'll take you on in anything," Marcus said, looking comically outraged.

"Just don't drop the soap in the showers," Ramirez replied. "Else, I might have to show you what a real man's like."

Marcus didn't laugh at that one; it seemed a little crass for his liking. Instead, he thought about all the challenges his squad had won in the day, and wondered if tomorrow they would have the same results. In reality, he didn't know how much better things could get.

"You know, I don't think I've heard you say much today Foley," Ramirez said as the group all stood in the chest-height shower cubicles washing themselves. "I mean, usually you have something to say when you're beaten by us girls, but today, you didn't really seem to take the bait. I don't want to say I'm proud of you for it, but, well... WHAT THE HELL IS THAT?"

The squad turned as one to look at whatever had caught Ramirez' attention, and when they followed her gaze onto Foley's naked body, it was clear that this was indeed cause for concern.

From the injection site on Foley's neck spanned purple-black tendrils that weaved their way like a spider web across the large man's shoulder and down onto his back. Whatever this was, it was clear that it wasn't anything good.

"I don't feel too good," Foley said, his head now starting to turn purple as though he was having trouble breathing. Then, he bent over and vomited right there on the floor of the shower.

"Get him to the doctor, NOW!" McCulloch announced, already pulling his underwear on. Marcus was hot on his heels, and the pair rushed over to Foley, taking hold of him and directing him out the door. A moment later, they'd made it to the room where they'd all met Dr. Kono.

"Kono, this soldier needs you," Marcus announced as he entered the room, and a few moments later, the alien doctor appeared in the doorway.

"What the hell is going on Kono?" Marcus asked, still holding up Foley with McCulloch, the larger soldier now hanging his head down like he had finally passed out. "Because this doesn't look good. It doesn't look good at all!"

"Is that your official medical opinion?" Kono asked. "That when someone turns purple, vomits and gets an ominous spidery rash on their body, that it isn't good? What do you know anyway, perhaps this is what's supposed to happen?"

"What? Is it?" McCulloch asked

"No," Kono said. "This… is bad."

"Then do something you psycho!" Marcus spat.

"Alright, alright, hold your horses," Kono said. "Lay him down here on the bed and step back."

The pair obliged, and Kono moved in, placing his stethoscope on various places on Foley's body.

"Well?" Marcus asked.

"It's definitely human," Kono said. "But quite sick."

"Are you freaking kidding me!?" Marcus asked. "I'm going to kill you!"

"Now, now, don't make me activate the self-destruct button in your coding. Let's all calm down here."

"The… what!?" Marcus almost shouted.

"Just kidding… or am I?" Kono asked. "But seriously, just give me some space and some time. It looks like the therapy is having a hard time with this one. I just need to make a few adjustments to the program, and he'll be as good as new… well, actually better, in no time."

"Are you sure?" McCulloch asked quietly.

"Well it's hard to say," Dr. Kono replied. "On the one hand, I would hypothesise that our friend Mr. Foley here was too far along his genetic path, so the therapy is pushing up against a metaphorical brick wall, and hard. But on the other, this kind of thing hasn't really been tested like this before, so it could just be the natural reaction of, oh, let's say one in five of you meatbags."

"So what you're saying is that you don't know," Marcus summarised. "Seriously, is this how things are done out there in the big bad universe? You just try things out and see what happens. These are people's lives we're dealing with here, not just numbers."

"Well, mainly yes," Kono said.

"Yes, what?" Marcus asked.

"Yes, we kind of just try things out and see what happens. The method is as old as time itself, and it's exactly how nearly every race of beings has reached the point at which they are now. It's called survival of the fittest. Or the luckiest, I suppose. Either way, advancement is not without its risks, and this is one of those situations. Now if you could excuse me for just a moment, I'm going to have to do some important work and tap on my terminal rather animatedly for a few minutes."

With that, the doctor produced some kind of glass device, and started prodding it rhythmically with his long lizardy fingers.

"And what's that going to do exactly?" Marcus asked.

"Please, can't you see I'm tapping on my terminal?" Kono replied sounding rather annoyed.

"Fine," Marcus growled. "But you better do what you can for Foley. Because if he dies, I promise you won't get away with it."

It looked like Kono was about to make another joke but managed to catch himself just in time.

"I promise I'll do everything I can for your friend," he said quietly and sincerely. "This wasn't something that I expected to happen."

Then Marcus was sure he heard within the muttering something along the lines of: "I always wanted a humanskin rug for my dining room."

Chapter 18 – Something Isn't Right

Foley didn't return to the squad that night, and the remaining members barely managed to get any sleep through the worry of it all. Sure, Foley could be an ass at the best of times, but in reality, he was their teammate and, above all else, their friend. It was scary too, because whatever had happened to Foley, whatever reaction he'd had to the gene therapy, could've happened to any one of them.

The squad took to their usual breakfast spot without saying a word en route. None of them felt like talking. Not until they heard something about Foley.

Marcus looked around the room and watched as others filled their plates with all the food they could fit on them. Towers of pancakes were balanced precariously, toast was stacked up to people's faces and bacon was stuffed into glasses so they could fit more food close by to them. It was like watching a pack of starving animals the first time they'd been allowed to eat proper food.

"They've all had it," Marcus said. "Everyone in this room has had the therapy, and that damn doctor doesn't even know how it's going to affect them. It can't be right, can it?"

"It's not right," Ramirez agreed. "Everyone in here could be in danger, but we have to keep it to ourselves. What else can we do? Quit? Because do you really think they're just going to let us go now we're filled with some alien tech?"

"Stop it," King said in a little above a whisper. "Stop talking like this was all a bad idea. I know what's happened to Foley, but I feel great. I'm fast and strong, so that's what I'm going to focus on for now. But please, don't talk like Foley's already dead or something."

McCulloch remained uncharacteristically quiet in all this, though Marcus could see he was under a fair amount of stress because of it. Foley was his friend too, but McCulloch was also the squad commander, and that meant that he was taking on a fair amount of responsibility for the safety of his team.

"Damn aliens," Marcus muttered.

The squad fell silent again, but the room around them was filled with an excited buzz. It was the same excitement that the Seventy-First had felt before Foley had taken his bad turn.

That was all to change; Callahan walked into the mess hall and stood looking out at the members of Operation Legacy.

"Listen up, recruits!" Callahan shouted, and the mess hall immediately turned still and silent.

"Now, before I begin with my announcement, I want you all to know that Colonels Whittaker, Armstrong and Johnson have, as of this morning, left this barracks and will not return. It's just you and me, boys and girls."

A silence washed over the room. Marcus felt the hairs on his neck standing on end like he was in danger.

"I bet they had something to say about the testing," Marcus whispered, but McCulloch shushed him.

"Now I am pleased to announce that we have moved along into phase two of this operation, you all now know what this is about, and have all received the treatment that will turn you into something more. With that being said, congratulations to all of you, you are all now hereby promoted. Squad leaders, you will find yourselves furnished with the rank of Corporal, and everyone else is, as of this moment, a Lance Corporal. You'll find your uniform updated later today. I hope you're already planning how to spend all that extra money you're going to get."

There were more than a few smiles in the room now, though Marcus and his squad weren't taken by the announcement; they were still thinking about Foley.

"Now it isn't all rainbows and butterflies," Callahan continued. "We have had some reports of mild side effects from the therapy, so if any of you has a headache, nausea or new and usual rashes appear on your body, it is important that you attend the medical facilities immediately. Is that clear?"

"Sir, yes, sir!"

"Good. Now, one last piece of business. Seventy-First. Your squad mate is doing well and will take the day to recover. You are to continue the day as though your squad is complete, and any squad you face will adjust their numbers down to match yours. That standing order goes for the rest of you too: if you lose a member through illness, you are to continue as usual, is that clear?"

"Sir, yes, sir!"

"Good. Now you may carry on, and I hope to see big improvements in your scores today."

"Crap, we forgot the check the leaderboard after yesterday!" King said once Callahan had left and the hustle and bustle of breakfast recommenced. "We'd better be top otherwise you lot have a lot to answer for."

"Us lot? You were right there with us," Marcus replied.

"Yeah, but I know I pulled my weight. If we aren't top, then it's not because of my performances."

"Don't worry," McCulloch said quietly. "We'll be top. Otherwise, I don't think Callahan would've bothered to single us out in front of everyone like that. He wants people to challenge us, and the only reason for that is to bring us down a peg."

Marcus did think that was a fair point, and indeed after breakfast when they approached the leader board on display just outside the mess hall, the Seventy-First were at the top of the pile. And by quite some margin.

Twenty-Third were second, followed by Eighty-First, Fifty-Fourth and Thirty-Eighth. Marcus didn't know any of the squads personally, though he was pretty sure he and his team had beaten them on their meteoric rise to the top.

"So how do you feel, Lance Corporal Cesari?" Ramirez asked as the squad left the leaderboard and crossed the grass to the pull-up bar. "Planning anything with all that extra money you're going to get?"

"Nope," Marcus replied. "Just keeping my head down to make sure it doesn't get bitten off by some alien monster."

It was weird, and the response came almost automatically. Once upon a time, Marcus knew that his response would've been booze, clothes and other things he didn't need. But now, his world just seemed like such a bigger place, and his outlook was simply on a different scale.

The squad then faced off on the pull-up bars against three other teams, beating them all without any trouble. Their opponents were clearly much better after the gene therapy, but Marcus and his squad's additional day of training was too much of a bridge to the gap – for now, at least. Interestingly, Marcus and the Seventy-First had continued to improve, with each of the squad passing one hundred pull-ups in a single session, whilst their opponents were maxing out somewhere around fifty.

Marcus wondered how long these improvements could continue on for. Could it be possible that without a genetic ceiling, the soldiers could just keep getting better and better? Or would they eventually come up against a wall, and something bad would happen? Like what had happened to Foley.

The question would remain without an answer, but something was about to happen that would change everything.

It was the last soldier that Marcus's squad was to face off against on the pull-up bars. They'd decided that after this round, they'd move on to hand-to-hand combat to really see how they matched up with the other teams. The man who hung from the bar from the Sixty-Seventh, however, did not look comfortable.

If Foley was to be taken as the benchmark for someone looking ill as a result of the treatment, this man looked twice as bad. His neck was a solid purple and his face sheet white. His eyes looked sunken and if anything, it looked like he wanted to be elsewhere. Perhaps in bed. A hospital bed.

The man leapt up, taking hold of the pull-up bar easily, and then started his movements. They were fluid, easy even and after the first fifty reps, Marcus wondered if he'd judged the look of the man a little too harshly.

It was when he hit eighty that Marcus realised he hadn't been too harsh at all.

The man pulled himself up once more, though now his once pale face was a deep shade of purple to match his neck, like he was being strangled. Then, like he'd been shot with a paintball gun, blood exploded from his mouth and nose, accompanied by a gargled cough. Losing his grip in the commotion, he fell from the bar and hit the ground hard, collapsing onto his side.

Marcus rushed in with the rest of the soldiers to tend to the fallen man, and he was the first to see what was happening. Blood was freely running from his mouth, nose, ears and eyes. It was like he'd had his head shaken and squashed, or perhaps juiced like an orange.

"Get a doctor, now!" Marcus shouted, and one of the soldiers darted quickly away in search of help. Another of the soldiers then knelt down and placed a hand on the fallen man's neck. Then he rolled him onto his back and began giving chest compressions and the occasional rescue breaths.

Marcus watched in horror as the soldier battled to save the man's life. The man who moments ago Marcus had seen as his opponent.

A minute passed, but eventually the soldier came to a halt, his arms falling to hang down by his sides and he moved away, shaking his head.

Nobody knew what had happened or how, but the man was clearly dead, and there was no amount of gene therapy that was going to fix that.

It was the first time that Marcus had ever seen a dead body, and he knew that it was something he wouldn't easily forget. The sense of loss, of complete and utter absurdity that human lives had to end, especially at such a young age and in fighting fit condition.

It was a lot to take. Marcus did his best to keep a brave face.

The soldier who'd run for help then returned, running with a doctor in tow. The two squads gathered around the dead man parted to allow the doctor access, though none of them looked up from the ground, from the life that had been lost.

The doctor spent a moment with the soldier, checking his pulse and conversing quietly with the man who'd administered CPR, but in the end, he too concluded the same thing the soldier had: the man was dead, and there was nothing that could be done.

Inevitably, the squad that the soldier had once been a part of picked up the body and carried him back to the main barracks, presumably for either Dr. Kono to have a look at for himself, or for a proper autopsy to be carried out. It didn't really matter what happened next to the man. Death was death, and that was a definitive.

It took a while, but Marcus and the Seventy-First eventually moved away from the pull-up bars after keeping silent, reflecting on what had just happened. It was all so sudden, so unexpected.

It was clear to Marcus that at least a couple of the others had experienced death before, but the whole situation had shocked him to his very core and he wondered just how close Foley had been to a similar fate. He shook the thought from his head.

"These things happen, Cesari," Ramirez tried to comfort Marcus, who was standing rigid and pale. "I know it sucks, but you're a soldier now and sooner or later you're going to see death. You might even be the one dishing it out," she added in a hushed tone. "It never gets any easier. You never forget, but eventually you learn how to deal with it, to move on and think about what's happening next, and why we do what we do."

Marcus looked Ramirez in the eyes. "And exactly why did that man have to die? You think when he signed up, he thought that one day he might be injected with some alien experiment, and the next day drop down dead? You'll forgive me if I don't see that as giving myself to queen and country."

"Actually, that's exactly what a soldier would do," McCulloch said calmly. "What's the difference if you get shot in battle or die right here? When a soldier becomes a soldier, they are accepting that they might just die sooner than they'd expected, and that it really isn't up to them. You might not think it's fair or just, but it's how things work here, so you can either get used to it or leave. It's your call."

"Leave?" Marcus scoffed. "You really think we're allowed to leave now? After what's happened, after what we know?" Marcus wanted to remind McCulloch about his condition and his father, but he managed to stop himself and just stare at McCulloch like he was challenging him to disagree.

"Then pull yourself together, Cesari. Act like the soldier I know you are and before you know it, we'll be out of this and through to the other side. Yes, what's happened was terrible, and we will all mourn the passing of a friend and a peer, but just shutting down or getting angry doesn't honour his memory. We don't let our friends die in vain. So we get back to work and we keep fighting, because that's what soldiers do. That's what makes it so our lives were worthwhile, do you understand?"

Marcus wanted to object. But he also wanted to shout and scream, to run out of this place and back to his home. But he knew that it would mean the end of his and his father's search for a new lease on life. He didn't know what would truly happen if he left the program either, though he suspected that if he tried, he would meet a resistance that he wouldn't be able to fight back against.

In the end, Marcus had no choice but to keep everything on the inside, and he wiped a single tear from his cheek before setting his shoulders, gritting his teeth and doing everything he could to focus on the path ahead, not what had just happened.

"I want to visit Foley," Marcus said quietly. "I want to make sure they're doing everything they can to keep him safe." He refrained from adding 'and alive' to that statement.

"That's a good idea," Ramirez said. "Then we can get back to work and keep our place at the top of the list. I don't think any of us want to see what King'll do if we start to slip."

King gave a half smile, but Marcus could tell that although Ramirez was doing her best to inject some humour into the situation, King really would be annoyed if they weren't top for the foreseeable future, though.

The squad then went back across the field again to the medical bays, though this time they didn't burst into random rooms. The last thing they wanted to see was the fallen soldier laid out on some bed being examined by Dr. Kono. At least he should have a little dignity in his passing.

Instead, the group knocked on the doors to the medical bays one by one until they eventually found Foley, and to their surprise and relief, he looked a lot better.

"Thought you'd visit me a bit sooner," Foley said as the squad entered the room. "But I guess you had better things to do, right?"

"Absolutely," King said loudly. "We're top of the leader board and nobody can touch us." She smiled and raised her chin a little.

"Well, that's something. And even with useless Cesari out there with you?"

"Shut up, Foley," Marcus said, though he was smiling. "When you're back on your feet, I think we need a little friendly competition, you know, to see who's the best once and for all. But no being sick out there again; I don't think I can stand the smell any more."

"Sounds good to me," Foley replied. "And I think I'm doing much better. I haven't been sick in hours, and the rash has gone. I hate to say it, but Doctor Zorgon seems to know what he's doing."

"Uh… I wouldn't be so quick to make that statement," Ramirez said. "There's something we need to tell you." She shuffled her feet on the floor, not wanting to speak about what had just happened.

"Don't tell me, there's an alien invasion and everyone out there is fighting for their lives and you've come here to collect me because you simply can't manage without the great Foley? Alright then, let's get to the armoury."

King scoffed and Ramirez forced herself to smile. Then she explained what had been happening in Foley's absence, and the entire feeling in the room turned sour. By the time she'd finished speaking, Foley had turned pale again, though it wasn't because his nausea was returning.

"That could've been me," he said quietly. "I could've just… been gone? Just like that?"

"As could any of us," McCulloch said confidently. "We all know what we are, Foley, so you'd better get over yourself and concentrate on getting back out there to work. If this little blip has passed, then you've got no excuse. And I presume this isn't something that's going to return?"

Foley took a second, and then nodded. "Kono said that he's fixed whatever the issue was. He said he didn't think I'd continue to benefit from the therapy as much as the rest of you, but… well, I guess that doesn't really matter anyway, does it? You've got a lot of catching up to do before you reach my level. That's if you ever do at all."

"Good," McCulloch said, ignoring more than half of what Foley had said. "I expect you back with the squad by tomorrow at the latest then. Oh, and you'll be happy to note that you've been promoted. Your new uniform will be awaiting you in the dorm."

"I knew it," Foley said. "I knew it would just be a matter of time before Callahan realised how superior I…"

"Everyone has been promoted, Foley," McCulloch interrupted him before he made a fool of himself. Then McCulloch stood to attention, turned a full one-eighty on his heels and marched from the room. The rest of the squad followed him, though not in the same rigid fashion.

"What's going on with him?" Marcus asked Ramirez as the pair and King followed McCulloch back onto the field, though they hung back to take their time where he was now jogging towards the firing range.

"I've seen this before," Ramirez said. "He might look and sound like he's dealing with all of this well, but he's just falling back to something familiar. He's regressing to something easy. It'll wear off in a while, but for now he's going to go into full 'soldier mode'," she air quoted. "That way, he doesn't have to have feelings about anything – he just has to follow orders and do what he's supposed to do. No thinking, no emotions."

Marcus hoped that it was something that he could learn in time because God knew that he was hurting inside. Hurting and scared. He still wanted to cry, to scream and to run, but he recognised that no good would come from that.

Not much was said between the squad as they carried out more of their challenges during the day. They didn't follow any plan or pattern, mainly because they already knew they could beat everyone at everything. Marcus did note though, that they steered clear from both the pull-up bars – no doubt too fresh a memory there, and the hand-to-hand combat areas. He internally agreed that this was probably not the time to actively try to hurt their comrades.

Everything changed once again though, when Marcus caught sight of a second soldier falling to the ground from across the parade square. His blood turned to ice in his veins.

Two deaths in as many hours. It was just too much for anyone bear. But that wasn't strictly true, Marcus knew. For a soldier, a couple of deaths was nothing.

But surely this was different; If they had been in combat or a war, then it was to be expected, but dying during what was essentially a training exercise was something that couldn't be easily swallowed.

Recognising that the day's work was over, McCulloch ordered the Seventy-First back to the dorms so they could regroup and decide on the best course of action. On the way, they passed at least ten other soldiers that looked far worse than they should, and with each McCulloch ordered them to report to the medical bays immediately.

Chapter 19 – Survival of the Fittest

"Do you think it's contagious?" King asked. "I mean, we touched a lot of those guys with the rashes and the ones being sick. Should we go and get checked?"

McCulloch shook his head. "They need the rooms, the last thing they need is for people to take up their time and space unnecessarily. Besides, we were in contact with Foley here, we even carried him down there and we've got nothing wrong with us. Best to just follow the orders and stay put until they decide what we're to do next."

"And by they, do you mean Callahan and Kono?" Marcus asked.

McCulloch nodded. "They're the only ones who really know what's happening down there and the only ones who can fix it. We follow orders, we do what we're told, and this whole thing will be over before we know it."

"Bit of a poor choice of words," Ramirez said. "But he's right, Cesari; if this thing could spread, then Mr. Sick over there would've passed it along already."

"That's Lance Corporal sick to you," Foley replied from his bed. He'd finally been given a clean bill of health and discarded to return to the dorms, where a new order had been given to all healthy soldiers in the barracks. They were to remain inside for the time being.

"How many do you think there are?" King asked. "I mean, how many have gotten sick from this therapy thing."

Nobody responded. Nobody had any idea how bad the situation could be out there, and they were under strict orders not to leave their dorms, so checking was out of the question.

Marcus had the fleeting thought that they could all go back outside and find themselves the only soldiers still alive in the place. But he shook it away.

What he hadn't realised, was just how much an effect emotional fatigue could have on a person. It wasn't something he'd experienced before, but now he was tired and all he wanted to do was sleep.

It wasn't until the following day that the squads would learn the gravity of the situation they faced. An alarm bell told them that their orders to remain in place had expired and that it was time for breakfast, which most of the soldiers were pleased about, given their insatiable hunger.

Marcus couldn't help but feel that sleep had gone a long way towards resetting his mental status, but not quite all the way.

The squads all made their way to the mess hall and had their breakfast as quickly as possible, but once they had finished and exited the main building to the outside world, everything changed.

Marcus and the Seventy-First arrived late after taking their time with their food. They were at the back of a crowd of soldiers just off the parade ground, trying to see what was happening.

Eventually, they managed to make their way to a position where they could see what was going on, and Marcus' had to pinch himself to check that he wasn't still asleep.

Over fifty black body bags zipped tightly closed lay on the hard, cold concrete of the parade square. And they weren't empty.

"Oh," Ramirez exclaimed and tried to run towards the mass graveyard. However, she realised her mistake a moment later when she noticed that Callahan was directing soldiers to pick up the body bags and load them onto an open-backed vehicle.

King quickly made her way back out of the crowd and threw up right there on the ground. The world turned silent as Marcus watched Ramirez. Callahan had seen her moving and had her help load the bodies onto the trucks with a handful of others.

McCulloch and Foley just stood there, watching the grim operation as it unfolded. Marcus couldn't help but let his mouth hang open as he stared.

He could feel his heart beating in his ears and hear the rushing of blood that somehow seemed in poor taste. It was like it was reminding him that at least he was still alive.

"H... how many?" Foley asked.

"Fifty four," McCulloch responded robotically.

"Do you think there's going to be more?"

"I don't know."

"I hope there aren't," Foley said. "I hope that's the last of them."

"So do I, Foley," McCulloch responded. "So do I."

The three stood silent for a long moment before Marcus managed to speak again. He'd been watching McCulloch and his stalwart determination to not show an emotional response to what they were seeing happen all around them.

"How do you do it?" Marcus asked.

"You just learn," McCulloch replied. "You push everything you think is right and just to the back of your mind and accept that you have no control over anything. And that includes your emotions."

Marcus nodded and fixed his eyes on the truck ahead.

When the vehicle had been loaded and it was ready to leave, it was Callahan who stepped in to drive it to wherever it needed to go. Presumably the bodies were top secret or of high importance or something, so the base commander had taken it upon himself to leave the barracks and accompany them. Either that, or this was his escape. Maybe he didn't like witnessing the pain, suffering and death just like the rest of them. Maybe they would never see him again.

Before he left, Callahan ordered the recruits to carry on as they had been, to return to their training though the leaderboard would remain frozen without anyone there to properly administer it. And that was it. The soldiers had been left alone, although Callahan had told them that medical personnel were still to remain in case they were needed moving forward.

Clearly that meant Dr. Kono, but it was unclear if any of the human doctors would remain along with the lizard-man.

The soldiers had been abandoned, and Marcus wondered if this was going to be a permanent thing – like the Operation had been shut down and the higher-ups just didn't know what to do with them all yet - or if Callahan really was going to come back and they'd continue along their new evolutionary paths.

The answer came to the soldiers loud and clear.

Three days passed and Callahan hadn't returned.

And there were three more deaths, but they happened early on, and after that, it seemed that the problems with the therapy had come to an end. There was no more sickness, no more rashes or headaches, just an insatiable hunger. It was a wonder that there was still enough food in the barracks to keep the soldiers well-fed; no food trucks were arriving, and if things didn't improve, it wouldn't be long before they'd have to begin rationing.

Some of the soldiers had searched for phone lines to call the outside world, but they hadn't found any. Or at least that's what they told the rest of the soldiers. It didn't matter anyway, what were they going to do, call for help? Surely the army or the government would've been keeping an eye on the place just to make sure everyone was doing as they were told.

Some of them spoke about leaving. Just opening the gates and making a run for it, but the majority overwhelmed them and convinced them to simply carry on as ordered. McCulloch had been vocal about that.

The whole place had the feel of something that everyone would like to just sweep under the carpet and forget about. Like the army had decided that what they'd done was wrong in so many ways, but they couldn't do anything about it anymore. To kill the soldiers would be inhumane, and not just because they were supposed to have been the best of the best, but also because nobody would ever have the stomach to give that order, let alone carry it out.

Most of the time now, the soldiers spent their time in their dorms contemplating what was going to happen to them next. They still showed up for meal times, and all of them used the grounds to burn off their excess energy, but the competition side of things was well and truly over. The leaderboard was stuck where it was, and nobody was there to update or change it even if they wanted to. The only saving grace for the Seventy-First, was that they had been top when the board was frozen, so the leaderboard would be a shrine, a testament to their strength and skill as soldiers.

Four more days passed, signifying a week without instruction. More soldiers talked about leaving but there still weren't enough to make it happen.

Marcus and his squad had searched for Dr. Kono, or any other medical professionals, but there was no sign of anyone except the soldiers in the base.

Nobody mentioned what they were all thinking: that they were all just supposed to die there. But they wouldn't let themselves believe it, even if they did wonder.

It wasn't clear when or how everyone had left, but again, it didn't bode well for anyone left behind. It was also a wonder where exactly an alien lizard creature could go, if not within a top-secret and locked-down army barracks. Marcus had the feeling that Kono wouldn't be too far away; he could tell that his experiments meant more to him than that. But perhaps he was forced to leave as a kind of punishment for all the deaths.

Food had started to become an issue. Most of the meats had been frozen and stored well, but fresh fruits, vegetables and bread were being rationed more and more. It wouldn't be long before the meat ran out either, because although everything was being portioned properly, the soldiers now needed daily calories multitudes higher than the average human being to fuel their ever-evolving bodies.

A part of Marcus wondered if the whole idea was for the soldiers to starve to death.

"I just want to eat what I want, when I want," King moaned as the Seventy-First sat in their dorm. They each sat on their own beds, and all wore their more than comfortable, alien-enhanced outfits. Contrary to how soldiers were supposed to reside, the room was filthy, and although Callahan had done a very good job at keeping the squad in line, day by day, it had become more difficult.

"We have our orders," Callahan said. "We carry on as usual until the commander comes back. They haven't forgotten about us."

"How many times do we have to have this conversation, McCulloch?" Ramirez said. "They left us here, they don't want to deal with us any more. They took the doctors away, and now the food is running out. Do you really think we should just sit around and wait?"

"Yes," McCulloch replied. "Because that is what we do. We are soldiers and we do as we're ordered, or have you forgotten that?"

"No, I haven't forgotten that, but have you forgotten that we're human beings and not some experiment? Besides, if we run out of food, we die."

"You don't know that," McCulloch said.

"What, that if we don't eat, then we die? I think I do know that, I know that very well."

"Well... what if we don't... need food any more..." McCulloch struggled, and Marcus took pity on him.

"Maybe it's a test?" he offered. He knew he needed to interrupt the pair because over the last few days, whenever the conversation had gone this way, it led to an argument and then to the squad sitting in silence for hours on end.

"What?" McCulloch asked. "You think they've done this to what, see if we'll disobey their orders and go rogue or something?"

"Actually, no," Marcus said.

"Yeah!" Foley interrupted Marcus before he could speak. "What if they want to see if we can go and find our own food? To make sure we can still function as regular people?"

"No!" Marcus objected, "That isn't what I was saying. What I meant was, maybe the test is to see if we'll all work together or something. Or if we continue with our training even if they aren't here to watch us? Maybe they just want to see what happens if we're left alone to do as we will?"

"I like Foley's idea better," King said. "I bet there's a few fish and chip shops around here, a few good pubs where we can get a drink. Maybe even see how friendly the locals are?" She raised an eyebrow, though her statement reminded Marcus of something.

That night in the Green Berry. He'd been the 'local', and the soldiers had beaten him to a bloody pulp. That hadn't been a fun experience, and being on the other side now, he still didn't think it would be very fun to cause problems in the community he'd grown up in.

Also, if the soldiers hadn't been there that night, if he hadn't got into the fight and the Colonel had seen him, then he wouldn't be in this mess right now either.

It reminded Marcus of how much he'd hated soldiers, but looking around the room, what he'd become and how the way he thought had changed, he felt like he was in a better place right now. Maybe not physically, but at least mentally.

"No," McCulloch said with an air of finality. "We stay here and we do as we're told. I'm not having this discussion again."

"But there are others..." King started.

"No."

The exchange was tense, but although it was getting closer and closer to the point where the soldiers could possibly outright rebel, for now, they were going to do as their superior commanded. Even if it was something that they didn't wholly agree with. And after all, that was a big part of being a soldier, wasn't it? You did as you were told, and if you didn't agree with an order, you kept your mouth shut and did it anyway. For the most part, at least. Until you died.

McCulloch sighed. It was like he'd just realised that he wasn't just a superior rank to the others but also one of the squad.

"I don't know what's going to happen in the long run, and don't get me wrong, I don't think they would just abandon us. But you might be right. We might need to think about how we're going to deal with the fact that we're going to run out of food pretty soon, and I really don't know what a lot of these guys are going to do if that happens. I know we're doing OK with the rationing system we've got going, but I feel like when we get hungry, we get irrational. And with what we can all do now, that's something I don't want to see the result of."

"And we need to talk about what happens if they don't come back for us," King said.

"Or if they just plan on dropping a bomb on us right here and saying it was an accident," Foley added with a smirk. Then he realised that what he said was a little less funny than he'd first thought, given their current situation.

"If things go from bad to worse," McCulloch said, ignoring Foley. "Then we're going to have to leave to get food. My suggestion would be for a few of the soldiers to leave the barracks so we don't raise any suspicions. We can go into town and find food."

"And pay for it with what? A song and a dance?" Ramirez asked.

"We do what we have to do to survive," McCulloch said in a low tone.

"Oh so we're the perfect, model soldiers until you want to go and pillage a nearby town?" Ramirez asked. "Why don't we rape the women and take their handbags while we're there, McCulloch? I mean, seriously, it's all just extremes with you, isn't it?"

McCulloch grunted but didn't reply. It was clear that he was trying to figure all this out as he went along, and perhaps his mouth was moving a little faster than his mind.

"I do think it could be a test, though," Marcus reiterated his earlier statement. "I mean, we could break out and steal what we need to survive… but what happens if they turn up right after and tell us we've all failed? I'm pretty sure that's something Callahan would do – especially after the backfiring paintball gun situation, right? I bet he can't wait to give us all a good ear bashing; it's like he gets off on it."

Ramirez answered first: "Well, we can hold out for as long as we can, but I don't know if we can convince everyone if they start getting too hungry. The gates aren't exactly going to keep us all inside. But I kind of agree. I say we go for as long as possible and then make the decisions later. I'm guessing the Corporals will get together and come up with something anyway. That's what ranks are for, right," she winked at McCulloch. "So you can decide what we do next, and we just follow the order. Ah, the benefits of being in the lower ranks, it's almost therapeutic."

The system of rationing was already being pushed to its limits. It was determined that there would only be enough food to keep them going at their current rate for another two days, and after that, they would start to feel the effects of malnourishment. Nobody wanted to experience that, though, given that they already needed much more food than usual, and the headaches that started to come with hunger over the last few days were some of the worst that any of them had experienced.

There was still no sign of Callahan, Dr. Kono, the Colonels or any of the other medical team. It really was starting to look like the barracks had been abandoned, and the members of Operation Legacy had been left to fend for themselves, or perhaps even starve to death.

But was that really possible? Could soldiers be so well trained that if told to simply wait and slowly die, they would? It was one of the questions that Marcus couldn't seem to shake from his mind.

The two days passed, and the entire barracks sat and ate their breakfast. Their last breakfast. Their last small breakfast.

Marcus looked down at his plate at the half a sausage, one rasher of bacon, one quarter of a slice of bread and eight baked beans. It was barely a mouthful. A mouthful that would provide just enough calories to keep him on his feet for an hour or two.

Over the last couple of days, the squad had spoken less and less, and not just with other the soldiers, but within the squad itself. It was like co-existing was just too much effort. The entire barracks seemed to have slowed down and quietened. Some of the squads refused to leave their dorms at all now.

The headaches had proven too much to handle.

They say that any civilisation is three good meals away from a rebellion, but for Marcus, he managed to hold out a little longer than that.

"I'm going to go see my parents," he announced suddenly as the squad relaxed in their dorm. It had been way too long since anything new had happened, and they had all finally agreed that they'd been left to themselves. Nobody was coming back for them.

They all knew that Marcus had lived just across the road from the main gates, but Marcus had always pushed back, saying that if he broke the rules and was removed from the program – or even disciplined – then the consequences could be too much to bear. Not just for him but for his father too.

But it had gone too far.

Marcus' body was still developing in line with the gene therapy he'd received from the alien doctor, but day by day as his ration of food had reduced, he'd become hungrier and hungrier, and the pain it was causing through headaches and an empty feeling in his stomach was almost intolerable. His muscles had grown, his body becoming stronger and more chiselled by the day, but he knew that eventually all good things would come to an end. The fuel had to come from somewhere, and he wondered just where that was going to be once he stopped eating.

If he didn't get food soon, and a lot of it, he would die. And so would everyone else in the barracks.

"I'm coming with you," Ramirez said. "There's no way I'm letting you go and get all the food you want while we stay here and starve to death. Plus, I don't trust that you won't just stay out there and forget about us." She smiled sweetly to ensure Marcus took those words as a joke, but she was being serious when she said she wanted to join him.

"And me," King said. "Now, I'm sure you don't plan on abandoning us here, but if you've got food over there, then I'm not just staying here and waiting for it to come to me. What about you, McCulloch?"

McCulloch grunted his usual non-committal grunt before he spoke. "I have my orders. I'm past stopping you from doing what you want to do, but I won't be leaving these barracks until I'm told to do so."

"Suit yourself, super soldier," Ramirez said.

"I never said you could all go. It's risky just one going but three?" Marcus said. "Plus I know you won't take your shoes off any my mum will go mental."

"I won't be going either," Foley announced like someone had asked him. "I take orders my seriously."

Marcus wondered where that had come from, but chose to ignore it.

"That's crap, Cesari," King said. "We're coming or none of us are going – including you, you got that? And by God, if you disagree with me, I'm going to break your arm the proper way, not like how Callahan did it, all rushed and haphazard. Like it'll really hurt. And you won't heal from that in a day, let me tell you."

"Fine, fine," Marcus replied, putting his hands up in surrender. "Not that it really matters anyway. Just try to remember to be on your best behaviour, OK?"

"No promises," Ramirez said.

"Just make sure there's food. Then we'll be good," King said, smiling again.

"There's always food at my house," Marcus said, standing up. "If not, mum makes a pretty good fish chowder, so there's always that."

"Oh hi mum," Ramirez mimicked Marcus' voice quite accurately. "Haven't seen you in a couple of months. Don't worry that I'm twice the size I was, and these are my two stunningly beautiful friends. I know it's two in the morning, but could you rustle us up some fish chowder? Also, we kind of eat a lot, so you might want to get a few pans out."

"Ah shut up," Marcus said. "You'll see. Just follow me."

Chapter 20 – Collected

Marcus took the key he'd always left hidden under a rock in the front garden and slid it into the keyhole on the front door. He silently pushed the door to his family home open and stepped inside, keeping his footsteps soft and the two soldiers, Ramirez and King followed.

The house smelled musty, not like the usual familiar smell of the home, a smell that had no real name, just a certain familiarity that Marcus had never known he enjoyed, but now without it, things felt different. Wrong somehow.

Ramirez sniffed audibly, and Marcus turned around to look at her. It was dark in the house, his parents must've been in bed upstairs, but the light spilling in from outside provided enough illumination for Marcus to see the look on Ramirez' face. She could smell it too. But she didn't make another sound.

The group crept down the dark hallway past the living room on the left, past the stairs on the right and into the kitchen. The dim light from out in the garden filtered through the window above the sink, though again there was something off. Something Marcus didn't recognise straight away.

And then he did.

There were no cups in the sink. There were always cups in the sink because mum and dad liked to have a cup of tea just before bed, then they'd wash them up the next morning – or perhaps sometimes just refill them if they were too tired to begin their day washing cups.

"Something's wrong," Marcus said quietly to King and Ramirez.

"I'll tell you what it is," Ramirez said at a normal volume. "There's nobody he-ere," she called out. "And I guess there hasn't been for a little while at least."

Marcus blinked. He knew it too, but he hadn't allowed himself to even think it, let alone believe it.

In a flurry of motion, Marcus pulled open the nearest cupboard, then drawer, then another and another. Then he pulled open the fridge, the freezer and took a large step back into the centre of the kitchen. There were no cups or plates, no cutlery or tinned food. The fridge and freezer were both empty. There was nothing. The kitchen had been cleared out.

Marcus ran from the kitchen and swung himself around the banister to ascend the stairs to where the three bedrooms and the steep steps into the loft conversion were. He ignored the other rooms and headed straight for his parents' bedroom. The door was partly closed, and he slammed it out of the way as he barrelled into the room.

And there it was. His parents' bed. Made perfectly as it always was, with nobody in it.

He stared at the bed like it had taken his parents from him, like he couldn't believe that it would've done such a thing.

But he knew the truth, and he let his head hand.

Slowly, he exited the bedroom and checked the rest of the rooms upstairs one by one, but the story was the same in each of them: the large furniture remained, but there was no sign of life in any of them. The drawers had all been cleared out, and anything small enough to carry had been removed. Even his own bedroom had been emptied.

This was just a house now, not a home. And it offered him nothing but questions and sadness.

Marcus walked downstairs and into the living room where King and Ramirez stood. He hadn't noticed it until now, but tears had filled his eyes and had spilt over onto his cheeks. His legs felt weak beneath him, and his palms were wet with sweat. He didn't even make it to the sofa or either of the two armchairs before he dropped to the ground on all fours, fell to his side and began to sob in a tight ball.

Ramirez was the first to kneel beside Marcus and offer him a comforting arm, and King quickly followed. They were saying something in a soothing tone, but Marcus couldn't hear them. He could barely hear his own thoughts.

'They must've left. They weren't forced to go. They must've gone quickly, or they would've let me know somehow. They're OK, wherever they are. I'll find them.' It was like a mantra repeating itself louder and louder, and eventually Marcus realised that the words were coming from the two soldiers, and somehow they had resonated in his mind.

Marcus had fallen to his side and pulled his knees up to his chest, wrapping his arms around himself and forcing his eyes shut. This couldn't be happening. All of this just had to be one long nightmare.

It was all too much.

And then Marcus drifted away into the darkness.

"Cesari?" Ramirez' voice broke through Marcus' internal darkness. "Are you OK?"

He didn't know when he'd fallen asleep or even how long he'd been out, but when he opened his eyes, it was still dark in the room, but the two soldiers were now standing over him.

"You aren't alone," King said in a tone Marcus had never heard before. "We're right here with you, and that's where we'll always be. You're never alone, you're a soldier, and soon you'll realise that you have a family bigger than you ever knew possible. We all look out for each other. I promise you."

Marcus pulled himself up to his knees and dried his cheeks. His body was aching and the headache was still there, but he felt like he could at least think a little clearer now.

"I… I just expected them to be here, you know. I haven't been away for very long, and my dad… I… I just don't know what would've happened to make them leave."

"Maybe they're on holiday?" Ramirez said, though she winced at the absurdity of that statement.

"Maybe they've been moved to a medical facility?" King offered. "It would make sense, wouldn't it?"

"Or maybe they've been moved, so they're far, far away from me and this program," Marcus said. "That makes the most sense, doesn't it?"

Neither King nor Ramirez could truthfully give an answer to that question, though anything any of them said would be supposition anyway.

"If they'd have just gone for a while, they wouldn't have taken everything they could carry," Marcus said. "If they'd have sold up and moved house, they wouldn't have left the furniture. I… I just don't get it," he said. "It doesn't make any sense."

"Well, what we do know," King said, "is that we aren't going to get any answers just waiting around here. I say we head to the nearest pub and get something to eat, how about that? I know it'll make me feel a lot better."

It was true, too. Marcus knew that food would make him feel better because most of the feelings of pain and discomfort had stemmed from the fact that he hadn't eaten anything but his rations for weeks now.

"I can't go in anywhere here," Marcus said. "Most people would recognise me, and I don't think that's going to be a good thing right now. So I say we head down to the beach, it'll be dark there and we can think about our next moves. Worst comes to worst, we're just going to have to steal what we need for now and apologise later."

"So now you want us to steal?" Ramirez asked. "First we go AWOL, and now we're going to turn into criminals?"

"What else is there?" Marcus asked. "If we don't eat, we'll die. And who can we turn to? Who can we ask for help?" then he added a little quieter: "And who would believe us anyway? If the army wants to keep us a secret, then you can be damn sure there's no record of us. Maybe that's why my parents aren't there."

"You don't think all of our families…" Ramirez started, then caught herself like the sentence was too difficult to finish.

"No idea," Marcus said. "But if they are, then we just have to believe that they're all being kept safe. Maybe it's just the way it had to be. But we'll sort that out later. First, we need food. And time to think."

"To the front then?" King asked. "And if there's a fish and chip shop open, we go there first. I feel like I need fat and carbs. A LOT, of fat and carbs."

"Then let's go," Marcus said. "There's nothing here for me any more."

Marcus felt that speaking with King and Ramirez was helping him deal with this new situation, but worried that if he stopped to think, then the pain and feelings of emptiness would all come rushing back in. He had to keep moving. He had to have a goal in mind. Then everything would be OK.

The group left the house and quietly closed the door. The streetlights that led up Canada road to the beach all cast a dull orange glow on everything beneath them, which made the smattering of cars all look brown. It was like nothing had changed since Marcus had called this place his home. But still, it felt different now. Empty. And he knew that without his family there, no place was truly home.

Walking quickly and quietly, none of the three soldiers said a word. They kept in the shadows as best they could, and Marcus took note of the fact that a few of the lights in the houses were on – so at least the entire street hadn't been evacuated on their behalf or anything like that. It went some way to assure him that they didn't just plan on bombing the place to wipe them all out.

They reached the seafront a few moments later, and Marcus crossed the two roads and the tarmacked path onto the stony beach. It felt like it had been ages since he'd felt the annoyance of a stony beach beneath his feet. But now he realised he'd missed it; it felt normal somehow. Like this was the way things were meant to be.

Marcus then slowly walked onto the beach and down the rolling pebbled hills with the ground crunching beneath him all the while. He arrived at the water's edge as it lapped quietly against the shore. And without stopping, he walked right into the ice-cold ocean.

"What are you doing, Cesari?" King called out from a few metres behind Marcus, though he didn't turn to answer. He just kept walking until the water was deep enough for his feet to no longer reach the ground, and he began to tread water.

"I missed this," Marcus said loud enough for the others to hear from the shore. "It's relaxing, isn't it?"

"Looks cold. And wet!" Ramirez shouted back.

"It is," Marcus agreed. "But it's calm. Right somehow."

"God damn it," Ramirez said loudly and stepped into the water. She hesitated a little as she let her body acclimatise to the ocean that was ten degrees or less, then waded into the water as Marcus had and caught him up within a few moments.

Then, with a loud splash, King joined the pair. She hadn't taken the time to wade out into the water, choosing instead to get it all over with as quickly as possible.

Ramirez' teeth chattered as she spoke. "I'd forgotten what it feels like to float," she said. "You're right. It is nice."

Ramirez and Marcus stayed floating in the water, treading water for a long while, all the time King seemed content to swim circles around them. She was always happiest when she was doing something active.

For Marcus, the cold, calm sea calmed his nerves and seemed to put the world back into order. The ocean between England and France had always done that for him. He could sit and look across the vast ocean and realise just how insignificant he was in a world filled with so much open space.

"But I am still hungry," Ramirez said. "Should we just see what we can find and make a run for it?"

Marcus wanted to object, to think of some better way, but he really couldn't figure out how exactly they were going to feed themselves, let alone provide something for the rest of the soldiers back at the barracks. The logistics of running such a place without the backing of the British Army just didn't add up whichever way he looked at it.

"I guess," he said. "Maybe if we eat something, we'll be able to think of something better?" There was no denying that his mind felt foggy still, and perhaps if he could get rid of this headache, something would come to him. A stroke of genius that would save everyone.

The squad then slowly waded back towards the beach and exited the water. Marcus was especially surprised at the fact that although he'd been entirely submerged and his clothes had been soaking wet whilst in the water, his boots and overalls seemed to repel the water somehow once they hit the cold night air, and within a few moments he felt dry once again. It was like a miracle.

The stones underfoot shifted as they walked, but where once the task of walking on the stony beach had been cumbersome and exaggerated, now it seemed like he was somehow able to anticipate the shifting in the ground beneath him, and he practically glided along like he was on a normal, stable pavement.

The squad moved back up the beach towards the shadows cast by sailing boats and their accompanying brick building, and once they made it there, they concealed themselves in the darkness just in case anyone had seen them.

"Right, so we..." Ramirez started.

And then they heard it.

At first, it sounded like a swarm of bees off in the distance somewhere, but as Marcus looked about himself to find where the sound was coming from, it got louder and louder until it was almost a deafening hum. Above them flew eight long-bodied, chinook-style helicopters. And it was obvious that they were heading towards the barracks.

"We need to get back!" Marcus announced quickly. "They're for us, and they might have food!"

The squad moved out of the shadow of the hut, but as soon as they did so, a helicopter hovering above them stopped, and a bright spotlight illuminated them like it was pure daylight.

"Cesari, King, Ramirez," Callahan's voice reached them a moment later and caused them to freeze where they stood. It was amplified by a megaphone, and between that and the spotlight, they knew they had nowhere to go.

"Stay right where you are, do not move a muscle," Callahan ordered.

The squad did as they were told as the rest of the helicopters continued along their path, and the one housing Callahan landed delicately on the stony beach a short way away.

Callahan beckoned the squad over to him, and dutifully, Marcus, King and Ramirez clambered into the helicopter and took a seat in the back, where Callahan had been sitting alone.

The roar of the helicopter's blades made speaking impossible, but it didn't matter because as soon as they were seated, the helicopter rose back into the air before any of them could say a word. Eventually, Callahan handed them each a headset so they could speak normally.

It was a surprise to Marcus, though, when the helicopter turned away from the barracks and headed back out to sea.

"Sir we..." Marcus started. He wasn't sure what he could say to explain why they had broken their orders and left the barracks, but Callahan interrupted him before he started.

"I apologise for my absence," he said. "After I left the barracks, I was called away and it was something that I had no control over. It was unfortunate that I had to leave you in the hands of that doctor, but I had no choice."

"Doctor?" Marcus asked. Then it dawned on him. Kono had been present at the barracks the whole time, and he had hidden himself away to watch what would happen to the soldiers if they were left to their own devices.

"He wasn't there," Marcus said quietly. "We were starving. Getting sick..."

"Oh he most certainly was there. Now you must believe that we wouldn't simply abandon the entire barracks and leave you behind to fend for yourselves, would you?" Callahan asked. "But the truth of the matter is that our mission schedule has been brought forward somewhat, so we're moving you all onto phase three of Operation Legacy and believe me, if you think what's happened so far has been mind-blowing, then you're about to have your entire world turned upside down."

Official Records – Thoughts from Marcus Cesari, Operation Phase Two

The moment I got onto that helicopter, my life was changed. I don't think any of us were expecting the things we were told or what was going to happen to us next.

Callahan explained to us that as soon as he left the barracks with the bodies of the soldiers who'd fallen during the initial injections in the gene therapy program, he had been contacted by the alien doctor Kono's superiors – the ones who were responsible for this testing – and had to leave for a while. And when I say that, I don't just mean leave the barracks.

The base commander was taken away from Earth, where he was given a briefing on what was going to happen next, and what all the members of the program were expected to do now that we had made it through to the other side.

We were told that Dr. Kono was present on the base for the whole time we were there, while we felt alone and starved half to death. Callahan didn't know what was happening at the time; he had expected us to carry on as we had been, but Kono had a different idea. Apparently, our new bodies needed testing for their resilience to menial things like starvation and boredom. They said we were eating the equivalent of a normal human being eating just one hundred calories a day, something that most humans simply wouldn't be able to cope with in the way that we had.

Yes, the headaches, nausea and fatigue had been ever-present, but it was clear that we weren't wasting away. Our bodies were leaning on our stored fat where necessary, and if anything, once the forced starvation study was finished, we were fitter, our muscles were bigger and harder, and our bodies looked like they'd been carved from stone, like Roman or Greek sculptures.

We were told that Dr. Kono needed to do this because of what we were about to face. The physical demands our bodies were about to experience and the mental difficulties we were all about to undergo. If I had known exactly what those difficulties were going to be before we had been told, I don't think I would've believed it.

On the helicopters, we were fed well. There were stacks of protein bars, high-calorie drinks and handfuls of fruits we could use to get ourselves back up to scratch, and I can't speak for the rest of the soldiers in the program, but King, Ramirez and I ate until we couldn't physically eat any more. It was like God had sent us a banquet, and to deny it would have been blasphemy.

I knew something was wrong though the moment Callahan spoke with us. He didn't give us an ear bashing or reprimand us for leaving the barracks in the face of his direct orders. He also didn't ignore the situation either; he seemed more understanding than I'd been expecting. Much more. And that was the worry.

Callahan told us that we had done what we needed to do to survive and that he would all just 'look the other way' while phase three of Operation Legacy began.

It just wasn't right. Everything I knew about the man told me that if he was being conscientious, then we were in real trouble.

I also managed to ask about my parents, and Callahan told me that he didn't know much about it, but that they'd been taken away to an undisclosed medical facility somewhere in the Midlands. He said that the word was that using my own tests along with my father's physical presence, they thought that they'd be able to do something to treat our shared illness. It wasn't some miracle cure, but it was significant, and that sounded good to me. Callahan didn't speak any more of our condition, what it meant or even the fact that I might've hidden it from him. I tired to ask for more specific information, but he either didn't have any, or wasn't going to share it.

I don't want to downplay the hardships of my time spent in the Canada Road barracks, the pain and suffering, the death that we experienced that seemed so unnecessary. It was truly like hell on earth. Something that will stay with me forever because you don't just forget about something like that. I know the nightmares will be there to remind me if I ever start to forget.

But what came afterwards in phase three, that's what truly changed me. That's what opened my eyes to the larger picture and what Dr. Kono had been trying to achieve. Why he had done what he had. Why it was all so important.

Because believe me, the universe that we experienced in phase three of Operation Legacy, was nothing like any of us could ever have guessed.

Chapter 21 – Talon Station

The helicopter that Marcus, King, Ramirez and Callahan rode in was the first to reach the platform in the middle of the ocean between England and France. A platform that Marcus was sure he'd never seen or even heard of before.

If someone had been watching in the daylight from either country's coastline, they might've seen the helicopters landing one by one on the floating platform, but at night, it was nothing more than lights in the distance.

It was a large metallic structure that remained steady on top of the open waters no matter how rough the waters were, even when the helicopters descended onto it to land.

In the centre was a round, conical shape, bordered by six flat platforms that the helicopters landed on one by one. If anything, it looked like a fairground ride by the way that bright multicoloured lights illuminated the thing.

Once the helicopters had set down, Callahan ordered the three soldiers to follow him, and he walked along an open pathway that led to the centre of the construction. As they walked, the wind whipped against them and Marcus felt the icy bite of an open-air platform in the middle of the ocean.

When they reached the central cone, It was like something out of a science fiction movie; right in front of them, a doorway that hadn't been there a moment ago slid upwards to allow the group to enter into whatever this thing was.

When they were inside, it was clear that what they had seen on the surface was just the tip of the iceberg.

Marcus' eyes bulged as he took in the sheer scale if whatever it was he was looking at; The inside of the cone was huge.

Everything seemed to be below them, on metal ladders and walkways, snaking down to a large open floor in the centre.

"It's…" Marcus said slowly, recognising the layout from the many hours of television he'd watched in his life. "It's a prison."

When he spoke, he saw Ramirez turn sheet white beside him, and he realised that maybe he should've kept his mouth shut. But it was already too late.

"You couldn't just leave us there to die – especially if we could just break out of the barracks – so you're locking us away in the middle of the ocean?"

"No," Callahan said with a half grin. "Do you really think if this was a prison and you were being placed here, there would be no teams of armed guards? Do you really think we're that stupid? I may have broken your arm and nose once before, Cesari, but I've seen what you people can do. I know how capable you all are. And I'm proud of you. No matter what you may think of me."

Again that was a strange thing for Callahan to say, and Marcus knew it. It was like he was being nice, perhaps overly nice to them on purpose, like he knew something bad was happening, or that he felt guilty about something. It made the hairs on the back of Marcus' neck stand on end, and he couldn't help but realise that the rest of his body had tensed in anticipation of a fight.

"Then what is this place?" he asked.

"Cesari," King said. "Do you really think it's our place as soldiers to…"

"No, it's alright," Callahan said. "You may be soldiers, but you're also human beings. And that fact is going to become even more relevant very soon." Then he turned to Marcus again. "If this place is not a prison, tell me, what do you think it is? Take a look around and tell me what you see."

Marcus did so, taking all the details he could from this vantage point. The walkways were all open, and rooms that were very much like cells skirted the walls. From what he could see at the bottom of the wide open space, it was clear that it was a mess hall of sorts. But then he looked at everything more closely. There were no guard posts or locks on the outside of the doors, and from what he could see, the whole place had a little more comfort than he would've expected to see from a prison.

"It's… it's a mobile barracks?" Marcus said. "Somewhere we can live but also move around in. In case people figure out where we are? Or want to target us?"

"That is actually very close to the truth," Callahan said. "Kono did say you'd be more perceptive after the therapy. But also, I don't blame you for not realising what this place truly is, given that it is the first time one has been present on earth. Well, almost," he added, rolling his eyes. "Cesari, King and Ramirez, you are the first members of Operation Legacy to find yourself aboard an honest-to-God, real-life spaceship. Welcome to the GSI Relentless. But uh… try not to break anything because this is kind of a loan from our friends and benefactors," he gestured upwards with his eyes.

Marcus' mind raced. If he had been told that this was what the inside of a spaceship was going to look like, he might've laughed. As it was, all he could do was stare in wonder, and try to see if he'd missed anything.

"That's where you've been, isn't it?" Marcus asked. "Why you haven't been able to get back to the barracks?"

Callahan gave another half-smile. "Please excuse me, the rest are arriving now and I think it would be best if everyone heard what I have to say at once."

Then a moment later, doors all around the central hub began to open, and the members of Operation Legacy began pouring into the spaceship and filling the metal hallways, all dressed in uniform and all looking as confused as Marcus had been when he'd arrived here.

Marcus could also see that Ramirez didn't seem to have recovered her colour as yet. And he could understand why.

"Listen up people," Callahan shouted from his position on the walkway, and everyone seemed to stiffen at the sound of his voice. "A few things for you to understand before we can move forward. What you have been through has all been a part of your training and testing, and I'm happy to report that you've all passed with flying colours. Dr. Kono and a medical team have been on hand this entire time, so you were never in any real danger."

Marcus wanted to scoff, and it took a lot of effort not to. Over fifty soldiers had died so far, not a long way off one in ten because of this operation, doctor Kono and his unique brand of care. He also wasn't sure if any of this had been a part of the training, or if Callahan was simply retrospectively covering his own mistakes.

"Now we move along to phase three and trust me, if you've been shocked so far, then prepare to hold on to your hats. Because what you're standing on right now, I kid you not, is an alien spaceship. Now it's on loan from a race of beings called the Bacchus - they're a lot like a typical alien, except their skin is blue and a little bit translucent. I'm sure you'll meet them soon enough and when you do, try not to stare, people."

There was a slight nervous shuffling from the soldiers, but none of them said a word.

"We will be travelling to Talon Station, where our illustrious sponsors will have a chance to see what their patronage has accomplished. And people, I expect you all to show the universe just what human beings are capable of, you hear me?"

"Sir, yes, sir!" The call returned and echoed throughout their metallic surroundings.

Marcus could hear the relief in the reply to the base commander. It was like they finally had a purpose again, a direction to aim in and there wasn't even the slightest sliver of resentment to be detected.

"Good. Now I'm pleased to let you know that this ship is stocked to the gills with good food, and lots of water, so take a dorm, remain in your squads and replenish those broken bodies. You're going to need all the strength you can get when we meet the Baccus."

There were now smiles all around. It was like Callahan had them all wrapped around his little finger, and the promise of food just sealed the deal. But Marcus couldn't shake the feeling that they'd been let down over the past few weeks. And the fact that if a little more time would've passed, then there might've been fewer soldiers standing there today.

With the announcement over and their orders given, the soldiers all filtered away from the upper walkways and laid their claim to empty rooms as they passed them. All the rooms seemed identical – which was one of the reasons it seemed so prison-y, but most just seemed happy that there was food coming, and Marcus couldn't blame them; knowing food was so close made his mouth water. His stomach yearned to be full again.

Foley and McCulloch caught up with Marcus, King and Ramirez on their way down the stairs towards the central mess area.

"Looks like I owe you an apology, Cesari," Foley said. "Maybe we're all going to get probed after all, just like you!"

Marcus smirked. "At least they're going to buy us dinner first this time."

Foley's face dropped slightly, and Marcus could tell he was trying to think of a witty comeback, but nothing was coming.

"I'd take an alien over you in a heartbeat, Foley," Ramirez said. "I think an alien being who's never had any previous interactions with humans before, would know its way around a woman better than I assume you do."

"Hey!" Foley said. "It's not my fault you can't seem to say what you mean."

"Alright Foley," McCulloch interrupted before Foley could dig himself a hole that he couldn't get out of. "Let's just get down there, eat until we feel sick, and see what this operation has in store for us.

"You know, that sounds like the best idea you've ever had," King said. "If they have steak down there… I hope it's measured in kilos."

There was indeed steak. And chips, all kinds of veg, salad, potatoes done however anyone liked, all kinds of drink – not just water, although no alcohol – and when Callahan had said there was enough for everybody, he hadn't been kidding. The food was arranged in the centre of the tables in veritable mounds, and although they were quickly cut into as the soldiers refuelled themselves, it was clear from the outset that nobody would be going wanting.

"What do you reckon they'll have us doing?" Foley asked through a mouthful that he'd been chewing for almost a minute already. "Teaching these Baccus things how to fight?"

Marcus frowned, but Ramirez managed to say what he was thinking before he had the chance. Also, Marcus might not have put it so harshly.

"Are you really that much of an idiot?" She said. "Or do you just think you're actually that good?"

"I am that good," Foley replied quickly.

"An alien race of beings have gone out of their way to genetically enhance a group of human beings. And you think you have something to show them? I bet we're nothing more than ants to these Baccus things. And if Kono is to be believed, then we really are nothing compared to what's waiting for us out there. The best case scenario, we're just some science experiment and worst case, they want to enslave us all. You can pick, I don't really care."

Foley raised his eyebrows and swallowed, but didn't reply. It really sounded like Ramirez had thought this through, and Marcus had to agree with her assumptions. This alien race wanted to use humans somehow, but he couldn't think that it was going to be for anything good.

"But still, it doesn't matter," McCulloch said. "We have our orders and no matter what happens, we follow them. Even more so now. We have to stick together and do as we're told if we're going to make it out of this alive, right? Just… don't do anything stupid, any of you."

"Ah, when have we ever done anything stupid?" King asked. As long as they keep feeding us, we'll be happy. Right big guy?" she tapped Foley in the stomach, which didn't give at all and if anything, King seemed surprised at just how hard it was. "Anyway, keep giving us food and we just keep doing as we're told. Like dogs… but with guns. Oh that reminds me, have any of you seen any guns around here? Because I don't like the idea of going to some alien space station without a gun."

"And I'm sure Callahan and the Baccus wouldn't like the idea of giving you a gun and sending you in amidst a load of aliens," McCulloch said. "Just stay calm, do what you're told and try not to shoot anything. Least of all because they might shoot back, and we have no idea what kind of weapons they might have."

"I bet they've got food we can't even imagine," Foley said.

"And there it is," Ramirez said. "He's in an alien spaceship, has met an alien doctor, learns about another alien race that's sponsoring our gene therapy program, and… he hopes they've got good steaks. I hope you eat one, and it makes you chuck up your guts."

"Whatever, Ramirez, I saw the look in your eyes when you were starving back there," Foley said. "You'd have eaten cat food if you could've got your hands on it.

"I… no I…" Ramirez fumbled, though she knew it was the truth, and she couldn't bear to force out a lie to the contrary.

"Can't we all just get along?" Marcus said with a smile.

"Sure we can," King said. "Once Foley here recognises his place."

"Oh, and where's that?" Foley asked.

"You see the bottom of my boot?" King raised her foot and pointed.

"Alright, that's enough," McCulloch said. "Now we're all one team here, so this is the end of it. No more fighting, no more bickering. We're God damn soldiers here, not… not…"

"Civilians?" Marcus offered. He knew it was what McCulloch had wanted to say but had stopped himself.

"Well, yes. Sorry Cesari," he added.

"Doesn't matter. It's true, isn't it? We do need to work together, so I'm with you, McCulloch. Let's just get through this as best we can, and when we get back home, we'll just arm wrestle it out to see who really is the best." Foley put his hands behind his head, clearly flexing his biceps. They must've been twice the size they were when Marcus had first met the soldier, and he wondered if anyone on earth would actually beat him in an arm wrestle.

And then as though to punctuate their conversation, a blue light filled the entire structure, accompanied by a siren that wailed in a pitch much lower than most alarm sounds the soldiers were used to.

"What the…" Foley said, but Callahan's voice interrupted him.

"All hands," the public address system in the structure barked. "Please note that we have now left earth's orbit and are on our way towards Talon

Station. If the shuttle is functioning correctly, then you won't have noticed this transition. There is no need to be alarmed, and during the next two weeks, we will be travelling through the vastness of space. This is not something that you should concern yourself with, so you may treat this time as though it is your vacation. On board the shuttle are gyms and cinemas, and of course all the food you can eat. If you need me, I'll be around. At ease soldiers and bon voyage."

"Well, that's odd," Marcus said.

"What?" Ramirez asked.

"It's Callahan. I've been thinking he's just acting too nice. Like he knows something bad and he feels guilty about it. And this down time? You'd have thought he'd make us run laps or work out until we bleed or something – but to just rest and relax? There's something going on here, and I'm not sure if I like it."

"So what?" Ramirez said. "There's always something going on around here, but like McCulloch says, there's nothing we can do about it. And if Callahan's going to give us some r and r, then I'm going to make the most of it. You think they've got Alien in the cinema?"

"It'd be a travesty if they didn't," Marcus said with a grin. "You know I'm partial to a bit of Rocky Four myself. I quite like the idea of some medicine enhancing the human body."

"Wait," Foley said. "Didn't the Russian lose in that one… so it's kind of like saying nothing beats pure one hundred percent human meat."

"My thoughts exactly," Marcus said. "Though in this case, what I'm saying is that films are made up stories, and I really like watching two men box."

The next few days quickly turned into weeks. It was inevitable that without anything else to do, the soldiers all seemed to treat this journey through the stars like it was one great holiday. The cinema did indeed have all of the popular movies from Back to the Future to Star Wars. Similarly, the food was varied and plentiful, and even King managed to set out a route for herself to run that didn't include too many awkward twists and turns. In short, the long journey from Earth to Talon Station – wherever it may have been - was nothing other than pleasant. And Callahan kept himself to himself, which was a bonus.

When it was finally announced on the public address system that the ship was entering the final approach into the station, the soldiers were all understandably excited, though with the absence of any windows on the GSI Relentless, it meant that they had to rely on their other senses to tell when they had finally touched down, and would meet their new alien allies.

It was clear that they had arrived. The ship lurched, clunked and banged as the landing clamps engaged and whatever else was happening happened between the ship and the station.

What followed, though, was not the opening of all of the doors around the upper walkways as they had entered. Now, the central cone of the GSI Relentless split in half, opening to allow a very large metal cage to descend into the centre of the mess hall. Through the opening where the cage had dropped from, there was only darkness. But it was clear what was supposed to happen next.

The cage was huge. It had clearly been made to fit hundreds of people within, though none of the soldiers wanted to be the first to step into the thing.

"Soldiers," Callahan's voice came over the speakers. Marcus could tell that it was different again though, uncertain perhaps. It was like Callahan was giving this order, but it wasn't something that he wanted to do. "Step into that cage."

"You heard the man," McCulloch said. "Into the lift and up into the station. Who knows, you might even find a girlfriend up there, Foley."

"Ramirez raised an eyebrow at that. It was the first time that McCulloch had teased Foley, and it was clear that he was only doing it to hide his own apprehension.

A few moments later, all of the soldiers stepped into the large metal cage, and the doors had closed themselves tightly around them. Then it began to slowly ascend upwards into Talon station, and to where the soldiers would finally meet real life aliens – other than the elusive Dr. Kono - for the first time.

But it was not to be a meeting as they had been expecting.

Chapter 22 – Put on a Good Show

"Friends! The time has come for you to see what our illustrious military and scientific minds have helped to create!" the voice reached Marcus as he tried to see what was happening above the elevator. It was high-pitched, almost whiney even, and Marcus listened intently.

"Some of the deadliest creatures known to the universe. These beings have performed heinous acts of war, death and destruction over thousands of years against their own people. They are the epitome of evolution on their home planet and would no doubt one day reach the stars on their own. But today they stand before you as allies, as weapons here to help us in our own plight. My friends, I give you: the human beings of Earth!"

As the last words were spoken, the elevator breached the ceiling and came to a halt at the new ground level.

The soldiers could only stand and stare as they had been raised into the centre of what looked like a giant, sand-filled arena, not unlike those of ancient Rome. Around the outside of the wide-open sands were large metallic doors and above them, long seats that rose high up and away. Even from this distance, it was clear that the absolutely filled arena was packed full of the smaller blue aliens that could only have been the Baccus. Marcus looked around at the crowds, his enhanced vision helping him to see the faces of the aliens that surrounded them.

"Holy crap," Marcus breathed.

"Now that's an entrance!" Foley announced, pumping his fists in the air. It seemed that he wasn't the only one to take the welcome as warm, and the crowd cheered like this was the most amazing thing they'd ever seen.

"Something's wrong here," Marcus said to Ramirez. "This isn't right. They've brought us here for something, and Callahan knows what. And he knows it's bad."

Ramirez didn't respond, she simply stared at the crowds in the arena who were clearly there just for them.

Then the announcer spoke again, though Marcus still couldn't see where he was. "But these aren't just your average everyday human. Oh no! These humans have been through a genetic enhancement program to make them larger, stronger, fitter, smarter, more perceptive and everything else that makes them stand out from the rest of their race. Through years of dedicated training, the small force you see before you has been hand-picked as the very best that humankind has to offer!"

Cheers rose up again, and not all of them just from the crowd. The soldiers from earth, it seemed, were excited at the prospect of being real-life action heroes to these beings.

"So to show what these beings are truly made of, we have an exciting demonstration for you today!" A door on the far side of the arena slid open, and the Baccus announcer walked forward - he was holding a microphone of sorts - flanked by two more of the alien beings. All three of them held long spears with two prongs at the end that looked very much to Marcus like cattle prods.

"I trust everybody knows what these are?" The announcer asked as he continued walking towards the humans. "Tafek Tolon!" He practically shouted. "Deadly to those of weaker dispositions but also hugely effective as a non-lethal deterrent, the Tafek Tolon has been designed to cause pain, to incapacitate and in some cases even blind an assailant with agony. So," he turned his attention to the soldiers still inside the metal cage, "I would like to ask for three human volunteers who think that they are better than the rest, to step forward and show all of these people here today just how strong you are. But for those of you who aren't aware, proving yourself through pain and suffering is one of the very best ways to show what you are made of. Let us all see how mighty these humans are!"

Marcus' eyes bulged. Were they seriously asking for volunteers for torture?

But then he noticed a sea of hands raised all around him. The tallest of which was Foley's, and by a few clear inches.

"What are you doing, Foley?" Marcus hissed. "Don't be an idiot."

"I'm going to show them all what humans are made of," Foley replied loudly. It was like something primal had been awakened inside of him. "Besides, they aren't going to kill us, and I want to be the one they remember.

The one they think of when someone says the word 'human' to them. They need to know we won't be beaten in a fight. Just in case one day we aren't friends anymore."

Marcus thought about pulling Foley's arm down by force, but before he had the chance to, the announcer spoke again.

"This one's a big one!" he said. "And these two have a certain fire in their strange human eyes that says to me, 'I'm ready!'" The gates at the front of the elevator cage swung open to allow Foley and the two others to walk out, then closed quickly behind them again.

Marcus knew the other two who'd raised their hands too. The first was a man from the Sixty-Second, Marcus had beaten him a couple of times on the pull-up bars and he didn't seem to be able to accept that he'd list even then. The second was a woman who Marcus couldn't remember the squad of, but she too looked determined to prove herself to these alien beings.

The three soldiers walked out into the centre of the sands with the announcer. Foley looked like he was loving every minute of it, again pumping his fists into the air and roaring like a Roman gladiator. The other two walked with a confident gait, though they didn't try to play the crowds as Foley did.

When they all came to a halt, the crowd turned quiet, and the announcer spoke to the soldiers without letting the microphone amplify his voice. A moment later, the three soldiers unzipped their overalls and let them hang around their waists, leaving the two men bare-chested and the woman in just a black sports bra. Marcus looked at Foley for signs of the black spidery rash he'd had before, but there was nothing there.

It had been a while since Marcus had bothered to notice the people around him, but their bodies were something else. Rippling six-packs, pecs that looked like they'd been chiselled from marble and arms that Hulk Hogan would've been jealous of. Dr. Kono's program had certainly been effective.

"And here we are, my friends!" The announcer turned his attention back to the crowds. "At almost twice the size of your average Baccus, I give you, human Beings!"

The crowds erupted into cheers again, eventually quietening down as the three Baccus moved to each stand in front of the presented humans, who were standing with their legs shoulder-width apart and their arms behind their backs.

Marcus couldn't help but admit that all three of them did look like they'd been waiting for this their entire lives. And all three looked like they were well over six feet now – possibly nearing seven feet, though the smaller

Baccus could've been giving the illusion that they were bigger than they were.

And then without warning, the Baccus all raised their weapons, and placed them against the soldiers' chests.

From each, a bright white light illuminated the space around them, not unlike that of an industrial welding machine.

The sound was firstly that of the crowd cheering at the show again, and then it was the soldiers that could be heard, even over and above the roaring crowd.

Marcus watched as the weapons touched the skin of his friend and comrades. He watched as each of them opened their mouths to scream in pain as whatever was in these weapons coursed through their bodies, causing every single one of their muscles to contract to their fullest extent. It looked like their skin was about to tear from their bodies. He watched as the first the two soldiers that weren't in his squad fell to their knees, and then Foley followed suit a handful of seconds later.

It was like a switch had been flipped inside the humans' cage. They instantly turned from expecting this to be some fun show to realising exactly what was going on out there: this was torture through and through. The ones closest the cage walls tried to grab a hold of what they could to free themselves to help their friends, but it was no use; the cage didn't move an inch. They were locked inside.

None of the soldiers fell any further than their knees though, and after a full minute of the weapons applying their clearly painful charges, the crowd had fallen silent. Nobody had expected these human beings to withstand such pain, such power, but they had. The three Baccus removed the weapons and the soldiers were still there, still on their knees and still conscious.

Foley was the first to bring himself back up to his feet, and when he was joined by the other two, he again roared and fist-pumped the air.

"We are humans!" he shouted. "We are humans!"

The crowd loved it. The cheers that erupted, along with whoops and the waving of arms made the entire arena feel electric.

The announcer then calmed the crowd down as he dismissed the man and woman, leaving just Foley out there on the sands. They were taken away somewhere out of sight, presumably to be checked by doctors.

The humans locked in the cage simmered down as they saw their kin well again and not enacting any revenge.

"We can't let this happen," Marcus said to Ramirez. "It's barbaric. They're going to kill him just to see how much it takes."

"No… they wouldn't, would they?" She said.

"We don't know anything about this race. What if they see dying as a good thing? What if their religion says if you kill someone of a different race, you get into their version of heaven?"

Ramirez stroked her chin thoughtfully. "It's not the vibe I'm getting from them. But anyway, what can we do? We're locked in here, and Foley seems to be having the time of his life."

"And we all know just how dangerous just one of the Tafek Tolon is," the announcer practically screamed. "So feast your eyes on this!"

Marcus watched in horror as the three Baccus encircled Foley and all of them as one placed their cattle prods against his skin. One on the chest, one on the side of his back and one on his neck. Marcus felt himself lurch forward like he needed to stop all this, but Ramirez had been right; there was nothing he could do.

Foley's body exploded into light. The electricity from the weapons illuminated his very veins, and as he opened his mouth to let out another roar of defiance, the light broke forth from within. This time, though, the large soldier did not fall to his knees.

It was over much quicker than the last time, and when the weapons were removed from Foley's skin, they'd left visible dark circles where they had touched him. Foley, to his credit and to the shock of everyone present, simply turned to the Baccus and smiled. His skin was smoking, but otherwise, he looked unharmed.

"You're going to have to do better than that!" Foley shouted, and again the crowd went insane.

"I knew he'd be OK," King said. "He's too stubborn to get killed here."

"I don't think…" Marcus started.

"Yeah, he's going to go out in a ball of fire," Ramirez agreed. "Like a daredevil of something. With loads of people watching."

"You mean like in an arena full of alien beings?" Marcus asked.

Ramirez smiled. "Well, maybe a different arena then. Probably one with more fire."

"Is this not amazing, friends?" the announcer bellowed with delight. "And now, just to push the point further…" he turned and waved an arm at an area of the arena where a second cage was now rising up onto the sands from somewhere below. Inside this cage wasn't humans, though. The creatures this cage held back were far more annoyed at their captivity. And they looked like giant, chitinous spiders.

When the cage came to a halt and the crowd could see what was within, there was a sharp intake of breath, followed by a worried hissing noise.

"Now there is no need to worry," the announcer assured. "The Scriven are locked away safely, and they have no chance of escape. In fact, these particular Scriven are ones that have been caught straight from the battlefields of Astati Three, so you might say they're rather slow."

The crowd laughed.

Then the announcer walked over to the cage containing the alien creatures, and the Scriven inside went ballistic. Their sharp, pointed legs clanged against the metalwork of the cage, and the ones at the front even tried biting their way through with equally sharp-looking beaks.

"Oh, they're angry," the announcer said, obviously not fazed by the aggressive reception. "They're big, they're strong. But they're nothing compared to our humans, are they?"

He then moved his cattle prod up to the bars, pushed it through and touched it against one of the Scriven trying to force its way out of confinement. There was a large flash of light, a high-pitched squeal, and the creature fell to the ground, dead and smoking.

"Jesus and they used three of those things on Foley?" King exclaimed. "I'm going to have to start working harder."

Marcus frowned. He still wasn't sure why everyone was taking this all so calmly. It was like they were simply acts in a circus, and the ringmaster had no regard for their safety.

"But they do have something of their own, too, these humans," the announcer said once the crowds had finished cheering. He pulled a new weapon out from behind his back and handed it to Foley. It was clear to Marcus and every other human in the room what this weapon was.

"They call this an S-A-Eighty," the announcer enunciated. "It's rather archaic but at the same time as brutal as the Scriven's own thirst for blood. The arena fell silent again, and Foley looked quite shocked that he'd actually been handed a weapon.

"If you would demonstrate by taking one of the Scriven down, sir," the announcer said loudly. "Try to make it a big one."

Foley didn't need to be told twice, and he raised the rifle to his eyeline. His firing stance was solid and his expression resolute.

Bang.

One single shot rang out, echoing around the arena, and a single Scriven fell to the ground. The crowd, again, went wild.

"And would you look at how accurate they are at such a distance! Amazing creatures!" The announcer cooed.

Foley's face lit up again, and he fired another shot into the midst of the alien creatures. Another fell, and the cage began to shake as the rest scrambled in either fear or blind rage.

"Careful now," the announcer said, and Marcus detected a very slight waver in his voice. "These Scriven don't like it when you push them too hard. In fact, I think they kind of like it. Am I right, friends?" He turned to the crowd, who gave a slightly more anxious cheer in response.

Foley, though, seemed to be having way too much fun. He popped off another three shots. Bang, bang, bang and three more Scriven fell down, killed instantly.

"Well friends, I know when I'm not needed," the Baccus said and he turned and scurried from the arena, his two accomplices quickly following.

Foley, not reading the situation kept firing one shot at a time into the alien beings, dropping them to the ground easily. Though with the sheer amount of Scriven within the cage, his efforts weren't making much of a dent in their overall number.

Marcus watched as Foley continued firing one shot at a time, but then he noticed something happening on the outside of the arena, between the sands and the crowd: a clear barrier, glass or possibly some kind of clear plastic was rising and shielding the watching masses from whatever they thought was going to happen next.

"Foley!" Marcus shouted. "You've got to stop; it's not what you think!"

"Oh, you'd love that, wouldn't you!" Foley shouted back in between shots. "Then you can come up here and…"

Crack.

The cage that held the Scriven was now vibrating with such ferocity that its base was leaping up and down from the ground. It didn't look like its structure had been compromised, but with each fallen Scriven, they were getting increasingly riled up. More than a few had begun screeching now, an ear-piercing sound that made Marcus want to cover his ears.

"Well, the more I kill, the less there are to scream!" Foley shouted over the ever-increasing cacophony, and he let off another shot.

That shot would be one of the biggest mistakes he'd ever made.

One of the Scriven creatures at the front, as soon as the shot rang out, covered itself with its legs and rather than break them or penetrate through, the bullet Foley had fired ricocheted off the creature and pinged into the locking mechanism on their cage.

Marcus' mouth dropped as the door that kept these terrifying alien creatures swung open.

It took just a few seconds for all of the alien creatures to scurry from their captivity, and it now looked like there were a lot more of them than anyone had assumed. Certainly, more than two or three times the number of humans still stuck in their own cage.

The crowd behind the glass gasped. Some even screamed and ran like they were in danger and the arena descended into chaos.

"Uh… I'm ready to swap with you," Foley shouted as he turned and ran towards the soldiers.

He still carried his rifle, but Marcus had seen him fire seven bullets, and in a thirty-round mag, it meant Foley only had twenty-three left. At least he had been firing one round at a time because if he'd been firing in bursts, there'd likely be no ammo left already.

Rat-a-tat. Foley had turned and fired during his retreat, but he'd now switched his weapon to burst fire and within a few seconds, the rifle clicked. It was the one sound that no soldier in the heat of combat wanted to hear. Even less one without cover, facing a quickly advancing enemy.

"Foley! Run!" King shouted, and she was quickly joined by all of the other soldiers shouting their encouragement.

"What do we do?" Marcus asked quickly. "They'll be here in a second. What do we do?"

"You stand your ground and meet your fate as a soldier," McCulloch replied through gritted teeth.

Then, like it was a gift from God, sections of the ceiling above the soldiers folded open, and hundreds of SA80 rifles descended on thin robotic arms. Clearly one for each of the soldiers.

"Scratch that order," McCulloch said, taking hold of a rifle. "We do our job as soldiers and engage the enemy."

By the time everyone had retrieved a rifle and Foley had ran around to the back of the elevator – still on the outside and stuck in the arena with the terrifying Scriven – the soldiers had arranged themselves into rows of prone, kneeling and standing.

Bang.

The first volley was a single shot from each of the soldiers and took out hundreds of the advancing Scriven. Their bodies littered the ground as the bulk of the force continued to advance, and the soldiers took their second and third shots to thin the ranks again. It was clear from the progression of the enemy and the speed that they were falling though, that at this rate they would reach the soldiers' elevator cage in less than ten seconds.

"Burst fire!" McCulloch shouted.

The soldiers, as one, obeyed.

Bang, bang, bang.

Another volley rang out, though this time each rifle fired multiple shots and the Scriven fell in so many numbers that their ranks visibly thinned in that one flurry. Some, though, at the front of the group, managed to defend themselves with their thicker frontal legs and kept coming.

Another volley.

There were few of the alien creatures left now, and it was clear that these were the greatest of their warriors. They were nothing compared to the well-armed, well-trained soldiers of the GSI, though, and after the next shot, the Scriven were all but gone.

That was, of course, all except for one. The spider-like creature had much wider frontal legs than the rest and by the way the concentrated bursts of fire ricocheted off the thing, it was clearly well armoured.

The alien moved cautiously under heavy fire, ensuring that it didn't present any of its vital parts as a target to the humans who were still trapped inside their own cage.

But their ammunition was limited, where its own methods of attack were not and Marcus could somehow sense that it knew that.

The Scriven moved slowly, but it moved towards them nonetheless. And then it was upon them, just outside the cage almost within touching distance. It reared up high on its hind legs, and the soldiers opened fire all at once at its unprotected undercarriage. It was clearly a softer target, and the moment the bullets started hitting home, deep red blood and black sprayed out and coated the frontmost soldiers in the cage.

The creature had been beaten, but it had one last sting in its tail. As it fell, it extended one of its razor-sharp legs and pushed it into the humans' cage. The leg skewered one of the soldiers straight through his heart and pinned him to the floor. He had been killed instantly, and it had seemed to Marcus like it had been the only objective of the Scriven warrior. To prove that these humans weren't immortal.

The entire arena filled with a deafening stillness and silence.

And then the announcer walked cautiously back onto the sands, careful not to step on any Scriven parts, and again carrying his cattle prod to the ready just in case any of them had managed to survive.

"My friends, would you look at that!" His voice carried around the arena but it still didn't sound very sure. "Two-thousand Scriven warriors – though let us not forget that these were the ones we managed to catch – and they traded their lives for that of one single human being. If you ask me, I think that's a pretty good trade on the side of the humans, no?"

The announcer spoke about how strong, precise and mighty the humans had been, but also made the effort to downplay the ferocity and strength of these Scriven in particular.

"This was a set-up," Marcus growled under his breath to Ramirez. "They knew this was going to happen. Did you see how the guns just dropped from the ceiling? Why else would they be in there?"

"Maybe," Ramirez said. "But wasn't it worth it to see Foley running and screaming?"

"Hey, I could've died out there," Foley said from just outside the cage. "But at least I killed more of those things than either of you did."

"How in the hell would you know that Foley?" King joined the conversation. "You killed what, seven before you ran like a little girl? I know for a fact that I hit at least twenty."

"Whatever," Foley said.

And just like that, the cage that had been keeping the humans inside – and mostly safe from the Scriven attack fell open. The soldiers all filtered out and took up formation on the sands, facing the announcer.

Marcus was one of the few who looked back at the man who the dead Scriven had skewered, left alone in the cage. He was still and quiet, but somehow it seemed so much worse than the bodies he'd seen back at the Canada Road barracks. Because something had done this on purpose. Something that was far worse than anything he could've ever imagined.

That last Scriven had been a terrifying beast, but Marcus couldn't help feel that even though the creature absolutely knew it was going to die, it was hell-bent on taking at least one enemy down with it. The thought was worrying. This enemy was clearly used to simply throwing numbers at an opposing force. An enemy which must've had so many numbers that losses didn't matter.

If this was the way things were done out here in the big, bad universe, then it didn't bode well for the tiny, insignificant human race.

Marcus gripped his rifle tightly, his knuckles turning white.

'I won't let this happen again,' he thought. 'We'll show the universe that we're not to be messed with.'

Chapter 23 – Truth

The next phase on Talon station, was to meet with a being that the Baccus seemed to simply call "The Overseer". The soldiers had been told that, every station had one, and they almost always belonged to a single race of beings. It was clear that this thing wasn't going to be a Baccus, a fact that the Baccus leading the soldiers – who had all been told to leave their rifles behind – couldn't help but reiterate on more than one occasion.

As they all moved through the station and the majority of the inhabitants moved out of their way to let them pass, Marcus realised something: most of the Baccus on the station didn't look like warriors. In fact, many of them were clearly women and children, and when he looked closer, he could see that most of them were wounded, too.

"Are you going to help us win the war?" A tiny voice caught Marcus' attention, and he turned to see a small blue Baccus girl asking the question in the general direction of the human soldiers. Nobody had stopped to answer her, though.

That was until Marcus reached her.

"What happened to you?" He couldn't help but ask the first question that came to his mind as he took a knee in front of her. The little girl that he'd presumed was just sitting on the ground, he now realised had no legs.

"Are you going to help us?" the little girl asked again, dodging Marcus' own question.

"I think so," Marcus replied honestly. "I think we've been brought here to do something for your people. But tell me, why are there so many hurt people on this station? And where are your parents?"

"My..." the little girl started to say but stopped herself. "The people are all here because of the war," she said. "Some don't come back when they go away, but I don't know what happens to them. Like my mum and dad. They went a long time but never came back."

Marcus' heart sank. The girl seemed so strong, like what she was saying was all just so normal to her. But he knew it was anything but.

"Did... did you get hurt in the war?" Marcus asked.

The girl nodded. "We were rescued by the soldiers before the big crawlers got to us. My mum said I was lucky it was just my legs, but I do not feel lucky. Would you feel lucky if you did not have your legs any more? I liked to play with my friends, and now they run much faster than me. They do not really talk to me any more." Then her eyes widened, "Do you think you can get me new legs so that I can play again?"

Marcus forced a smile. "If there is ever any way that I can do that for you, I promise I'll do it," he said. "What's your name?"

"Toria," the girl said. "I do not like the Scriven. And I saw what you can do with your guns."

"You saw that?" Marcus asked, shocked that anyone would allow a child to see such a spectacle, though in reality he had no idea of the customs of these alien beings. Or come to think of it, how old this Baccus was.

Toria nodded. "They are not nice," she said with a grimace. "But it will be OK because you are here now?"

"Cesari, pick up your feet!" McCulloch called from the group of soldiers slowly moving away from him.

Marcus stood up to his full height again and gave Toria a smile and one final promise: "We'll do whatever we can to help you. I have a feeling that's why we're here. Now I want you to stay out of trouble, OK?"

Toria smiled and nodded. "I will," she said.

Then Marcus had a thought. "You should go and ask to see Dr. Kono. He's a really good doctor, so he might be able to help you. If you find him, tell him Marcus Cesari sent you, and he wanted to make a six million dollar man, he'll know what that means."

"I will," Toria repeated. Then added: "Thank you," before turning away to watch the soldiers as they left.

The soldiers all continued along the maze of corridors that comprised the station, past door after door until they all came to an elevator, though this time it was more traditional – solid and a lot smaller than the cage had been. So much smaller, in fact, that to get all of the soldiers up to where they needed to be, it took twenty trips, and as Marcus was at the back of the pack, he had been in the last. At least each trip only took twenty seconds or so.

When it was Marcus' turn and the elevator came to a halt, the doors opened to a large open, carpeted room. There were sofas and chairs all around, and it looked like it was a place that had been made specifically for someone important. A far cry from what Marcus had seen of the place so far.

The soldiers had all been waiting for the last group to arrive, and they all stood in the large room facing what Marcus instinctively knew to be 'The Overseer'.

Sat on a red velvety sofa, was the thin grey-skinned alien with slits for nostrils and a tuft of dark grey hair atop his head. And it was nothing like the blue-skinned Baccus. This one looked like it thought itself royalty, and there were no two ways about it.

When the creature saw that the entirety of the human complement had made it up in the lift, it stood up to its full height of a long seven feet. Not a soldier in the room made a sound nor a move.

"Welcome. Please feel free to take a seat and wait here. I would like to have a short conversation with each of you if I may?" The creature gestured with a long open hand to the sofas in the room. Its voice was smooth and official, which was what was expected from the look of the thing. "I am The Overseer, and I am pleased to welcome you… humans… to my station, please feel free to eat and drink anything that takes your fancy; our supplies here are bountiful and I believe that everything we have to offer is compatible with your physiology."

"Speak with each of us?" Foley whispered. "That'll take all day, won't it?"

Marcus nodded. "But if they're giving us all the food we can eat, then it's fine by me. Not like we have anything better to do, right? I'd rather be up here than back in the arena with those Scriven."

"You know what Foley, I think it's about time we had that arm wrestle," King announced. "We've got time, there's food, and a load of witnesses."

Foley grinned. "Yeah, I'm up for that," he said. "Right here on the floor?"

The Overseer spoke again, apparently having heard what Foley and King were saying.

"Ah yes, please help yourself to whatever you like. I'm sure you'll find things to your liking within these quarters."

A long time passed. Arm wrestling and eating soon became the soldiers' two favourite things to do in the world, but it quickly became apparent that many of the arm wrestling matches were more like wars of attrition than showcases of actual strength. Foley had beaten King twice, then she had returned the favour and won the next two battles. Calling a truce, the rest of the soldiers got in on the act, and within hours, everyone was a part of the competition, with multiple contests going on all around the room.

Every few minutes, The Overseer would bring one of the soldiers back and take another, and the group quizzed the one who returned, but never had anything interesting to report. The Overseer would ask questions, they would chat, then he would return them. By the time it was Marcus' turn to be called through, he was almost happy to go so that he could ask exactly what all of this was about.

When he got the call, Marcus followed The Overseer into another much smaller room where two small sofas faced each other. The Overseer immediately sat on one and gestured for Marcus to sit on the other. It was very close and perhaps a little uncomfortable, but Marcus kept a straight face.

"It is a pleasure to meet you," The Overseer said. "What is it that you like to be known as?"

"Marcus," Marcus replied. "And you are The Overseer. I want you to tell me why we were brought in like cattle to be showcased, and now one of us is dead."

The Overseer peered at Marcus in silence for a long moment before he spoke again.

"I am afraid that I am not of the Baccus and have no direct dealings with them nor the humans on the station. Would you like to have a conversation with me where we can both learn something about the other?" It asked.

"Yes," Marcus said. "That would be helpful." He sighed but could tell that The Overseer had been truthful - he didn't have anything to do with the treatment of the human soldiers.

"You are not like the others," it said.

"Why do you say that?"

"Because when I asked you your name, you are the first to reply without a rank or title, and I am also assuming that you have given me your first name, and not your family name."

Marcus blinked. He hadn't even thought about giving a rank and surname, though it could well have been a natural reaction for the others.

"Do not misunderstand me," The Overseer said. "It is not a bad thing, nor a good thing. It is just… a thing."

"Do you have another name? Is The Overseer your title or…" Marcus asked.

"I once had a name a long time ago. However in my race, we are often known by our titles. If I were to be in a room filled with other Overseers, my specific label would be Overseer four eight two. What is your family name?"

"Cesari," Marcus said. "My full name is Marcus Cesari."

"Ah, I shall remember that, Marcus Cesari," The Overseer said. "It does have the ring of a hero, does it not?"

"Hero?"

"That is what you are here to become, is it not?"

"Honestly, I don't know what we're doing here."

"Then why not have a guess?"

Marcus closed his eyes and thought about everything that had brought him to this very moment. And then he opened his mouth and the words just came out.

"We are here to help the Baccus in a war against the Scriven. They seem to be having trouble with it, but I don't know why. The soldiers from earth have been sponsored by this race of aliens as a last gasp… or at least, that's what this all seems like to me."

"That is very perceptive of you, Marcus Cesari," The Overseer said, overtly not confirming or denying the supposition. "So tell me, what led you to this place?"

"Well, the Scriven in the cages first," Marcus started.

"I apologise, but I have moved on to the next part of our conversation," The Overseer said. "I am now asking specifically why you decided to become a soldier."

That was a question that Marcus hadn't been expecting, and it felt like it gave him whiplash. He was about to spill his deductions of why he thought they were going to be thrown into a war, but apparently that line of questioning was over.

"To help people in need?" Marcus said slowly. It was a bald-faced lie, and he knew it, but he wasn't about to give this creature his entire backstory.

The Overseer blinked and steepled his long grey fingers.

"Interesting," it said.

"Does it matter?" Marcus asked. It was something the old him would've said. He knew the words came out like a challenge, not like something a soldier would say at all.

"I thought that we would have a civilised conversation, Marcus Cesari," The Overseer said. "But how can that be when we do not have trust between us? A lie, no less."

"I… uh," Marcus stuttered.

"You see, my race makes for exceptional diplomats, and that is the reason we are often asked to become Overseers of ships, stations and even, in some cases, entire worlds. The reason that this is so is because of our natural ability to tell the truth from lies. So I will give you one more chance to answer my question truthfully."

Of course the alien was talking about his last question, though in that moment, Marcus saw what was happening as clear as day. This Overseer was interviewing every soldier to ascertain what kind of threat they all posed to themselves, to others, the station, and possibly even the universe as a whole.

"I became a soldier to help my father," Marcus answered truthfully this time. "I haven't been with the army very long, but the program gave me a way to get medical aid for him, so I agreed to join."

"Ah, that sounds like a much better answer," The Overseer said, relaxing somewhat. "And do you have any malice aimed towards your comrades, any alien races, or this station perhaps?"

"No," Marcus replied flatly. Then added: "Although I would like to punch Dr. Kono in the face if I ever see him again. And perhaps the Scriven. Oh and the Baccus announcer, he seems like the type to need a good punching. But from what I have seen since being here on the station, the Scriven are the bad guys in all this, right?"

The Overseer nodded.

"They are indeed being portrayed as the 'bad guys' to you," he said. "Though as my race is impartial to all of this, I cannot say that I would share that view one way or the other."

"One of them killed one of my friends," Marcus said. "It would be hard for me not to blame them. And then there are the women and children, the walking wounded right here on the station. Surely you can see…"

"As I have said, I am impartial in this matter. But I would offer you this question: When you were in that cage in the arena, if one of the Scriven had been freed to kill you one by one like it was a show or a sport whilst you were locked away and unable to retaliate, would your people not have responded in the same way given the chance?"

"But I saw the people on the station…" Marcus replied. The question swirled around his mind, though, and it raised a very good point.

"The Baccus are on this station because they have paid for it. It is as simple as that. If you were to visit a Scriven-controlled system where their young and females had been wounded by the horrors of war, I wonder, would you feel the same way?"

"I… uh…" Marcus struggled.

"But do not misunderstand me, Marcus Cesari. My race are genetically programmed to search for truth, not to take sides. I provide hypotheticals in this and not facts. I do not believe that either side in this is wrong or right, I only know that it is happening and that you are here right now."

Marcus opened and closed his mouth a few times, searching for something to say.

"Our conversation has been interesting, Marcus Cesari. Different to the others, for sure. I hope that you will return someday so that we can have another."

The Overseer then stood up in the universal gesture for: 'I'm done with this conversation, please leave', and Marcus turned and left the room without another word. His head was spinning and he didn't know if it was something that being in the presence of The Overseer had done, or if his mind was still analysing everything that had happened to him thus far.

Chapter 24 – Prepare to Fight

"Do you see, friends?" The Baccus announcer from the arena cooed as he walked past the ranks of the human soldiers, followed by an entourage of similar beings. "Aren't they marvellous up close? Like titans, ready to fight and kill, untouchable by even the mightiest Scriven warrior."

The soldiers had been arranged in formation in a large, brightly lit room so that the Baccus could parade them around. Callahan had appeared momentarily to warn the soldiers not to react to anything they did, and to follow orders from the announcer as though he was their CO.

Marcus pondered the fact that the one Scriven who had made it into close quarters with a human soldier had seemingly killed him without much issue, but on the other hand, the humans had taken down literally thousands of the belligerent spider-like enemy for just that small cost.

The Baccus were relatively small beings. Well, at least compared to the ever-growing stature of the members of Operation Legacy. The humans towered over the aliens as they walked the line, surveying the beings that they had been told about, but before today had never seen.

"I wager one battalion of human soldiers against an entire hive of Scriven, complete with queen and guardians any day," the Baccus continued speaking.

"Are you sure they'll fight for us?" Another of the Baccus asked. They were talking like the humans couldn't hear them, or perhaps that they weren't worthy of their direct attention.

"Why don't you ask them?" The announcer replied. "I understand that as part of their gene therapy back on their home planet, they were equipped with our universal translation technology."

The other Baccus looked shocked by the fact that the humans were all listening to them talking about them and turned to face the soldier nearest her.

"Can you understand me, human?" she asked. Her tone was polite, and if anything, Marcus thought, quite well-spoken.

"Yes, ma'am," the soldier replied. "We understand you like you're all speaking English."

"Well, doesn't that just make things a lot easier," the Baccus replied with a smile. "Tell me though, such an astute fighting force… are you happy to fight for an alien race that you didn't even know existed a week ago?"

"As soldiers, we act as we are ordered, ma'am," the soldier replied.

"But what if you disagree with an order you are given?"

"It is not our duty to question orders, ma'am," the soldier replied again.

The Baccus appeared intrigued and perplexed by the soldiers' unwavering dedication to following orders. They exchanged glances, as if silently communicating their thoughts amongst themselves.

"I find it truly fascinating," the announcer mused aloud. "These humans, so disciplined, so obedient. They follow orders without question, even when faced with the unknown. To have such an asset on the battlefield will be a great boon to our war effort."

The female Baccus replied, "But can they truly be trusted, even with their impressive capabilities? We have seen their strength, but we know little of their motivations." Then she turned back to the soldier. "Tell me, what would happen if you were given an order to kill me right now?"

The soldier opened his mouth to reply with an immediate answer, then appeared to change his mind and say something else.

"Our standing orders are currently to treat this Baccus," he gestured towards the announcer with a flick of his eyes, "as our commanding officer. Therefore, the order would have to come from him directly."

"Right," the female alien said. "So if it was ordered by your own… Callahan," she recalled, "or Salek here, you would do it? You would kill me without hesitation?"

"If such an order was given, it would not be within my position to question the relevancy or reasoning of such an act," the soldier replied.

"So you would do it?" the alien pressed.

"Yes," the soldier replied, not having anywhere else to go in this conversation.

The Baccus regarded the soldier with a mixture of curiosity and concern. "You would take a life without hesitation, even if it went against your moral code or sense of right and wrong?"

The soldier paused for a moment, his expression unreadable behind his disciplined demeanour. "My moral code is to follow orders, to serve and protect. That is what I was trained for."

The Baccus nodded slowly. "Your loyalty is unwavering. It is a trait we find both admirable and troubling. Loyalty to one's comrades and mission is commendable, but blind obedience can also lead to great harm. I want you to remember this."

"Ma'am?" the soldier replied.

"I want all of you to hear this," the Baccus raised her voice. "When you are out there on the battlefield, facing a field full of the enemy, it is not their sharpened legs nor their beaks, nor their acidic blood that you should fear above all else. There are those within the ranks of the Scriven, those with an enhanced intelligence that are able to fog your mind. Incept concepts that you believe to be your own." Then she lowered her voice again to speak to the soldier directly. "What would you do if a Scriven has invaded your mind, and you are unsure as to where your orders are coming from? Perhaps you are being told to kill your friends, your comrades, but it is in the voice and tone of your commanding officer?"

The soldier then lowered his head to look the Baccus dead in the eye.

"There won't be any Scriven left to cause such trouble," he said. "Not once we arrive on the battlefield."

The Baccus looked a little shocked at that, but eventually nodded and moved away. The announcer continued speaking loudly about how well-trained these humans were, and that the Scriven had no chance against them. Marcus couldn't help but find the whole situation strange – like it was nice to be admired, but this was just a little much. Even Foley started to look uncomfortable.

Then, the announcer rounded off his speech with an announcement that turned heads.

"And we have decided that in order to aid our war effort as swiftly as possible, these soldiers will be briefed and sent along on their way to the front lines, today."

Nobody said a word, and the announcer's voice quietened as he and his entourage left the room. Then a second later the door swung open again and Callahan entered.

"At ease, people," he said. His voice wasn't as enigmatic as it usually was, and Marcus could tell that he didn't want to say what he was about to. It didn't matter though, everyone in the room knew what was coming.

"Are we going to war, sir?" Someone asked, and Callahan's head whipped around towards the soldier who'd spoken out of turn. The room turned cold.

Then Callahan exhaled loudly.

"Yes," he said. "Tonight is the night of nights, so to speak. And I know that this wasn't what many of you had expected. Hell, if you'd have been told about everything that was going to happen to you six months ago, I bet you'd look at me like I owned a box of frogs. Or whatever that saying is. It doesn't matter, I suppose."

Callahan was speaking like someone without a true purpose, and it made Marcus nervous.

"The thing is, this is what we were made for. And I say we because I will be joining you on the field of battle. Our sponsors, the Baccus central government, need our help, and that is why you have all been a part of this special operation. Now I know it may seem strange – why would an advanced alien race need us for anything, and the answer is simple. We are warriors, the best of the best and the Baccus seem to have forgotten that particular art. The Scriven have not."

"So they can just buy us?" Another soldier asked, clearly bolstered by the fact the first hadn't been shouted at for speaking out of turn.

"This is bigger than us, son," Callahan replied. "Bigger than all of us, myself included. The advancements made by Dr. Kono and the equipment promised to earth are for the benefit of all mankind, and forever. What we have promised the Baccus is a small contingent as a token of good faith between our peoples. Up until recently, none of us had any idea how big the universe actually is out there. Any help we can get, frankly, is sorely needed."

A moment of silence passed.

"Are they giving us better guns?" Foley's voice rang out, and Marcus winced.

"Now you saw how effective your weapons are against this enemy we are to face," Callahan said. "And you tell me what would be better than the weapons you have all trained with, and plainly speaking, are the very best in the universe at wielding."

"Have you been modified?" Someone else asked.

Callahan smiled and turned away. "Now that would be telling, wouldn't it," he said.

Over the next few hours, the soldiers were all given a little time to themselves, and also a briefing of what they were to expect when they entered this unknown alien war. It was a Baccus that was giving them the rundown of the situation, after they had already been shown the transport ships that would take them from the station to the planet, and how the escape pods worked should they need them. It was all very much the same as on earth in regular ships – if the thing was going down, then you jumped in a lifeboat and away you went.

"There are multiple transports that will take you into orbit, and from there you will be transported to the surface in individual drop pods. In the years that we have been fighting this war, we have not encountered any resistance to our orbital or flying machines, so we have found this the best way to send reinforcements down to the planet's surface."

Next to Marcus, King raised her hand and the Baccus pointed to her.

"If there's no airborne resistance, then why don't you just wipe them out from space?" she asked. "There'd be no risk then, lives saved and all that?"

"That is a very good question, and one that is frequently posed. It is always an option for us to do so, but we are not quite there yet. We have many tens of thousands of troops on the ground scattered across the planet, and the Scriven have a tendency to… well, burrow. When we have conducted small, contained orbital strikes in the past, the Scriven have managed to evade total destruction, and their nests are so deep in the ground that they remain largely undamaged. You must also remember that this planet was recently home to many of our people, so mass destruction is not entirely palatable. Lastly, this planet does have large yet infrequent deposits of natural gasses deep below the surface. Scanning for these has proven time-consuming and difficult, though safe to say that if one of these pockets is high with large enough ordinance, well, it would be goodbye planet."

King grimaced and didn't ask a follow-up question. The response had been a pretty resounding 'no we aren't going to do that', and to press the subject wasn't going to help anything.

"The distance from Talon station and the planet is less than a day, which is why this place was chosen as an operation station in this war," the Baccus continued. "In your drop pods, you will find supplies enough for a prolonged conflict should they be required."

This time, Marcus couldn't help but raise his hand. "How long are we expected to remain on the planet for?" he asked. "I mean, if you're giving us long-term supplies, then are you expecting us to dig in? What are the victory conditions here? What are our objectives?"

"All very good questions," the Baccus replied. "The supplies are there in case they are needed for you, but primarily they are to resupply our warriors already on the surface. But from what we have seen of your combat prowess, we do not expect them to be needed for very long. Your mission is as follows: You will arrive at a Baccus stronghold – that is a prefabricated forward operating base on the surface that has automated defences and other deterrents designed to ward off the Scriven. From there, you will co-ordinate your attacks on the surrounding nest or enemy combatants until the area has been cleared. Then you will be collected by a troop transport and taken to a second location, repeating your task over and over. There are a total of ten of these operating bases on the surface of the planet, all of which were placed centrally to known hive activity. Each hive will have a queen, and it has been determined that if we kill these queens in quick succession, then the Scriven will not have time to regenerate, and the entirety of their race on the planet will be unsustainable, and will eventually fall. We do not need you to be a part of what we are calling the clean-up operation, but understand that ultimately, your job is to kill the ten queens that we suspect are active under the surface near these locations."

"Right," Marcus said. "So you drop us into the enemy homes and hope we can kill the queens, where hundreds of thousands of your own people have been unable to do."

"That is the gist of it," the Baccus said. "But understand that inside the perimeters of these forward operating bases, you will be more than safe. The Scriven are base creatures, unable to break through. But the Baccus are not a warring race and we have thus far only been able to kill one hive queen, and it took over a year of careful planning and battlefield manipulation."

"So again," Marcus said. "If it took you a year to kill one, how long do you expect it'll take us to kill ten?"

"Like a day or two?" Foley piped up. "Give me two flame throwers, a handful of grenades and point me to their caves. They'll be on their backs and curling up their legs in no time."

"Didn't look that way to me when you were running away from them in the arena," King said.

"We anticipate," the Baccus said, interrupting the soldiers, "that given your tactical knowledge and battlefield prowess, you should be able to advance on each of these hives and clear them out in no more than an earth week or two each. Does that answer your question?"

Marcus nodded, but his mind was still whirring. There was still something that wasn't adding up. Some piece of information that he instinctively knew was being hidden from them all. And whatever it was, it was dangerous. Something that could get them all killed.

But mainly, he still didn't understand why a few hundred human soldiers were going to be sent into a warzone of hundreds of thousands of Baccus and expected to do what the Baccus couldn't. Unless, of course, they were simply seen as the suicide squad in all of this. Or worse, perhaps even a decoy.

"Now, if you are ready, I will explain to you and show you how our storage systems work and where you will find your supplies in your pods once you arrive on the planet. But there will be teams of Baccus on the surface ready to help you once you arrive, and I believe that you will find them all most hospitable. You are all something that can end this war for us, and that is something that we will be forever grateful for."

The Baccus then led the human soldiers into another section of the base, where a ring of troop transports were sat idle. On the sides of each of these were cylindrical shapes about the right size for one person, if they stooped down a little and it didn't take much explaining from the Baccus for the soldiers to understand what they were and how they worked.

"I don't like this," Marcus said under his breath, just loud enough for Ramirez to hear. "They can't expect a few hundred of us to win a war for them that they've been fighting for years, and they have technology that we could only dream of. Doesn't that sound a little off to you?"

Ramirez nodded subtly. "It does. But what do you want to do? Tell them thanks but no thanks, and by the way, please drop me off at earth whenever it's convenient?"

"We could kill them all?" King said as she clearly overheard the conversation. "You know, when we get our guns just turn around, take the station and live here in happiness forever. Like pirates."

"Will you three shut up," McCulloch growled. "I know you think you're being quiet, but I can hear every word you're saying. Nobody is conducting a mutiny, nobody is deserting. We're here to do a job, and the quicker we do it, the quicker we can all go home."

"Sir, yes sir," Foley said. "But just out of interest, do you think we're actually going to make it home? And if we do, what do you think they're going to do with us? Don't we know too much or something?"

"Maybe they'll send us to America, you know, Area Fifty-One or something?" Ramirez said. "You know, cut us open and see what's happened to our organs out here in space."

"Maybe they'll throw you a God damned parade," McCulloch said. "Just for you two, Foley and Ramirez, because you're such damn heroes. Now shut up and listen to what we've got to do next. I don't want to die because you pressed the green button when it should've been the red."

"Jesus McCulloch," Ramirez said. "We were just talking, no need to go all do or die on us. We know the deal: land on the planet, go to a base surrounded by a nest of alien war spiders, kill the queen, get picked up, rinse and repeat ten times. Seems pretty simple to me."

"You haven't seen them run at you," Foley said with a shiver. "I never did like spiders."

'Then it's a good job we're about to go to a planet of probably millions of them, but they're massive and all want to kill you, specifically," Ramirez said.

"At least they won't hide in my shoes," Foley said.

"I just hope they aren't the kind that lay eggs in your stomach," King said. "You know, then later they eat you from the inside out and burst free from your chest cavity?"

"You watch too much TV," Marcus said. "These ones probably just pin you down with four of their legs and then bite your head off. You know, real spidery stuff."

Foley had stopped responding by this point and the colour wasn't returning to his face, though he was making a definite effort not to look worried.

"I'll kill them all," he muttered. "Guns, fire, knives, whatever." Then he added as an afterthought: "Hey, maybe we should've brought some insect repellent!"

Ramirez face palmed.

"Just… if a little one gets inside your clothes, don't come to me for help," she said. "Run the other way, as far and as fast as you can, you got that?"

The group laughed, but their fun and games were to be short-lived, because a moment later, they'd boarded the troop transports and were on their way.

A dozen hours passed, and the troop transports were all hovering over the dusty orange planet, ready to drop the humans at their first designated forward base. They had been told that the atmosphere was breathable for the most part, though it was best to wear a helmet for long periods of time, which the soldiers all wore during the journey. Their overalls would connect with the helmet and provide them with clean air almost indefinitely, and they weren't in full space suits so they didn't have any communications issues to overcome or bulky gloves to deal with. In fact, they still wore the same overalls and boots they'd trained in.

The Baccus had adapted to survive without the need for purification on the planet.

There were six troop transports, each equipped to hold up to one hundred humans – a number dictated by the number of drop pods attached to each. Once the area had been cleared and purged of any Scriven activity below, the transports would then land in the newly safe area and pick them all up manually, along with their pods.

Everything was going to plan so far, and the humans were stuck somewhere between anxious to go to war, and wanting to see what they could really do out there to make a difference in the wider universe.

Official Records – Thoughts from Marcus Cesari, Into the Frying Pan

When we arrived at the planet where the main war against the Scriven was being waged, we had no idea what to expect. No frame of reference for what was about to happen to us. But in reality, I don't think we could've ever been prepared for what faced us. All we knew was that there were ten bases, ten nests and ten queens. Oh and we could see that it had two suns. That stuck with me, the sight of two burning balls of light in the sky. It was like a constant reminder that it wasn't earth.

Even from high above, we could see that the face of the planet had been battered and scorched over a long time, because there were ruins everywhere and no signs of life. Well, none other than the rumble of gunfire and the flashes of explosions all across the landscape. Presumably the Baccus had been doing their job at keeping the Scriven at bay, but from what we'd been told, this whole conflict was in a deadlock.

The landing had been a disaster from start to finish. I don't know if they'd been expecting it to go down like that, but we lost a lot of soldiers, good men and women before they even had the chance to show the universe what they were made of. We ended up spread out and in unfamiliar territory, and that was a bad position to be in.

We were all ready to drop, waiting in our pods for the green light, when they started firing the pods out like we were missiles. I could see through the little window all of us launching, and more than a handful of them shot straight down at the ground below and exploded on impact. Some flew up into space, and some even collided with each other. It was a miracle that my pod didn't seem affected by whatever the malfunction was that was causing us all this trouble. It was clear that we weren't yet in position either because I couldn't see any sign of a forward base below us. Where some landed successfully, they were nowhere near where they were supposed to be. I tried shouting through our comms network to anyone who could hear me, but I got no response. In fact, the moment we arrived in orbit, all of the comms equipment went strange.

It was far worse for some of the others though, because I even saw two of the transports crash into each other, bursting into in a ball of fire. So many must've died right there and then. It was like the world had turned insane, and it was doing everything it could to take us out before we could touch down on the planet.

At least some of us made it, that was the only positive I could take from all of this, but I had no idea how many. Eventually, when my pod launched, all I could do was grit my teeth and hope and pray that I didn't go down like so many of the others. I needed a landing so that at least I'd have a fighting chance. That was the worst part of the others falling: that they didn't have the chance to fight back, to have a chance of survival no matter how slim it might've been.

It was a Godsend that me and the other pods in the Seventy-First remained together, and we were joined by a few others whose pods had taken them close by to where we'd landed, but it was a far cry from the hundreds we'd been expecting. In the end, we were few. But at least we were alive.

Once we'd landed and regrouped, we concluded that the volume of our arrival would've alerted the enemy to our presence, so we knew that whatever we were going to do, we needed to do it quickly.

Thank God that the escape pods from the transport were equipped with armouries, so we stocked up on everything we could. And it wasn't just weapons, but also there were strange meal bars that could fill you up in one bite – Foley took a liking to those - and flasks that pulled moisture from the atmosphere. I guess those Baccus really knew how to equip a soldier for a long war. A long war they told us they hadn't been expecting. We all just hoped that it wasn't going to be too long. In some ways, we were right.

I took an SA80, a long-range rifle and a pistol. Of course, as many bullets and magazines as I could carry, and we took turns carrying the crates of supplies between us. The weapons were all of earth design so we all knew what we had, which was helpful. If we hadn't, then I don't know if we'd have lasted as long as we did.

We tried to communicate with anyone we could through our radios, but they weren't working and it didn't seem to be temporary because we tried regularly. I guess whatever happened to the transport ships had broken the comms too. And that meant for the foreseeable, we were alone.

Oh, the others who managed to join us were Johnstone, Carter, Asimov, Hernandez, and Hunter. There had been another, his name was Wilson but he didn't make it, his body was just too broken when his pod had impacted the ground. We were a grand fighting force of ten. Ten from hundreds, and we didn't know why or how any of this had happened.

The women, Ava Hunter, Sofia Hernandez and Olivia Carter seemed quieter than what I was used to in Ramirez and King, but I think it might've just been the trauma in watching our friends die out there so senselessly, miles away from the enemies they planned to fight. Honestly, I didn't know what they'd used to hit us, or what their capabilities were because we had all been under the impression that the Scriven were a basic race, not one capable of manufacturing defences or using weapons. But even then, we hadn't seen any evidence some weapon had been used against us; it was like everything just went wrong somehow.

We knew we needed to take cover and fast, so we moved quickly towards the only place we could see that looked like it might be OK to set up a defence should we need it while we regrouped. It was a huge concrete tunnel littered with large blocks scattered around that looked like they'd provide good cover. Leading up to the tunnel, too, were the remnants of a road that had once been on stilts, like a bridge. Most of it had been destroyed, but it was intact enough for us to walk up to the tunnel entrance. If anything, it would make it an easier position to defend, having a narrow corridor up to our front door.

Once we were set and sure that there weren't any Scriven hiding out in the tunnel, McCulloch ordered us to cover the entrance. It wasn't something I would've thought to do at that point; I wanted to go out and try to save as many humans as we could, but McCulloch was the highest rank of all of us so we had to do what he said. I don't think any of us envied his position though. I know I certainly wouldn't want to make the decisions he did over the coming days.

In hindsight though he was probably right, I doubt that anyone would've survived out there in the open for very long. Not with those things out there.

So I moved into position behind one of the makeshift barricades, picked up my long-range rifle and watched the world outside the tunnel, hoping to be greeted by hundreds of human soldiers making their way towards us, and the rest followed suit. What I saw, though, would be something that would stay with me forever. It was not our friends and allies coming to join us.

In the distance, I could see the ruins of an old city, and between our position and the ruins was a wide-open space littered with twisted metal and bodies, both humanoid and Scriven, like a war had been fought there between the Baccus and the spiders.

It only took a moment, but I was the first to see movement out in the field and relayed the information to the rest. I hadn't actually used a long-range rifle before, but the weapon felt familiar in my hands. It wasn't too different to the SA80, and the scope was clear and well-magnified. I knew that firing on target wasn't going to be an issue, and actually anticipated the first kill somehow. Not that I was bloodthirsty or looking for a fight, but holding that weapon right then in that moment, with allies beside me and within a fortified position, I felt safe. How wrong I was.

The movement, however, could not have been mistaken even if the scope hadn't been so useful. A huge, mottled yellow spider leg raised itself over a burnt-out old, twisted piece of metal and then followed another, then the black beaked head of the first grotesque spider-like Scriven that I would ever see out in the wild. And somehow I knew that where there was one, there would be more.

Like the few others I'd seen, the thing had eight legs, all at least two metres long if they weren't bent at the middle, with its angular head sat atop them like a turret. A long beak that split right down the middle and culminated in a pincer-like point looked as deadly as every single other part of the creature, and at the same time, it looked heavily armoured – as though there was going to be no going tette-a-tette with the thing.

As I watched through my scope, it seemed to be sniffing the air like a dog. And then it turned its turret-like head to pierce my vision with its own three eyes. It raised its head to the sky, let out a deafening screech much like the war cry that I'd heard before, and started scuttling towards us with murderous intent.

McCulloch was the one that ordered us to hold our fire until they got closer.

I can remember now how sweaty my palms were and how fast my heart was beating. I wanted to turn and run. Everything inside of me was telling me to flee. But I didn't. None of us did. This was what we were here for and it didn't matter that the circumstances had changed; the result would be the same: a smoking barrel and a whole pile of dead aliens.

And then more Scriven appeared behind the first and joined the charge. All of a sudden there were so many that I couldn't count them all.

And then we opened fire.

The first round I fired with the sniper rifle barely took any time at all to fly through the air in a perfectly straight line before impacting my target, obliterating it entirely. Blood and gore erupted from the creature as it was struck down, or I suppose more accurately, blown out of existence, but that did nothing to deter the rest of the mob that were quick to overtake their fallen ally and continue toward us. If anything, they seemed invigorated at the loss of their fallen kin. Just like they had been on Talon station. I remember my legs shaking at this point, like they just couldn't control the adrenaline coursing through them.

I fired a few more shots as the others began to join in with their own fire, a mixture of single shots and burst, then more bursts as the enemy came closer and closer. It was like the battle was building and building, and somehow I couldn't wait for the final crescendo.

Scriven were falling by the dozen but even I could tell through my scope that they were still advancing towards us, up the narrow bridge. I gritted my teeth and looked down at my finger turning white as I pulled my trigger so hard, like it would somehow make it fire even faster. The gun creaked under my newfound strength, and I had to make an effort to ease off on it.

It was pure luck that none of these creatures managed to realise that they could withstand our fire if their legs were strong enough like on the station. Though judging by the damage my new rifle did, I guessed that even their hardened shells would be unable to save them from that.

The enemy still advanced. It was like an endless stream that came from seemingly nowhere. I wondered if they were just popping up out of the ground at the sound of battle.

With their increasing numbers, the sniper rifle, I knew, would quickly become obsolete.

This led me to conclude that it was time to swap out for the SA80. I knew that this was the case as soon as the wave of enemies had become so dense before me that I no longer needed to aim to hit them, just shoot over and over. What I was thankful for, though, was the fact that without the long scope of the sniper rifle – the assault rifle did have a degree of magnification, but it paled in comparison – the enemy now seemed a bit further away from me. Like I could let go of the breath I'd been holding from the moment I saw that first creature tearing towards us.

You have no idea how horrifying it truly is to watch an army of Scriven baring down on you, screeching their war cry with nothing but bloodlust in their evil black eyes.

I fired in bursts like the others, but either because of the distance or the inferior power of the weapon compared to my long-range rifle, the shots merely wounded the creatures, and not even that badly. There was only one thing for us to do, and that was wait for them to get closer, just as McCulloch had said.

We still fired, though, with increasingly well-placed shots, aiming at the heads or the joints in the legs. But they were still coming. For days, I would dream about the noise of their cries, the sound of their feet and the gunfire.

Their bodies piled up at the entrance to the tunnel as our gunfire resumed in quick bursts. The proximity made them easier to kill again, but they didn't seem deterred. They were frenzied.

We were all firing as fast as we could, I was just thankful we had so much ammunition with us otherwise, the whole thing would've been over much sooner.

It was Foley who broke first. I don't know why he thought it was a good idea, but he threw two grenades simultaneously towards the tunnel entrance. It killed all the Scriven that had made it inside, bar a few, which we easily picked off. But it also collapsed the entrance, trapping us inside.

We had to illuminate the tunnel with the torches attached to our helmets to make sure none had survived and lurked in the darkness.

Something told me that these creatures enjoyed a lack of light. It was what they lived every day. And fighting an enemy on their terms was never going to be a good thing.

But something kept nagging at me. If this was how the Baccus conducted themselves in a war zone, it was no wonder they were struggling.

Chapter 25 – Hidden

"Jesus Foley," McCulloch called out. "How about next time you wait for the order to throw explosives? Or at least let us know that's what you're doing! There's protocol for a reason."

It was hard to see who was who in the darkness and with the headlamps darting about from person to person, but thankfully everyone was accounted for, and everyone was still pretty much where they had been a couple of minutes ago.

"Ah, don't shout at Foley," Ramirez' voice cut through the darkness. "He probably saw the spiders running towards him again and crapped himself. But seriously, can you blame him?"

"No, it wasn't... I..." Foley started to say, but gave up.

"Well, as long as we're all OK," McCulloch said. "Looks like he's done us a favour anyway. I'd say it'll take them a while to get through all that."

"You think?" Marcus said. "A race of alien beings that we're pretty sure live underground... and you think they're going to have trouble with a cave-in?"

"You... could be right," McCulloch agreed. "At least this tunnel seems to have caved in at the back at some point too, and the concrete above looks pretty sturdy... so we'll at least know which way they're going to come from. Again I mean."

"We already knew where they were coming from," King said. "Right, God damn there," she pointed to the newly caved-in entrance. What we don't know, is how many there are, if they're out there waiting for us, where the nearest base is, and how we're going to get out of here!" her voice rose with every sentence, and when she finished, it echoed all around them in the darkness.

Marcus knew she was right. They needed to come up with a plan, and for that they needed more information. In a position like this, information – or the lack thereof - could mean the difference between life and death.

"Let's assume that they're primal creatures above anything else," Marcus said. "From what I've seen so far, they don't seem to strategize; they just see an enemy and use their numbers to try to overwhelm it."

"Thank you Mr. Preceptive," Ramirez said. "And can you tell me what colour they were? Perhaps their mating habits in the winter months."

"What that means," Marcus continued pointedly, "is that there's a good chance when they don't have an enemy to rush at, they get bored and go home. So maybe if we're quiet, play dead and all that, they'll just go back to where they came from."

"And then what?" Ramirez asked, "We sneak out while they aren't looking and go in search of the nearest base… which is in which direction, by the way?"

"Actually, they said something about there being a tracker or something in the crates, you know, with the rest of the supplies," Foley said.

"What?" three voices said at once.

"Yeah… I mean, weren't you listening to the briefing? Each crate has its own tracking thing on it. I forgot what he called it actually, but apparently if you find one of these crates out in the field, then one of the things inside is this tracker. It'll point you in the direction you're supposed to go, along with the distance too."

"If Foley is the reason I get out of this alive, I'm going to kill myself," Ramirez said.

"Are you guys OK?" Asimov asked in a small voice.

"Don't worry about them," McCulloch said. "Foley's a bit sensitive, and Ramirez and King both like to take the mickey. Marcus here is a bit more perceptive, but sometimes his military prowess leaves something to be desired. What about you guys?"

"Not much to tell, really," Asimov said. "My name's Benjamin, and before all of this, I was a Major. I'm a bit of a fan of astronomy and the universe in general, so you'd think I'd be loving all of this… but it's not quite how I imagined it."

Each of the newcomers then introduced themselves to the team.

Sergeant Olivia Carter was a strong-looking woman who could give King a run for her money, though she seemed less interested in actual sports and fitness and more intrigued by camping, the outdoors and photography.

Lieutenant Sofia Hernandez was a much smaller woman with curly black hair who said she enjoyed reading and cooking. Captain Liam Johnstone was tall and thin with short black hair and piercing green eyes. He had an analytical mind and liked to play strategy games in his spare time. And last was Captain Ava Hunter, another athletic woman, though she enjoyed close combat, unarmed fighting and other things that Marcus thought would be useless when facing the Scriven.

Together, though, the group of ten seemed like they would make an acceptable band – even if they were probably outnumbered by thousands to one.

"We need to take stock of everything we've got," McCulloch said. He might not have outranked the entire group before Operation Legacy, but right now, he was still the highest rank, though more than that, he was a natural-born leader. "And get a hold of those trackers. At least we'll know which way to go with those."

"Got it," Foley announced a moment later, holding up something that looked like a palm-sized illuminated screen. "And I have good news and bad news."

"Is the bad news the fact that God has decided you really are the one to lead us all to salvation?" Ramirez asked. "Because I was serious, you know, if Foley is the one to save us, I'm going to shoot myself right here, right now."

"Nope," Foley said. "Good news is that it shows us which way to go, assuming that it's showing the closest base. It also has a readout telling us how far it is."

"OK sounds suicidey so far," Ramirez said. "And the bad news?"

"The thing that tells us how far away we are…"

"The distance to the POI," Ramirez corrected Foley.

"Yeah that, it's in a language I don't know."

"What?" Ramirez said. "Give it here."

She took the device from Foley and looked it over. "Son of a bitch," she said under her breath. "They give us universal translators and it doesn't extend to actually reading the language?"

"Does it matter?" Marcus asked. "If it was one mile or fifty, we'd still have to make the trip."

"That is a fair point," Asimov said. "So you think we should just wait around for a few hours, dig ourselves out – quietly – and then head on out in the direction that thing says? And you're sure it's pointing us in the right direction – like it isn't an alien thing that displays what direction not to go in?"

"Well, that'd be pretty stupid, wouldn't it?" King asked.

"Pretty stupid yes, but the Baccus have been fighting a war for a long time against an enemy that doesn't use guns. And they just got us all blown out of the sky… so come to your own conclusions."

The cave fell silent for a long moment as the group thought on that.

"Well, I can't think of anything better," Ramirez said, walking over to the newly formed dirt wall. So I say we go with that. Wait around, have a nice bite of meal bar and then dig our way out through the mud and dead bugs." She kicked a flattened Scriven leg as she spoke. "Once we're out of here, we sneak like cartoon robbers across no man's land in the direction the alien telly thing says, then we all have a nice cup of tea once we catch up with the Baccus in their nice cosy base."

"Ramirez, move!" McCulloch shouted.

As Ramirez had been speaking, she hadn't noticed that the Scriven she'd kicked had slowly and silently risen back up to its full height. In fact, nobody had noticed until now as it towered over her. Without the direct light from their headlamps, it was difficult to see anything except what they were specifically looking at.

The creature looked groggy, though, listing from one side to the other, and just before it regained its senses, a rain of fire descended on the Scriven to tear it into pieces. Its blood splattered Ramirez as she watched the creature's obliteration, dumbfounded. Thankfully for her, this one didn't have acidic blood like the Baccus had suggested.

The cave eventually turned quiet again once the Scriven was well and truly dead.

"I think I had it," Ramirez said. She hadn't even raised her weapon.

"Don't worry, little sister," Foley said. "We're here to look after you."

"Call me that again and you'll be the one curled up on the floor with his arms and legs ripped off."

"Alright guys, let's not make this a thing," McCulloch said. "Let's just take a good look at this bug and see what we're dealing with."

The group surrounded the Scriven body, though not before searching for other hidden dangers or Scriven bodies playing dead. It would do them no good to be killed by an enemy they thought they'd already dealt with.

The Scriven was nothing special. It was just like the others, terrifying, huge, full of bullet holes and splattered with blood. That was until Marcus noticed something odd.

"It… it looks like it's sharpened its legs," he said slowly, shining his light on one of the pointed legs that were still intact. "Look at the score marks here," he gestured to the leg. "Like they've been rubbed up against a stone or a wall or something. You know, how you used to hold a penny against a wall when you were a kid."

The group moved closer.

"Could've just got it from digging tunnels, or living in a cramped nest?" Hernandez offered.

"No, look at how the marks all go in one direction, and are all around the back of the leg. It would have to have done that on purpose," Marcus said. "So… these things know what they're doing. They're here to fight, and I think we need to give them a little more credit than the Baccus have."

"You're saying they're intelligent?" Asimov asked.

"I don't know if I'd go that far," Marcus said. But they aren't just seeing an enemy and charging. They're preparing. And that's bad news."

"Jesus Cesari, they're bugs. Give me two grenades and point me at the nest, and I'll show you how to deal with a termite infestation."

"They aren't termites," Johnstone said. "And have you ever heard the expression 'don't kick the hornet's nest'? I mean, technically they aren't hornets either, but you get the idea."

"They'd get the idea," Foley said.

"Something happened to you back there in the barracks, didn't it Foley," Ramirez said. "You seem smarter somehow, like you're completely switched on."

"Really?"

"No."

"I hate you Ramirez."

"It's OK little brother, family often dislike each other."

"Anyway," McCulloch pressed. "Does anyone think this changes anything, or do we stick to the plan?"

"I don't think it changes what we've got to do," Marcus said. "Just that maybe we need to give these things a little more credit. If they aren't stupid, then they're even more dangerous than we thought."

"Got it, smart spiders, can we go?" King asked.

"In a hurry?" Foley said.

"Shut up, Foley," King said.

As planned, the group waited two hours before they made any moves to start digging. They weren't equipped for the task, but thankfully, the dirt and small stones covering the entrance were loose, and it didn't take them long to break through. When they did, there were no signs of living Scriven anywhere, just the dead that they'd felled during that first battle and the ones littering the previous battlefield beyond.

The suns still shone, the world around them was once again a dirty, sandy affair and for once, everything seemed peaceful. There wasn't a Scriven in sight.

"Alright. There's ten of us and three crates to carry," McCulloch announced. There had been more crates, but the soldiers had all placed as much of the contents on their bodies and into the remaining three crates as possible. Their enhanced strength meant that carrying them wasn't going to be a problem, but they were large, so required two people to carry.

"I want six of us rotating the crates and four on the lookout for threats as we move. That's one forward, one on each side and one to the rear. I don't want these things sneaking up on us."

"And what do we do if they spot us? Hernandez asked. "Out there we'll have no cover… and if they swarm us like they did the last time…"

"Let's hope they learned a lesson," McCulloch said. "But if things start going that way, we wait until the last moment before we open fire. We place the crates down as stable firing positions and focus on the Scriven closest to us. Don't use grenades until we're sure there's no other option," he peered at Foley, who shrugged.

"You don't think the noise will attract more of them?" Marcus asked.

"Nah, they make enough noise on their own," McCulloch said. "Unless anyone else has something to add?"

Marcus scratched his chin. "We should stay away from the wide, flat areas," he said. "Try to stick to hills. If we can see as far as possible, then we'll know which ways to avoid. Plus, we'll have the higher ground if something does go bad."

"Sounds like as good a plan as any," McCulloch said. "We'll make a soldier out of you yet, Cesari. Everyone ready?"

He got a simple nod in response from each of the soldiers.

"Alright folks, move out."

Ramirez stopped.

"Actually, I think this might be a bad idea. Maybe we should wait here in case they send rescue teams for us. They must know what happened out there, and there's loads of Baccus at the bases, right? We're safer here than out in the open, aren't we?"

McCulloch shook his head. "We're never going to be safe out here away from the others. For all we know, the Scriven are out there gathering reinforcements to storm this place…"

"For all we know they're hiding six inches under the ground waiting for us to step outside," Ramirez interrupted.

It was clear to Marcus that nearly being killed by one of the alien creatures sat heavily on her, and he could sympathise. If he had been the target of that close call, he didn't think he'd want to go outside either.

"McCulloch's right," Marcus said in a soothing tone. "We don't know enough about this place or about our enemy. For all we know, it'll get dark in five hours, and something even worse will come for us. We need to get to somewhere safe, somewhere where they can tell us what's really happening around here."

"Oh, and when did you become such a brilliant tactician, Cesari," Ramirez asked.

"Does it matter?" McCulloch said. "There are ten of us here right now, and I know it doesn't seem a lot but it could be much worse. I'm not going to sit here and let our environment take us one by one. We go now, try to make it to the nearest base or we all die trying."

Everyone went quiet at that.

"I mean, obviously, I don't want that to happen," he added quietly.

"It really is the best way," Asimov added. "The likelihood is that if we stay here, we die eventually anyway because it means relying on someone else to rescue us. If we wait and nothing happens, we'll be weaker when we eventually do have to make our move."

"And if the enemy is intelligent, they can just whittle us down to nothing," Johnstone said. "It's quite clear that we have to move as soon as we can and as fast as we can."

"I know," Ramirez said. "I know all of that. But it doesn't make it any easier, you know?"

"Oh, don't worry, Ramirez, I'll look after you," Foley said.

"Foley, if you touch me, I'm going to cut your balls off and put them in a Scriven nest like they're eggs."

"Well they are…"

"If you say 'pretty big', I'm going to kill you."

Foley shut his mouth; it was clear that it was exactly what he had in mind to respond with.

The group had decided, regardless of how they were stalling and as one they broke forth through the newly re-opened tunnel entrance and out into the bright light of the twin suns. They all kept close together and carried the crates between them, though none of them had the courage to speak, knowing that if they made too much noise and drew the enemy in, it could mean the end of them.

It didn't take long for the group to leave the concrete tunnel well behind them and thankfully, their methodical movement across the empty plains did nothing to draw out any Scriven. In the end, Marcus felt like the whole thing was more of a training mission than a real life or death situation, with alien enemies potentially always just feet away from them.

It was when the group had made it to the top of a pair of hills straddling a valley that they finally had the chance to take a good look at their surroundings.

It had been an odd ascent to the top of this particular hill; it seemed steeper than most of the others in the area, and the texture was considerably different. Where in other areas, the orange-brown dirt and sand seemed to be compacted together, making traversing the landscape easy, this hill seemed like it was made of a fine, loose sand. In fact, it was so loose that as the group moved, it shifted underfoot and the ones carrying the crates found they were unable to climb the shallow hill effectively.

"OK, chain up," McCulloch ordered, and the soldiers instinctively formed a line that effectively elevated the crates to the summit of the hill by passing them hand to hand between themselves. Marcus had never done this, but knew what was happening immediately. After all the crates quickly made it to the top, he was amazed at just how effective the manoeuvre was.

The soldiers reached the top having crossed what was effectively a desert. Before them, it was something that none had been expecting.

A city stood dark, ruined and smoking in the distance. And before it, a huge basin between wide rolling hills. In front of the city and indicated clearly by the tracking devices from the crates, stood a fortress. High stone walls, metal fences, watchtowers and firing positions. This was the first of the forward operating bases that the human soldiers had come to make their new temporary home. And they were so close.

Chapter 26 – Close but no Cigar

"Stop," McCulloch ordered and lowered himself to his knees. The rest of the group dutifully followed suit. They had taken the opportunity to drop the crates, so lying down on the top of the hill would've been a great protected vantage point should they have needed it for defensive purposes.

McCulloch pointed into the open space between their current position and the forward operating base.

"That's where we're going," he said. "But look at all that…"

Marcus followed McCulloch's point. He saw the fortress in the distance, probably only a couple of miles away and then he traced his vision down to the valley between them and it.

The ground was like a blackened, charred graveyard, and if he hadn't looked directly at it, he might've missed it. It was filled, covered almost entirely by the charred, dead bodies of the Scriven.

"Is that… are those…" Hernandez asked under her breath.

"It's a graveyard," Johnstone said. "But… it's a good thing. It's common for animals and insects to understand what this is. If so many died before then it's a dangerous place to be, and they'll give it a wide berth."

"Sounds like a good idea to me," Hernandez said. "I don't think we should be walking through that place either."

"Oh, come on, Hernandez," Hunter said. "You've got to look at this in a different way. If the Scriven aren't going near it, then they won't come in to attack us."

"Yeah, and what if they aren't all dead?" Hernandez replied.

"Have you seen it down there?" Foley asked. "The place looks like it's been dead for weeks. The ground's scorched but not smoking, so whatever happened, it's been done with for a while."

"Yeah, and let's see how you feel the next time one plays dead next to you and then miraculously comes back to life," Ramirez spat.

"All I'm saying," Foley said, "is that I'd rather walk through a field of dead bugs than somewhere I can't see the alive ones."

"And you know they're all dead for a fact then, do you?" Ramirez asked.

Foley looked back across the charred remains of the battlefield and nodded.

"Pretty sure, yeah."

"Ramirez… you know I hate to agree with the great oaf," King said. "But I don't think we really have another choice here. What would you have us do, turn back and go hide in the tunnel?

Ramirez exhaled.

"I know… it's just, give me a minute, OK?"

The squad all remained still and quiet for a good thirty seconds before Ramirez announced that she was ready to move. It was clear that her close encounter still weighed heavily on her, but she also knew that she would have to try to put it all behind her if she wanted to survive.

The soldiers watched the valley below for a long while through the scopes of their rifles, searching for even the tiniest movement that would betray a Scriven still alive down there, but in the end, there was nothing, so they began the difficult descent down the loose ground, once again daisy-chaining the three crates so that they wouldn't simply get stuck in the sand.

When the ten soldiers reached the bottom, it was clear just how destructive whatever had happened to the creatures had been. When viewed from head height, the alien bodies towered up over them where they lay fallen. Their chitinous skin had been burnt like the entire valley had been engulfed in flames, and the bodies were packed so close together that the soldiers almost brushed shoulders with them as they moved. The only positive about any of this was the fact that because of the size and density of the graveyard, it meant that they didn't have to keep low or quiet as they moved. Nothing would be able to find them out there at all, and nothing would see them moving.

After a few minutes, Marcus managed to relax a little. The suns were both still high in the sky, though the planet must've resided well within the Goldilocks zone of at least the closest one, because the sunlight was bright but not too bright, and warm but not overbearing. And although it initially seemed like the valley of the dead Scriven was a horrible place to be, it seemed like it was relatively safe compared to being out in the open.

Of course, all good things had to come to an end.

From the front of the group, McCulloch held up a fist, and everybody stopped. He lowered his posture slightly and drew his rifle up to his eyeline. The soldiers carrying the crates: Marcus, Ramirez, Foley, King, Hernandez and Johnstone, slowly lowered them to the ground and silently replaced them with their rifles. Hunter, Carter and Asimov had already taken up a defensive posture, but not a single one of them had made a sound in doing so.

After a good minute of the group all searching for whatever had caught McCulloch's attention around them, Marcus was about to ask what was happening, when a rustling sound made his stomach drop.

It was a strange noise, like someone was cracking the shell of a lobster to get to the meat in the tail or the claws. And then it dawned on Marcus what that meant, and the hairs on the back of his arms stood on end.

Something was alive out there.

McCulloch again raised his fist to keep everyone from making any noise, and he slowly began walking to whatever it was that had garnered his attention.

Marcus didn't move, but raised the scope on his rifle to his eyeline and followed McCulloch's slow movement. For the soldier to be moving towards the thing, it was clear that it either hadn't noticed him, or didn't look threatening and eventually Marcus saw what it was, though it wasn't easy.

On the back of a fallen Scriven warrior, facing away from the soldiers, was a much smaller spider-like creature. It was obvious that the thing was another Scriven, given its shape and markings, though this one was more like the size of a rabbit – tiny in comparison to its kin. And this little thing was cracking open the armoured plate of its larger kin, and eating whatever it was finding inside.

Marcus tapped Ramirez and pointed towards the creature and made sure she could see what was happening. Within a moment, everybody was watching the little Scriven take its dinner, and a moment later, McCulloch arrived just behind it and drove a long, sharp knife through its head. It didn't even manage to let out a scream before it curled up and died right there, skewered.

The group moved towards McCulloch, who'd straightened up now that the imminent danger had passed.

"You think there are more?" Hernandez whispered.

McCulloch shook his head. "I don't know," he whispered back. "But I don't hear anything, and this thing didn't sound the alarm, so we might be good. But maybe we should get back on track before more show up."

The next few minutes were tense, with the soldiers remaining on edge, waiting to hear another telltale sound of life amongst the graveyard. And eventually, their caution was rewarded as they came upon another of the smaller, rabbit-sized Scriven. McCulloch, again at the front of the group, took the creature out with his knife without causing any alarm.

"Just keep watching for more," McCulloch whispered. "If they're spread out like that, then it's not going to be a problem, but if they all come for us at once in here…" he trailed off, but in truth he didn't need to finish his sentence; everyone knew what would happen if the Scriven knew they were there.

Again they waited to ensure there were no sounds coming from nearby, and then again the soldiers picked up the crates and moved slowly forwards, towards the base and to their salvation. They knew that if they could keep going for just a little longer, then they could relax for a moment and catch up with the rest of the soldiers who'd made it.

They continued silently, with Marcus following behind Foley and with Ramirez to his side. Marcus and Ramirez carried one of the crates between them and had their weapons slung over their shoulders.

But the universe had other plans than to make this easy for the soldiers.

Marcus saw it first. From above them, one of the smaller creatures had been walking along one of the fallen Scriven's legs and had taken its opportunity. It fell down and landed on Foley's shoulder. Then Ramirez saw it, and just before either of them could draw their knives, Foley turned his head to see what had just tapped him. He came face to face with the little yellow and black, three-eyed monster.

Foley screamed.

Then he swiped the thing off with the back of his hand, and it went flying onto the ground. It reared up on its hind legs like it was about to pounce, and Ramirez raised her rifle.

"No!" McCulloch half-shouted, half-whispered, but it was too late. Ramirez opened fire.

Pop, pop, pop, three single shots rang out and the Scriven fell onto its back and curled up into a ball. Then Ramirez lowered her weapon and turned to see nine stunned faces staring at her.

Nobody moved. Nobody made a sound.

And then they heard it. Like hailstones on a flat roof, the cacophony of tiny footsteps started quietly, but grew and grew until it rang out from all around them.

"Run!" McCulloch shouted and turned back in the direction they'd been heading, pounding his feet into the ground.

Marcus thought about leaving the crate behind, having dropped it when Ramirez had done so to draw her weapon, but when she picked it back up and started pulling the box along the ground, he knew what they needed to do.

Catching quickly up to Ramirez to run alongside her and helping her with the crate, Marcus focused all his attention on the path before them. It had been OK to move within the graveyard when they were taking their time and remaining quiet, though now that they needed to move quickly, it seemed like the whole place was closing in on them.

And to make things worse, the appendages of the fallen Scriven were so sharp that if anything even touched them as they moved, they would slice right through like there was nothing there at all.

But it wasn't just that it seemed like the space between the Scriven was getting smaller. It was. In fact, after a few moments of running, the path was so tight that they had to move in single file.

Then the path closed entirely, and Marcus and Ramirez nearly ran into the back of McCulloch, who looked like he had finally run out of ideas.

"There's no way out," he breathed. "Ready your rifles!" he ordered loudly and the entire squad prepared themselves, raising their weapons.

The rumbling sound of the Scriven sounded a little further away than it had before they'd started running, though they all knew that it would only be a matter of time before they were discovered again; the little beasts knew there was something hiding within their meal, and it was unlikely they were going to give up the chance for fresh meat.

Foley was practically bright red, though Ramirez was visibly shaking. Marcus could see that as she held her rifle up, her arm was bleeding where a leg must've nicked her on the run. He couldn't see how deep the wound was, but he knew it would most likely need attention soon by how it dripped continuously.

The rumbling, tapping sound started to grow louder again as the enemy turned a corner and bore down on them, yet still the soldiers could see nothing.

"Here they come!" Foley growled as his knuckles turned white around his rifle. "Don't give them an inch!"

And then the first of the advancing, rabbit-sized Scriven came into view. It was just like the ones they'd already seen, except this one had friends behind it. Lots of friends.

Marcus didn't see who fired the first shot from his position crouched down behind one of the crates, but as soon as he heard it, he joined in with fire from his own rifle. All ten of the human soldiers, in fact, began firing in bursts, and the Scriven fell in waves like some invisible forcefield was pushing them back.

And they were still coming.

Halfway through their magazines, McCulloch, Asimov, Johnstone, Hernandez and Hunter held their fire so that when the others needed to reload, it wouldn't result in everyone pausing at the same time. It did, of course, allow the enemy to push forward a little further when they did so as the wall of gunfire was thinned, but they only had to wait a few moments before they restarted their defensive fire to allow the rest to reload. The action was perfectly timed, like they'd done it a thousand times before.

"Reloading!" Foley announced and took a knee to allow the rest to cover his act.

Marcus, too, followed suit and pulled the empty magazine from his rifle so that he could replace it with a fresh one. In training, this had been such an easy task, but with thousands of large spider-like aliens rushing at him with intent to crack his skull open and feast on what was within, combined with the deafening sound of rifle fire all around him, he couldn't help his hands from shaking.

"Get back in the game Cesari!" King shouted as she resumed firing. "We can hold them off, but not if we start falling behind!"

Marcus took a breath and clicked his magazine into place, resuming fire an instant later. King had been right; they weren't losing any ground and the enemy kept falling. It was a miracle that they were all coming at them from one direction, if they hadn't, Marcus didn't want to even think about how they would've defended themselves.

And then everything changed.

From somewhere above, in amongst all the firing, the killing, the screams of the Scriven as they die and the roars of battle from well, mostly Foley, a single, small spider-like Scriven silently fell down from above and landed right on the barrel of Ramirez' rifle.

The soldier screamed, the creature reared up on its back legs like it was about to pounce and Ramirez slammed the barrel of the rifle down onto the top of the crate. Then again and again.

The Scriven – or at least what was left of it, did not survive.

"Jesus woman," Foley shouted. "Remind me never to let you handle my barrel like that! I tell you what, if you ever want to find a husband after this..."

"Foley, if you don't shut your mouth, I'm going to..."

Ramirez didn't get the chance to finish her sentence because just as she was speaking, another Scriven leapt at her. This time, it was straight in front of her, so she pulled the trigger on her SA80 and let loose.

Or that's what she tried to do, because she hadn't realised that when she had crushed the one that had landed on her barrel against the crate, she'd inadvertently damaged her rifle so badly that when she pulled the trigger, all it did was click.

"Fu..." was all that she managed to scream before the two frontmost legs of the alien creature punctured her neck and threw her backwards onto the ground.

Marcus saw the movement from beside him and without thinking, turned his back on the enemy whilst the rest kept firing, retrieved his knife from his side and skewered the beast. He pulled it away from Ramirez and discarded it, immediately applying pressure to the two tiny wounds on her neck.

Marcus looked down at his best friend in all of this, her eyes wide and searching, her mouth open like she was so shocked that something had managed to make it through to her.

"It'll be OK," Marcus said. "It's nothing really. Just stay here, keep the pressure on and it'll be over before you know it. We'll be away to the Baccus base and they can help you. Just... stay with me, OK?"

Ramirez opened her mouth to speak, and Marcus shushed her, though she forced her words out anyway. They were strained, and just hearing them made Marcus' stomach twist into knots.

"When... you... tell... them... about... us... tell... them... Foley... was... a... tiny... girl."

"Hey!" Foley called back, having overheard Ramirez' words. "You make sure you tell them I'm a man, you got that?"

Marcus looked at Foley and then back at Ramirez. But it was too late. Her arms had fallen limp, the wounds on her neck were leaking blood faster than he'd ever seen blood pouring before and he knew. He knew that for Ramirez, her fight was over.

And then he saw red.

Marcus picked up his rifle and switched the firing mode to full automatic. He emptied the first magazine in seconds, and then another, and another, not stopping to wait for the squad's firing pattern to clock on and off. He couldn't hear anything, even the sound of his own rifle as it fired over and over. The whole world had just died for him, along with Ramirez. He couldn't hear McCulloch and the others shouting at him to stop. He wouldn't have if he had, because this was his act of revenge.

When he didn't have another magazine to hand, Marcus let his rifle click a few times and then fell back to the ground with his mouth open in a silent scream. He hadn't noticed the tears streaming down his cheeks, and there was nothing else he could do other than curl up in a ball on the ground and hope that he wouldn't have to wait too long to join Ramirez wherever she had gone.

Chapter 27 – Hello Darkness

The Scriven had just torn apart Marcus' entire world. Everything that he thought he knew about what was right and wrong had changed, just like that. It was like he had become deaf to the sounds around him and he just didn't care if the Scriven were still bearing down on them or not.

"Snap out of it Cesari," Foley's voice broke through Marcus' cloud of dark thoughts and finally he could hear again.

"If I have to reach down there and pick you up myself…" Foley said, and Marcus felt the brute's large, rough hand on his shoulder.

Marcus' rigidity faded, and he uncurled himself to lay on the ground, looking straight up through the graveyard of Scriven legs curling up high above them and to the bright sky above. It was like the world was mocking him with its brightness, given the darkness he felt inside, the sense of loss that had already consumed him.

"Get. Up," Foley ordered. "You don't get to lay down on the ground in a fight, and if you do it again, I'm going to shoot you myself."

Marcus realised now that the gunfire had stopped, and that could mean only one thing: that there were no more enemies nearby. Then, as he sat himself upright on the soft, warm ground, King and Carter knelt beside him and offered him their comfort.

"Don't worry, Cesari," King said. "I know it's hard seeing something like that happen up close, and even harder when it's someone you care for. Trust me, it doesn't get any easier, but you kind of just have to push it all to one side…"

"Or better yet, down deep," Carter added.

"Yes…" King continued. "Just whatever you do, you can't let it consume you like that when it matters the most. We're in a nightmare here, the worst position I could think of, and it's going to get worse before it gets better. You know that, right? This isn't the end of anything. It's just the start. And Ramirez... she'd want you to keep fighting as best you could. She'd wat that for all of us."

Marcus nodded slowly but he wasn't really listening. He could only see Ramirez's face as she choked on her own blood.

He wanted to reply, to reassure King and the rest of the squad that he had what it took, that he wouldn't let this happen again. That he wouldn't let Ramirez' death be in vain. But he simply couldn't. Because he knew that if he opened his mouth, all that would happen is that he would sob.

"Heads up, there's more coming," McCulloch's announcement ripped Marcus' attention from the morose situation at hand and he raised himself to his feet, looking all around.

"There you go, now stop being a girl and do some real work," Foley said. "Take it like a man."

Marcus ignored Foley. He had no headspace to deal with the great oaf right now and instead he focused on the last words that Ramirez had spoken. He couldn't help but let it comfort him, thinking about how Foley would've hated being remembered as a woman. It was a silly notion, and he knew it, but it helped him shake away a little of the pain he was feeling and refocus on the fact that he would have to fight to survive.

"Same direction," McCulloch said.

"I hear something from behind, too," Johnstone added. His voice had a slight tremble to it, but he pushed down on it. "They must've regrouped and circled around. But there's no way they could be that smart, right?"

"Never assume anything about the enemy," McCulloch replied, pulling his rifle up to the ready. "And if you have to, assume they're smarter than you. But we have one advantage…"

"What's that?" Johnstone asked.

"We have me! Foley said.

"No," McCulloch said. "You don't have to think; you just have to point and shoot in the direction you're told. You got that? Cesari, are you back with us?"

Marcus nodded.

"Good, now ready your weapon."

The rumbling sound was rising again, coming closer and making Marcus' feet sweat. He had already seen the chaos that a battle against these small Scriven caused, and if they were to do it all over again, he wondered how many more soldiers or friends he would lose by the end of it. And then, if the enemy continued the tactic with numbers that seemingly had no end, then eventually, this battle of attrition would only go one way. He suddenly sympathised with the plight of the Baccus on this planet.

"Weapons ready!" Foley ordered as the rumbling had once again got so loud that the wave of creatures could only have been yards away.

"Permission to throw grenades?" Foley asked.

"Not yet," McCulloch replied. "We might need them later. And try not to waste any bullets this time Foley, I saw you spraying and praying earlier."

Marcus couldn't help but feel his spirits raised by those words. It gave him renewed hope that this wasn't the end, and although he knew McCulloch had no idea how any of this would pan out, his underlying hope was infectious.

Raising his weapon, he tamped down on any feelings he thought were human and readied himself for what was to come.

The sounds of the enemy approach were concentrated mainly to the front of the group, but the sounds from behind were still there, although they were mostly drowned out now. It made Marcus think that whatever was coming from behind was a much smaller number than they'd already dealt with. But he knew all too well that it only took a single Scriven to end the life of one of the human soldiers.

"King, Carter to the rear," McCulloch ordered. "I don't want them sneaking up on us while we're preoccupied with all their friends."

The pair dutifully turned around and faced the rear, while the remaining seven soldiers all took up ready positions to face the oncoming onslaught. Marcus knelt down behind the crate that Ramirez had used to smash one of the alien creatures. It still had multicoloured ooze on it where the last Scriven she'd killed had faced its end.

And then the firing started.

Marcus heard the gunfire from all around him before he actually saw any of the Scriven, but once he saw the first signs of movement coming through the graveyard towards them, he too opened fire. This time he kept his rifle on its single-shot mode, choosing to elect targets as they presented themselves. It wasn't just so that he would save his ammunition, though; Marcus wanted to know that each time he pulled his trigger, an alien creature met its end. He wanted them all to understand and feel his pain as he enacted his surgical revenge. It was more than they deserved, he knew, to be given the space in his mind, but a big part of him ached for justice. For Ramirez.

But one soldier down was a noticeable change. And with the two at the back having their attention occupied, it meant that where last time there had been ten soldiers to shower the advancing Scriven with gunfire, this time there were only seven.

The wave of enemies seemed to grow and advance even through the alternating gunfire and within a few seconds, Marcus had switched his rifle to fully automatic once again, just as the others had. The rifles popped and rattled without pause, over and over, but there was little more that any of them could do.

"Get those grenades ready, Foley!" McCulloch shouted over the noise. "How's our six, people?" he added.

"Wait!" King shouted. "It's not..."

And then all hell broke loose.

Flames shot forward from behind Marcus and the squad, engulfing the graveyard on both sides of them. The heat was intense, like he was caught in the centre of a swirling fireball. His ears filled with the whooshing sound of the force of the hot air that passed by him, and he instinctively turned his head away from the brightness and the heat. Whatever was doing this, whatever had caused this wildfire that now seemed to be spreading out all around them, it was to be the end. The end of everything. The Scriven, the soldiers, the graveyard.

And then he realised.

The fire was not closing in on them. It was not coming closer and closer until it eventually engulfed them. It was directed somehow at the Scriven.

"Woooh yeah!" Foley shouted. "The cavalry's here, boys!"

Marcus turned his head to see what Foley was talking about, and when he did so, he felt a strange mix of emotions. Ambling forward were a handful of blue-skinned Baccus, holding strange-looking flamethrowers and wearing comically large backpacks. They were the ones belching fire into the approaching Scriven. They were the ones who'd just saved the lives of the humans. They were the ones who'd arrived as salvation for their allies.

Only a moment passed and the battle was once again over, because the SA80's had stopped firing, and the Baccus' flamethrowers died down until they didn't squirt out any fire at all. In the end, all that was left was the stench of smoke and burning Scriven flesh in the air. Even through his helmet, Marcus could smell that smell. It was something that he would never forget. It stung his nostrils, but it was the smell of victory. Of vengeance.

"I am glad that we managed to arrive just in time, it seems," one of the Baccus announced as it moved to the centre of the group. He looked down firstly at Ramirez's still body, and then at the three crates placed on the ground. "And it seems that we have not experienced much of a loss."

"What!?" Marcus shouted, though he hadn't meant to. "How can you say that!?"

"Cesari!" McCulloch said in an official tone. "Stand down! Our friend here was referring to the crates we brought."

"That is correct," the Baccus said. "I understand that you are upset at the loss of your squad member, but please know that it is not an uncommon thing for us any longer. We have lost many hundreds of thousands of friends, family. And to mitigate future losses, we need supplies. Supplies like the ones you have brought in those crates for us."

Marcus opened and closed his mouth a few times, but no words came out.

"Now, please, know that it is not safe here," the Baccus said. "We must return to the forward operating base before more arrive and there are too many for us to deal with."

"Hell no!" Foley exclaimed. "Let's go take them down with those flamethrowers of yours!"

"I am afraid that it is not possible," the Baccus said. "The flamers we have are only equipped with enough accelerant that they will be rendered useless after a short while. If we remain out here for much longer, we will be rendered helpless and unarmed."

"The hell?" Foley said, but a look from McCulloch cut him short.

"Let's get out of here," McCulloch announced. "I think we could all do with a little safety." He shot a glance at Marcus. "And perhaps a little time to unpack everything that's happened so far."

The Baccus made a strange clicking sound, and then the other Baccus, of which there were now ten in total, picked up the crates and turned away from the humans. They left Ramirez on the ground where she had fallen.

The humans all followed, except Marcus, who had a strange inability to leave Ramirez behind.

A hand landed on Marcus' shoulder, and he turned to see Asimov's face in a forced half-smile.

"She would have wanted to stay," he said. "We have to get used to the fact that we aren't going to bring everyone home. She died, and it's a terrible thing, but she would not have wanted to be a burden."

Marcus nodded and closed his eyes. It was true; she wouldn't have wanted to put anyone out for her. Not now.

He wondered if he was supposed to say a prayer, beg that Ramirez would be safe in her journey wherever she had gone or was going, but he had never believed any of that. Right now, he wished that he did, wished that he could take comfort in the knowledge that she would be going to a better place. But his mind wouldn't allow that. She was gone, and whether she stayed there or was buried someplace else under a cross and a prayer, it would make no difference. Because she wasn't coming back.

He forced the tears away and swallowed the lump in his throat. They had more important things to do.

Marcus walked alongside Asimov, and although he had been straight and tough, Marcus found him surprisingly warm. Once they were walking without any threats around them, Asimov told Marcus about his own time within Operation Legacy, about the changes his body experienced and how hungry he was all the time. It took Marcus back to a place where things were more tangible for him. Where everything that happened wasn't new or terrifying. They didn't mention the Scriven, the Baccus or this alien planet as they walked. It was like nothing else in the universe existed beyond the Canada Road barracks.

Once the combined forces had made it through the graveyard and out the other side, there was a flat, clear area of about a hundred metres before the impressive structure of the forward operating base stood.

Made of what looked like thick concrete and standing at least twenty feet high, the base was encircled by an impenetrable wall with ringlets of wire and metallic outcroppings that prevented anything from trying to climb up and over the thing. In front of them, where Marcus assumed the main gates should've been, was a fifteen-foot gap in the wall, and when he looked closer, he could see no gates at all. The position was defensible but not impenetrable, and he wondered why it'd been made like that. It seemed odd to him that the whole place would be so formidable, and then the doors would be left wide open. Perhaps they'd been damaged or destroyed in some battle, though he could see no evidence of that.

"Please, everyone inside the walls," the only Baccus to have spoken said. "The deterrent is currently not active, so you can pass through freely."

Marcus had no idea what 'The deterrent' was, but it sounded like it was something powerful, something that could keep them safe.

"Please wait here," the Baccus said once they had made it through to find that the forward operating base was built like a large tower within the walls. The walls themselves had steps on the inside so they could be manned from the top, and there was a gap of a few yards between the walls and the interior building, which looked like a large rectangle with no windows and just a single door from what Marcus could see. It actually looked like a prison more than a fortress, though upon reflection, Marcus realised that there wasn't much difference between the two. One was designed to keep people in, whilst the other was designed to keep people out.

The Baccus all filtered away and left the soldiers to themselves just inside the walls. Foley was looking out at the graveyard holding his rifle down by his hip like he was guarding the place, Johnstone, Asimov, Carter, Hunter and Hernandez were talking amongst themselves – they'd arrived together so presumably they were still most comfortable huddled together, King was pacing back and forth and that just left McCulloch, who was approaching Marcus with a strange look in his eye.

"Come with me," McCulloch ordered. "We need to talk."

Marcus didn't reply, but walked alongside McCulloch for a few paces until they were out of earshot of the rest of the soldiers. McCulloch turned, pushed his back against the inside of the wall and slid down into a seated position. Marcus followed suit next to him.

"It never gets any easier, you know," McCulloch said when the pair hit the ground. "Losing someone you care about, a friend."

Marcus remained silent.

"But there are ways of dealing with things. What you did back there… it could've put us all in danger, got us all hurt, or worse: killed…"

Marcus' eyes widened and he felt the blood rise in his cheeks. He couldn't help it.

"Ramirez was a person," he growled and his voice began rising involuntarily. "You seem to be forgetting that. And her name was Ramirez!"

"I know who she was!" McCulloch's own voice raised in tandem. "Can't you see that I'm hurt too, though I suppose that's the point, isn't it? I knew who Ramirez was, I knew that she was a soldier, and I knew that there were seven other soldiers plus me and you to think about, so I'm sorry if I didn't fall down to the ground and let the enemy take me!" Then his voice lowered significantly. "I can't just stop and hope that the world around me follows suit… there's too much on the line here, too many lives. I know it hurts, Cesari, but you have to get a handle on this."

Marcus looked up at McCulloch, who he could see had tears in his eyes. It was like he had changed in that moment from an uncompassionate ass, to something that mirrored much of Marcus himself.

"How do you do it?" Marcus asked slowly. "How do you switch it on and off like that?"

"The truth is," McCulloch sighed. "Is that it's always with me. The weight of everyone I've seen killed before their time. And no, it doesn't get any easier, you just kind of find a way to deal with it. A way that you can't see from the outside, but you still feel everything on the inside. I deal with it by falling back on being a soldier; that's what I am, so that's how I act. But it doesn't mean for a second that I care any less or that I don't wake up in the night and still see their faces. This is who we are, Cesari, and the sooner you realise, accept and embrace that, the easier it's going to be for the rest of us. Because we all hide something deep down, and the more that we see what it is we're afraid of mirrored back at us, the harder it is for us to hide it. So be a soldier, Cesari. Be a soldier and realise that in doing so you can make a difference for the future, even if you can't change the past."

McCulloch stood up and walked away from Marcus, back to the other soldiers and joined in their conversation. Marcus reached up and placed his head in his hands for a long moment, then raised himself to his feet, steeled his expression and followed McColloch back to the others.

Chapter 28 – Home Away from Home

Marcus replayed McCulloch's words in his mind over and over. But he knew he was right. There was nothing he could do to change the past, but he could put everything he had into making a better future. In reality, it didn't take more than a minute for Marcus to tamp down on his true feelings and put on a new face as he approached the rest of the human soldiers, but it felt to him like it had been a lifetime.

The soldiers were chatting about their favourite sports, something so far related from the situation they'd found themselves in that it was almost comical. As Marcus walked towards them, three Baccus carrying weapons similar to the humans' own rifles exited the main doorway of the interior of the base and walked straight up to the group.

"How many more are out there?" the lead Baccus asked. He was slightly taller than the others and the fact that he was covered in scars – which were a slightly deeper blue than the rest of his skin – was something that told Marcus that this individual had been in this war a long time.

Nobody answered.

"Answer the question," the Baccus said.

"We are all that's left," McCulloch replied, taking the lead for the group. "Our transports crash landed…"

"We know what happened, do not take us for fools," the Baccus said. "You were sent here to reinforce us, reinforcements which we are sorely in need of. And you are telling me that these reinforcements total nine?"

McCulloch nodded slowly. "We came in the hundreds," he explained. "But after the failed landing, we're all that's left."

The Baccus seemed to look McCulloch up and down for a moment with an expression that seemed somewhere between confused and angry.

"Well, what can you do?" the alien asked. "If it has been decided that you few humans are able to turn the tide of this war so effectively?"

"What can we do?" McCulloch asked, now equally confused. "I apologise, but we are humans, and where we are skilled soldiers, fighters, I don't know what you expect us to be able to 'do'."

"Then you are useless and you have wasted our time," the Baccus said. "You have put us all in danger, what few remain here and all you can say on the matter is that there is nothing special about you, except that you have brought us new supplies. Which one of you is called Callahan?"

"Callahan didn't..." McCulloch started.

"Put you in danger?" Foley shouted. "We didn't ask to come here and join your war. We didn't even know aliens existed a year ago, so you should be thankful that we're even here to help you!"

The Baccus looked at Foley, then away again, seemingly ignoring him.

"You are a loud and aggressive race, are you not?"

McCulloch looked back at Foley and gave him the 'shut up' look. "Some of us are, sometimes," he said.

"Then perhaps you are not without your use," the Baccus said. Then he visibly softened. "I have been here for many years, and although I may seem direct, perhaps even crass, it is not the way of my people. We are no longer fighters with steely determination where are enemy is exactly that. And when you are a fear-filled race pit against an enemy without such convictions, you have already lost the battle. It is my assumption, then, that the humans, yourselves and the ones who did not make it here, are here to be what we are not. To do what we cannot."

McCulloch nodded. "We're all trained soldiers here," he said. "We will always do what we can to follow the orders we are given as fully as we can."

The Baccus nodded in a very human-like gesture.

"I was not a soldier before I was sent to this conflict," the Baccus said. "But I feel that this war has changed me, and I do not know if I will be able to change back when it is over." Then he turned and looked at the crate the soldiers had cared for until they had been rescued. "These supplies will be useful to us, though if more aid does not arrive in the coming year, then I do not think this is a war that we will be able to win."

"Year?" King asked, astounded. "Three crates of supplies are going to last a year?"

"Indeed," the Baccus replied.

"Three crates for thousands of soldiers? What the hell's in them?" she asked.

"Ah, I see that there has been a miscommunication of information," the Baccus said. "Because within this forward operating base, our total strength is around one hundred. Of course, we had thousands when we arrived here, but this war for us has been mainly one of attrition. I do not believe that the Scriven suffer the same rate of which that we unfortunately do."

"I think we need to talk more about what's going on here," McCulloch said. Marcus was going to say the same thing, but McCulloch had beaten him to it. "Because I think we haven't been told the whole story about this place."

"Of course," the Baccus said. "Please follow me inside and we can talk away from all of this," he waved his hand and in that moment Marcus could tell that although this creature seemed to have a tough exterior, he just wanted to be inside and away from anything that reminded him of war, or the Scriven. He didn't entirely blame him.

The squad all followed the three Baccus inside the main building, and Marcus was immediately surprised at how bright the interior of the place was. From the outside, it was clear that it had no windows – no doubt a security feature - but inside it had the feel of a hospital, with corridors and stairs snaking away, each straddled by small rooms, some of which had doors, some had curtains and some had nothing at all. What was evident as they moved through the building though, was that not only were most of the rooms empty, but when they did see Baccus sitting alone in their little spaces, they looked injured, downtrodden, broken almost. If the Baccus had been there for years, it was anyone's guess at how many had lost most of their families, friends and kin.

"It is through here," the Baccus leading the way said. "I must apologise for my brash tone outside of this place. It has been a long few years and I am afraid that once I step outside into the sunlight, there is a change in me. A desire to get back into safety as quickly as possible. Though I fear that this place may not be as safe as it once was in the coming days and weeks."

"What? Why?" McCulloch asked as they continued to traverse the hallway. "This place is a fortress designed to repel enemy attacks, isn't it?"

"That is correct," the Baccus said. "But like most of our technology, this place relies on power – and in this case very much power. The entranceway that we came through on the outer wall is a very intriguing design that has worked well in testing and other conflicts. But… it is permanently open."

"What the hell?!" Foley asked from the back of the group. "Just leave the door open, yeah that's a great idea!"

"I understand your apprehension," the Baccus said. "But our testing showed that enemy combatants would often search for a weak point in our defences and attack there. The idea of our open door is that they do not need to search, therefore we already know where an attack will originate from. Then, there is a repellent attached to that open doorway, which can be turned on and off as we see fit."

Marcus quickly understood what was happening. "It's like a giant bug zapper," he said. "But… that must take a lot of power?"

"Indeed it does, and power is costly, is it not?" The Baccus said. "But regardless of that fact, our forward operating bases utilise a form of energy that borrows upon a combination of the gravitational field of a planet, and photovoltaic cells. In normal circumstances, power would not be an issue, but as the repellent has been used so frequently in this particular war, time has taken its toll, and our battery reserves have been falling steadily since the day we arrived."

"Hang on," Marcus said. "What do you mean 'arrived'? I thought this was your home planet?"

The Baccus let out a short laugh, not unlike a snort or a scoff.

"Of course not! Calatea Four is but one of many worlds inhabited by my people. As is the way with all expanding races across the universe and as shall the human race one day it is presumed?"

"Wait," Asimov interrupted, not grasping the gravity of Marcus' line of questioning. "How much power do you have remaining?"

"At the current rate of skirmishes against us," the Baccus replied. "We are at a point where our longevity is now measured in days rather than weeks."

"Damn," Asimov breathed.

Marcus spoke again, clearly not interested in the power situation. "So you're saying that you came here as an expanding civilisation, and that it isn't your home world?"

"That is correct," the Baccus said.

"And can I ask, were the Scriven here when you arrived?"

"In a small way they were," the Baccus said. "They lived in small colonies across the surface of the planet. They were in no way belligerent at that point, but as we stayed, it seemed their race evolved into what it is today. Something more akin to a feral beast."

"So you're the invaders ," Marcus stated rather than asked.

"Let me be clear, human," the Baccus practically hissed. "Calatea Four is, has been and will be forever a home to the Baccus who inhabit it. As soldiers, it is not our place to question the orders we have been given, but to follow them to the best of our abilities."

Marcus shut his mouth with a click. Of course, the Baccus was correct; whatever had led to this very situation didn't really matter, but it certainly left a bad taste in his mouth.

"And as I was saying," the Baccus continued. "The Scriven are a plague, though one that is constantly expanding and adapting. They are an intelligent race, although we do rather see them as base creatures for the most part. They spread, take over and are vicious beyond anything our race has encountered before."

"Then give me one of those flamethrowers and point me at their nest," Foley said, punching a fist into his own open palm.

"Of course our weapons are available for you to use and the flamers have been useful in keeping the Scriven somewhat at bay. But I must tell you up front, once the Scriven take a foothold underground, they are impossible to uproot. That is why we had to destroy the city along with every Scriven within, and that is why we scorch the earth as we fight."

"You… destroyed your own city?" Hernandez asked.

The Baccus looked down at the ground. "We had no choice," he said. "It is something that I wish never to witness again. However short the remainder of my life may be."

"What about retreat? Rescue?" McCulloch asked.

"Lifeboats came periodically, though I do not know if they will come again after the destruction of the fleet that you were a part of. In truth, there are many here that would do well to leave, though we have no method of contacting our people any more. They simply do not respond."

"I'm… sorry," Hernandez said softly. "I'm sorry you had to do that."

The Baccus nodded once. Then added: "This world is but one of many colonised by my people. It is a sad thing indeed, but in the greater scheme of the universe I suppose that it is inconsequential."

"Can you tell us more about the Scriven?" Johnstone asked. "Knowing your enemy can give a great advantage in battle. For instance, we've seen both large and small versions of the aliens. Why is that?"

"Of course," the Baccus said again. "The Scriven used to be more like the smaller ones that you were fighting back out there, though there were many fewer than that in the past. These smaller creatures are a mixture of the young and the members of the race not designed for war. They can fight and swarm, of course, but it is not their main function. Through our own observations, we have seen that when a threat to the Scriven race is identified, they begin to breed warriors, and these large versions do not allow the smaller ones to eat if they are nearby. This means that the smaller Scriven are forced to scavenge. Typically, we know that if we start to see more scavengers on the surface, it means there is a full nest nearby. We do not know how all of this is determined, but it is the reason that we attribute intelligence to the Scriven race. They are reactive to any threat to their nests."

"We were told that our job here is to destroy the nests," McCulloch said. "I take it that's a difficult task?"

"It would be," the Baccus said. "If you were able to find it, and so far we have not. It is clear that it is close by, judging by the activity of scavengers, though we believe that they move periodically and that is providing us with difficulties."

"So what you're saying," Foley said, stepping forward. "Is that you don't know where your enemy live, there are more and more every day, and you're almost out of people and power. That about sum it up?"

The Baccus nodded. "It is not an easy thing to admit defeat. But I do not see a way out of this for us if something does not change, and soon."

"Nuke the planet and leave," Foley said nonchalantly.

"Foley!" King shouted. "That's not funny. What if somebody said that about earth?"

"Well, if there were giant spider creatures scurrying about and killing almost all of the population, then I guess we wouldn't have much of a choice either."

"Please understand that we will do everything we can to remain on this planet," the Baccus said. "Retreat is not an option for us. The cost has already been too great."

"Then we must do what we can to help," McCulloch announced. "But first, do you have a shower or washroom or something? I can smell Foley from here."

"You haven't smelt anything yet!" Foley announced and unlaced his boots one by one. Then he made a show of removing them from his feet and slowly turning them upright to allow the sand that had collected within them to fall to the ground.

Marcus watched the show, but he saw the look in the Baccus' eyes as the alien, too, watched Foley. The look was one of shock and amazement.

"Where did you get that?" The Baccus asked, his eyes still wide.

"What? They gave us the boots back on earth. I know there's something about them, but I don't know how they did it. Don't your people have similar tech?"

The alien was indeed wearing boots similar to the soldiers, though it was clear when he took two steps forward that he hadn't been talking about Foley's footwear.

The Baccus fell to his knees and began picking up the sand Foley had tipped onto the ground, letting it flow through his fingers over and over again.

"You… don't have sand?" Foley asked. "There's loads of it out there…"

"Out where!?" the Baccus shouted. The alien looked up at Foley, who looked extremely confused by what was happening.

"You have no idea what this is?" the Baccus asked.

Foley shook his head. The Baccus then looked at the rest of the soldiers, who each shook their heads.

"These are the fresh tailings that the Scriven create as they dig the tunnels for their nests! This is what we have been searching for for months!"

Foley looked at the ground, then grimaced and stepped back.

"That's so gross," he said, pulling a face.

"No! It is an amazing thing! With this, we will know exactly where the closest nest is and we can make our attack! Do you not see how important this is?"

Foley still looked a little disgusted but managed to force his mouth into a smile. "You hear that King? My feet might've just saved the planet. Jealous?"

"Nobody in their right mind would be jealous of your feet, Foley. And that goes for the rest of you, too, for that matter."

"Whatever. You wish you saved the world."

"I wish you'd get bitten by a spider," King said.

"Woah… too soon!" Foley complained.

After a short back and forth, and a detailed description of the nearby hill that the soldiers had traversed, it was decided that they would indeed shower in the facilities that the Baccus provided, and then immediately go in search of their first nest. The Baccus was clear that the soldiers were to be escorted by at least two of their own, which McCulloch agreed to, mainly for their situational knowledge rather than their combat prowess – of which he had no clue.

The showers were less a cascade of water and more a high-powered fine mist that did an excellent job at washing the general stink off the soldiers. They were also set in individual cubicles too, so Marcus took the first opportunity in as long as he could remember, to stand alone. It gave him a moment to remember Ramirez, and think about what he was going to do without his friend once all of this was over.

Chapter 29 – Into the Fire

The shower was pleasant in the end, that was after Marcus allowed himself to close his eyes and forget everything he'd experienced in the last few months. He imagined that he was back at home in his parent's house without a care in the world, his mum making him toast and tea in the morning, even getting fired from his job, whatever it was that week. He found himself thinking about Helen, too. He wondered if she thought about him or about where he might've gone after that night in the Green Beret.

Of course there would be no way for him to find out, but replaying the normalcies of his time back on earth turned out to be an excellent way of forgetting that he was stuck on an alien planet, that he didn't know where his parents were, that he'd just lost his best friend, and that he didn't know if they were going to survive the next few hours. All in all, this was a bad time for Marcus.

As Marcus emerged from the shower, he felt like the cleansing mist had washed away not only the physical grime that had coated him during the battles with the Scriven, but also some of the mental weight he had been carrying. He knew he couldn't dwell on the past; he had to focus on the present and the tasks ahead. Just like McCulloch had said.

The soldiers were provided with fresh sets of uniforms that although weren't exactly like what they had been wearing, and were perhaps a little smaller if anything, but Marcus couldn't help but marvel at the advanced technology of their Baccus hosts as the fabric was lightweight and breathable, and as their old uniforms did, seemed to refit itself around the wearer.

McCulloch gathered the team in one of the larger rooms within the Baccus facility, where a large holographic display table stood in the centre. It hummed to life, projecting a detailed map of the surrounding area for the squad to look at, as well as the small group of Baccus who were there to watch. The leader of the facility was also present, but it seemed that he had passed the torch to McCulloch, who spoke in a very official tone.

"Our primary objective is to locate and neutralise a Scriven nest," he began, pointing to an area on the display. It was the hill that they'd had so much trouble crossing. "According to our Baccus allies, we're close to one. They've been searching for these nests for months without success, but now, thanks to Foley's feet, we have a lead."

Foley gave a mock salute, clearly pleased with his contribution. Then added a "Huzah!" for effect. "But… don't we have radio yet? I mean it might go a bit easier if we had a battalion of Baccus behind us."

"Nothing," King said. "Both us and the Baccus have been radio silent since we arrived. It's… worrying."

McCulloch continued, ignoring that grim assessment, "We'll all stick together, but if the situation called for it, we'll be working as two teams, with a Baccus guide accompanying each team. We'll head out towards the location indicated here," he pointed to a spot on the hologram. "It's the most likely place we're going to find a point of entry, but it might also be guarded, so we're going to have to stick together and watch our backs."

Hunter then asked: "What if we encounter heavy resistance? There could be tens of thousands of those things in there and there's only going to be what, a handful of us?"

McCulloch nodded. "Good question. We'll engage outside only if absolutely necessary and if there's no other option. We need to get inside unnoticed if it's at all possible."

Hernandez looked uneasy. "What if we find ourselves trapped? You know if we get inside and they surround us or something?"

"We'll all stay as close together as we can, but we think that if we stay quiet and unnoticed, we can make it in and out without ever being spotted. If it goes really badly, then the Baccus will do what they can to extract us."

Those words didn't seem to pacify Hernandez.

Carter frowned. "What if we find civilians, Baccus perhaps, held inside or in danger?"

McCulloch sighed. "We think that it is… unlikely. The truth is, the Baccus have never seen any evidence that the Scriven take hostages. If we find anything at all, it's likely to be remains at the very most. We leave them be."

Marcus felt his eyes redden at the thought of seeing the lifeless body of Ramirez in there, half cocooned in some ridiculous ritualistic way, but he shook the thought away.

"Then, when we're deep enough inside the nest, we set explosive devices that have been designed specifically to obliterate the Scriven living underground. I don't think I need to tell you that we don't want to be inside when these things blow."

"And then we move onto the next base and do the same thing all over again!" Foley said. Marcus couldn't tell if Foley was actually excited for that prospect, or if he was putting on a front to hide his fear. Marcus could understand it if that was the case because he, too, was scared of what they had to do next.

"Right," King said. "So we're going to go and do what the Baccus have been trying to do for years… with nine soldiers… and that's normal is it? When they've had hundreds of thousands at their disposal?"

"Eleven," McCulloch corrected.

"What?" King asked.

"We have eleven soldiers, counting the two Baccus escorts."

"And that makes it better?"

"Not really, just factual," McCulloch said. "The thing is, is that the Baccus aren't really a warring race…"

"I can explain," the Baccus in command interrupted. "I know it may seem from our weapons, our bases and the fact that we rescued you from the smaller Scriven earlier that we know how to fight. And in some ways, we do – when the battle is against our own people, organised and familiar. But here, we have fallen in the hundreds of thousands because we are not warriors. We are not soldiers, and when faced with an incoming horde of enemy combatants, most of us will turn and run. From what we have already seen of the humans, you will fight until your very last breath. It is something unfamiliar to the Scriven, and something that we believe will give you the ability to carry out this task."

"That is true," Foley said. "We are unstoppable killing machines."

"Killing the will to live of everyone around you," King said. "And I get all that, but does it really change anything? We go into a nest, lay explosives and run? We already know if we get swarmed, then there's not much any of us can do to stop it."

"But there is a difference," the Baccus said. "When we have fought the Scriven, we have found that they will press their advantage, swarm as you have seen and not hesitate to do everything they can to destroy their enemy. But in a nest, there is a slight difference. When in the nest, we believe that if the Scriven view you humans as an unknown, they hesitate. They have learnt over time that the Baccus are not a threat to them, so they attack immediately. It is our belief that human soldiers, as a new and unknown, combined with your fearlessness, that you will be able to carry out this mission. We believe that your presence will cause the Scriven to stutter, to strategize, and therein lies opportunity."

"Right," King said again. "So the plan is for the Scriven not to attack immediately or to stop and think about who we are… and then we blow the place up?"

"Yeah! Sounds good to me!" Foley announced with a fist pump.

King placed a hand on her forehead. "You're a God damn idiot."

McCulloch listened to the banter between King and Foley, a wry smile playing on his lips. He appreciated the levity, even in the face of the grim task ahead.

McCulloch then turned his attention back to the holographic map and cleared his throat to regain everyone's attention. "We'll return here if everything goes according to plan," he said, pointing to the forward operating base on the map. "If someone gets separated or needs extraction, head back here. The Baccus will do their best to retrieve you. But if you're left out there alone, well, there's not much anyone can do to help you. And this probably goes without saying…" he looked pointedly at Foley: "Don't try to be a hero. We're a team and we will act as such."

Hunter leaned in, studying the map intently. "Are there any known weaknesses or vulnerabilities we should be aware of in the Scriven nest? Anything that could help us at all?"

The Baccus leader nodded. "Based on our limited observations, the Scriven nests are vast underground networks. They have a central chamber where their queen resides, and the rest of the tunnel networks always seem to lead away from there. Destroying the queen is the key to dismantling the nest. However, reaching her is incredibly challenging due to the labyrinth of tunnels and the aggressive nature of the Scriven."

"So you've been inside a nest before?" Hunter asked.

The Baccus leader shook his head. "None of us here; we haven't had the means to do so effectively. We've mostly focused on holding our ground and defending against Scriven incursions, and as you can see, we are at breaking point, days away from destruction. This is the first time we have an opportunity to strike at the heart of the problem, and your presence gives us that chance."

"Alright, team," McCulloch announced. "Let's get ready. Gear up, check your weapons, and meet back here in fifteen minutes. We'll head out as soon as we're prepared."

The soldiers dispersed to prepare for their first real mission since arriving on this dying planet, and Marcus couldn't help but feel a profound sense of anxiety. He was about to face a deadly and unknown enemy in an alien environment and in their own home, no less. But he was also part of a team that had a chance to make a difference. A team that had already lost a vital member. One that he would never forget.

The two Baccus that joined the human soldiers were named Sarin and Torlen, and other than introducing themselves and pointing the way forward, they didn't say much. It was apparent that the moment they stepped foot outside of the base they felt unsafe, and that was a position that everyone felt.

The Baccus carried weapons of alien design that Marcus couldn't identify, but he could see that they weren't the flamers that he'd already seen in action.

The soldiers and the two Baccus quickly made their way to the exit of the Baccus facility. Marcus couldn't help but think about the incredible and yet so dire situation they were in. They were strangers on an alien world, facing an enemy they barely understood, with the fate of this planet resting, at least partially, in their hands.

Foley slapped Marcus' back as the larger soldier made his way to the front of the group.

"Look sharp, Cesari," he said. "This one's gonna be fun."

"Seriously, Foley, if you don't quit it, then me and Carter are going to pin you down and feed you one of those spiders!" King announced, catching up to Marcus.

"Didn't hear you!" Foley said as he continued walking, but Marcus was sure he heard something in Foley's voice that suggested he had.

"Are you OK?" King asked quietly so that only Marcus could hear as she caught up to him.

He simply nodded in response to her question.

"I'm hanging in there," he whispered back. "Just trying to focus on what we've got to do... and surviving this. But I guess that's what it's always like being a soldier, isn't it?"

King nodded but didn't answer.

As they walked, Marcus couldn't help but again be awed by the alien landscape surrounding them. Calatea Four was like nothing he'd ever seen before, a barren place that must've once been so full of vibrancy and life. But war had destroyed all that. Marcus always knew that in war there was no winner, and this war was no exception.

The soldiers and the two Baccus moved slowly. They knew that if they were discovered en route, they probably wouldn't get into the nest, and even if they did the noise they'd make would alert the Scriven to their proximity. With that in mind, they had to choose between skirting the outside of the Scriven graveyard, thus taking longer and increasing the risk, or going back through. Marcus' skin crawled at the very thought of going back in there.

But not because he was scared of the little Scriven. It was simply that whenever Marcus looked at the graveyard, his mind returned to the last time he'd seen Ramirez. And then her lifeless body on the ground.

Foley, from a few paces ahead, called back: "I wonder if the Scriven have a nightlife. Maybe we'll find them partying in their underground nest, and we can just sneak in and plant those explosives while they're all dancing."

Marcus couldn't help but raise a single eyebrow at Foley's attempt to lighten the mood. Humour was clearly his way of coping with the tension – or any tension, for that matter.

"I doubt it," Marcus replied. "But if they are, maybe they'll invite us to join the party."

King rolled her eyes but gave a small smile.

"Alright," McCulloch announced loudly. "We think it's going to be best to avoid the graveyard for now. We don't think it'll be a problem, but we don't want to make that much noise again, right? So just stay low, stay quiet and we'll be six feet under in no time."

"Great choice of words there, chief," King called back, but McCulloch just smiled awkwardly.

The group did seem to take some note of McCulloch's instructions though. Their speaking volumes were reduced to little more than a whisper, and their footsteps somehow seemed lighter. The route around the graveyard was much longer than the direct path they'd taken before, but they could at least all be sure that nothing was sneaking up on them.

It was still light out and visibility was good. The rolling hills around them hampered it, but there was enough distance between them that anything approaching would give themselves up long before they could attack. That was the only positive of an enemy that didn't use ranged weapons.

Marcus' pulse quickened the longer nothing happened. It was like he could sense danger from all around but just couldn't see it yet, and the longer they were out in the open, the worse it got. In fact, when Marcus thought about it, it would just take one Scriven, big or small to see them and alert their kin, for their whole plan to be thrown into disarray. He knew they would fight if they had to, and do what they could to breach the nest. But it wasn't a pleasant prospect.

And eventually, there it was.

Ahead, the entrance to the Scriven nest loomed, a dark, foreboding opening in the ground. They would never have found it if they hadn't been right on top of it and Marcus could see why the Baccus'd had so much trouble finding it.

But it was time to put their plan into action, to venture into the unknown and face the Scriven head-on. They had made it to the place that the Baccus hadn't been able to find, and it was time to descend into the belly of the beast.

The nine human soldiers and the two Baccus stood facing the entrance. Marcus wondered why they didn't simply get inside as quickly as possible, but staring down into the darkness, he realised that this could very well be the last time that some or all of them ever saw daylight again. And then he let himself enjoy it. The warmth on his body and the embracing light of the strange and unfamiliar planet. This was the calm before the storm.

And he was going to make the most of it.

"You ready for this Cesari?" Foley asked quietly.

"Never been less ready for anything in my life," Marcus replied.

"You ever see Foley naked?" King asked.

Marcus stared at her.

"Still less turned on for that, than I am for going in there," she said.

Chapter 30 – Dark Times Ahead

The two Baccus and McCulloch took the lead. The opening in the ground was large enough for the entire group to walk together shoulder to shoulder, though it seemed like it would've been safer to Marcus that they didn't all bunch up like that.

It was dark almost immediately, and the atmosphere was much colder than it had been outside. A memory flashed through Marcus' head of a series of caves he'd once visited in Wales, but he'd been so small. He ignored it but recognised that it perhaps wasn't something that he should've been able to remember.

As the group walked on, Marcus began to have the distinct feeling that they were being watched. Like there was always something lurking in the darkness just out of sight, and every now and then, when one of the soldiers made a slightly louder noise than the rest – perhaps a boot had hit a rock or a heel had scuffed the ground – Marcus held his breath as the sound echoed away into the tunnels ahead.

They walked for a long time before anything seemed to change. The cold darkness remained, the large tunnel walls around them remained large and overbearing and they didn't come across a single Scriven, neither big nor small. Marcus was just about ready to wonder if this really was a Scriven nest or not, when McCulloch held a fist up to bring them all to a halt.

Marcus couldn't see what was happening or what had caused McCulloch to stop, but he peered forward into the darkness where the leader's headlamp was shining.

And then he saw it.

Unmistakable, like it was taunting them, daring them to do something about it, sat an egg about one foot high. It was alone, sticking bolt upright out of the ground.

McCulloch took a tentative step towards the object, though both Baccus quickly took hold of the soldier to silently convey their disagreement at the idea of approaching the object. McCulloch stopped and turned to face them, shrugging as though he was asking what he was supposed to do next.

The Baccus didn't breathe a word – presumably so that it wouldn't carry into the nest proper – but simply gestured forwards as though to say they should continue. Then one of them, it was difficult to tell them apart really, gestured to his weapon, and then cut through the air with his arm and shook his head. Even over international language barriers, it was clear that the Baccus was telling them not to shoot anything.

McCulloch nodded and again stepped forward, the Baccus letting him go. He held his rifle in one hand with clear intent not to use it and walked right up to the egg with seemingly not a shred of apprehension. Then he knelt down and shone his headlamp directly onto the thing.

Even from where Marcus was, he could see that the light from the headlamp was clearly illuminating the contents of the large egg as it passed through, and it was clear that the contents were both spiderlike and moving. He had to admit begrudgingly, that the movies had actually done a pretty good job at portraying the things. A fact that he hoped didn't carry over to their contents.

McCulloch slowly and silently removed his knife from his belt and held it against the shell of the egg for a moment, the entire complement of soldiers and Baccus watching, waiting to see what he was going to do next.

Marcus felt his palms begin to sweat again, and his heart beat out his chest as the group waited in silence for McCulloch to make his move.

But then it happened. McCulloch forced his strength into the knife and it cut cleanly and quickly through the shell of the egg, and into the creature within. It didn't make a sound, and when McCulloch pulled his knife from the egg, the Scriven within was clearly not moving any longer.

Marcus let out a breath that he hadn't realised he'd been holding, and he felt the tension in the air dissipate as McCulloch wiped away the dark blood that had collected on his knife. The soldier turned to look back at the group with a grim expression on his face. Not the expression of happiness that Foley seemed to be displaying at the killing of an enemy combatant, more the expression of someone who had just taken the life of a civilian, a child whilst they slept. The thought clearly disturbed McCulloch.

But then the slightest movement in the darkness above McCulloch's head drew Marcus' attention, and as his gaze travelled upwards, so did the light from his own headlamp.

And there it was. A full-sized, adult, armoured Scriven warrior, towering over McCulloch and as soon as the light from Marcus' headlamp illuminated the creature for all to see, it lunged.

It had been way too fast for anyone to draw their weapon and fire. It was only inches away from McCulloch, after all, and even with their enhanced reflexes, aim and tactical awareness, this was a battle that they simply couldn't win.

The Scriven chose to lead with its beak-like mouth, it's terrible maw opening ready to sever McCulloch's body, or perhaps remove his head from his torso.

But McCulloch was still holding his knife in his hand and in the fraction of a second before the Scriven warrior struck, McCulloch had followed the light from Marcus' headlamp along with the gaze of everyone present, turned around and stood bolt upright to drive his knife into the tiny area between the Scriven's head and its body.

The Scriven opened its mouth to screech, but to Marcus' surprise, not a single sound emerged from the creature. But even though it was hurt and attempting to sound the alarm, it wasn't dead. It thrashed its head about, and McCulloch did everything he could to remain rooted to the ground, but the Scriven had the size advantage, and his feet were beginning to slide. Without his enhanced size and strength, there was no doubt he would've been tossed aside like a ragdoll.

McCulloch had no choice but to change tact. Still holding his knife firmly inserted into the Scriven with one hand, he used his free palm to smash the butt of the blade as deeply as he could manage into the creature. This time, it reared up on its hind legs, and McCulloch travelled up into the air with it.

A moment later, the Scriven was on its back, its legs flailing wildly in all directions and McCulloch was standing atop it, pulling the knife from it and plunging it back in over and over. The silence was maddening. It seemed like the fight lasted a lifetime, but when it was over, McCulloch was the only man standing.

He was coated in the Scriven's blood, but it didn't seem to be doing him or his clothing any harm. Marcus sighed in relief at that, although he was still sure that they would eventually find an alien creature with corrosive blood or spit, as had been suggested.

McCulloch walked back to the group, having wiped his knife again and replaced it in its holster. The only thing now was that he seemed to be holding his arm in a rather awkward way. He showed it to the group, and Marcus saw that he had been nicked in the forearm by the Scriven as it had struggled. He was lucky; had the appendage impacted much deeper, he might've lost his arm. The wound was sickeningly deep as it was.

King quickly wrapped a long piece of cloth around McCulloch's forearm, and he grunted as she tightened it. It wasn't exactly a medical-grade solution, but it was the best she could do with the limited time and resources they had to work with.

After the group scanned the tunnel once again with their headlamps, and after seeing that the Baccus now seemed to fear the human soldiers somewhat after seeing McCulloch kill a much larger Scriven warrior in hand-to-hand combat, they set off again, moving onwards to what they hoped would be the belly of the beast.

Through more dark tunnels and past vast caverns, the soldiers walked. Occasionally they would come across an egg or two and one of them would remove the inhabitant from the field of play whilst the rest stood watch – and thankfully no more warrior Scriven seemed to be lurking in the darkness – and although Marcus felt the pang of guilt each time they took one of these lives prematurely, he understood that when they came back this way the last thing they needed would be those small aliens causing a scene.

The first vast cavern they saw nearly caused Marcus to exclaim. It was over a hundred metres long, twenty metres high and filled from top to bottom with the larger Scriven. It took him a second to control himself before realising that these creatures, although looking large and very deadly, were clearly sleeping as they didn't move and were mostly curled up on the ground. He didn't know if they had simply got lucky with timing, or if this was their natural state until they detected a threat. He didn't want to wait and find out. Thankfully the light from their headlamps didn't seem to rouse the sleeping enemy, though they all made a conscious effort not to look directly at the Scriven.

Each time they found one of these caverns, of which they eventually passed five, the Baccus laid charges at the entrance with remote detonators. They gave McCulloch the detonator once they had set the first charge, clearly accepting him as head of the operation. Though it could also have been out of fear.

Once these chambers had been passed and the group moved further along the path, they began to see subtle changes in how the tunnels were arranged. Where once they were large enough for the entire group to walk comfortably side by side, now they seemed to be closing in until eventually they were not much larger than a single human soldier. Evidently in this part of the nest, the larger Scriven wouldn't have even been able to fit inside.

And that was something that was confirmed when the group came across the next alien creature along their path.

About twenty metres in front of them, a creature the size of a large dog seemed to be scraping away at the tunnel walls. It wasn't brightly coloured like the warriors, bearing a more beige-coloured exterior and where the warriors had hard outer carapaces, this one seemed softer somehow. One of the main differences with this one, though, was that it didn't actually have a turret-head sat atop its body, everything just seemed more compact somehow. After a few minutes of watching it, Marcus also assumed that it was blind, and relying on its senses to dig in the right places for whatever its task was.

But that didn't mean that the group weren't in any danger from the creature because Marcus knew that in most creatures – humans included – if they were deprived of one sense, the rest could be greatly amplified.

Marcus stood and watched the smaller Scriven that he mentally entitled a 'worker ant'. It was the best he could think of after watching it for a short while because he could see what it was doing. It was not expanding the tunnel system, rather it was picking through whatever the walls were made of and collecting something from them, discarding the rest. After the creature scurried away, Marcus realised what the thing was doing: it was collecting minerals from the walls, and must've been taking them back to the centre of the nest where they were needed. Or more importantly, where the queen or new-born Scriven needed them.

The thought then occurred to Marcus that if this was indeed the case, it meant that the Scriven were not specifically carnivores, but rather a species that could at least in part live on what they found underground. It was almost fascinating to him, actually. So fascinating that he almost got left behind once the group had resumed along their path and he hadn't been paying attention. He didn't risk voicing his assumptions with anyone else now though; if these creatures could sense sounds or movements to a greater degree than the others, the last thing they wanted to do was to make any unnecessary noises and give themselves up.

The group kept moving and, on occasion, saw more of Marcus' worker ants, though each time they remained still, allowed them to carry out their tasks and scurry off again. It became clear that they either couldn't detect the soldiers, or otherwise didn't care about their presence at all when one passed by the group almost within touching distance. It was a small miracle that it hadn't caused anyone to have to move from its path. They had their theories but they were just that, and nobody would want to test them.

It didn't take the group much longer to reach their intended destination and the central chamber of the Scriven nest was much larger than anything that Marcus had been expecting.

The tunnel they had arrived from opened into a colossal chamber, and the sight that greeted them was both awe-inspiring and deeply unsettling. The walls of the chamber were like solid rock, dwarfing everything beneath them and all around the sides, tunnels spread away in all directions, some of which contained the flashes of the worker ants as they carried out their duties – which Marcus could see that he had been correct about; they were bringing minerals for the inhabitants of the central chamber to consume as they carried out their own tasks.

But that was the most horrifying part.

What must've been hundreds of thousands of eggs covered the entire chamber, packed so tightly together that the soldiers would have no hope of walking through them even if they wanted to. But then they still weren't the worst of it.

In the centre of the chamber, atop a massive, elevated platform, lay the queen of the Scriven. She was a grotesque and colossal creature, easily ten meters in length. Her body was a mottled blend of dark greens and browns, covered in a thick, slimy secretion. Her head was adorned with a crown of writhing tendrils, and her six limbs twitched and flexed with a strange, insect-like grace. She wasn't rigid and pointed like the warriors were, nor was she pale and softer as the workers were. The only thing this creature resembled to Marcus' mind, was a wasp, mixed with a spider, mixed with a slug. And even as they watched, more eggs slipped from her grotesque rear.

Around her on the platform, yet more worker Scriven scurried, attending to her needs. Some were feeding her morsels of food from beneath, though Marcus could see no mouth there, while others were carefully removing the eggs as they arrived and were placing them in clusters around her. The new eggs were translucent and pulsated with a sickly green light from within, and Marcus could only assume that they received their harder outer shell later somehow, like it developed out in the open air.

But this whole nest had Marcus thinking again. There were just so many, and the entire place worked like an organic machine that simply pumped out fighters over and over. It was no wonder the Baccus couldn't fight them properly, it was no wonder they were losing this war. After all, how could a force like the Baccus stand against an enemy that was not only within, but could produce a seemingly unlimited number of soldiers.

"You have entered my home," a voice filled Marcus' head and it took him a moment to realise that it was actually coming from within him somehow and had not been spoken aloud.

None of the Scriven in the chamber were acting any differently, so at least there was something.

The voice was rasping, though, and most certainly feminine. It had a confidence to it that Marcus didn't like. A confidence that betrayed the fact that whatever was speaking did not sense any danger from them.

Marcus glanced at his fellow soldiers, and it was clear that they, too, were hearing the voice inside their heads. Their expressions ranged from confusion to fear, mirroring the uncertainty that had settled over each of the group.

Nobody replied to the voice.

"Why don't you come out into the light so I can see who it is that has become bold enough to visit me here in my home?" the voice continued.

Marcus frowned, entirely sure that the command was something that he wouldn't be obeying in a million years, when he saw that the two Baccus had dropped their weapons to their sides and had begun walking forwards much like mind-controlled zombies.

He wanted to grab them, but he was too far away and McCulloch, who was closer, tried to do exactly that, but the Baccus had moved before he had the chance, and he wouldn't risk walking after them.

"Ah, here are my two new toys," the voice said as the Baccus walked out into the chamber. Still nothing made any moves to suggest that they had been seen, and Marcus even thought that the Scriven queen wasn't looking even close to their direction, though he suspected the voice was coming from it.

The pair of Baccus continued walking forward until they reached the edge of the sea of eggs within the chamber and then stopped.

"Did you come here today to sacrifice yourselves to my nest? Or did your pitiful race finally conclude that the Scriven are your superiors in every single perceivable way?"

The voice was speaking and then leaving gaps as though there was a two-way conversation happening, though if there was, then Marcus wasn't privileged to it.

The soldiers exchanged alarmed glances, realising that the Baccus had now become completely submissive to the Scriven queen and were not in control of their actions. Marcus watched as McCulloch's grip tightened on his weapon, but he hesitated to take any action. Then his attention turned to the rest of the group.

Foley had turned sheet white, Asimov, Carter, Hernandez, Johnstone and Hunter had huddled closer together like they were expecting a fight to come, and King was still within touching distance of Marcus, though none of them made a sound.

But then Marcus watched as McCulloch pulled out one of the explosives that the Baccus had prepared for the centre of the Scriven nest, and seeing him do so, Asimov followed suit.

They'd been told that the explosives would be strong enough to completely obliterate the Scriven nest, though upon seeing how large it actually was, Marcus doubted that anything that could fit into packets so small would be able to deliver such damage.

McCulloch apparently had the same thought, and gestured animatedly for Asimov to take his explosive to a secondary location.

Of course, they'd discussed this plan previously, but they hadn't really thought about what it would mean up until this point. In truth, even Marcus had simply thought they'd find a hole in the ground and throw the explosives in. This was just on a completely different level.

the fact that the tunnel system in the nest was centralised at this point made things easier to plan though, so Asimov, along with Johnstone, and Carter shuffled away from the main chamber and disappeared along the tunnels until they would appear at another point in the chamber, hopefully far enough away from McCulloch and the rest of the soldiers to make the pair of explosives effective. After all, from what they'd been told, all they needed to do was kill the queen and do as much secondary damage as possible to call this mission a success.

Then the voice rasped again.

"I am so thankful that you chose to come and visit my home. My workers bring me the meat of the dead, and it has been a very long time since I've had the pleasure of tasting a fresh kill."

And then the Baccus stepped forward. The crunching sound from the first egg they'd each stepped on echoed throughout the cavern, and Marcus winced as he thought about what was to come next: the awakening of hundreds of thousands of tiny, aggressive and hungry baby Scriven.

But that didn't happen.

When the Baccus had stepped on the four eggs they'd broken once they again came to a halt, the baby Scriven inside immediately popped free from their crushed former home and scattered away to disappear in all directions. They did not immediately attack and devour the Baccus and Marcus could only wonder if it was because they were new-borns, perhaps they simply didn't have the killer instinct yet. Or perhaps they recognised a threat when they saw one.

Another set of eggs cracked and the babies scurried away again, then another and another until it was clear that the Baccus were clearing a path through the eggs and approaching the central platform step by step. It was actually a miracle that the babies were surviving with their eggs prematurely broken, though again, Marcus didn't know anything about these creatures so perhaps this was just the way they were supposed to hatch.

"I am glad you are here," the voice reiterated through Marcus' mind and presumably everyone else's. "And I thank you both for being such accepting minds. But I am afraid that your tour of my home has finally come to an end. And I am afraid that the end will not be a pleasant one for either of you."

Then Marcus watched as the Scriven queen raised her body up like it was moving in slow motion. The gunk and goo that she seemed to be covered in fought back against her movements, but she was simply too large and too strong to be held down by it. Then two unfathomably long, needle-sharp legs unfolded themselves from beneath her body and hung in the air for a moment as if they were taking a moment to steady themselves after being trapped for so long.

In the blink of an eye, the two legs then shot forward and punctured straight through the Baccus' skulls. They remained in place for a moment, before the Scriven queen picked up the bodies with seemingly no effort at all, then placed them on her platform beneath her and just out of sight.

The Baccus were no more, and Marcus was glad that he couldn't see what was now happening to their bodies on the platform.

Chapter 31 – Revenge

It was not like when Ramirez had fallen. Marcus didn't feel shock through to his very bones and he did not feel like life simply couldn't go on any more. He didn't know if it was because Ramirez was his good friend, that she was human where the Baccus were not, or if he simply dealt with this better the second time around. If he were to think long and hard about it, he might have concluded that it was all three.

The group knew they had to wait though. No matter what happened to the Baccus, it was too important, and they'd come too far not to complete their mission. Johnstone, Asimov and Carter were still making their way around to another section of the queen's central chamber and as soon as it was clear that they'd done their work, they could all retreat and blow the explosives from a safe distance.

Marcus could only watch the queen and the rest of the Scriven as he waited to ensure that they weren't discovered or would come face to face with some new danger.

From where he stood, Marcus could see all around the egg chamber and nearly all of the tunnels that led away from it, so he was sure that when the others reached a suitable destination, he would see them. What he hadn't expected though, was for the voice to return to his mind.

"I can still sense more… faint, but certainly more…" the voice rasped. "I know that you can hear me, so why don't you come and say hello? I promise I don't bite…"

Marcus did everything he could to ignore the voice, and then the burning desire to walk out into the chamber like the Baccus had. He looked at

McCulloch, who was in turn staring back at all of the soldiers still remaining hidden in the shadows and although they looked more than a little worried, not one of them followed in the footsteps of the Baccus.

There was a lull, and then the voice came again. "A resistance then… that is interesting. Something new perhaps? Something that I have not seen before… but now that I have sensed your presence and felt your mind… I will not forget and in time, I will break through whatever your meagre defences are because in time, every being and every race will bow down before the might of the Scriven."

Again, Marcus and the other soldiers remained in position and gave no indication that they were going to do anything that the voice commanded.

Another moment passed.

"Well then, perhaps if you will not come to me, then I shall send my children out to find you? Please try not to struggle too much though, because I do so enjoy my food still wriggling."

This time, when Marcus looked at McCulloch, the squad leader's eyes were bulging. Then Marcus followed his gaze back out into the egg chamber and watched in horror as the eggs, which at some point had begun shaking, were now beginning to crack open and the small baby Scriven were slowly crawling out.

Marcus shut his eyes for a moment, trying to force the image out of his mind, but he knew that it wasn't going to be a long-term solution. Instead, he opened them to see McCulloch moving towards him. It was time to go.

The Scriven babies were slowly radiating out from the central platform where the queen still sat and it was clear that they didn't know which way to go because if they did, they would've made a beeline straight for the soldiers.

McCulloch waved his hand to tell the squad to get moving and shook his head silently at the unanswered question of what to do about the three who'd gone to set their charges elsewhere. They would have to make their own way out of this mess, and quickly.

It had taken a while for the soldiers to make it to the central chamber, and they could only hope that if they traced their steps back out of the nest, they wouldn't meet the Scriven warriors on the way out, awakened by the voice and ready to greet them.

But they had no other choice. And no matter how much any of them wanted to stay, to wait for the other three to return before they made their mistake, they each knew that they had no time. And any time they wasted could possibly have meant the death of them all, not just potentially three.

"Oh come now, you know your lives will be over soon," the voice hissed. "Why not just come out now and get it done quickly rather than starve in your stone building."

Marcus knew that not only was this the queen speaking, but also that it thought he and the rest of the humans were just more Baccus, ones who could resist her mental attack.

The Queen had some telepathic ability, and that was how it was controlling the rest of them. How it had controlled the Baccus. But the humans were immune to its persuasion, and if they hadn't been, they'd all be dead already.

None of the soldiers said a word as they moved as quickly as they could back to the nest entrance whilst still remaining as silent as they could. They passed worker Scriven again, the chambers of sleeping warriors - which thankfully hadn't yet been awakened - and they made it closer and closer to their salvation, all the while knowing that the queen and the baby Scriven were actively searching for them – which was bolstered by the voice in their head switching between polite invitations and outright threats to their lives.

"Aha," the voice rasped. "There you are."

Marcus' blood turned cold and he chanced a look behind himself as the group began to move faster. They were no longer silent but they each could almost feel the hot breath of the enemy touching the back of their necks as they no doubt approached.

Marcus saw nothing. But then he remembered Johnstone, Carter and Asimov back there, further into the nest and more at risk of discovery.

Then he heard the first gunshots. Then the shouting.

"Move!" McCulloch broke the silence to give the order. There was no need to try to remain stealthy any longer because the gunfire was sure to have awakened every Scriven, warrior or worker in the entire nest and sent them all along to their location.

The squad broke into a sprint. It took everything that Marcus had within him to press down on the urge to go back and help his allies, but he knew it would be no use.

The burst fire echoed through the nest in three distinct waves, each signifying one of the three soldiers as they fought off the Scriven.

And then there were two.

And then just one.

Then silence.

Carter, Johnstone, and Asimov had fallen, and Marcus pressed that fact into a deep, dark corner of his mind as he willed his legs to pump harder and faster. All that he thought about now was surviving this, escaping so that he could enact his revenge on the Scriven.

And then there was light streaming in from before them, it was the entrance to the tunnel system. They'd made it.

But then a handful of large, armoured Scriven stepped into view, dark with the light shining behind them. The gatekeepers of the outside world. The one barrier between the soldiers and their freedom.

Within a second, Marcus, McCulloch, Foley, King, Hunter and Hernandez had drawn their rifles to the ready and after no more than two paces running at full speed, they each squeezed their triggers.

The tandem gunfire was deafening. There was no time to arrange organised fire in waves and even if there was, the soldiers knew they couldn't stop moving because if they did, they'd run the risk of being trapped inside the nest. And that would mean triggering the explosives while they were still inside. Either way the nest would be destroyed, but Marcus felt that he'd rather survive this ordeal than become another loss in the war. A loss that would most likely be forgotten with all the rest. Another number. Another failure.

The Scriven covering the entrance were utterly obliterated in seconds. There were too few of them to mount a reasonable defence against the wall of bullets hailing from the human soldiers and their bodies had broken into chunks and pieces by the time the soldiers reached them. They didn't even have to slow down.

"Take cover!" McCulloch ordered as he dove to the side of the entrance and as soon as the rest of the squad had followed suit, he activated his detonator.

Nothing happened for a short pause. And then the world shook.

Like an underwater earthquake, the explosion that would have been earsplitting otherwise sounded more like a muffled thud. And then the ground behind the entrance to the nest began to sink.

It was a slow process at first, and then a vast crater over a mile in diameter began to descend into the ground, which in itself had turned a deep shade of red with the molten dirt and rock. There was no chance that anything within the nest would've been able to survive such a blast, no matter how far away from the centre they might've been.

Marcus thought about the three lives that'd been lost in setting the second explosive charge, and wondered if just the one would've borne the same result. But he knew it didn't bear thinking about. It was something that couldn't be changed.

There was a rumbling sound coming from the tunnel entrance and it was getting louder. Marcus looked towards McCulloch for some kind of instruction but he knew what the answer was when he saw the squad leader cover his ears and brace himself.

A second later, a column of fire erupted from the nest, followed shortly by an immense shockwave that threw each of the soldiers away from the entrance and hurtling through the air. Marcus landed with an oof at least twenty metres away from where he'd been stood and thankfully on a self-inspection he hadn't been hurt as far as he could tell. The rest of the squad, given that they were tentatively raising themselves back to their feet, seemed to have been similarly unaffected by the sudden blast.

Marcus looked back at where the entrance had stood and could see that it too had been absorbed by the blast. Now, all that remained was a vast fiery crater in the ground and not even the slightest sign that there had once been an insectoid home just beneath the surface.

And where the ground had been flattened and all of the tailings from the previous work the Scriven had put into their nest had fallen into the abyss, Marcus could now see the Baccus forward operating base in the distance, stood proud and victorious. A testament to the resilience of the Baccus. The victors against this one Scriven nest and its queen.

But it was the human soldiers who'd made the difference in this case.

Marcus looked back to the rest of the human soldiers, and noticed for the first time that McCulloch hadn't returned to his feet like the rest of them. He wondered if the squad leader, being closer to the entrance to the tunnel and therefore the blast, had taken the brunt of the force from the explosion, but he could now see that on the ground surrounding McCulloch was an expanding pool of blood.

"McCulloch!" Marcus announced and ran to where the squad leader was lying. The rest of the squad followed suit and then all helped to gently turn McCulloch into his back. It was then clear what was happening.

Where the Scriven had managed to cut into McCulloch in the cave, although McCulloch had emerged victorious, the soldier's arm where he'd been scratched was now displaying a deep, wide gash that had turned a necrotic black, with dark tendrils jutting out and up the rest of his arm.

"McCulloch I..." King started to say but Marcus interrupted her by picking the squad leader up, who seemed unresponsive and pulled him across his shoulders.

Marcus didn't need to think about what needed to happen next and he immediately set off running towards the Baccus base as close to the edge of the burning crater as possible. He didn't wait for anyone to offer their aid as he ran as fast as he could, focused on the singular destination that he thought might've been able to help.

Official Records – Thoughts from Marcus Cesari, A Bitter Pill

It was a bitter pill for me to swallow. Ramirez falling was something that would stay with me forever. Something that I still wake up thinking about sometimes, a vision that I can't seem to erase from the back of my retinas. It was in the heat of battle, the way a soldier was supposed to go.

But McCulloch was senseless.

I managed to get the squad leader back to the forward operating base and the Baccus there took him away from me and off into the medical centres they had there. They told us that they had medical technologies in advance of our own and that we were to wait while they tried to stem the infection through his body. They told us that this kind of thing wasn't common, but in the few instances that they had dealt with this poison, it had led to amputation.

I felt bad for McCulloch, but it would be worth it knowing that losing an arm would always be better than losing a life.

I thought about my dad. He'd lost the ability to work and that seemed to have broken him. Did he share my own belief that continuing to live would trump any other loss? I wondered how much a single human being could endure. The loss of my friends… I wondered how much I would be able to take the loss of my own limbs, or even the ability to walk after everything I'd been through.

Somehow I knew that I wasn't the only one struggling. Not physically but mentally. I noticed that Foley and King had been arguing less and less and although that might've sounded like a good thing, to me it felt like a warning sign. A sign that either they'd stopped caring, or that they were worried. Either way it was bad news for all of us.

The Baccus celebrated the destruction of the nest. They still hadn't had any contact with the other bases on the planet but they assured us that an entire nest and a queen being removed from the battlefield was a big deal. They were pretty sure that it meant this base and the Baccus within were going to be safe, and that was something they hadn't been able to say for years.

I wish I could say the same for McCulloch.

I don't know if it was because the Baccus didn't know enough about human physiology, or if it was just the way things were. They said that the infection had spread and caused a fever. Within a day they'd pronounced McCulloch dead. I didn't feel much about it. I remember feeling numb if anything.

We hadn't heard anything from any of the other humans that'd been sent to the planet. From hundreds, we were now a total of five. Myself, Foley, King, Hunter and Hernandez. I understood why Hunter and Hernandez were quiet – they were the interlopers to our squad and their own had almost certainly all died. Foley and King worried me with their quietness.

The Baccus explained to me that some of the more intelligent of the Scriven race had developed a kind of telepathy somehow. Nobody seemed able to describe it properly, or even how they might've been able to evolve in such a way.

But I knew.

I knew that the queen had this power and that it was much more significant than anyone could imagine. That voice alone was enough to give me nightmares, and that was on top of everything else that'd happened. Everything else I'd seen over the last miserable few months.

My worry was that if the queens - or whatever else had already developed this ability - found a way to infiltrate the human mind, we wouldn't last another day.

Chapter 32 – Secondary Objectives

"It's time we left this place," Marcus announced as the group sat around the square metallic table eating their breakfast bars. It had been a week since there had been any Scriven activity in the area, and there was still no word from any of the other Baccus settlements or from any of the other humans that had landed on the planet. The only assumption of the humans was that they had indeed perished. And that included Callahan. But for all of the bases to have fallen was unlikely, given that this one had held out for so long.

"Where do we go?" Hernandez asked.

"We continue our mission," Marcus said. "We go from this base to the next, wherever it is, and we do the same thing all over again. It's what we're here to do. Besides, you saw the difference it made when we cleared that first nest. A few more days like that and we'll be free of the Scriven in no time – then it's back home."

"Maybe they'll throw us a parade?" Foley asked. It was a far cry from the confidence he'd displayed before, but at least he was talking again.

King smiled, but she didn't add anything. Nor did she give Foley a hard time. The silence made Marcus' heart sink.

"Now the Baccus don't have any transport here, and the closest operating base from here is about nine days' travel in that direction if we go on foot," he pointed over his shoulder. "So you know what that means. We've got a long walk ahead of us."

King looked at Foley, expecting him to say something snarky so that she could retort with something sarcastic, but the faraway stare in his eyes told her that he wasn't in the mood for any of this.

"Anyway," Marcus continued. "The Baccus have been monitoring the situation with the Scriven for some time now, and it appears that they have been evolving quickly. The latest advancement is this kind of telepathy we all heard. The one that made the two Baccus back there walk up to the queen and well, you know." He paused for a moment. "They're saying that it's what could've caused the interference in the landing, why it was such a mess. The whole planet's gone dark, no comms, nothing. Just the GPS systems left, and with the bases so far apart the Baccus haven't even attempted going out to search for the rest."

"So we're the canaries down the mine," King said. "Send us out there to see if we get eaten, or we make it to the next base."

"Pretty much," Marcus said. "But the mission remains the same. You saw what a difference it's made taking out that nest. The Scriven activity in this part of the planet has been reduced to nothing, it's like we won this battle with a single explosion and if we can do that over again, then this whole thing's going to go a lot smoother than we thought it would a week ago."

"I don't know, it sounds pretty dangerous, just walking out in the open like that," King continued. "What happens if we come up against a ton of those big freaks? There's going to be nowhere to run to and nowhere to hide."

"That's why the Baccus are lending us these," Marcus said, picking up three large Baccus-made flamethrowers from the ground and placing them on the table. "You saw how effective they were at repelling the Scriven, so in our hands they should be even better. I say that you, Foley and Hunter should take them up; I know how you all like a good bit of competition. Me and Hernandez will keep the rifles and the explosives because well, I don't think we should keep the explosives next to the flamers, not after seeing how effective they are."

King smiled at Foley. "You think you're better at barbequing than me big boy?" she asked.

Foley returned her a half grin, but didn't reply and his eyes weren't in it.

"And we can now select the destination that the GPS takes us to. It's been pre-programmed with the other nine forward operating bases, though the bad news is that they're very, very far apart. I mean, if we left now and walked in a straight line to the tenth non-stop, we'd be going for a month. So that means we're carrying enough supplies and ammo to keep us going for much longer than that. At each base, we can resupply and rest, but we'll also be resting along the way. The Baccus have provided us with tents and also assured me that the temperature here is pretty stable, even at night."

"And what other creepy-crawlies come out at night on this planet?" King asked. "You know, this is getting more ridiculous by the second, Cesari. Now we're supposed to hike and camp?"

"Yes, and actually, thanks to the Scriven, no creepy-crawlies come out at night. They've torn up pretty much everything they could lay their claws on, so as long as we remain hidden from them, we should be safe."

"Well, that's reassuring," King said.

Marcus nodded and smiled.

"Or," King held up a finger, "is it so damn terrifying to think that a race of aliens can just wipe out everything else on a planet, just like that? It really makes you think, huh?"

Marcus nodded again. "But the point still stands either way. If we don't get caught by the Scriven…"

"IF," King interrupted.

"Yes if. IF we don't get caught by the Scriven between bases, then this whole mission could go down exactly to plan."

"And IF we do get caught?" King asked.

Marcus smiled. "Then we have you and Foley to compete for who sets the most Scriven on fire. He looked at Foley for some sign of agreement, and the large soldier simply nodded.

"I can't believe we made you squad leader," King said. "But then again, we're all technically the same rank, Hernandez and Hunter are new to the squad, Foley looks like he's seen a ghost, and well, I just didn't want to take on the responsibility."

"You are gracious indeed," Marcus said. "So, are you ready to go?"

King closed her eyes, paused for a moment and then nodded.

"Just… try not to get us all killed out there, Cesari," she said.

"No promises," Marcus replied.

King smiled.

The journey across the planet's surface was long and boring, and although Marcus felt like that was the best way for it to be, he couldn't help but wish for something to happen after the first few days. He itched for the chance to take out another of the nests, and as the squad walked and walked and walked, he couldn't seem to shake the feeling that with each passing day there were more and more lives being lost.

It was a strange layout, too, for a planet that had been inhabited by the Baccus and one that they wanted to defend so vehemently. It was like whatever had been there before had simply been wiped from existence.

There were no smouldering ruins, no outlying towns, no vegetation, simply dirt, sand and sunlight. Marcus wondered that if the war had caused this, then was there really anything left worth fighting for?

It was only after the full nine days that Marcus eventually saw the second Baccus base that they would encounter during their participation in the war, and it was exactly like the first. A dominant square, grey construction that stuck out from the landscape like a sore thumb.

Foley had remained quiet as the group had walked across that planetscape at their singular, monotonous pace, but King, Hernandez and Hunter had been chatting away and Marcus decided to let the women have their time together. He had bigger things to worry about, like how they were all going to get out of this war alive.

"Do you think this one'll have those mist showers like the last one?" Marcus could hear Hunter asking the other women.

"I hope so, but you know what I really miss?" King replied. "Toilets. Every time I squat down to take a crap, I'm worried that something's going to jump up out of the ground and bite my ass."

The women giggled at that.

"I just want to sleep on something that isn't a thin piece of material covering the ground," Hunter said quietly. "And maybe eat something that isn't in bar form and keeps me full for a day. You know it's all well and good not having to eat proper meals… but I miss potatoes."

Then, there was the sound of agreement from the others that potatoes were indeed superior to all other foods.

"What about you, Foley?" King called to the large soldier who was walking alone between the group of women and Marcus. "What are you hoping for up there?"

Foley glanced back to the others and said: "Meat. And sleep, maybe."

"I think I've seriously underrated chairs!" Marcus called back, trying to pull the focus from Foley. "If I don't get the chance to sit down soon, I don't think my feet will ever forgive me!"

They all laughed again.

Soon after, the group found themselves at the next Baccus base, and again they found that the power to the entrance pathway was out. This time, they simply walked straight inside without a second thought.

Once they were through, Marcus planted his back against the interior of the perimeter wall and slumped down to the ground as he had done the last time he'd arrived in one of these places. He felt, for the first time in nearly two weeks, that he was safe. For the moment, at least.

On the journey from the first base to the second, they hadn't had to fire a single bullet.

The Baccus base had chairs. And beds and showers, it even had some food that it took Marcus and the squad a long time to determine if it was edible or not, but the one thing that it didn't contain, was any Baccus. Either the place had been evacuated not long ago, or the Baccus had simply moved on. It didn't look like there had been a battle though, because in the surrounding wastelands there wasn't a graveyard like there had been at the last base, and inside there was nothing that suggested there had been any fighting.

It took a day for the squad to search every inch of the base for anything they could find useful, which did include a small amount of weapons and more food, though beyond that, the place seemed to have been deserted.

It then took a week for the squad to search the area surrounding the base in concentric circles to see if they could find any sign of a Scriven nest, though eventually they concluded that the Baccus must've abandoned this base once they figured out that no Scriven were nearby. Either there was never a nest in the first place, or they'd managed to destroy it somehow. Whatever it was wasn't clear, but in the end, Marcus made the decision to move on.

Marcus and the rest of the soldiers took the opportunity to reset themselves, taking advantage of the comforts that the base provided. It was never going to be a home away from home, but it would at least allow them to lower their guard significantly and relax where they hadn't been able to for what felt like a lifetime.

After securing additional supplies and restocking their ammunition, Marcus gathered the squad to discuss their next move, because they all knew that this place was comfortable, but they weren't there for comfort. They had a mission to complete.

The GPS system they'd been following was already indicating the location of the next Baccus base, and it was time to resume their journey. Again, with each passing day, the guilt inside of Marcus built, knowing that time was not on their side. But he also recognised the necessity for rest if they were going to remain an effective fighting force.

"We've got a mission to complete, and we can't afford to rest any longer," Marcus said as they sat around a table, the food that they'd found to be edible spread out before them. "The Scriven aren't going to wait for us to catch our breath. We've seen how quickly they adapt and evolve. Our success so far has been due to our speed and efficiency. Let's not lose that momentum."

Hernandez, who had been playing with one of the GPS devices, spoke up. "According to the GPS and if I'm remembering the Baccus numbering system properly, the next Baccus base is a several-day journey from here. We should start early tomorrow morning and make the most of daylight. If we can get there without any trouble like we did here, then I'll be happy."

"So what, we just keep finding empty bases?" Foley asked in a gruff tone. "I thought the plan here was to aid the alien bases in their struggles against the nests. Well, we found a base, but we haven't found a nest. So is our job done? Or is this something else we should be worrying about now?"

"Oh shut up Foley," King said sharply. "You've done nothing but moan and complain for weeks, so why don't you just keep it to yourself for once, alright?"

Marcus expected the confrontation to turn into a full-blown argument, but again, where Foley had once been happy to fight his own corner, he simply slumped back into his chair and muttered under his breath.

"Dropped into a damn alien world… everything's been a lie."

Marcus continued, doing his best to ignore Foley. "So we've got enough supplies to sustain us for the long haul, but let's not waste them. Foley, I want you and King up front when we move out. You've got the biggest guns, and though I really hope we don't have to use them anytime soon, you'll be best to have a clear path to use them properly. Hernandez, Hunter, stick close to me. We'll take rifles so keep them ready, and remember, our goal is to reach the next base safely. So try not to make too much noise."

It was the same drill as before, but it felt like the right thing to do to reiterate what they were doing and why. Marcus couldn't help but feel like Foley was going to let him down at some point though, like he was on the verge of disobeying his orders or just going out there alone.

The squad spent the rest of the day preparing their gear and resting. It was a much-needed break, but the tension in the air was obvious. They knew that each step they took towards the next base would bring them closer to another potential battle with the Scriven, another nest, and another queen.

Marcus watched the twin suns dip below the alien horizon, casting long shadows across the landscape. He remembered the Baccus in the last base who'd told them that the nights were peaceful and warm. A fact that he was thankful of now, and knew he would be again tomorrow.

With their weapons and supplies in tow, the squad set out early the next morning, leaving behind the comfort of the abandoned Baccus base.

They had been heading toward the next base for a short while when a sound made Marcus halt suddenly.

But it wasn't a sound, he had misheard. It was a voice.

"Leaving me so soon? But I was hoping you would join me for dinner..."

The squad froze, each of them evidently hearing the voice from within their own minds. It rasped just like the last time they'd heard such a voice and Marcus' hairs stood on end at the very tone.

"There's a queen," Marcus announced quietly. "And it has to be close."

He remembered the last queen they'd encountered. It wasn't until they were practically within the central chamber that it could communicate with them telepathically, and he could only assume that this was the same. And that meant it was close.

"I am ever so hungry... " the voice continued. "Why don't you stay a while?"

"We can't stay here," Marcus said. "We need to move, but stay alert. Keep your eyes peeled for any signs of a nest or a queen. We need to find it, but we can't be taken by surprise."

Foley, despite his renewed grumbling, took the lead, his massive flamethrower at the ready. King followed closely behind, her own flamer held facing the ground as though something was going to jump out at them any minute. Hernandez and Hunter flanked Marcus, their rifles also aimed outward.

The voice continued to rasp in their minds, growing louder and more insistent with each step they took. It came from all directions, making pinpointing the queen's exact location impossible. The squad moved cautiously, their senses on high alert.

"I will make you a deal," the voice said suddenly. "If you unearth me, I will only feast on half of your number and let the rest run free."

Marcus stopped.

"What?" he said aloud. "That's not right... since when did a queen want to make a deal?"

"I know that I cannot control you," the voice said almost in answer to Marcus' statement. "As I have been attempting to do so... though perhaps in this weakened state it is not currently possible. Unearth me, and I will reward you with some of your lives..."

The squad exchanged puzzled glances at the bizarre offer from the queen. It was clear that this Scriven queen was different from the previous one they had encountered. This one did not sound like it was going to outright kill them all, or set its babies on them; it almost sounded desperate somehow.

"Don't trust it," Marcus ordered. "Remember what we're here for - destroying the nests along with the queens. This could be a trap, a trick to get us closer. You saw what happened to the Baccus back there."

Foley grunted and took two steps forward, continuing to lead the way, though he kept a watchful eye on the ground.

The voice persisted, growing increasingly desperate. "You don't understand. I am different. I am not like the others. Unearth me, and you will leave with most of your lives intact. You are so close now I can sense it, and moving closer with each step you take."

And then the world changed. Foley took another cautious step forward, and the ground beneath him fell away as a great sinkhole had just opened up to swallow him whole. Marcus and the rest of the group watched as Foley silently disappeared from their view, and they all ran to where he had stood to try to rescue him. But it was too late, he was gone.

Chapter 33 – Curled Up

King had been the closest to Foley before he'd disappeared, swallowed up by the ground beneath him, and Marcus was not far behind, arriving next to her as she peered down into the hole that seemed to have opened up out of nowhere.

King stared into the abyss, her face a mixture of shock and disbelief. One moment, Foley had been leading the way, and the next, he had vanished into this sudden chasm. The voice of the Scriven queen continued to echo in their minds, a haunting reminder of the bizarre situation they were in.

"What the hell just happened?" King asked aloud, her eyes fixed on the dark void below. She cautiously knelt down and peered into the hole, but there was no sign of Foley. Even using her headlamp to illuminate the cavern that had opened below bore no results. She opened her mouth and inhaled, ready to call out to Foley, but Marcus placed a hand on her shoulder to stop her; the last thing they needed was to alert any Scriven in a nearby radius – including the queen – that they were nearby. Especially if this was indeed a nest.

Hernandez and Hunter hurried over to join Marcus and King, their rifles trained on the surroundings in case of any further surprises. The ground seemed stable around the newly formed pit, but Marcus had the feeling that this event was far from natural.

Marcus tried to keep his voice steady as he spoke. "Foley's down there, he might need help and he might be hurt."

The fact that Foley hadn't called for help had him worried, but he knew better than to simply run head-first into enemy territory. That would be a sure fire way to get them all killed.

"Then let's go," King urged.

"Just… wait a minute," Marcus said. The voice in their heads had been quiet since the ground had swallowed Foley, and that was just one thing holding Marcus back. The other was the fact he could see that the squad could descend into the chasm and follow Foley, but he couldn't see an easy way out of there. They could do it, but it'd take time and effort. Time they might not have if they needed to make a quick escape.

"Forget that," King announced and leapt into the hole in the ground.

Marcus almost called out after her, but then caught himself and realised that they had no choice now but to follow, regardless of the consequences.

He shook his head and followed King down into the darkness, with the other pair following closely behind. King had been rash, but she'd been decisive. It was the kind of decision that needed to be made when someone's life was potentially on the line. The kind of decision Marcus should've been able to make for himself.

Marcus' feet slipped on the loose ground as the edges of the newly opened sinkhole were uneven and sloped. It was a wonder that the hole wasn't simply straight up and down.

Marcus managed to kind of fall-run his way down the newly made tunnel entrance, much like he was running on a sand dune. And now he recognised the ground beneath his feet. These were almost certainly the tailings of a Scriven nest.

"Yes! That's it! Come closer!" The voice rasped. "I can almost taste your presence in my domain… but what are you? You are something different to the Baccus… I have heard… but it is only a matter of time, is it not? Come to me… I want to see you… I want to taste you and to know…"

Marcus shut his eyes tightly and mentally shook the words away. They were nothing different to what had already been said, but as it spoke in his mind, he couldn't help but feel a weight upon him. Like he wanted to listen, to obey, but his stubborn humanity was keeping him from it, and that in turn was taking its toll.

"It is futile to resist," the queen rasped in Marcus' mind like it had read his thoughts. "Come to me, and all this will pass."

Marcus picked up the pace and caught up to King, who was jogging just up ahead. Nobody mentioned the fact that Foley hadn't been there on the ground, unconscious. And the fact he wasn't calling out for help was still worrying.

As the group ran, their headlamps bounced on the walls around them, illuminating the poorly formed tunnel walls. It was nothing like the last nest they'd been in, rather this one looked like it had been abandoned, or at least left to decay.

And then they finally came to a halt because standing before them, upright and still, facing away was the unmistakable hulking form of Foley. He was staring at something before him. Something that Marcus saw too when the group caught up to their large squad mate.

It was the nest's central chamber, and the queen.

But this chamber was much smaller, only a handful of metres high and wide, and the queen barely fit inside. The chamber had all but collapsed, and immediately Marcus could see the problem that'd caused: the queen was trapped within.

There were no eggs around her, and she wasn't coated in the slimy goo like the last one. She had the thin, pointed legs as before, the wasp-like body and tail and the pointed turret-head with three black eyes sunken into it, but seeing her like this Marcus did not sense power and authority, he sensed fear.

The squad all came to a halt alongside Foley, who was still yet to say a word.

"You are strange creatures…" the queen said. "Why don't you approach your queen and we can discuss how we can help each other?"

Marcus peered around the cavern and then the tunnels behind him. There was no sign of any other alien creatures. Not a single one.

So he spoke aloud.

"You're trapped, and alone, right?" He said. His voice did not echo, which he had guessed it wouldn't have, but King whipped her head around to stare at him like this was the stupidest thing he'd ever done.

There was a moment of silence where Marcus felt the very air thicken.

"I am your queen and you shall obey!" The voice rasped. She had heard Marcus' words. He smiled.

"Why don't you come out here and show us why we should obey?"

There was a silence again.

"What are you?" the queen asked with a very different tone now.

"We're the cavalry," Marcus said. "Here to show you what we think of oppression, murder and war."

"Interesting…" the queen said. "That you would make such a proclamation when you are clearly not of this world."

King snorted. "She's got you there."

"Shut up," Marcus said. Then turned his attention back to the queen. "We're going to kill you, you know that, right?"

"I do not think that it is within your capability…" the queen started, but was then suddenly cut off by an intense heat exploding from next to Marcus. The roar of Foley's flamer, accompanied by his loud shout of distaste filled the dark tunnel, illuminating everything like they were within the very flames of hell.

The flames washed over the queen, and she reared up only to be restricted by the low ceiling above her. She screamed a high-pitched squeal and did her best to cower from the attack, but there was nothing she could do, and nowhere she could go.

Marcus placed a soft hand on Foley's shoulder, and the soldier let the flames recede back into the barrel of his weapon. Marcus was awed by the destructive power of the weapon when used in such an enclosed space.

The queen's body was sizzling and smoking, but she was still alive.

"I am going to ask you some questions, and you are going to answer me. If you do not answer, then you have seen what will happen to you. Do you understand?"

No answer.

"Foley," Marcus said and again the soldier obeyed, coating the cavern and the queen with the flames from his appropriated weapon before letting them die back down again.

There was again no answer after a moment, and Marcus said: "Foley…" but before the soldier could wash the Scriven queen again with fire, she answered.

"Yes," the rasping tone returned to Marcus' mind, and it sounded annoyed.

"Where are the rest of the Scriven from this nest, and where are your eggs?" Marcus asked. "Are we going to be ambushed?"

"I am all that is left of this place," the queen said.

"What happened? And what happened to the Baccus in the base nearby?"

"I was victorious against the Baccus," the queen replied. "I pushed my influence to them and they simply walked here. Such is the way of war. They were delicious…"

"So what happened to you then? If you're such a victorious and powerful queen, why is it just you?" King asked, joining Marcus' interrogation.

"Once my children feasted on the Baccus as they arrived, the minerals that this land provided was not enough to sustain them," the queen said. "I attempted to push my will onto them, but I had already spread myself so thin. I was weakened momentarily and my nest turned on me. They chose to bury me here, not wanting to face me directly."

Marcus thought about what the queen was saying. The Scriven didn't obey her unconditionally, and it was likely the same for the rest. He wondered if that was something that they could use ink the future.

"So what, they just left you here to die?" King asked.

The queen did not answer.

"No, it's worse than that," Hernandez said stepping forward. "They left her here as a punishment, didn't they? They could've swarmed you, could've killed you, but they wanted you to starve at the bottom of the hole you dug for yourself. The Scriven don't want to be controlled, do they?"

Again, the queen didn't answer.

"Because you're nothing. You're weak," Hunter continued. "You couldn't even keep a hold of your own nest, your own children!"

"I WILL SHOW YOU TRUE POWER!" the queen roared in all of their minds and attempted to rear up again.

Foley again engulfed the Scriven queen in fire from his flamer, and again it seemed to calm her back down. Marcus wouldn't admit it out loud, but the simple fact that the queen wasn't killed from just one of these attacks was amazing.

"You have no idea of our power," the queen said, though her telepathy seemed strained. "We knew you had arrived…"

"You knew we had arrived?" King said. "Yeah, we know because any time we come close to one of you queens, you start talking in our heads."

"That's… not what she meant," Marcus said. "She means in the beginning…"

"The…" King started but froze. "It was YOU!" she practically screamed. "You were the reason the transports malfunctioned! But how?"

Kind was clearly upset and angry, now pacing about trying to piece it all together whilst waving her arms in the air as she spoke.

Marcus looked at the ground. "They must've controlled the pilots somehow. If they can extend their telepathy… but it must've weakened them, right?"

"Yes!" the queen rasped triumphantly. "No reinforcements for the Baccus!"

"YOU!" Hunter shouted and fired her rifle into the midsection of the queen. The bullets made a sickening wet sound, and their impact caused small red holes to appear. The queen seemed less affected by this than she did by the flamer, however.

Marcus was quickly losing control of the situation, and he could feel it. He needed his people to remain calm, so he did the only thing he could think of.

"STOP!" he shouted, and the gunfire dutifully obliged. The cavern fell quickly silent again.

"Nobody is to fire their weapon again unless ordered to do so by me, you got that?"

"But this fu…" Hunter started.

"Do you understand?" Marcus reiterated before she could finish.

Hunter closed her mouth with a click and nodded.

"Now I know how you all feel. How we all feel about this. The Scriven killed our people, but it's no different to what they did to Ramirez, McCulloch or any of the Baccus for that matter. But now we need to do things in the right way. We need information and a plan, not to just kill everything we come across. So I say again. No shots. Not yet, at least."

"Yes!" the queen rasped again. "We took control of your pilot, all of us! But it weakened us… some did not return alive from this, but more will eventually take their place, as is the way with the Scriven for we are eternal."

Marcus listened to the queen's words, his mind racing with the newfound knowledge. The Scriven queens had been responsible for sabotaging the transport ships, leaving the stranded humans to fend for themselves on this alien world, or killing them in fireballs of ruined lifeboats. It was a revelation that left a bitter taste in his mouth, but he knew that the longer he kept this going, the more information he could gather.

"Tell us more," Marcus demanded. "How did you take control of the pilots? What's your connection to the other queens, and where are they now? Have any of them been killed? Have any been abandoned like you?"

The queen hesitated for a moment before responding. "We share a connection through the vast network of our kind. It is how we communicate, how we exert our influence. But controlling the pilots, that was a collective effort, a sacrifice. We reached into their minds, manipulated their thoughts, and caused them to malfunction. Just know that each moment you spend here with me, my kind are preparing a new way to interact with your species, and when we find a way to break through, you will belong to us."

"Can you do it again?" King asked, ignoring the queen's proclamation. "If they come back to rescue us, will they lose control again?"

The queen's response was raspy and strained, though sounded sincere to Marcus. "Not from this weakened state. And not without time to recover."

"Where are the other nests?" Marcus pressed. "And how many queens are there?"

The queen's three black eyes seemed to glint in the dim light of the cavern. "The other nests are scattered across this world, hidden from your kind. There were ten of us…"

"Not were," Marcus pressed. "How many are there?"

The queen hesitated again, and Marcus raised a hand towards Foley, who readied his flamer.

"There are three left, including myself," the queen said. "The rest have fallen. One recently you may well know. But they will be replaced in time."

Marcus smiled. The Baccus had thought there were ten queens out there, and after the one they'd killed already, It would've left nine. Things had just got far simpler, or so he assumed.

"So you're losing," Marcus said. "Your nests are being destroyed and your queens are dying. Sounds like we got here just in time to finish the job. Now tell me, Are there other humans here?"

"There were," the queen replied, and Marcus could sense the smile in her voice. "And I have to say, they were very useful to our kind. And not just as dinner."

"What's that supposed to mean?" King asked loudly. "What, you lay your eggs in their stomachs and they burst free after the babies inside have taken their fill?"

"An interesting concept…" the queen replied. "But no. The Scriven are an advanced race, far more advanced and adaptable than you seem to comprehend. So I will enlighten you. Our knowledge is shared within our race through our natural links as well as passed to our young through our genetics. So when we learn something, we can easily adopt it, and devise new ways to deal with new situations. Be that a particular evolution to better survive a harsh new world, or military tactics. You are not Baccus, and you have brought us something new, something we can use."

Marcus' blood ran cold. He mentally ran through everything that the Baccus had told them about how the humans were different, about how they had been brought into this war because they were soldiers. And it sounded like their presence was just feeding the Scriven new information. Information they could use.

He searched for something the Scriven could have learnt, but as much as he searched, it was simply too difficult to take an outside view of something he was already so close to.

"What have you learned from us?" Marcus demanded, his voice firm.

The queen's response was chillingly confident. "We have learned much. Your tactics, your strategies, your weapons. You have brought us knowledge that will make us stronger, more efficient. Your race is not yet just another species to be treated as prey. You are a valuable resource."

Marcus exchanged fleeting glances with his squad. The implications of the Scriven using their knowledge to enhance their own abilities were grave. It meant that not only were they fighting against a formidable enemy, but one that was becoming increasingly intelligent and adaptable.

"But it is already too late. We have absorbed your knowledge, and there is nothing you can do to stop us. Your fate is sealed."

As Marcus contemplated their situation, something in the dimly lit chamber caught his eye. A subtle movement, a shadow shifting against the rocky wall. He raised his weapon and pointed it at it, his headlamp too illuminating the place where he was sure he'd seen the movement.

"Did anyone see that?" he whispered.

The squad members all turned their headlamps toward the wall, and there was nothing there. But then something moved. It wasn't that there was nothing there, in fact, the wall was completely covered, every single inch of it with tiny Scriven, camouflaged almost perfectly when they remained still. These were different from everything Marcus had seen so far. These were like a cross between insects and chameleons, blending seamlessly with the rock and dirt of the walls. The Scriven had learnt to hide.

"Scriven!" King shouted, raising her flamer and immediately setting the walls ablaze with her stream of flames. The tiny Scriven squealed in distress as some of them began to sizzle and burst. They fell to the ground, their chameleon-like abilities disrupted by the flames and the gunfire that had joined the attack.

But more tiny Scriven revealed themselves where their kin had fallen, skittering away from the squad in a desperate attempt to escape the sudden assault. The cavern filled with the sounds of gunfire and panicked Scriven cries, and not a single human soldier was not firing their weapon. Foley though, he was concentrating his fire on the queen, who was already writhing and screaming in agony.

"Watch the ground!" Marcus shouted as he fired at the remaining camouflaged Scriven on the walls. He could see out of the corner of his vision, that some of the tiny creatures were working their way across the floor towards them. He remembered McCulloch and how a single wound could prove fatal.

Some of the shots around them turned to the ground, though it was a tough decision to shift their fire when there just seemed to be so many of the Scriven advancing on them.

King then turned her flamer onto the queen and as soon as her flames joined Foleys' and lapped at the large alien creature, Marcus noticed a definite ripple in the advancing tiny Scriven on the ground.

"Kill the queen!" He shouted above the booming gunfire. "It'll break the control and we might just make it out of this!"

The three rifles turned on the queen, all of them firing in bursts and in unison. The queen, unable to move, could do nothing against the onslaught of fire and bullets cascading into her and within just a few moments, her legs curled up underneath her, and she slumped to the ground without another sound. Marcus' nostrils stung with the scent of burning flesh, but it was a smell that gave him at least a little comfort. Because it was the smell of another queen falling, never to kill another human or Baccus again.

The Scriven on the floor seemed to pause as the telepathic link to their mother was severed. The soldiers watched as the insects tried to decide what to do next, almost frozen in position.

But then the Scriven did the only thing they could when they had been stripped of their unifying direction. They scattered, and did everything they could to get to their food.

The problem was that the only food in the tunnel system, was the humans.

Chapter 34 – Attrition

The tiny Scriven, where once they'd been an orderly mass making their way towards the humans, were now scattering in all directions and all at once and the cavern descended into utter chaos. If they'd been any smaller, then they would've looked like fleas, leaping and jumping, fighting each other to get closer to their meal. It was immediately obvious that they didn't care how much bigger than them the humans were – they simply needed to attack, to feed, so that was what they did.

The disorderly fashion of the Scriven without their leader was an entirely new challenge to Marcus, who identified that they needed to change their tactics quickly, before they lost the advantage of their tandem gunfire. What made matters worse, was the fact that King and Foley's flamers were only effective at dealing with the Scriven who weren't moving too fast or close by – it had been a lot easier when they had all been bunched closely together, or attached to the walls.

"We need to go!" Marcus shouted loud enough to be heard.

"Where?" King shouted back, looking all around for an exit.

"Where we came in! We can boost each other out if we have to, but we can't stay here!"

It wasn't a particularly well thought out plan, but Marcus knew they had no other choice. The tiny creatures were leaping about, climbing the walls, the ceiling and scurrying across the floor just to get at the humans. It was a small miracle that one hadn't made it through to them yet.

Outside of this nest they hadn't seen any Scriven, so if they were going to retreat, that was the only option.

'The gunfire might be drawing more Scriven towards us,' Marcus thought. 'But we can deal with that later; we just need to get out of here'.

"Foley, you take the lead," Marcus said. Burn anything that comes our way. King, you flood the tunnel behind us with fire, and the rest of us will shoot blindly through the fire. Just keep your rifles aimed at the ground, you got it?" It wasn't the best use of ammunition, but if it kept them safe for the few minutes it'd take them to escape, then it was their only option.

There wasn't a reply of acknowledgement, rather Foley skirted his way around the group so that he would be at the front during their journey out of the place. King continued to fire her flamethrower into the cavern before them and Marcus, Hunter and Hernandez emptied their magazines in full-auto mode through the fire and across the ground. The formation was effective, but Marcus knew it wasn't going to last forever.

A tiny bug leapt at Hunter, and Hernandez took the shot, disintegrating the Scriven with a single well-aimed shot no more than an inch from Hunter's head.

"Hey, that was too…" Hunter said, though she was forced to return the favour when a second Scriven lunged in much the same way at Hernandez.

"Move!" Marcus shouted and the squad obeyed, following the path illuminated by the flamer fire belching from Foley's weapon.

The group condensed between the two flamers, and when fired into a narrow tunnel, they proved more than effective at destroying everything they shot at. Nothing could breach their defensive line because nothing could pass through the flames without being burnt to a crisp.

The journey back to where Foley had fallen through the ground was short but punctuated with constant gunfire. Not a single Scriven had managed to break through their line, and Marcus could only marvel at the combat prowess of each and every one of his friends and comrades.

Eventually they saw daylight again, and Marcus sighed a breath of relief; the constant fireballs that were erupting from King and Foley's weapons had been sapping the oxygen from the cave system, not to mention making him sweat more than he'd ever thought possible.

"Good job we've got these advanced overalls," Marcus said. "Keeps the sweat from sticking and I can barely smell Foley from here!"

With the hole in the ground finally above them, Foley and Marcus both ceased their fire. Foley moved to the unstable ground that led up and away to daylight, and Marcus stood behind him to brace himself and push the large soldier up and out, just like they'd done against the wall in The Gauntlet.

"Clear," Foley said once he was out and had searched the surrounding area for any sign of the enemy. Marcus smiled. At least, that was something.

Foley lay down on his front and dangled an arm down for Marcus to grab and pull himself up with. Marcus had almost forgotten how strong the gene-editing program had made them all, and the wrench he experienced when both he and Foley pulled caused him to shoot upwards and land perfectly on his feet with almost no effort.

Marcus turned to dangle his own arm into the hole for the three women to grab and pull themselves up with, and he watched as they all fired continuously back into the tunnel where he could no longer see the approaching enemy.

"Ready!" Marcus shouted to be heard over the sound of the gunfire. "Give me your hands and I'll pull you up. Foley, you take Hernandez and I'll take King and Hunter."

King's flamer was still belching flames into the narrow corridor, which in itself was surely taking care of the lion's share of the Scriven. But Hunter and Hernandez, too, were firing non-stop, seemingly aiming their shots to choose precision over King's area of damage style of fire. They would have to cease fire to escape the cave.

Both Marcus and Foley's hands dangled down for the women to take, and they knew that when they had the opportunity - a lull in the enemy advance - they would need to take their shot.

And then Marcus' heart stopped.

It stopped in tandem with the very moment that the flames spurting from King's flamer died down to nothing seemingly in an instant. She had run out of fuel for the flamer, and she wasn't carrying a backup.

Hunter and Hernandez both immediately switched their rifles to burst fire and began firing wildly, and King took a second or two to see if there was any way she could reignite her flamer.

But it was no use.

Marcus watched as King turned to look up and him and Foley through the hole where they hung, awaiting their squad mates. He watched as Hunter and Hernandez' rifles trilled their dire melody. He watched as a wave of tiny Scriven flooded the tunnel below, cutting the rattle of the gunfire to nothing.

Marcus' ears rang with the new silence.

He watched as the three soldiers disappeared.

Foley roared, standing up to his full height and pointing his own flamer down into the nest, unleashing a wave of fire that filled the cavity and the tunnel system beyond.

Marcus' world slowed to a craw.

He could see that Foley was screaming, but he could hear nothing.

And then it was over.

Foley had spent the fuel for his flamethrower just as King had. But he still kept screaming.

Marcus slumped to the ground. First to his knees and then he fell onto his back. He knew that it was finally over. They'd tried their best on this alien planet, in this alien war. But they'd lost. They simply hadn't been enough. He awaited the surge of tiny Scriven from the tunnel entrance and didn't even have the frame of mind to hope that they'd end him quickly. He just lay there, waiting.

But the end didn't come.

Foley had gone silent and he was looking down into the nest, but there were no Scriven bursting forth from it. Marcus rolled over onto his front and peered down into the hole.

King's face flashed in his mind, looking up at him in those last moments, but he forced it away. This was another face to be reserved for his nightmares. Not for now. Not when there was still so much work to be done.

The tunnel beneath them was now littered with smouldering, smoking corpses of the tiny Scriven. It was a gruesome sight, the aftermath of Foley's fiery assault. The air was thick with the acrid stench of burnt flesh and chitin. But there was no sign of the three women who'd stood their last stand just moments ago, and Marcus didn't know if that was a good thing or not.

Foley's last desperate act had bought them a reprieve, at least for the moment. The Scriven had been decimated, and their advance halted. But Marcus knew this was just a temporary respite. There was always something coming for them, right around the next corner.

"Get up," Foley's voice was hoarse as he helped Marcus to his feet. "We need to move. They won't stay away for long."

"They won't?" Marcus asked, not entirely present in the conversation.

Foley shook his head. "This is hell, isn't it? And when did you ever hear about hell giving anyone a break."

Marcus shook his head slowly. "This… isn't hell, Foley. This is an alien planet and a war that we've been roped into."

"Same thing, isn't it? Pain, suffering. The only difference is that we've got a way out. Because when they get us… and they will eventually get us, our jobs done, and there's no more death."

Marcus squinted at Foley. The once jokey, happy soldier had been affected, changed by everything that had happened to them. And Marcus couldn't blame him. In truth he felt his own sanity slipping away from him too.

Suddenly, the GPS device from the crates they had been carrying beeped. It reminded Marcus that with just the pair of them left, they'd only be able to bring one of them along, leaving the other behind. Also, it was the first time the device had made a sound, which was interesting in itself.

Marcus peered down at the device after withdrawing it from one of his pockets. There was the usual directional indicator flashing, though now it was pointing in a new direction.

"What do you think of this?" Marcus asked Foley, pleased to be given an opportunity to change the subject.

Foley stepped closer and looked at the device.

"Suppose it's telling us where to go, just like always. I'm guessing when we make it to the next base, we'll be sent out to take another nest."

"It's… what we're here to do," Marcus said.

"Maybe after this one, there won't be any of us left," Foley said. "Looks like they get a few of us each time."

Marcus closed his eyes. Every time he thought about the people he'd lost, it hurt. Like a deep pain in his heart, but more than that, he felt guilt.

He remembered the words McCulloch had said to him at that first base: they were soldiers, this is what they were here to do and everything else was irrelevant. Soldiers were supposed to put their lives on the line, and if they died in the line of duty, then so be it. Marcus wondered how McCulloch felt in his own last moments – inside, in a hospital bed and without an enemy combatant in sight. It wasn't a soldier's death.

"Just two more," Marcus said. "Two more queens are out there, and after that, we can go home."

He saw the look Foley gave him. It spoke of the same feeling that Marcus had: that even if there were just two left, and even if they destroyed them, this war wouldn't be over any time soon. And all the while the war continued, so did their participation.

"So let's go. It'll be a while before we get there, and I don't want it to take any longer than it has to."

Foley nodded, looking back at the crate they were to carry with them. He stopped over and opened the lid, producing an SA80 that matched Marcus' own. There was no sense in carrying the flamer anymore as it was entirely spent. He left it on the ground.

"This one's yours now, King," Foley said. "Just try not to break it." He shouldered his new rifle and turned away from the hole in the ground.

Marcus and Foley each took hold of one of the handles at either end of the crate and began the long march in the direction indicated by the GPS system.

The first time they saw a Scriven warrior on their journey, it had been alone. The pair were cautious of it, watching it through their rifle scopes with their fingers hovering over their triggers, but they waited before they opened fire to see if it had any friends nearby.

But the creature seemed alone, aimless even, and while they watched, they found that it had already seen them. It just wasn't doing anything about it.

Marcus and Foley watched as the alien being skittered back and forth but made no moves to approach them. Eventually, Foley was the first to stand up and make sure that it knew they were there, waving his arms back and forward at the creature. It didn't respond.

Then Marcus had an idea. He pulled a meal replacement bar from his pocket and launched it as far as he could towards the Scriven. It flew through the air and landed practically at the feet of the creature, causing it to leap back in surprise as it landed. Marcus could only smile as he watched the Scriven stab a sharp appendage at the bar before it plunged into it head-first, eating the whole thing in one go. When it had finished, it looked on the ground to see if there was any more.

Marcus pulled another bar from his pocket and launched it into the expanse between them and the creature, closer to them this time. As soon as it hit the ground, the Scriven scurried towards it and devoured it in a second. When it was done, it fixed its eyes on Marcus and Foley, clearly anticipating more food.

Marcus opened his pocket again. He knew throwing away food wasn't the best idea, but with just him and Foley left, they had enough of the bars to last years.

Bang.

The Scriven's head exploded into a mist of deep red and black blood as its legs curled up beneath it and it fell to the ground, dead before it even knew what hit it.

Marcus whipped his head around to see Foley, gun still raised and barrel smoking.

"One less to deal with later," Foley said, lowering his weapon.

Marcus didn't say anything. The shock was enough to keep him silent.

They continued along their path.

Along the way to their next destination, the pair found a handful of Scriven of differing sizes wandering around the barren planetscape. It was only after the third group they found that Marcus realised what was happening.

"These are the ones without a queen," he said to Foley. "Like, once their link to the nest is gone, they're just animals. They want food, but that's about it, they aren't soldiers and I don't think they're intelligent."

"Don't make a difference," Foley grunted. "They kill us or we kill them, that's all that matters."

"Is it, though?" Marcus asked. "What happens if we take out all the queens and all that's left are peaceful creatures just wanting to survive? What then?"

"Then we kill them," Foley said. "Or they come back again to kill us in our sleep. We don't make the rules here and these aren't our decisions to make. So don't try. Just kill."

"You really think that…"

"I don't need to think!" Foley raised his voice. "And that's the point! When you start to think, you start to doubt, and there's no room to doubt, Cesari. So shut your mouth, stop trying to give purpose to everything and concentrate on keeping yourself alive."

Marcus shut his mouth. In a way, Foley was right because when he allowed himself to think too much, in his mind's eye all he could see were the faces of Ramirez, McCulloch, Hunter, Hernandez, Johnstone, Asimov, King and everyone else who he recalled from the gene editing program that now felt like a distant memory. They'd become soldiers, warriors, sent far away from home and most had lost their lives before they even had the chance to fight back. And he and Foley were the last two left, for whatever reason the universe had decided.

And then the radio attached to Marcus' arm crackled. It was the first time it had even made a sound since they'd touched down on the planet and now it was crackling. In fact, Marcus had forgotten that it was still switched on.

He clicked the button twice to signify he was receiving a signal without saying anything. His heart was racing and his mind was immediately filled with all the possibilities – there were rescuers inbound, there were other survivors – whatever it was, having human contact was the best news he'd had in months.

Then the radio burst into life.

"We're pinned down!" The male voice shouted. Marcus could hear the distinct fire of at least a handful of guns in the background, and that meant survivors.

"We need help! We're holding them off, but they keep coming! Is anyone out there?"

Marcus held the radio up and replied.

"We're here. Where are you?"

The radio spluttered now, cutting off much of what the other man was saying. "Over… coordinates… help," it crackled between interference.

Then Marcus' GPS pinged again. It was so coincidental that he knew it had to be related. The soldiers must've found a way to ping the GPS system to let them know where they were.

Marcus looked at Foley, who nodded. They picked up the crate again and began running in the direction the GPS system indicated, the crate occasionally crashing against their legs, but they ignored it. This was too important.

Chapter 35 – Alone

"Can't you just run in a straight line?" Foley said loudly as the crate crashed into his already sore leg. For five straight hours, the pair had run with the crate clattering between them. And for five straight hours, the blip on the GPS didn't seem to move. Not even a little.

Marcus' arms had begun to burn with the constant weight bobbing about, but he pushed it from his mind and told his body to obey for just a little longer.

"The radio's been silent since we started," Marcus said, ignoring Foley's annoyance. "But the GPS is still telling us where to go, so that's a good thing, right?"

"Yeah," Foley replied. "Unless they switched it on, called for help and then were killed. The Scriven, not knowing what the GPS was, just left it there… and that's where we're going now."

Marcus hadn't thought of that, and slowed his pace a little. The change caused the crate to crash into Foley again, who nearly fell over.

"That's enough!" The large soldier announced. "I'm sick of running. I'm sick of carrying this God damned crate and I'm sick of this planet!"

Foley dropped his end of the crate and fell to his knees. Marcus had no choice but to stop, too, as the heavy crate dug into the ground. He then sat on it behind Foley as though it was a seat.

"I know how you feel," Marcus said. "I didn't ask for any of this, you know? But we're soldiers…"

"I don't care," Foley growled. "Just… shut up will you." His shoulders slumped, and Marcus didn't say another word.

"Ramirez, king… McCulloch," Foley muttered.

Marcus closed his eyes. He could see their faces again, shrouded in the darkness of his mind's eye.

And then the guilt returned.

It was so clear now: this was all his fault. If he had been a proper soldier in the first place, if he'd been a better leader, they might all still be alive. But he wasn't. And they weren't.

"This is all my fault," Foley said, still not turning to look at Marcus. "Just… if I stayed at the back like I was supposed to, if we fired in bursts…" he trailed off. It didn't take Marcus long to figure out Foley was talking about how King had died, and then Hernandez and Hunter.

"No…" Marcus said. "It's on me. It's all on me; you only did what you were told… what I told you to do."

"And you don't think I could've questioned that?" Foley asked.

Marcus shook his head to himself, but he didn't respond.

The radio burst to life again. "We're pinned down!" The same male voice they'd already heard shouted. Marcus could still hear the distinct fire of more than a couple of rifles.

Foley didn't react to the sound, seemingly lost in his own misery. But Marcus was looking down at the GPS again, because it was beeping.

But something didn't add up. The voice that had come through the radio wasn't just the same one that he'd heard before; it was exactly the same. Even the gunfire was the same, because again he found himself picking out the different firing patterns of the soldiers pulling the triggers.

And then it dawned on him: this was not a live transmission. And that was why he received no reply when he tried to respond.

"It's… not real," Marcus announced. "None of this…"

Foley didn't move a muscle, and Marcus stood up from the crate and placed a hand on the larger man's shoulder. Foley was still on his knees facing away from Marcus, but with the contact, Marcus could now feel from the jittering of the man's shoulders, that Foley was sobbing.

"Foley I…" Marcus started, but Foley let out a cry.

"I'm sorry!" he wailed. "King… Ramirez… I'm sorry!"

"Foley, snap out of it!" Marcus quickly turned to try a new approach, and he pulled hard on Foley's shoulder to turn the man so they could speak face to face. But when he did so, Marcus saw that Foley's eyes were both bloodshot and milky white.

A cold shiver swept over Marcus as he realised what had happened. The Scriven must've managed to break through Foley's mental defences. And that meant they were both in danger.

Marcus let go of Foley and backed away from the soldier. He didn't know exactly how far this mental control would extend or even if it was somehow contagious, but he knew he needed to move away from it.

What he didn't want was for this thing to consume his friend, to force Foley to turn on him. He didn't know if his already pressured mind would be able to take it if he had to take another human life, even if it was the only option available.

Thankfully for Marcus, Foley just kept sobbing and apologising, and it was like Marcus wasn't even there with him at all.

Marcus shut his eyes tight enough to block out all the light from the world around him and did everything to keep his mind set on the present. He wouldn't allow himself to be caught up in whatever was happening to Foley. And then a thought occurred to him.

Opening his eyes again, he banged the side of the GPS device, concentrating on the directional arrow.

"This isn't real," he said to himself. "Just see through it."

The arrow on the GPS, the ping that'd been leading them to this very location and beyond, abruptly vanished.

Marcus stared at it in wonder. It was like his eyes had been opened.

"I know you're here," Marcus thought as loudly as he could. "And I know what you're doing, so you can just save your effort and stop."

He waited for a response, sure that he had concluded correctly: that there was a queen out there doing this, getting into their heads.

But then he thought about why that might be. The queens he'd met so far had thought themselves all-powerful; even when pretending to be caught or trapped, they'd still exuded an air of confidence and authority. If another queen had indeed manufactured this situation, then this one was different.

But then, if it had managed to get into their heads well enough to cause them to think or even see things, it meant that the Scriven were evolving. And that was a worry.

Marcus closed his eyes again to think again. The queen must've been nearby to be able to get into their heads as well as it had, and it must've had the time to do so. He knew that the queens had managed to bring down their transports, but if the other queen was to be believed, that was a draining, one-off experience. So far, they'd only experienced the mental attacks of the queens when they'd been close by. Very close by.

But they'd already seen that the Scriven could evolve quickly, and this could just be another type of enemy they had to deal with.

Marcus looked at Foley, his mind racing. He had a mental image of alien eggs in their stomachs, but he pushed that thought aside not even wanting to even entertain it.

Then he turned and saw the large supply crate sitting on the ground behind them.

The crate that had been right there with them the whole time. The crate they under no circumstances could leave behind.

"Foley…" Marcus said, slowly backing away from the crate and touching his friend's shoulder. "There's a bug here… and I need you to snap out of this…"

Foley didn't respond.

Marcus raised his rifle and pointed it at the crate. Sure, if he destroyed the thing, it would mean loss of supplies and ammunition, but if there was something inside of it that could affect Foley the way it was, then it needed to die, whatever the cost.

"Foley!" Marcus shouted, but again he was left standing alone.

"I'm sorry…" Foley sobbed louder now. "If I could go back, if I could do things differently… I'm sorry!"

Marcus shut it out. He shut everything out and took a tentative step towards the crate with his rifle still trained on the inanimate object like it was a bloodthirsty creature.

And then the radio buzzed into life again.

It was a voice he didn't recognise, but if he had to guess from the accent and cadence, it was that of a Baccus.

"We need those supplies now! We have civilians here in need of urgent medical attention!"

"Not good enough," Marcus said and took another step towards the crate.

The radio clicked again, and this time a cold sweat encapsulated Marcus' entire body, and he froze in place. The voice coming from the small black box belonged to Ramirez.

"God, if we don't make it out of this… I hope someone hears this…" rumbling, the sounds of explosions filled the transmission. "Something's gone wrong… I… please… it can't end like this. Not now. Not here."

Marcus couldn't help but match those words in his mind's eye to the vision of Ramirez' face as she'd perished.

It was just too much. All of this was too much.

Marcus couldn't see anything any more. Not the world around him, not Foley, not the rifles they each held, and not the crate. It was all blank now. Everything except Ramirez's face and the echo of her last words replaying in his mind over and over.

But there was something. He could still hear Foley sobbing. It was a chilling sound and one that reminded Marcus that the world was still there beyond this darkness. This wasn't real, and somewhere deep down he knew that.

"You will not break me."

Marcus furrowed his brow and forced his eyes to open back to reality. The world was bright again, too bright, and it caused him to wince in pain.

"Hold… on… Foley…" Marcus gasped as he took two steps towards the crate. His entire world was now pain and it grew with each step he took towards the crate. But he knew he needed to end this before it consumed them both. Before it was too late.

He kicked out at the crate, but the heel of his boot skimmed it. His vision was blurry and wavy, and he took another unstable step closer.

Mustering all the energy he could, begging for his enhanced body to give him this one respite from the pain and confusion clouding his mind, he kicked out again.

This time he made contact with the crate, and the lid swung open with a loud crack. Marcus peered down into the open crate through his failing vision and finally saw what he hadn't before. He didn't know when it had happened, but there, squashed into one corner inside was a creature that looked very much like a fist-sized wasp, with eight long, pointed legs spread out to steady itself.

Marcus didn't know why he knew, but his instincts told him straight away that not only was this Scriven the reason for both his and Foley's mental anguish, but also that this was a queen. One of the two queens still left out here.

It didn't make much sense to him; the Scriven queens had always been so huge, but this one was one was so tiny in comparison. He could tell that it was certainly queen-esque because its segmented body mirrored that of the queens he'd seen already, but he'd never thought they'd find one outside of a nest.

Whatever this was, and however it had got there, Marcus took immediate action. He raised his rifle and aimed it at the body of the creature. Ignoring the waves of pain that came faster and more intense as he set eyes on the queen. He could feel it was trying to stop him, pushing him away, but he already knew he had won this battle. He'd already managed to aim at his target.

The world hazy, his head pounding and not entirely sure he could shoot straight, Marcus took a deep breath, shut his eyes and squeezed the trigger. The bang reverberated around his mind and rang in his ears. He was sure that this single shot had obliterated the Scriven queen, and as soon as he opened his eyes and saw the fine mist of death puff up out of the crate, he fell to the ground and lay on his back just like he had done before.

He could see Foley. The pain was still there, but it was receding. He only hoped that Foley's pain and anguish would follow suit.

But then Marcus noticed something. Although Foley was facing away from him, he was holding his rifle. But not how he should've been holding it. Marcus could see that it was upside down.

He knew what this was. Marcus scrambled to his feet and lunged at Foley, but before he could cross the short distance between them, a single shot cracked from Foley's rifle like thunder and lightning. He'd been too late. He couldn't save him.

Marcus fell to the ground, his face and shoulders wet with Foley's warm blood and his friend's body landed next to him a moment later.

Foley had made a way out of all of this for himself. But it was not the way Marcus would've wanted.

"It wasn't my fault," Marcus repeated to himself over and over through his tears and anguish. "You idiot Foley. You just had to hold on a minute longer... how could you leave me like this? Just a minute longer..."

But no matter how hard Marcus tried to talk himself around, something kept nagging at him, telling him that all of this could've been avoided.

"We should've checked the crate, or I should've realised what was happening..." he moaned.

But really, he knew that Foley had been changed long before the little Scriven queen had gotten involved. Perhaps he could've done something about it earlier, but perhaps this was the way it had always been destined to be.

Whatever the cause, and whatever could've happened differently, the situation remained the same for the foreseeable future: Marcus was alone. And there was still one queen left out there.

Official Records – Thoughts From Marcus Cesari, Last Man Standing

Once Foley was gone, I didn't know what I was supposed to do. All my friends, everyone who had arrived on that godforsaken planet had all been trained soldiers. And where had it got them?

They were all dead, and I was still alive, and that had to mean something, right? The only thing that I could think it meant was that at some point, for some reason, the choices they'd made had been wrong, and that was the reason they weren't there anymore. I could do better.

I did everything I could to ignore that making me their squad leader after McCulloch had gone could've been one of those wrong decisions, but if that was one of the reasons the rest had died, then I didn't want to think about it. They weren't there anymore so it made no difference if I called myself squad leader or God-damned Emperor of the entire planet.

The Scriven queen that had managed to get in the box… I didn't know how it had managed to do it. Maybe it had snuck in when Foley took out his rifle in place of the Flamer. Maybe it had been there for much longer. What it meant, though, was that I couldn't trust anything around me. Not even my own two eyes or the thoughts running through my own head. And that was a terrifying realisation.

The thing was much smaller than the other queens too. I mean much, much smaller. It was strange to think it was a queen, but something inside me told me that was exactly what it was, like it had some kind of royal presence or something. Either way, it was dead, and like Foley had once said, it was another one dealt with now that couldn't come back for me later. That was good advice, and I understand it now.

I laid next to Foley for a long time, and it would've been longer if the sun hadn't started dropping. I didn't want to leave him out there all alone for the Scriven to find. But it eventually dawned on me that he was the one who'd left me alone out there, and I needed to look out for myself.

Sifting through the supply crate for everything that I could carry, I took food, water, ammunition, grenades and anything else I thought might be useful because I knew that after I left this place, I'd never return. Not to Foley's bloodied dead body, not to the dead Scriven queen, not to the supply crate. At least with what I took, I knew I could survive for a long time. Long enough for someone to come and rescue me – if they even knew I was still alive.

My situation could have been better. I still had no communications, which meant that even if someone wanted to come looking for me, they'd have no way of knowing that I was still alive.

I had learned something from my last day or so running across the landscape, though – at least it wasn't all a waste of time. Firstly, when a queen was killed, if it had a nest, then the rest of the bugs within that nest would scatter. The Scriven aren't a naturally warlike race as far as I can tell, so without the influence of a queen, they kind of turn into wild animals, just out there looking to survive. And they don't seem to travel in groups either. It makes me wonder how this whole war got started in the first place.

Second, I had some time to think about what the smaller queen had planned for us. It didn't seem like the kind to attack on its own – given the fact that it chose to hide rather than try to eat us or whatever. With this in mind, I guessed it was using the GPS system to guide us somewhere. And I could only assume it was to another nest, as this queen didn't seem to have one of its own. Maybe these two worked together. Hell, I didn't know how they operated but it made sense.

That also brought me to my next problem. I still had the GPS device, and it was still indicating a direction to travel, but I couldn't trust it. The Scriven Queen was able to either influence it directly or make me see things that weren't there. I could only assume that I'd been told the truth by the other queen who'd claimed responsibility for bringing the transports down.

But all of this had just one outcome. I was lost in the middle of nowhere. I could see some hills nearby and not really much else. I could only hope these weren't more of those tailings caused by the Scriven digging up another nest.

But hell, why not? That was pretty much how my luck worked, wasn't it?

While I was alone, I had some time to think about what had happened to me and what had brought me to this place. I thought about my mum and my dad. I thought about Helen again, out there wondering what happened to me. But my dad. I hoped those doctors kept their word, especially that lizard-thing Dr. Kono. I never trusted him, but I guessed he was a good doctor; otherwise, I wouldn't even be here right now.

My dad. I hoped he was alright. No, scratch that. I hoped he could walk, and he was sat having a Sunday roast with my mum.

But those were thoughts for another time and another place, because where I was now, was on an alien planet, in the midst of an alien war, and alone. Really, it couldn't have got any worse for me.

I decided to roll back the days to where all of this started. Given the thought that my friends had all died because of their poor choices, I chose to go back and undo one of them: I made my way to the hills in the distance and into the mouth of the first cave I found. Of course, I made sure it didn't lead into a nest or tunnel system or something – the last thing I wanted was to find myself within another nest or something – but I couldn't help but feel if I had no one to watch my back, then at least I would have a solid wall behind it to lean on.

How right I was.

Chapter 36 – Last Man Standing

The cave that Marcus had found was only twenty metres deep and ran in a straight line from its opening halfway up the hill. The hill itself seemed solid, which suggested that it hadn't been formed from nest tailings, which gave him a little relief.

The cave was only a few metres wide and tall, so Marcus knew that none of the larger queens would be able to walk straight in if they so chose to. But beyond that, if he found himself having to fight off the warrior Scriven, only a handful of them would be able to fit inside his tunnel at a time. On the flipside, if he found himself trapped, then he would have no escape route either.

Escape routes were unnecessary though, when you had nothing left to fight for.

For the first few hours, daylight streamed into the cave as the planet's twin suns completed their arc to allow the night's rest to approach. This was Marcus's first thought about what would happen when he finally fell asleep, because he had no traps or objects to make any, and no one to watch his back while he was slept. The only thing he could think to do was to stay away for as long as possible. Not that he would've been able to fall asleep easily as it was.

He hoped that the Baccus had been right when they'd said that the night time wasn't particularly dangerous.

Marcus had three grenades, two SA80's - one as a spare, more ammunition than he cared to count, meal replacement bars that would last him a decade if he took a bite a day (which was all that was necessary), and a water bottle that could draw an indefinite amount of drinking water from the atmosphere. He would've been rich as a king if he'd been back on earth in the early nineteen hundreds.

But this wasn't even earth. And Marcus knew that he was one wrong move away from death.

With the thought of how impossible it would be to survive alone in his mind, he began to do what he could to turn that around.

"This is Marcus Cesari of the Seventy-First squad, uh… human soldiers," he said into the radio. "I've been stranded alone here and I don't know how long I have left. If you receive this message, I don't know how you'll find me, but there's a supply crate about two klicks away from the cave I'm hiding in. The Scriven can get into your heads, make you see things, feel things… but I guess you already know that." Marcus let go of the button on the radio and let it hang down by his side as he looked out over the barren landscape. He'd think of something better to say next time, on the hour, every hour until this was done, one way or another.

He didn't hold out much hope for rescue but knew that anything to improve his odds of surviving this, no matter how small, had to be attempted.

When the first darkness had set in completely, Marcus took the decision to keep his headlamp switched on. It was a tough call because if anything outside saw the light coming from within this cave, then it would surely betray his position, but that could also prove true for allies out searching for him. Besides, he knew that the Scriven didn't seem to have any problems moving around in the darkness, and they could very well sneak up on him in the darkness if they so chose.

It was a good job Marcus kept his light on, because no more than an hour later, a large, warrior-type Scriven skittered into the cave entrance. It seemed like it didn't really have a purpose, and perhaps it was alone as Marcus couldn't see any others, but he couldn't run the risk of taking Foley's advice and shooting it so it wouldn't be a problem later.

He had set himself up with his feet against the cave's back wall, lying on his front. Remaining still and ready, he would present little of a target for the Scriven to home in on.

So far, his plan was working; the Scriven walked back and forwards along the cave mouth as Marcus watched silently through the scope of his rifle, his headlamp illuminating the creature – something it seemed to assume was just another natural occurrence. It was like the creature knew something was off nearby, but couldn't exactly pinpoint it.

And then it locked its three black eyes on Marcus.

Marcus made no moves; perhaps it was a coincidence.

But perhaps the Scriven had realised that the light from the headlamp should not have been there.

The Scriven still didn't move, still peering at Marcus' position with its three piercing black eyes. They were locked in a standoff.

Then as though it had made up its mind, the creature opened its mouth, screeched an ear-piercing scream and launched itself in Marcus' direction, all eight legs moving in tandem, clattering across the ground.

Marcus had no choice. He hadn't wanted to turn this into a thing; he'd hoped the Scriven would've just turned and walked away, but now he had to. He waited for the Scriven to halve the distance between them, and then he squeezed his trigger to let one single shot ring out.

Bang.

The Scriven slumped over and curled up on the ground, a pool of blood expanding beneath it. The gunshot echoed through the cave and out into the world beyond.

Marcus hadn't wanted to fire a shot. Not when he didn't know what dangers that would bring his way, or how many Scriven it would draw the attention of.

"You were supposed to be sleeping at night," he berated the dead Scriven. "Now look what you made me do!"

After the echo of the single shot repeated for what seemed like forever, Marcus listened to the silence that followed, trying to hear if anything was coming his way.

He did not have to wait long to find out.

The next Scriven to arrive at the cave entrance didn't stop to assess the situation like the first had; this one knew there was something inside, something that it would very much like to eat and by the time Marcus had dispatched this new enemy, another had entered, and another.

Marcus left his weapon on single-fire mode to save his plentiful ammunition. It wasn't that he was worried about running out; rather reloading the weapon would take precious seconds that could very well mean the difference between losing his life and downing another enemy as it charged. Besides, the tunnel was narrow and the Scriven were streaming in one or two at a time, so he had the time to aim and fire with accuracy rather than firing in bursts and praying for hits.

This new stream of Scriven came in fits and starts, with a random number of anything from nothing to three enemies arriving every minute. Marcus imagined that out there in the barren lands, the Scriven remained scattered and came from far and wide to see what enemy – or food – was nearby.

He didn't care. He knew exactly what he needed to do: survive. And in this defensible position, surrounded by ready magazines and a handful of meal bars, he knew that if nothing changed, he would make it through this. Barring a situation where the enemy numbers were infinite, of course.

Hundreds of Scriven bodies had piled up within the tunnel within the first couple of hours. Some of the bodies had been trampled or cut apart by the following Scriven and their sharpened, devastating legs. Some had even managed to act as a kind of natural trap, the appendages of the fallen Scriven impaling the live passers-by. But it seemed to make no difference to the wave after wave of alien beings that sought their prey.

Time passed slowly, and Marcus didn't know when the sun had risen, but like it had happened suddenly, he realised that light was streaming into his cave. He'd made it through the night, though whatever internal relief he felt for that fact, he knew that night or day made little difference to the Scriven.

But it had been hours since he'd fired his last shot, and that gave him the sudden realisation that he'd made it. There were no more coming, and so he released his iron grip on the rifle, noticing that his trigger finger was white and numb with effort. His ears also rang from the gunfire, but he knew it would all pass after a short while.

He picked up his radio and spoke slowly and clearly.

"This is Marcus Cesari. I am the last human survivor on this waste of a planet. If you're out there and want to rescue me, follow the bugs. If you're a Scriven and you can somehow listen to this message, then know that I am going to kill every last one of you. So whoever hears this, come and find me. Honestly, I don't care either way. Send your best."

He let his head hang and stared at the ground. He was tired, but he knew he wasn't tired enough to require sleep just yet. The genetic enhancements that had been made to his body had given him the ability to not only function with reduced sleep, but also to be able to fight against the urge for it.

And that meant all that he could do was wait.

Walking towards the tunnel's entrance whilst all the time keeping an eye and a raised weapon on all of the fallen Scriven – he knew all too well how sneaky they could be – he wondered what he would see when he looked outside into the new day. Would there be a horde of Scriven warriors out there just waiting for him to emerge? Could there even be a rescue convoy there to save him from this hell?

But in the end, when he carefully passed the lethal corridor out of his defensible position, he saw nothing. No bugs, and certainly no rescue.

And then he heard a beep.

It was just like before when the GPS had wanted to get his attention, and Marcus held up the useless device, wondering what could possibly happen to him next.

The device was flashing, indicating a new direction.

"Not this time," Marcus chuckled. "You don't get to trick me twice."

And then he heard gunfire.

It wasn't exactly the same as the gunfire he was used to from the SA80's, but it was certainly gunfire.

He tried to peer out into the barren wasteland to see if he could discern where it was coming from, he even readied himself to leave the cave to go and reveal himself to whoever was nearby.

But then he stopped. And he laughed again.

"You nearly had me there for a second," he said aloud. "But I don't fancy walking into your dinner party as the guest of honour today. Maybe you should try again tomorrow."

Marcus turned his back on the outside world and returned to where he'd set up his defensible nest. He wouldn't be tricked into making the wrong decision ever again.

Lying there with his hands on his rifle again, Marcus listened to the changes in the world around him. The gunfire in the distance ebbed and flowed as it tended to do, getting louder, stopping entirely for minutes on end, but he still wouldn't be tricked or swayed; he knew what this was. But he also had the thought in the back of his mind that if he was being infiltrated in such a way, then there might've been something nearby that he didn't want to even think about. Something that he didn't know if he could deal with alone.

The day drew on and eventually Marcus found himself in the darkness once again, peering down a scope for the second time in as many days. During the light, there had been no sign of the Scriven, and every hour he'd sent out his distress call in one way or another.

But with the darkness, Marcus switched on his headlamp and took a deep breath, ready for whatever would come his way.

And his second night of fighting for his live began.

It was like the darkness was sending the Scriven to Marcus, like they knew that humans couldn't see in the dark so everything would be so much harder for him. But he fought back again. His headlamp illuminated the ever-decreasing entranceway to his temporary home with each new Scriven body that fell there.

The Scriven arriving were once again the larger warrior kind, and that was a good thing as far as Marcus was concerned. The entranceway being filled with Scriven corpses meant that eventually only one at a time could make it through, and it was slow at that. He shuddered to think about how difficult this would all have been if the smaller ones arrived. He didn't have a flamer and with just one rifle to fire, he doubted it would be something that he could cope with for very long. Especially whenever he would have to reload.

But nothing changed. The Scriven that came streaming through the entranceway remained large and lumbering. That was of course, until they learnt that simply walking to their deaths was unsustainable.

After a lurch and lull in activity, Marcus was just about ready to stand up and stretch his legs, waiting for the next Scriven to arrive and sacrifice itself, but then he sensed something different. The sounds coming from the entranceway were still there, but they had changed. There was a scratching, digging sound and when he finally realised what it was, he knew it didn't matter; there was nothing he could do about it.

The Scriven were digging.

He couldn't tell exactly where they were digging and the darkness certainly didn't help, but he didn't need to know, because a moment later he saw a long Scriven leg pierce the wall to the side of the blocked entranceway – they were making the tunnel entrance wider.

And then the pile of fallen Scriven began to shift and Marcus could see that more Scriven had started pulling away the corpses so that the new, larger entranceway would be clear for more of them to rush in at him all at once.

Marcus chanced a look at the grenades to his side, but he knew this wasn't yet the time. If these creatures were intelligent, then he just needed to give them a reason not to bother with him, that he wasn't worth their time.

So Marcus switched his rifle over to burst fire and rattled off bullets in triplets.

The cave had been loud before. His ears had been ringing, and his trigger finger had been numb with overuse. But that was nothing compared to what was happening now.

The Scriven were entering the tunnel at three times the speed they had been before, now streaming in through the larger entranceway. But they were falling three times as fast, too, and within minutes, their bodies were starting to pile up again.

But the Scriven had anticipated this, and working in waves, they both cleared the entrance and sent new warriors into the tunnel to devour their prey.

"Why don't you just leave me alone?" Marcus shouted over his rifle. "Can't you see I'm just not worth it?"

He grit his teeth, kept firing and reloading over and over. He had no choice but to carry on, to prove to these creatures that human beings were far more trouble than they were worth.

And then something changed again.

Where Marcus had been able to mostly keep the alien bugs at bay as they streamed into his home, he found them edging closer somehow and it took him a moment to realise that they were now coordinating their approach from both sides of the tunnel as well as the centre.

If he didn't do something drastic, then he wouldn't last much longer.

He picked up one of the grenades, pulled the pin and threw it into the leftmost expansion to the entranceway.

"I hope you like explosions!" he shouted, but inside he hoped that he hadn't just made a huge mistake.

The grenade exploded with a loud thud, and Scriven appendages and blood fountained into the air. By some miracle, the cave remained intact, and the tunnel entrance was reduced in size by a third.

Marcus smiled and rose to his feet, firing all the time. Then he began walking towards the Scriven as they scrambled in confusion. He kept firing over and over, driving the creatures from his home and from his mouth he let escape a roar. A primal sound. A sound that the Scriven recognised as one that was simply too much for them. The cry of battle.

The Scriven retreated, and Marcus let his rifle turn silent.

Then he returned to the rear of the cave, slumped his back against the cold, hard wall, and shut his eyes. He had no more fight left to give. No more energy to keep him awake and fighting.

This planet had finally managed to break him.

Marcus awoke some hours later. Opening his eyes he was shocked to find that he'd survived and hadn't been eaten in his sleep. In fact, everything was right where it had been when slumber had claimed him.

The radio was on the floor next to him, crackling periodically, and the gunfire he'd been hearing somehow seemed louder.

Marcus stood up, rubbed his face, picked up his rifle and the pair of grenades before once again making his way tentatively towards the front of the tunnel.

Again he had to be careful not to skewer himself on the Scriven corpses, and he made sure none of them were still alive, waiting for him to come closer, but he sensed no movement.

That was until he reached within a couple of metres from the entranceway, and he was suddenly confronted with a wave of Scriven, both small and large, flooding in. They were heading straight towards him.

Marcus inwardly wished he had a flamer; it would've been so much easier. But all he could do was pull his trigger, firing in bursts over and over whilst backing away again.

But he could already see there were too many, and they were too fast.

This fight was to be his last, and he could no longer see another way out.

His attention fell on the two grenades he had left, but that was all he had and if he used them now, then what? But he didn't have a choice.

Continuing to retreat until his back hit the wall, the Scriven drew nearer and nearer until their splattering blood began to coat him from just inches away.

He bent down, still firing with one hand.

He picked up a grenade.

Still firing.

He placed the pin in his mouth.

Ready to pull the pin and put an end to the fight and be damned the consequences.

And then, like somebody had flipped a switch, there were no more Scriven.

Somehow, through some miracle, the last Scriven had fallen at the end of his rifle, and there were no more behind it save for the bodies of its kin on the ground.

Marcus had won to fight another day.

And then he heard the radio crackling again.

"Marcus Cesari, this is the Baccus ninth division. Can you hear me? We have received your communications and have arrived to extract you to our forward operating base. It seems we have located you, as you have put it, by following the 'bugs'. There are many more on their way, but if you move quickly, you will be able to reach our transport."

Marcus looked at the radio again. Could he trust this thing? He replaced it in his pocket, not wanting to think about how it'd tricked him before.

But did it make a difference either way?

Marcus concluded in but a moment: if he was going to die, he was going to do it in a blaze of glory, firing his rifle at anything that came at him. It was how Ramirez went. And it was how Foley would've wanted to go.

With the grenade in one hand and his rifle in the other, Marcus carefully made his way back through the Scriven corpses towards the entrance to his tunnel.

He hadn't realised that it had become so dark inside with the Scriven bodies blocking out the sunlight, so when he arrived at the ledge of his temporary home, he had to wait for his eyes to adjust.

And then he saw.

To his right were hundreds of Baccus soldiers and vehicles where there had been a sea of nothingness before. His heart leapt at the sight of them, waiting there for him to join them. They were his escape. His freedom.

But then he turned his head to the left and saw the colossal wave of thousands upon thousands of Scriven hurtling towards him at speeds he had no idea were even possible.

Marcus didn't stop to think. He turned, and ran.

He didn't know how fast his tired body could run, but his genetically modified muscles pulsated at the request for them to push him harder and faster and with each step he took, he came closer to salvation. But behind him, he could hear the thundering roar of the alien creatures approaching.

The Baccus began shooting towards Marcus, their fire surrounding him, keeping him as safe as possible from the Scriven so close to him.

He dropped his rifle and grit his teeth, pulling the pin from his last remaining grenade and throwing it over his shoulder. He heard the explosion and the squeals of the Scriven as they perished, but he kept running, not even taking the time to look behind him.

He watched the Baccus firing as they began retreating and Marcus approached the back end of a transport open, ready and waiting for him to leap inside.

He was ten metres away.

The Baccus gunfire whistled over his head.

Five metres.

He only had to reach out his hand and take the wrists of the Baccus who was reaching out to him.

Two metres.

He heard the enraged screech of an angry Scriven right behind him.

One metre.

"Aarghhh!"

His world turned to nothing but pain.

Marcus lurched forward as he felt the two front legs of a Scriven slice across his back. An angry 'X' that spoke of just how sharp the Scriven could make their legs.

They had caught up to him. And the Scriven had finally made their mark on the last remaining human on the planet.

The world around Marcus was gone. No more Scriven, no more Baccus. No more guns.

Just darkness.

Official Records – Thoughts From Marcus Cesari, Closing Statements

I made it onto the troop transport and we got out of there as fast as we could. My back was torn up and I knew without being told that if I had been an inch closer to the Scriven when it had attacked, I wouldn't have made it. Life can be funny like that, can't it? Like how I'd been so lucky where the rest…

It made me wonder if the lives of my friends, of Ramirez, King, Foley and McCulloch, or any of the other soldiers for that matter had been decided on the narrowest of margins. There were the thoughts of a man dying within a transport, being hurried away from an enemy he had no business fighting in the first place. There was no glory there.

But the Scriven had made me their enemy, and I wanted nothing more than revenge.

The Baccus told me they'd launched an attack on a Scriven nest. It was so close to where I'd made my last stand that the coincidence was almost laughable. That's why there were so many of the things nearby, and once the Baccus'd managed to take out the queen, they heard my distress call loud and clear. It was also them who had sent the GPS signal – it had been real all along. But how was I supposed to know that?

If only the Baccus'd been so good at wiping out nests before we got dragged into all of this.

The Baccus weren't good at fighting, that was for damn sure. But they were good at rescuing, running, and healing. And that was what I needed more than anything else. To lie down, rest and recover. And a little medical attention for my back didn't go amiss either. The pain almost killed me alone, even with my genetically enhanced body.

I was told that I would wear the scars for the rest of my life unless I decided to have cosmetic surgery to remove them.

I know that I never will. I wear these scars for my friends, and I will wear them well.

The Baccus offered me the chance to leave with the next rescue boat, along with the last of the civilians and the wounded. The planet had been rid of all of the queens so they felt it was safe to restart orbital transports. I still wasn't sure about it, given what I knew about those sneaky bastards. And if they were going to get me, it sure as hell wasn't going to be as I tried to run away. Besides, there was still work to be done.

I chose to stay on the planet.

There were no queens left, but that didn't mean they weren't going to make more of them. I didn't know exactly how it worked, but I wasn't about to let the bugs rebuild and have everything we'd done be for nothing. Our lives were worth more than that. My friends lives were worth more.

And then, of course, I wanted revenge.

My anger was what consumed me for the longest time. I roamed the planet, joining and leaving groups of Baccus as we cleared the landscape of any Scriven we came across. They were disorganised when we found them and it wasn't hard to kill them. Other than the fact that there were so many.

I had no idea it was going to take so long. But I think I needed the time to arrange my thoughts and come to my senses. Time to grieve.

I didn't make any friends of the Baccus. They were allies in this war for sure, but it was their fault that we were there in the first place, and that was something that I would never be able to forgive. Every time I looked at them it reminded me of Ramirez, King, Foleys and McCulloch.

When I finally returned to earth, I'd spent a total of two years on that planet. Two years killing alien creatures as revenge for what they'd done.

But I saw it as something else too. I saw it as my sentence. My penance for being the one to survive where the rest hadn't been so lucky. Because that's all it was in the end. That's all anything is: luck. And I just happened to be luckier than the rest.

Their names and faces will be forever etched into my mind.

I don't know how long it'll take before I stop seeing them. Or hearing their voices.

All I do know, is that when I do, it'll be all too soon.

I'd never heard from Callahan again because presumably, he'd fallen before he'd even made it to the planet's surface. I'd hated the man, but now

I understood. He'd been so hard on us because it was what would best prepare us for what we had to deal with. In some ways I owed him my life. In other ways I owed him a punch in the face. But still, I vowed that if I was ever in his position, I'd be the same. Because in his position, I'd want to do whatever I could to help those I knew would be in trouble. I just wish we'd been told what was happening before everything went the way it did.

The way I saw it, his way had been the best way to prepare soldiers, to save lives and hopefully take the sting out of a situation that no human being should ever have to endure.

Because in war, there are no victors. Only death, loss and pain. A pain that lives within you forever.

Epilogue

Dr. Kono watched on the cameras that covered the Canada Road barracks and the surrounding streets. It had just turned dark and everything was still and quiet, but he knew that Marcus Cesari had finally made it home after his heroics fighting alongside the Baccus. Marcus Cesari was the very last surviving member of his gene editing program.

It had been a long two years, but those were the costs for an experiment that could, in time, change the very course of the universe.

He'd been awaiting Cesari's return for a long, long time, and he knew that although the human was unlikely to go directly to the barracks, there was a good chance he would visit his old house to try to find his parents. That was the whole reason he'd joined up, wasn't it? That annoying genetic anomaly that wouldn't disappear no matter how hard Kono had tried.

It had been a conundrum. Kono saw himself as the pinnacle of medical science, able to give human beings the ability to smash through their genetic ceilings and become Gods among their race. But this one single anomaly just wouldn't die like it should.

But then it was something he didn't want to dedicate too much time to, so treatment over cure seemed to be the logical conclusion whilst the doctor worked on more important projects. Projects to benefit the many and not just the singular.

And there he was. Marcus Cesari. He was walking down Canada Road from the beach end. He had been debriefed, sworn to secrecy and sent along on his way for an extended period of shore leave. He'd also been given the right to sleep inside the Canada Road barracks if he so chose, given that he had no home of his own.

Cesari wore jeans and a white t-shirt, a far cry from the combat gear he'd worn nonstop for the last two years.

As he walked, he rearranged the clothing more than a few times, and it was clear that the high-tech combat gear the Baccus had supplied had been far more comfortable for him. But of course it was; that's how it was supposed to be.

Marcus approached the Green Beret, stopping outside. He held out his hand and peered down at something within. Curious, Kono zoomed the viewscreen into the object and it automatically focussed on the plain silver star and golden ribbon within.

It was the single medal Cesari had been presented with once he'd returned. It had been a private ceremony, and this was the only medal that had ever been awarded to have no name, no inscription and no official record. It was the medal that said to Cesari: 'You know what you did, and you know we can't talk about it, but we thank you, and you did a good job'.

Marcus slipped the medal into his pocket and pushed the door open to the Beret, walking casually inside.

"Gadd's number seven," Marcus said as he sat on the barstool facing the barman. Chris hadn't seen Marcus enter the pub and started speaking before he stopped himself.

"No problem, mate, it's a bit early for…"

Marcus looked up and made eye contact with the barman.

"Jesus…" Chris said slowly. "I almost didn't recognise you.

Marcus was surprised by that. But when he thought about it, he hadn't looked at himself in a mirror in a very long time.

But now he could see the changes he'd gone through because at the far side of the bar, behind bottles of liquor attached to the wall, was a silver-framed mirror.

Marcus barely recognised the man sat at the bar, staring back at him either.

His once black, untameable hair hadn't grown into a mane as much as one might've assumed. It was short and remained in position of its own accord. But where it had been entirely dark before, it now carried a streak of white, like he had aged years and years beyond his actual station.

His body was huge. Way over six feet tall and it was the body of a soldier, honed into size and strength through training and hardship. His arms pushed at the fibres in the arms of his t-shirt.

But his eyes. They were the real object of interest. He stared into them, and what returned to him was a stare as equally as piercing. As equally as harrowed. Because those eyes had seen things that would haunt most people for the rest of their lives.

Then Marcus turned back to Chris, who was still staring at him.

"It's been a long couple of years," Marcus sighed.

"Jesus, I'll say!" Chris exclaimed. "You look twenty years older. I mean, talk about a hard paper round!" Then Chris bit his lip, remembering the fuse that Marcus had on him and the fact that the man looked like he could crush a watermelon between his bare hands.

But Marcus smiled. And then he laughed. He laughed like he hadn't laughed in years because that's exactly how it was.

The door swung open behind Marcus, and he heard a voice he hadn't heard in a very long time.

"I picked up the antibac wipes but they didn't have any toilet cakes..." she was saying as she pushed the door open with her shoulder and fumbled with a carrier bag, handing it to the barman.

Chris gestured with his eyes and a smile to Marcus and Helen realised they had company with a start.

"Oh, hello," she said, still not giving Marcus her full attention. "You're in early. From the barracks then?"

"Kind of," Marcus said as he met Helen's gaze. Then he saw the spark of realisation of who he was ignite within her, the happiness along with all of the other emotions that cascaded through her in that very moment.

Helen dropped the bag and threw her arms around Marcus, hugging him as tightly as she could.

"I knew you'd come back," she whispered in his ear. "I missed you."

~

As Marcus pushed open the door to his family home, he couldn't help but feel like he was once again walking into the unknown. The last time he'd been here, it had been marred with sadness, loss and confusion. This time though, he'd already been through so much he wondered why exactly all this was making him so anxious. His heart raced and his hands were sweaty, but there would be nothing on this planet that could hold him back from the hope that still lived within.

It was still dark outside, but as he'd approached the house, he'd seen lights on inside. And that could only mean one thing: his parents were back.

He walked through the corridor leading from the front door into the house and took a left into the living room. And there they were. Like they'd never even left. His mother and father sat watching the TV.

Marcus stood for a moment before clearing his throat to gain their attention.

His mum leapt to her feet with a squeal of glee and ran to him, throwing her arms around his neck. Tears had already filled both their eyes.

And then he looked at his dad. He was still sitting in his chair, but as Marcus watched, Francis Cesari planted his hands on the arms of his chair, and pushed himself up to his feet.

Marcus couldn't help but watch with wide eyes as his dad walked across the room to him as though it was the most normal thing in the world.

"D... dad... you're..."

Francis nodded. "Thank you so much son. It's so good to see you. We've missed you more than you could ever know."

"I can't believe they cured you..." Marcus said, taking a step back to look at his dad.

"Oh... I'm not really cured..." his dad replied. "More like... just treated in the right way. Apparently, it's not going to cause me any problems, and the same goes for you, right?"

Marcus nodded. "I think I'm fine. But... where did they take you? and did you see anything... weird?" Marcus knew he couldn't outright say that he had seen an alien doctor, but he could at least ask leading questions about it.

"They took us up to the midlands," Marcus' mum replied quickly. "We were really well looked after, but they didn't know how long we'd have to stay for, so we took most everything with us."

"I'll say," Marcus said. "But you know you left the kitchen sink behind."

"Anyway..." Marcus' mum replied. "They did a lot of tests, took a lot of samples... you know how it is. Eventually, they came back with a treatment plan, and within a few months, there we were, back home, down the beach and both standing, watching the waves. I don't know how you convinced them to do it... but it's made such a difference. It's so wonderful and we're so happy to have you home!"

Marcus looked at his father in the eyes. He didn't want to say what he'd had to do for this, but Francis could see that it wasn't anything good. His son had been changed forever.

"Whatever it was," Marcus said pointedly. "It was worth it."

~

"Jesus I've wanted this for so long," Marcus moaned.

He smiled as he looked down at his burger. It was greasy, the meat looked cheap and unappetising, and the chips were slumped on the plate like they had been cooked twice and microwaved to within an inch of their lives for good measure. But this was what he'd wanted. To be sat in the centre of the town he'd grown up in, in the burger place he'd been into a few times when he was much younger. It wasn't about the food. It never was.

"You… really like that?" Helen asked as she watched Marcus take a bite of the burger and close his eyes in pure ecstasy.

"Mhmm," Marcus replied. "You know when I was up there," he gestured to the ceiling with his eyes," I ate meal replacement bars and drank only water for two years. You have no idea what that can do to a man…"

"I'm surprised you didn't just shoot yourself," Helen replied, then wished she hadn't said those words when she noticed something flash in Marcus' eyes.

"But I'm glad you didn't," she added quickly, placing a hand on top of his.

Marcus smiled, and Helen returned the gesture.

"So what do you have planned next?" she asked.

"I have a few ideas," Marcus said. "But for now I just want to relax, take some time off and spend some time with the people who matter the most to me."

Marcus punctuated his statement with a wink and Helen blushed.

"But honestly, it's so good to be home. And it's good to be here with you, right now. I wouldn't rather be anywhere else in the universe."

~

The End.

A Thankyou

Again, your investment of your own time and money is always well appreciated and again, I ask that you **rate** and **review** everything that you read as it makes a huge difference!

Also, check out my website, it's usually kept up to date with current works, reviews and a few extra little bits. You'll find it at:

www.davidlingard.com

If you have enjoyed this book, please consider signing up to my mailing list on my website – there's no spam, just updates of new and upcoming stories.

PLUS, Click HERE to get a FREE eBook!

Other Books by David Lingard

I love to write what I read, and love LitRPG (Gamelit), Fantasy, Sci-Fi and Historical Fantasy genres, though this is not strictly limited as time goes by. I write what he loves and that means sometimes writing outside of the lines!

LitRPG is my passion though, so have a look at Don't Call Me Jack, The Freedom Online series, as well as Welcome to Eden, three LitRPG stories available right now on Amazon!

LitRPG
Freedom Online: The Copper Rose
Freedom Online: From the Ashes
Freedom Online: Birth of a New World
Welcome to Eden
Don't Call Me Jack

Sci-Fi
Cascade Failure
Legacy of Man
Celestial Secrets

Historical Fiction
Baldur's Children
Lanista: Wrath of the Gods

Fantasy
Atlantis Rising
The Hidden Academy
Flames of Rebellion
Skyward Ascension

Please rate and review this book!

www.ingramcontent.com/pod-product-compliance
Lightning Source LLC
Chambersburg PA
CBHW071413200726
48294CB00002B/379